Suffolk C

24

THE POLKERTON GIANT

Also by Ian Ogilvy

Loose Chippings

THE POLKERTON GIANT

Ian Ogilvy

SUFFOLK COUNTY LIBRARIES & HERITAGE	
H J	17/09/97
	£17.99

HEADLINE

Copyright © 1997 Ian Ogilvy

The right of Ian Ogilvy to be identified as the Author of
the Work has been asserted by him in accordance with the
Copyright, Designs and Patents Act 1988.

First published in Great Britain in 1997
by HEADLINE BOOK PUBLISHING

10 9 8 7 6 5 4 3 2 1

All rights reserved. No part of this publication may be
reproduced, stored in a retrieval system, or transmitted,
in any form or by any means without the prior written
permission of the publisher, nor be otherwise circulated
in any form of binding or cover other than that in which
it is published and without a similar condition being
imposed on the subsequent purchaser.

All characters in this publication are fictitious
and any resemblance to real persons, living or dead,
is purely coincidental.

British Library Cataloguing in Publication Data

Ogilvy, Ian
The Polkerton giant
I. Title
823.9'14 [F]

ISBN 0-7472-1608-8

Typeset by
CBS, Felixstowe, Suffolk

Printed and bound in Great Britain by
Mackays of Chatham PLC, Chatham, Kent

HEADLINE BOOK PUBLISHING
A division of Hodder Headline PLC
338 Euston Road
London NW1 3BH

To Aileen, Francis, Kerry-Jane, Betty, Tig and David – all of whom contributed, in one way or another, to my education, which learnt me proper grammar and how to spell words like serendipitous correckly.

Chapter 1

From Megan's and Derek's point of view – their vantage spot was some two hundred feet below – the shape was unmistakable. The mass of multi-coloured tents pitched two and three abreast all the way up its length – and clustered just as thickly all over the bulge beneath – brought the outline into kaleidoscopic relief. It was an image of festive, bunting-wrapped virility and, to eyes less disappointed than Megan's and Derek's, a sight to lift even the most dismal of spirits.

Megan and Derek stood close together and stared miserably up at the hill. They'd come such a long way for this, and now it wasn't going to happen – at least, certainly not tonight.

Megan had worked it out so carefully, even using Derek's pocket calculator to make sure of her sums. Her sums had told her that tonight was definitely the night. Everything had gone so well: they'd both managed to get the same week off work, Derek had agreed to Megan's plan much more quickly than she'd thought he would, the Morris had given no trouble at all, and she'd even managed to feel a little sexy along the drive and put her hand companionably on Derek's knee (but no higher, of course, because that sort of thing could cause a nasty accident).

They'd stopped in Bath for lunch at a very nice pub, and Megan had allowed herself a half of lager and a crème de menthe for afters, because crème de menthe made her a little reckless; it also made her breath smell nice, and that was going to be important later on – although probably the taste would have worn off by then, in which case she would just have to rely on her Colgate for the same effect. Of course, by the time they arrived, the recklessness might have worn off too, and she had nothing to replace that with. But the drive had been lovely all the same, what with the weather being so splendid and all the trees out and everything.

Derek had been quiet the whole way. Not his usual chatty self at all. When they left the pub, Megan put her hand back on his knee and gave a little squeeze.

'Penny for them?'

Derek kept his eyes on the road. 'Just listening to the engine, love. Fingers crossed, touch wood . . .' He knocked on his skull with his knuckles. 'The motor's behaving quite well – so far.'

Megan didn't know very much about cars. She left all that sort of thing to Derek, who knew lots about them. She liked the way he called it the 'motor' – it sounded so professional – but even Derek's mechanical proficiency didn't seem up to keeping the Morris reliable. It was quite old, of course, and the milometer thing read 85,000 miles, which was a lot. It had belonged to Megan's father and he'd given it to them when he bought his new Rover, which was kind of him because he could have used it for part exchange. Derek said that Megan's dad hadn't bothered with part exchange because the Morris wasn't worth the paperwork, and he'd said it in such a sneery sort of way that Megan had got quite cross with him; though now she had to admit that he'd probably been right about it – the Morris went wrong an awful lot and several of Derek's friends from work called it a heap. Still, here they were, whizzing along at fifty miles an hour, and the engine sounded fine to her.

She gave Derek's knee another little squeeze. 'Isn't this fun?'

'Mm.'

She looked at him and saw that he wasn't just listening to the engine. She knew him so well, she could tell when something was bothering him. She shifted sideways in her seat so that she could look at him without twisting her neck.

'What's the matter?'

'Nothing.'

'Yes, there is, Derek. You've got that look on your face.'

'What look?' Derek put a little laugh on the end of his question, as though he thought she was just being silly –

The Polkerton Giant

but Megan wasn't going to be fooled by that.

'Something's bothering you, Derek Baines, and I want to know what it is.'

Derek sighed. When Megan got like this, there was no denying her – so, although it was going to sound silly, he knew he'd have to tell her. Maybe she'd understand a bit how he felt. On the other hand, maybe she wouldn't. There were lots of things Megan didn't understand about him, and they were all to do with him being a man. Sometimes Derek thought Megan didn't try nearly hard enough to understand him.

'Come on. Out with it.'

Derek glanced sideways quickly and then back straight ahead, because Megan didn't like it when he took his eyes off the road, even for an instant. In that stolen look he saw that she was smiling and happy, which meant that she'd be as understanding as was humanly possible.

'Well, it's just I feel a bit funny about it.'

'Feel funny about what?'

'Well, you know – camping on it.'

'*It?*'

'Yes. I mean, actually going to sleep on it. Lying on it. Not to mention doing the other . . . you know.'

'No, I don't, Derek. I don't see the problem.'

'Well, it's a man's thing, isn't it? I mean, it's a man's private part.'

'A penis.'

'Yeah. That.' Derek felt a little trickle of sweat slide out from under his arm. It always embarrassed him, this insistence on Megan's part to refer to unmentionable parts of the human anatomy by their medical terms. She said *testicles* and *vagina* and *labia* and *urethra*, and once asked him if he was sufficiently *tumescent* for their *congress* and Derek had had to go and look up tumescent in the dictionary and, by the time he'd found the word, he wasn't tumescent any more and wasn't in the least interested in congress, which he looked up straight after finding out what tumescent meant.

'Well, what of it?' said Megan, staring hard at Derek's profile, and he felt the blush starting at the base of his neck, felt the flooding of colour move steadily up into his face. It was awful how Megan could make him blush.

'Well, it's a bit funny . . . you know . . . going to sleep on a man's thing – not to mention the other.'

'On his penis.'

'Yeah. I mean, being that close – it's a bit sort of . . . homosexual, if you see what I mean.'

'It's only a picture of one, Derek. Just an outline. It's not an actual one.'

'I know, but – all the same – I feel a bit funny about it. That's all.'

Megan thought what weird things men were and how tenaciously they clung to their manliness. As if camping on a crude representation of the male organ could possibly bring a man's virility into question. But it had with Derek – and that was bad, because the last thing she needed tonight was a reluctant lover.

'You won't feel funny later on, I promise.'

'Won't I?'

'Not with what I've got planned, Derek Baines. You won't have time to feel funny.'

'Whoooaaarrgh.'

Megan winced. She wished Derek wouldn't make that noise every time he contemplated an erotic interlude. In truth, Megan had no erotic plans at all, leaving all that sort of thing to Derek, who never seemed to have any either. Derek wasn't very imaginative, she had to admit that. Oh, it was lovely, being in bed with him, all snuggled up and cosy but, when it came to the actual act of doing it, Derek was a bit single-tracked about what exactly they were supposed to *be* doing. He'd go straight for her breasts at first and nuzzle at them for a bit, and Megan would stroke the back of his head where his hair curled up and she'd moan every now and then because Derek liked it when she moaned. Then, his face still buried against her chest, he would slide his hand furtively down her tummy and rummage about down there, like a woman feeling in her handbag for her lipstick. Two minutes of that, then he'd climb up on her and shove his way into her and batter away for another couple of minutes. Then he'd gasp and tell her he was coming –

The Polkerton Giant

and sometimes he'd tell her so loudly that the rest of the neighbourhood must have known he was coming too – and with a great sigh he'd sink down, all his weight on her, and expect her to stroke his back for hours and hours – which she did because he had a nice back and, besides, it gave her time to think. To plan. Megan liked making plans.

She had made the plan that had brought about this expedition a week before. She'd sat up in bed suddenly, half an hour after the end of the stroking, and had pushed hard on Derek's shoulder, waking him.

'Wha'?' he'd slurred, turning half-way towards her. 'Wha'? I was asleep.'

'We ought to go and do it on the giant,' Megan had said excitedly.

'Do wha' on the giant? What giant?'

'The Polkerton Giant. We ought to do it on the giant, Derek.'

'Wha'? Do wha'?'

The television programme had been on that afternoon while Derek was at work – and Megan had been home because she had a bit of a sniffle. Her supervisor, Mrs Troughton, had said that you couldn't be too careful – so Megan had come home at lunchtime and had sat down in front of the television. This programme was really interesting, particularly the bit about the Polkerton Giant. The Polkerton Giant, if the presenter was to be believed, seemed the answer to their prayers. Well, her prayers; she could never be sure what Derek really thought about it all. About their Situation.

She'd looked up Polkerton in their *AA Roadmap Of Great Britain Atlas* and had found it buried in Somerset. Quite a long way from them – but anything worth doing was worth doing well, and doing something well included driving two hundred and fifty miles to do it.

'Do wha'?' Derek had said again, and this time Megan had detected a slight testiness in his voice. Ordinarily she would have raised her eyebrows and looked down her nose at him and said, 'I beg your pardon?' in her haughtiest voice but, this time, she'd decided on a gentler strategy. This was probably the strangest thing she'd ever suggested to Derek and there was going to be some resistance, she was sure. She'd settled back against her pillow and curled her fingers in his hair, tugging gently now and then to make sure he was listening.

'I saw this programme,' she had said. 'On the television. Ever so interesting it was. All about the Polkerton Giant. It's this great big drawing of a giant on the side of a hill. Drawn in the chalk, you see. It's ever so old, too. Prehistoric. Are you awake?' Tug, tug.

'Ow! Leave off, Meg. Yes. I'm awake.'

'Anyway, it's a sort of outline, you see. They cut away the grass, exposing the chalk underneath.'

'Who do?'

'*Did*. Thousands of years ago, it was. These prehistoric people, Derek. They made this drawing by cutting away the grass and it's been there ever since. On the side of this hill. Outside Polkerton. Polkerton is in Somerset. It's huge, Derek.'

'Yeah?' said Derek, wondering *what*, exactly, was huge.

'Yes. And the funny thing is, Derek – the funny thing is – when they made it, these prehistoric people all these years ago, when they made this pictorial representation of a human being – a *male* human being – they drew all of him. Every little bit, if you get my drift. Every little detail – although from the picture on the television it didn't look *little* at all. Quite the contrary, in fact. It's enormous. A bit exaggerated, if you ask me. I mean, it's a lot bigger than yours and yours is quite big enough, thank you very much.'

'What's bigger?' asked Derek and Megan had sighed. He was always slower than she was and sometimes that was annoying. Having to explain everything.

'His *penis*, Derek. It is an erect one, of course.'

'Wha'? On the side of a hill? So everybody can see?'

Megan had sighed again. 'It's not realistic, Derek. It's more like what a kid would draw. Actually, it's a bit like what they do when somebody's been murdered – you know, that sort of silhouette on the floor.'

'But with a bit of a whoo-haa, right?'

'With an erection, Derek. Yes.'

Derek had drawn up his knees under the sheet, making a

The Polkerton Giant

tent of the bedclothes so as to conceal any erection (or lack of one) from Megan. This question of size had been bothering him lately. The trouble was, like most men, he didn't know if he was big or not. Megan was a virgin when they met at the Polytechnic and hadn't been with any man other than himself, so her understanding of what constituted big was, Derek thought, likely to be influenced by her limited experience. Perhaps the giant's proportions weren't any bigger than what was considered normal, and Derek was going to turn out to be on the small side. It was all very worrying.

'Anyway, there was this lady talking about it on the television and she said that there was an ancient belief – an ancient belief that could help us, Derek. With our Situation.'

'How?'

'Well, apparently, the ancients believed that having congress actually on the penis itself made conception that much more likely.'

There had been a long silence while Derek mulled this over. Megan kept quite still and quiet while he thought it through. Then Derek had said, 'Are you saying we ought to go and do it on a hill in Somerset?'

'Not *any* hill, Derek. The hill with the giant on it. Yes. And there's lots of couples with our situation who've been there already, so there must be something to it, you see.'

'Ah.'

Megan's will being what it was – and Derek's being what *it* was – a week later they had loaded up the Morris with all their camping gear and set off for Polkerton. As they approached the outskirts of the small town they saw crude signposts; every two hundred yards or so there was a square of yellow cardboard tacked on to whatever upright piece of wood was handy. Drawn on the cardboard were little stylised representations of the Polkerton Giant and arrows pointing the way. Derek followed the arrows through the town and out the other side, and quite soon there was another square of cardboard nailed to the trunk of an oak tree, with an arrow pointing off to the right. They turned into a narrow lane, driving between two high banks of earth veined with exposed tree roots. The Morris began to labour a little as the road steepened upwards, and the springs squeaked and groaned as the wheels bounced in and out of the potholes.

'Come on, old girl,' Derek muttered.

Trees arched thickly overhead, making the narrow lane gloomy. Megan and Derek, used to the relative openness of the skies over Chester, sunk a little lower in their seats. They turned a corner, then another, and followed a yellow plaque with an arrow pointing left. Derek swung the Morris wheel and they emerged suddenly from under the canopy of trees, rattling over a cattle grid, into a field.

The field had three lines of cars parked on it. An old man in a waxed cotton jacket and an old corduroy cap waved at them like a policeman, beckoning them forward and into a space next to a muddy Volvo. Derek switched off the engine and the Morris had shuddered for a few seconds before shutting itself down. They could hear the ticking of cooling metal. There was a rapping on the window and Derek wound it down. The old man in the corduroy cap was holding a pad of tear-off tickets in his hand.

'Camping or just for the day?'

Megan leaned across Derek and looked up at the man. 'Excuse me,' she said. 'Are all these cars here for the giant?'

'Yurr,' said the man. 'Camping or just for the day?'

'And are they all camping?'

'Mostly, yurr. Camping or just for the day?'

'Camping, please.'

'Roight. That's foive pound for the car and ten for the camping. Fifteen altogether.' The man held out his hand and Megan saw that it was quite dirty, with black stuff under his fingernails. She wrinkled her nose in disgust, nudged Derek and whispered, 'Fifteen, Derek,' and Derek pulled out his wallet and gave the man the money with a sick look on his face because fifteen pounds seemed an awful lot of money just to camp on a hill. And talking of hills, where was it? The field was surrounded by trees and there didn't seem to be a hill in sight.

The old man stuck one ticket on their windscreen and thrust another through the window, and Derek took it and put it in the pocket of his jacket where he kept his biros. They got out stiffly, smelling the grass and the mud and the

The Polkerton Giant

hot oil stink from the Morris. The man was walking away and Derek said, 'Oi!' The man turned.

'Where do we go, then?'

The man pointed across the field, and Megan saw that the grass had been beaten into the semblance of a path. The path led to a break in the trees.

'Is it far?' asked Megan.

The man said, 'Quarter of a moile. Through the woods. Lovely walk.' Then he grinned ferally and turned away and walked off down the line of cars.

It was quite an effort, Megan found, carrying all their stuff through the woods. The path was muddy in places and their gear was heavy and there seemed to be an awful lot of it too. Derek was right. 'You don't need all that stuff,' he'd said. 'Not for just one night, you don't.' But she'd insisted, so here they were, struggling along with a tent and two sleeping bags and a groundsheet and a storm cover and the stove and the pots and pans that clanked together with every step they took. And they'd left all the food in the car to be picked up on a second trip, so it was no wonder that Derek was a bit quiet, since it was he who would be coming all the way back down again to lug all the tins of food to their camping site.

The trees started to thin and they could see open ground ahead and within a few minutes they were out of the wood and standing at the foot of a steep hill. The Polkerton Giant lay, foreshortened somewhat from their angle of sight, but impressive all the same. His feet were about fifty yards from where they stood; his legs, splayed wide, rose up the side of the hill, the outlines showing starkly white against the grass. Then came the startling penis, stylised but unmistakable – and Megan's heart sank as she looked at the tents covering every inch of it and those spilling over on to the bulge of the scrotum beneath. In fact, there was a scattering of tents all over the giant – some dotted here and there on his torso, two or three on his head and several more pitched on his thighs. There was plenty of room if you simply wanted to camp on his body, but the prime site – the site they'd driven two hundred and fifty miles to camp on – was fully occupied.

'My word,' said Derek, feelingly. 'It's ever so big, isn't it?'

Megan glanced at him sharply to see where he was looking, but Derek's eyes weren't focused on any particular spot, merely roaming about over the expanse of the hill. His mouth was open too.

'It's full up, Derek,' she said in her kindergarten teacher voice. 'It's all full up.'

Derek didn't reply. He didn't have enough confidence in his ability to mask the relief in his voice, so he remained sensibly silent, hoping that Megan would take his reticence as a sign of disappointment.

They stood, mute, for several more moments, then Megan said briskly, 'Well, we'll just have to wait for a spot, that's all there is to it.'

'Wait where?' said Derek.

'We'll camp somewhere else on the giant and wait for one of the tents to go away. Then we'll move.'

'You mean we'll spend more than one night here?'

'If needs be, Derek, if needs be.'

'We've only got six more, you know.'

'I know that, Derek Baines. I know that quite well, thank you very much, and if needs be we'll stay here for all of them.'

She had dropped her kindergarten voice; now she was one of those starchy hospital matrons, and Derek knew that this was not the time to make any objection. Now was not the moment to bring up anything at all, other than compliance with Megan's plan for their holiday, for Megan, Derek had learned in the two years of their marriage, had a will of tempered steel. His will, in comparison, was like a stem of wilted celery. Megan's way always came first – then, if she was happy with the outcome, Derek could put in his two penny worth, and if she was really happy with her results they might even implement his plan, or parts of it at least. His plan had been to make love to Megan as vigorously and as frequently as time and the environment would permit, thus giving the giant every opportunity to resolve their Situation and keep Megan from wondering (should the giant fail them) whether perhaps they could have done more to guarantee success. Then, the next morning, while she was still post-coitally rosy, he was going to suggest (ever so hesitantly and with ever so many little observations that

The Polkerton Giant

they didn't have to if she didn't want to) that, having come this far, might they not consider going on to Birmingham, where they could probably stay for a few days with her brother Paul, who lived in the suburbs in a very nice flat with two bedrooms, and who liked cars almost as much as Derek did . . . and while they were staying with Paul, might they not perhaps look in at the Exhibition Centre, where there just happened to be a rather splendid motor show running? And if Megan had looked a little doubtful at this point, which she almost certainly would have done, Derek had planned to mention the many other cultural attractions that Birmingham had to offer – the museums and the art galleries and the theatres – all of which they could visit as often as she liked (just so long as Derek and Paul could have a quick look at the motor show).

All of this wonderful plan would now have to be put on the back burner, just because a whole bunch of idiots had decided on the same strategy as Megan's to resolve their Situations. (Unless, of course, the double rank of tents that was squashed within the outline of the penis was inhabited solely by frivolous people, merely there for the salacious fun of it and without any serious intent at all. If that was the case, then perhaps they wouldn't have to wait any longer than this one night to get a place on the coveted spot.)

Megan was thinking how cramped and crowded the coveted spot was, and how the lack of space between walls of the tents and their completely inadequate soundproofing was going to make lovemaking very difficult indeed. She, of course, could be as quiet as a mouse, but Derek occasionally howled. Sometimes, after a noisy session, their neighbour Mrs Cogan would greet her across the fence with, 'You two made a night of it and no mistake,' the observation delivered with such excruciating roguishness that Megan wanted to smack her.

Well, Derek would just have to be quiet, that was all. If she had to, she'd put her hand over his mouth. Meanwhile, there was plenty of room elsewhere on the giant and the shadows were getting long, so she tapped Derek on his shoulder and said, 'Come on, then. We can pitch on that foot over there. It looks flatter than anywhere else. And it's near those Portaloo things as well.'

While the space was indeed flatter than anywhere else on the giant (and only fifty yards from the blue plastic conveniences) it wasn't really flat at all, and pitching the tent was difficult. When Derek had finished it looked a little skewed, listing like a sinking ship. They arranged their sleeping bags inside and Derek tried lying down on his. He felt as though he was going to slide out of the tent feet first and frowned at the silliness of it all – they could have been tucked up in a comfortable flat in Birmingham. Megan, popping her head through the flap to see what he was doing, saw the look on his face and cut short any objection he might think of raising by telling him to get the food from the Morris before it got so dark that he couldn't find his way.

When he got back with the sack of groceries, Megan had set up her stove and had arranged her pots and pans, and had even hung her little enamelled sign that read 'Home Is Where The Heart Is' on one of the tent's uprights. Derek saw that she was in one of her cheerful moods, during which everything was to be made the best of. While he felt unaccountably depressed, he had to admit that he loved Megan a lot more when she was like this. She could even be quite affectionate. So he said, 'Phew, what a slog,' in so jolly a way as to show her that he would gladly repeat the trip ten more times if she asked him to, then he helped to unpack everything from the bag (and managed to give her all the right things a second before she got exasperated with him for not handing them over precisely when she needed them), and his efficiency kept the atmosphere between them as warm as it ever had been.

Megan heated up a tin of beef stew and they had individual apple pies as afters, and Derek drank two light ales because Megan didn't show any sign of objecting when he reached for the second. Quite soon it was dark, so they turned off the stove and Megan went into the tent alone to have a little freshen-up, and when she was ready she called to Derek and he crawled inside and tried to get into her sleeping bag.

Megan kissed him on the end of his nose and said, 'Not tonight, Derek. Let's save it for when we need it, shall we?'

Derek said, 'Righto, love,' and, a little relieved, slipped

into his own sleeping bag. Megan reached out and held his hand, for which he was doubly grateful – not just for the friendship she was extending but also for the tether that attached him to her like an anchor chain and stopped him sliding feet first out of the tent.

Chapter 2

The Polkerton Giant had lain, certainly dormant by the nature of its being, on the side of Giant's Hill for a very long time. The hill itself, useless for anything other than grazing the most sure-footed of sheep, rose steeply out of the surrounding land, most of which was composed of old timber woods which had been protected from cutting by an act of Parliament. This legislation had enraged old Mick Jenson, the owner of the acres, to such an extent that, when the environmentalists' bill had passed, he'd very nearly sold the farm that had been in his family for eight generations. Then came this sudden unexpected interest in the giant, and now he was raking the money in by charging five pounds for parking and ten for camping – and any idea of selling the land had gone clean out of his mind.

Until the publicity started – outside the boundaries of Polkerton and those few villages that squatted nearby – the giant had been hardly known. The hill where he lay was nowhere near a main road and couldn't even be seen from any nearby lane. To find it at all you had to follow the route taken by Megan and Derek (and all those who had gone before), driving down the rutted lane that led to the Jenson farm and turning off into a field a hundred yards or so before you reached Mick's sagging gate. Then there was a quarter-mile walk through the woods – pleasant enough if the day was fine but tough going if it wasn't – and only then, breathing hard, would you come to the foot of Giant's Hill and glimpse what was, in truth, better seen from a low-flying aeroplane.

While Polkerton and its satellite villages boasted an eclectic collection of residents, there were two opposing elements that seemed to dominate the social, political, economic and artistic scenes – and it was the collision of these elements that brought the Polkerton Giant to the front pages of the tabloid press, the back pages of the family press, and into the tag stories, mostly of humorous content, of the evening television news . . .

On one side stood stout little Viola Pomfret. Viola Pomfret was determined to do something – anything – to stem the rising tide of immorality among the Polkerton youth (and the Polkerton middle-aged and the Polkerton old, although Viola rarely mentioned them). On the other side – and as passionate a disbeliever in everything Viola Pomfret stood for as it was possible to be – was tall, stork-thin Rapunzel Beaufort-Lyons, who was equally determined to stop her.

Viola Pomfret was a short, fifty-fiveish sort of person, with a tight perm, a bright smile and a wardrobe of smart little two-piece suits. She was (in her own mind, at least) impeccably bred and of sound common sense. She saw herself as an honest, down-to-earth, no-nonsense sort of Christian woman, who just happened to possess the keenness of eye that could see instantly to the heart of any problem and, in the merest twinkle of that same eye, also see the solution. It puzzled her that so few of her fellow human beings were possessed of the same attributes. Thus, believing herself to be the kindest of creatures and altruistic to the marrow, she had elected herself many years ago to be their spokeswoman, their shepherd, their adviser and their friend. She had scores of friends, all of whom detested her – but such was the power of her personality, with its winning little ways, that none of her friends ever dared to voice so much as a whisper of dissent.

Her husband, Victor Pomfret (Viola had been so pleased that his name also started with a V), was the chairman of a large company that made lawn mowers. They lived on the outskirts of Polkerton in an Elizabethan manor house called the Grange, and Victor commuted daily to London by train and was seen only at weekends. This was a relief to his friends and his wife, because Victor had the habit of speaking very slowly and on subjects of no interest to anybody, like the correct gearing for self-propelled mowers as against the

The Polkerton Giant

motorised kind. Since Victor was unaware that he was considered the dullest man in a radius of twenty miles and so continued to drone on whenever the opportunity presented itself, everybody was pleased that his work took him to London and not to their dinner parties – parties that, among the Pomfrets' circle of acquaintances, were always held, inexplicably to Victor, during the week.

Viola was on lots of committees and had even started one of her own, of which she was Chairman. It was called the Association of Women Against Rape (Except Nuptial) and Extramarital Sex in Somerset, otherwise known as AWARENESS. In fact, Viola (with a little help from Uther Tregeffen) had thought up the acronym well before working out what the letters stood for, but she had a general idea what she wanted the committee to promote. While the Women Against Rape bit was pretty obvious and hardly seemed to warrant a committee to persuade anybody to that opinion, and although the Except Nuptial part had caused Viola some problems with one or two female acquaintances (she was determined to keep it in if only to complete the acronym), the rest of the message of AWARENESS was very much to the point and, in Viola's eyes, a crucial influence on the lives of the Polkertonians.

Viola was very proud of AWARENESS and all it stood for – morality and God and the Conservative Party, a sort of holy trinity in Viola's mind that had last been manifested in the utterly perfect mind, body and soul of Margaret Thatcher, whose enforced retirement by the traitors in her own cabinet had so powerfully affronted Viola's sense of justice and fair play that uttering the name of her successor was, for a time, quite hard for her (of course, uttering the name of his political rival on the other side of the house was entirely out of the question).

Viola was on the Polkerton Town Council, which was unfortunate for both the town and the council, for Viola cared nothing for the practical side of politics, unless the side had some bearing on her ideas of how things should be. So, while the council debated the cost of refurbishing the municipal swimming pool, Viola was working up a speech – and later delivering it with a passion that made her short, stout frame quiver – about the disgusting brevity of the swimming costumes worn by most of the Polkerton girls who used the pool, and the terrible effect such displays had on the young men who came to ogle them, all of which was very interesting (and even instructive and important for the council to know), but quite irrelevant and time-wasting with regards to the proposed budget for the coming year, a topic on which Viola had nothing to say at all.

Sometimes Gerald Barker, Polkerton's mayor, wondered why Viola Pomfret was on the council at all. Her presence in the chambers was a hindrance and her election a mystery. However, after an initial skirmish of the most trivial sort, Gerald had found himself being nice to her, simply because life, it turned out, was easier that way.

The skirmish had occurred within the first month of Viola's appointment to the council. She had risen one day, unbidden and out of order, smiling the most winsome of smiles and silencing with her first few words the current speaker, who was just getting warmed up on the subject of fire engines.

'Don't you think, dear Mr Mayor, that we ought to plant some new roses in the flower beds? You know, the ones either side as one walks up the steps to the town hall? The darling, brave ones that have been there for so long are quite worn out with giving us pleasure all these years and, lovely as they once undoubtedly were, they now, frankly, seem rather sickly to me. Perhaps they ought to be removed to rosy heaven to make way for some younger blooms.'

Gerald had muttered that perhaps Viola would like to bring up the matter at the appropriate time – when they were on the Parks business and not discussing the purchase of a new fire engine – and Viola had taken affront at this and had engaged three jobbing gardeners, at her own expense, to remove the old roses and plant a lot of splendid new ones. Shortly afterwards, Gerald (and anybody else who happened to be passing and who happened to glance down at the fine new roses) noticed a heavy metal plaque, mounted on a stake stuck deep in the soil in front of the roses, heavily embossed with the words: 'The Victor And Viola Pomfret Rose Garden'. When Gerald nervously brought the matter up at the next council meeting, intending to question the Pomfrets'

The Polkerton Giant

right to annex an admittedly small portion of council property and name it after themselves, Viola rose to her feet before he could get to the nub of the matter and made a most gracious speech of acknowledgement, thanking the council for its gratitude and saying that if there was any other minor business that the council would like her and her husband to attend to, then she, Viola Pomfret, would be only too glad to take the financial burden upon herself.

'After all,' she finished, 'surely it's up to the more fortunate members of our society to help those who are not so similarly blessed?'

That, thought Gerald, was something of a joke. Viola's own sympathies hardly ever seemed to lie with those less fortunate than herself; indeed, those less fortunate than Viola Pomfret were usually consigned by her to the back row of her consciousness, where their voices were less likely to be heard.

'I cannot understand,' she said plaintively, to anyone who would listen, 'why we have to have an unemployment department at all. Why, just the other day, Victor and I wanted some work done on our lovely old stables – several Derby winners are known to have been bred there, you know, and the National Trust has expressed great interest – and, try as we might, we couldn't find a single, solitary workman who was prepared to do it for us. Not one! Can you believe it? One would think, wouldn't one, that with all this so-called unemployment about, working men would be falling over themselves to take the job? But no. It's beneath them, it would seem.'

Viola had omitted to mention that she and Victor only ever accepted tenders from firms that paid their workers well below the minimum wage, and only accepted the next lowest tender long after it became obvious that unless they did so the work they wanted done would never even be started.

After the incident with the roses, Gerald was always warmly polite to Viola and listened to everything she had to say and that made Viola happy, and she remarked to Victor, on more than one occasion, what a very pleasant man Gerald Barker seemed to be, and how very little of his yeoman accent remained – although, of course, while one could take the accent from the man one could never lift the man from the class he was born into. 'But you know, Victor,' she said, her head on one side, like an intrigued chaffinch, 'I think it's acceptable for the mayor to be a little common. It allows him a closer degree of contact with the lower orders and, as a public servant, I think that's quite as it should be. I myself – and you too, of course – have always had a firm contact with the lower orders. You with your thousands of employees and I with the ordinary people of Polkerton through my committees.'

'Um,' said Victor, agreeably. He was looking at the stock prices in the *Financial Times* and was only dimly aware that Viola was talking to him.

'I do think it's terribly important to keep some sort of line open between ourselves and working people, don't you? If only to know what it is that they actually want – otherwise, how could one possibly tell?' Viola finished off with a tinkly laugh of her own invention, which was supposed to indicate the girlishness of her nature but which, in reality, sounded like coins being dropped into a china piggy bank – and, in fact, there was something a little porcine about Viola, enough to have given her the nickname 'Piglet' while she was at Roedean.

Viola's brand of snobbery was tainted with an unattractive passion for wealth. For her, old blue blood was simply not enough – the family had to be stiff with money as well. After Roedean – and the sudden, unpleasant intrusion of the real world – Viola was forced to temper the worst of her snobbery down to a level that was at least practical, given that she had to acknowledge the presence of people she disapproved of simply in order to get anything done. Thus Mr Jarvis the fishmonger and Mr Havers the butcher, and all the other tradespeople Viola came across in her day-to-day living, were treated with an icy charm that was so obviously insincere that it had earned her several nicknames in the high street much nastier than Piglet.

Victor Pomfret, while not of the absolutely bluest blood (although his aunt, Lady Stebbings, was married to a baronet) had lots of money and had seemed, as a young man, malleable enough for Viola's ambitions. The one thing she hadn't wanted was a man who would interest himself in her affairs, so Victor, who seemed uninterested in everything except making money, was the perfect choice for a mate. Viola got on extremely well with him. He was pleasant, portly, plain – and patient as a cart-horse. He wore dark blue pinstripe suits, and had a round, pink face, with small pink eyes set a little too close together on either side of a small, pink nose; he looked like a strawberry blancmange.

Whatever Viola wanted was all right by him, so long as she didn't interfere with his business. Since lawn mowers came dangerously close to being horribly common things – their saving grace lying only in the fact that the Duke of Dunderton had one of the Pomfret machines and actually used it himself – Viola was careful to distance herself from the company, and pretended (to herself at least) that Victor's money was terribly old money and had little or nothing to do with those noisy green machines.

Victor gave her plenty of his money and, since Viola had exaggerated the amount she needed during the first week of their marriage and had continued to exaggerate ever since, there was lots to spare every month, which was why Viola had more smart little two-piece suits than anybody she knew, and better pearls too. Victor never complained about anything at all; indeed, he rarely spoke, which was pleasant for Viola, who rarely listened.

They had no children. Viola didn't like sex, and neither did Victor very much – least of all with Viola. On the rare occasions they'd tried it, she'd claim that every fumbling move Victor made was hideously painful, and these complaints would lead to a torrent of tears and accusations that he was nothing but an animal. After a few weeks of unpleasantness, they'd both agreed that sex wasn't for them; thereafter, they slept in separate bedrooms and never spoke of it again.

They gave at least ten cocktail parties every year, six dinner parties, and one débutante ball for some local girl whose parents were of sufficient breeding and who had showed the Pomfrets the respect due to them over a sufficient period of time.

Viola had many enemies, none of whom were

acknowledged as such because, as far as Viola was concerned, everybody loved her – but there was one enemy that even Viola had to admit detested her, and who represented a danger to everything she held dear. Rapunzel Beaufort-Lyons was, physically at least, the antithesis of Viola Pomfret. The only factor they had in common was that neither would see fifty again – but there the similarity stopped. Where Viola was short and stout and smart as a new pin, Rapunzel was tall and thin and ragged round the edges. She had a long, narrow nose, inclined to redness, her bony head was covered with a crop of grey hair so short that it was almost a stubble (all her acquaintances had, at one time or another, remarked on how inappropriate was her name), and she moved in an odd, jerky sort of way, her head thrusting forward at each step so that she looked like a Marabou stork. She wore long, shapeless, brown dresses, small, round steel spectacles, ropes of amber beads and, when the weather was warm enough, she would put aside the stout brown hiking boots she usually wore and slip her feet into a pair of rope-soled espadrilles, with canvas ribbons that criss-crossed their way up her shins.

She lived, with her husband Eric, just outside Polkerton in an ugly, aggressively modern house called Grassmere – a picturesque name for a building that was all steel and concrete and glass. There were rows of solar panels on the flat roof and more in the wild, untended garden, where weeds and sickly wild flowers struggled for life. It was obvious to any who passed by the place that neither Rapunzel Beaufort-Lyons nor her husband possessed a Pomfret mower, and possibly no gardening tools at all, because Grassmere rose out of a wilderness of undergrowth.

'We prefer it like this,' Rapunzel said to anybody who showed curiosity about their horticultural taste. 'It's so much more natural than those awful shaved lawns – and, of course, it's an absolute magnet for wildlife.' To the visitor, the ranks of stinging nettles and burdock didn't look like a magnet for anything, and nobody could remember seeing wildlife of any kind or at any time in the Beaufort-Lyonses' garden. Perhaps the magnet worked best at night, one neighbour had suggested, and Rapunzel had confirmed this, relating in a breathy, excited voice how a badger had actually come

The Polkerton Giant

snuffling right up to the plate glass window the night before, so close that she could count the hairs on its back.

Although Rapunzel and Eric breathed raptures over the animal kingdom, their real passions lay elsewhere. Rapunzel was an ardent supporter of the arts and a defender of all the latest trends. On her trips to London, she would seek out the gallery that was displaying the most controversial pieces and stand, entranced, before a bath filled with bricks. When anybody expressed doubts about the artistry of the piece (or wondered whether there was any artistry being displayed at all) Rapunzel would shake her head gently and say, 'Well, there's a depth, you see. A profundity of implications.' And if the doubter continued to doubt she would thrust her head forward, tilt it slowly to one side and say, 'Art moves ever onwards and one simply has to keep up if one is to understand it. It's not given to everybody, I'm afraid.'

Her devotion to the arts extended to her own creations, and her paintings hung on every wall in Grassmere. Another interest was drama, and Rapunzel was the founder, president and artistic director of the Polkerton Players, who put on three productions a year. Rapunzel had been seen most recently (and most triumphantly) as Masha in *Three Sisters*. Eric, too, was active in the Players and his portrayal of Vershinin had been widely praised by all their friends. 'How clever,' they had said, 'to play Vershinin with a Welsh accent,' and Eric had smiled modestly and said that the idea had come to him quite suddenly in rehearsal and, yes, he thought it had been a good choice, and how good of his friends to have noticed.

Eric was as tall as Rapunzel, but not as thin. He had a round, cherubic face with a button nose, and he combed his white hair forward on to his forehead in a short fringe (he thought it looked senatorial in a Roman sort of way but in fact it gave him the appearance of a swottish schoolboy). He wore shapeless corduroy suits and smoked a meerschaum pipe filled with aromatic tobacco.

Eric had no money at all, but that was all right because Rapunzel had plenty. It had been left to her by her father, who had inherited it from *his* father, who had inherited it from *his* father, and so on back several generations to an obscure pirate called John de Leonboules, who had stolen it with startling ease from an ineptly-led Spanish treasure convoy. John, the most startled of all his crew because up to that moment his career as a pirate had been going nowhere, had come home, changed his name to Lyons (a pretentious descendant added 'Beaufort' for no other reason than he liked more syllables than just the two that Lyons offered), and retired to an even more obscure private life than the one he'd led as a pirate. The money had grown steadily over the generations, and by the time Rapunzel had inherited it the sum was enough to support her and Eric in considerable comfort.

All this money meant that Eric didn't have to work for a living, so he didn't. Instead he wrote poetry and published it himself, through a small and exclusive publishing house in a small and exclusive Polkerton side street. The publishing house, which doubled as a small and exclusive book shop, was owned by Eric and Rapunzel and was called Verse and Versatility, and Eric's slim volumes, bound in Moroccan leather with gold-leaf titling and a purple silk ribbon to mark the place, could be seen in the book shop's windows.

Eric and Rapunzel had produced two children, now adults with children of their own. They lived in London and came to Polkerton only at Christmas, when the unkempt vegetation at Grassmere was obligingly dead, or better still, covered with snow. They stayed for as short a time as was polite and then left for London; Rapunzel and Eric got on their nerves.

Whatever portion that was left of the Beaufort-Lyonses' affections, after the arts and the animal kingdom had taken the greatest share, was reserved for the working classes. Rapunzel and Eric were anti-monarchy (and pro a vague sort of Republicanism), and one of their greatest feats of self-delusion was the idea that the working classes shared their beliefs. Another delusion was that the working classes were as fond of the Beaufort-Lyonses as the Beaufort-Lyonses were fond of them.

'They're the only *real* people,' said Rapunzel.

'You know where you *stand* with them,' said Eric.

'We've always felt a great *affinity* with them,' said

The Polkerton Giant

Rapunzel – and Mr Havers and Mr Jarvis and all the other tradespeople with whom the Beaufort-Lyonses did business were forced to waste time standing about in their shops while the Beaufort-Lyonses talked to them, at length and in their friendly and informal way, about the irrelevance of the royal family – and the names that Mr Havers and Mr Jarvis and all the rest of them up and down the high street had given to the Beaufort-Lyonses were almost as nasty as the ones they'd given to Viola Pomfret.

Viola Pomfret and Rapunzel Beaufort-Lyons had hated each other on sight.

When the Beaufort-Lyonses had first moved to Polkerton, they'd armed themselves with a list of names supplied by their estate agent and invited everybody who was anybody in the area to a sprawling, unstructured party, where the only thing to drink was mead that Rapunzel had made and the only things to eat were bowls of unsalted sunflower seeds (Rapunzel encouraged her guests to throw the shells on the floor). Eric read some of his poetry, and Rapunzel did a majestic but strenuous dance on the back lawn based, she claimed, on the Aztec welcoming ceremony. All of this left Viola narrow-eyed and purse-lipped – but what Rapunzel and Eric had hanging on their walls left her gasping and, temporarily, speechless. Viola disliked most art, apart from pleasant, unobtrusive landscapes (and she had several pleasant, unobtrusive landscapes – large, dark and Victorian – hanging on the walls of the Grange), so what met her eyes at Grassmere (and there was no looking away because they were everywhere) upset her terribly.

That evening, her voice returned, she'd complained to Victor. 'One might perhaps expect that sort of thing abroad, from foreigners with different values from ours – but not, surely, in Somerset.'

'Expect what, old thing?' said Victor.

'Their pictures – Victor – although I hesitate to call them pictures at all. Great splashes of paint, the most garish colours imaginable . . . and I was looking at one of them when Mrs Beaufort-Lyons crept up behind me and tapped me on the shoulder – I almost jumped out of my poor skin –

and said I ought to move back a bit in order to get the full effect. And when I did all those awful colours sort of swam into focus and I found myself looking . . . It's too upsetting, it really is.'

'What is?'

'The picture, Victor – and again I use the word in its broadest sense – was of a naked man, exposing everything in the horridest way.'

'Mm,' said Victor – and then, very slowly, as if the words were being handed to him one by one by a more-than-usually-stingy muse: 'Thing is . . . you – can – see – that – sort – of – stuff – in – museums . . . can't you?'

'Of course you can, Victor, although I prefer not to. But the point is, you see, that the picture was of *Mr* Beaufort-Lyons. Of course, it didn't actually look like him at all because it was so very badly painted, but I could tell it was *supposed* to be him because of that ridiculous way he wears his hair.'

'Ah.'

'And there were more, you see, all over that dreadful house! And they were all of Mr Beaufort-Lyons in the nude, and Mrs Beaufort-Lyons insisted on showing me *every single one*. At the end, I don't mind telling you, I felt quite queasy.'

'Don't – um – blame you. Know – *I* – would.'

Several weeks later, and only as a gesture of social reciprocation (tinged with a desire of Viola's to show them how things were really done), the Beaufort-Lyonses were invited to a Pomfret cocktail party at the Grange. There was dry sherry, served by men in white coats and white gloves, and the guests, all aching to be somewhere else, stood in small clusters while Viola trotted gaily from group to group, introducing everybody to everybody else, and including (if it was worthwhile), small details of pedigree in her introductions.

'Have you met Lady Stebbings? You haven't? Oh, but you must. She's Victor's aunt, you know, and married to Sir Jeremy Stebbings. They have the loveliest house deep, deep in the Cotswolds. Victor and I stay occasionally. Oh, here she comes. Mary! Mary! Do come and meet these delightful people – Mr and Mrs Carstairs. He's related to the late Lord Bungay. Mary, the Carstairs have the sweetest little jewel of a house just down the road, with the tiniest of rooms. One feels one is in a doll's house.'

When Viola reached the group that included the Beaufort-Lyonses, Eric caught her eye and said a cheery, 'Well met by moonlight, proud Titania!' Viola froze for a moment, like a mouse meeting a snake. Then she smiled gaily and, looking just over the tops of everybody's heads, said to nobody in particular, 'Oh, and here's the artistic group. All talking about things that poor little me couldn't possibly understand. You're all very naughty to do such a thing and I shan't forgive until you break up and mingle.'

This was unfair of Viola. Apart from Rapunzel and Eric (who were, admittedly, painfully artistic), the other members of the group consisted of a retired commodore; a stockbroker and his wife; a small, elderly woman who had whispered that her name was Evie and who might or might not have been the wife of the commodore (it was hard to tell because the commodore refused to look at her and kept her at a distance of several feet); and Uther Tregeffen, who was perhaps a little artistic, but was also certainly the most financially secure of anybody in the room apart from the Pomfrets and the Beaufort-Lyonses – and art, of course, had had nothing to do with that. Fairness, however, had no bearing on the matter as far as Viola was concerned; not when some sort of punishment had to be meted out, which was what she intended for the Beaufort-Lyonses. Those who behaved in a manner that was beyond the pale should be placed there themselves, and these people had certainly done that by flaunting their tastelessness in such a manner. They were to be put in Coventry, Viola decided, and to that end she began to chivvy the other members of the group, like a border collie nipping at the heels of sheep, separating the individuals and driving a wedge between them and the Beaufort-Lyonses, until the members broke away and drifted off to join other groups. Uther Tregeffen moved away too, but didn't join another group. Instead, he stood under a large oil painting of a mist-shrouded mountain and pretended to examine the patina of the paint in the extreme bottom left corner. He was careful to stay in earshot.

With the Beaufort-Lyonses to herself, Viola smiled her

most winsome smile, carefully avoiding any eye-contact with Eric by staring fixedly at a spot somewhere between Rapunzel's eyes, and said, 'So glad to catch you both alone for a moment. I did so want a quiet word. In private. A friendly little word about how things are done hereabouts, and all the problems that can arise if they're not quite *comme il faut*, if you understand me? It's always best to be open about these things, isn't it?'

'What things?' said Rapunzel, the end of her red nose twitching.

'My dear Mrs Beaufort-Lyons—'

'Do call us Rapunzel and Eric,' said Eric jovially. 'And we shall call you Vi.'

There was a pause, during which Uther, several yards away, detected a lowering of the ambient temperature. Then Viola let out one of her tinkly, coin-on-china laughs and said, 'Oh, Mr Beaufort-Lyons, Mrs Beaufort-Lyons, I couldn't *possibly*. Not until . . . well, I don't have to tell you, do I?'

Rapunzel and Eric looked blankly at Viola, and she smiled tightly, her head tilted so far to one side that Uther wondered if she might not be in danger of getting a crick in her neck. A master-stroke of ambiguity, he decided, and a classically Pomfretish move. One that deserved a reward. Besides, the poor old hippies were in obvious need of rescue.

'Darling Viola,' he called, staring at the picture in front of him. 'Do come here. I believe I've found the most extraordinary thing in your magnificent painting.'

Viola turned her back on the Beaufort-Lyonses and trotted to Uther's side. 'What, Uthie? Do tell little me.'

Uther pointed to the corner where a tangle of tree roots coiled like painted snakes. 'You see there? The initials? G.W.?'

Viola couldn't see anything but tree roots, but she nodded enthusiastically and said, 'G.W. Yes, yes – there they are. How clever of you to spot that.'

'Exciting, isn't it?'

'Frightfully,' said Viola, trying her best to sound excited.

'Fancy it being a Gerhardt Winkel, eh?'

'Fancy.'

'Of course, I might be wrong.'

'No, no. I'm sure you're not. And even if you are, well, lovely

The Polkerton Giant

landscapes like this are still wonderful, aren't they?' Viola half turned away from the picture and raised her voice just enough so that the sound of it would carry the short distance between herself and the Beaufort-Lyonses. 'I cannot abide all that dreadful modern stuff. All this aimless splashing about with horrid colours, and this silly emphasis on nudity – so unnecessary and crude, when one can have a lovely picture of woods and fields instead. I certainly don't want to look at naked people hanging on my walls.'

'Beastly,' murmured Uther, who had several marvellous nudes hanging on his.

Viola loudly asked Uther to luncheon on Friday, then went off to tell everybody about her painting. When she reached the far side of the room, Uther sidled over to Rapunzel and Eric.

'You mustn't mind Viola,' he said. 'She has her little ways and we all put up with them for a variety of reasons. I do because I'm a collector; Viola is a rare creature indeed and one of my most treasured possessions. I'd put her in a glass case if I thought she wouldn't suffocate.'

Rapunzel had been feeling quite angry at the woman's rudeness, and had been gearing herself up for some suitable retaliation, but now she felt the chill in the air dissipating, replaced by a warm glow that seemed to radiate from the man in front of her. She had noticed him in the group, listening attentively to what she had been saying, and she had been encouraged by the look in his eyes, which had seemed to be telling her that everything she was saying was absolutely right and he couldn't agree with her more, and that he didn't want to join in the discussion, being perfectly happy to take on the more passive role. And now here he was again, standing before her, smiling engagingly down at her, languid as a well-dressed giraffe.

Uther Tregeffen was tall, well over six foot, and slim as a reed. His pale grey suit hung on him creaselessly as if he were a shop-window mannequin (Rapunzel felt a sudden need to go round and look at his back to see if the jacket had been safety-pinned into its present perfection), and his slightly protuberant grey eyes gave him the air of a man endlessly interested in everything you had to say. His nose was attractively broken, giving his otherwise fine-boned face an unexpected touch of manliness. (Nobody knew – and Uther would never reveal – that his nose had been broken years before in Sainsbury's by an airborne tin of tomato soup. A tall stack of cans had collapsed when, too idle to reach for the top one, he'd tried to remove one from near the bottom. When the swelling had subsided, Uther decided that he rather liked his new look and had done nothing to repair the damage.) A gold-rimmed monocle, which he didn't need, hung from a black silk cord round his neck. He wore no jewellery, apart from a signet ring on the little finger of his left hand. He never wore a watch but was always on time, and whenever he appeared at a gathering such as this one, every man in the room coveted the tie that he was wearing.

The only jarring note in his appearance was the glaringly obvious toupée that sat, like some small woodland creature, on top of his head. The colour of the hair so mismatched what was left of his own (the toupée was a bright straw blond while Uther's own strand of hair, running from temple to temple in a two-inch strip, was a mousy brown) that even from a distance there was no doubt that he was wearing a wig. Everybody who knew him, and knew how much money he had, wondered why he didn't replace it with something that looked a little less like a crushed canary.

The truth behind the business was that Uther knew quite well his hairpiece was so glaringly apparent, but he didn't do anything about it because he preferred it that way. There were a number of reasons for this: he'd had it a long time, and was attached to it rather more strongly than the simple bond that the tape that held it to his head provided; he liked the aura of eccentricity that wearing it lent him (only an eccentric or a blind man could ignore its manifest artificiality, and Uther had eyes like a hawk – so he had to be doing it on purpose), people talked about it and therefore talked about him and Uther liked that; he liked the warmth it generated on cold days; but perhaps more important than anything else, Uther enjoyed the company of *everybody*, without exception, and wanted everybody without exception to be completely at ease with him. A really good matching toupée would have put him in the awkward position of having to

The Polkerton Giant

pretend that the hair on his head was all his own – a position that might have made his friends uncomfortable, and Uther would rather be dead than allow that to happen. So Uther not only retained a toupée that had long since given up any pretence of reality, but he also cheerfully acknowledged that the yellow mat on his head was a wig. He'd even given it a name so that, if perhaps Viola Pomfret rang him up to ask him to lunch one day, Uther could reply that he would have to give Quentin a good brushing and get out his heavy-duty industrial tape, because the day seemed a little blustery and he didn't want to be seen chasing Quentin down Polkerton High Street. Viola would trill with laughter and tell all her friends how deliciously funny Uther was, and how quite without any vanity too – which was wrong because Uther Tregeffen was one of the vainest men in the world, although careful to conceal it.

Nobody knew how old he was. He looked about fifty, forty-five in candlelight; without the yellow toupée (and only his mirror saw him like that) he looked fifty-five. But Uther was in fact sixty-seven – a secret that seemed unlikely to be revealed since he had no living relatives, never invited anybody to his house, and kept all papers and documents that referred to his date of birth in a safe under his bed. Nobody knew how rich he was, or what he'd done to earn the money he obviously possessed. Nobody knew where he'd come from or who he was. Nobody knew much about him at all, except the fact that, if you wanted to be in Polkerton society, it was necessary to be his friend (which wasn't difficult because Uther was everybody's friend). In fact, Uther Tregeffen's circle of friends was enormous. He knew and had influence with an eclectic mix of people, most of whom were unaware of each other, and of the common thread of his friendship that bound them so loosely together.

Rapunzel and Eric found themselves staring, with an awful fascination, at Uther's head, where the marcelled yellow waves lay unconvincingly across his scalp. Uther smiled down at them and said, 'Oh dear, has Quentin slipped out of alignment again?'

'Quentin?' said Rapunzel.

'My frightful wig. Has it gone askew?'

'Oh, no – not that we noticed . . . um . . .'

Uther patted Rapunzel on her hand. 'My dear, of course you noticed. You'd have to be in Cornwall with glaucoma not to notice. It's perfectly all right. I rely on my friends to tell me if Quentin is not quite where he should be, and my friends are kind enough not to yield to the temptation and say "in the dustbin", which of course is where he belongs. But I've had him for so long and we're such good friends that I really couldn't bear to part with him. You must come and get better acquainted with him – why don't you dine with me tomorrow evening? Say, seven o'clock? Not at my house, of course, because I never entertain at home. Too sordid for words. No, I shall buy you dinner at Zucchero – you know, the Italian restaurant in the high street . . .'

The next night, after the best that Zucchero's could provide, Rapunzel and Eric had found themselves not only with a new best friend but also an entrée, whether they liked it or not, to at least a part of Polkerton society.

And Uther Tregeffen had added two more delicious absurdities to his collection of delicious absurdities. For the next four years he shuttled happily between Viola Pomfret and the Beaufort-Lyonses, gently stroking the egos of both parties and watching, enraptured, as Rapunzel, with Eric in tow, rose steadily onwards and upwards through the ranks of Polkerton society.

Chapter 3

The invitation to lunch that Viola had noisily extended to Uther was unnecessary, since Uther always went to lunch at the Grange on Friday. Now, four years after the subtle but definite battle lines had been drawn between Viola and Rapunzel, Uther was sitting as usual next to Viola at one end of the Pomfrets' long dining table, and over the poached salmon, Viola brought up the subject that was pressing on her mind.

'Uthie, dear, I've been meaning to mention this for ages...'
'Mention what?'
'Well, you know that awful thing on the hill...?'
'What awful thing on what hill?'
'You know, that disgusting giant thing. It's off the Bath road, just outside town.'
'You mean Polkerton Pete?'
'*Pete*, dear?' This was news to Viola. That the horrid object had a name at all implied that certain people had become attached to it, and that was a bad thing.
'Well, that's what they call it, I believe. By "they" I mean of course the lower classes, the ones who go to pubs. The jocular crowd. Naturally I call it the giant, if I call it anything at all – which, on the whole, I don't.' Uther injected a note of censure into his voice because he'd noticed that Viola, when mentioning the giant, had wrinkled her nose as if there were a nasty smell underneath it. Uther had never seen the giant – because he disliked woods and grass and open spaces he'd never ventured off the main road to take a look at it – but he'd seen postcards of the thing. They were sold at several of Polkerton's antique shops and all newsagents too. Uther thought it looked rather a jolly sort of giant, with a keen interest in orgies and a careless disregard as to how many

people knew about it. He wondered if Viola had actually been out there to take a look for herself. Probably not: like him, Viola preferred paving stones under her feet. Whatever, she had shown her disapproval and that had given Uther a clear lead to follow. So he wrinkled his nose too and said, 'Not my favourite landmark, I must say.'

'Indeed not,' said Viola. 'I'm so glad you see it my way – and now you'll help me, won't you?'

'Help you do what, you naughty thing?'

Viola wriggled again. 'Why, help me get rid of it, of course. It's nothing more than graffiti of the nastiest kind, a blot on our lovely environment, not to mention an outrage to the sanctity of marriage and a dreadful example of immorality to the local youth.'

'Which particular youth is that, Viola?'

'All of them, Uthie, all of them. We've put up with this nasty thing for quite long enough. It's high time we on the town council stopped shilly-shallying about and did something.'

'But I'm not on the town council, Viola.'

'I know you're not – but you have a great deal of influence in Polkerton and your voice would lend the cause considerable weight.'

Uther doubted this; his voice was light and high, with clear, bell-like tones, more suited to the dissemination of slander than the promotion of causes. He said, 'Now, Viola, you know my rule . . .'

'Yes, Uthie, of course I do. But surely, just this once . . .?'

Uther shook his head and a strand of Quentin fell across his eyes. He brushed it back and said, 'No, Viola, not even this once. You know I never get involved in anything at all other than gossip, and I don't intend to start now. What I *will* do, however, is be your eyes and your ears. I shall report back anything I might see or hear on the subject – but that's all, I'm afraid.'

Viola sighed in a way she hoped might soften Uther's heart, but a quick glance at his stony face convinced her that there was no chance of changing his mind. She sighed again and said, 'Well, I do think you're unkind not to help little me. I shall be all on my ownsome, you know.'

The Polkerton Giant

'Nonsense. You'll have hordes of people on your side, all keen to smite the devil where it hurts him the most. The churchmen for a start, and Commodore Billingsworth. And then there'll be all those frigid Polkerton wives and repressed Polkerton husbands – mobs of them . . . What fun you'll all have.'

'But you do *agree* with me, don't you, Uthie?'

'Oh, absolutely. Disgusting thing. Let's have it down by all means.' Uther didn't agree at all. Polkerton Pete had never bothered him, so he saw no reason to bother with Polkerton Pete. Besides, his idea of morality was quite different from Viola's, although she didn't know that. She thought Uther held dear all the things that she held dear, and she thought that way because Uther had made her think that way. In fact, whenever Viola expressed an idea Uther purposely adopted the opposing view, although he was careful to make Viola believe he was on her side. That was the fun – believing in one thing but making everybody think you believed in another. Having established a firm rule for himself that precluded all involvement in anything more serious than a dinner party (a rule that he'd convinced everybody to respect if they wanted to retain his friendship), Uther was able to ally himself with all conceivable points of view without ever having to put his money where his mouth was.

'Well, it's very exciting,' he said now. 'How are you going to start?'

'Well, I thought we'd start with Geoffrey Pargiter, who will agree with us simply because of the Church's position on these matters. Then Father Roget, of course – we must have the Roman Catholics on our side as well – and then dear Commodore Billingsworth, of course . . .'

'Of course.'

'. . . And once we've got the support we need, I shall bring up the matter with the council to have it removed.'

'You must have a committee,' said Uther. He liked other people's committees and often helped them choose a name for their cause. He'd helped Viola with AWARENESS and it gave him endless pleasure whenever he saw mention of it in the *Polkerton Press*. 'You could call it CROSS,' he continued, 'the Campaign for the Removal of Obscene Signs and Symbols.'

Viola nodded enthusiastically and fetched a pen and a piece of paper and wrote C.R.O.S.S. at the top. Then they pored over the paper together, adding a name here and removing a name there, until Uther looked at the ceiling and said, 'Good Lord, it's four o'clock. Time I was going.'

Viola air-kissed him on both cheeks and saw him to the front door. His shiny black Morris Minor was parked in the gravelled drive at the foot of the stone steps, and Uther's equally polished shoes twinkled as he trotted down to it. He waved as he got in, and Viola waved back and watched until he turned the bend at the far end of the rhododendrons. Such a dear man, she thought. A little eccentric to drive that old, common little car when he could so easily afford something better, but that was Uthie all over. Such a pity he wouldn't openly ally himself to her – but his value as a spy was probably greater than his worth as a confederate, so perhaps he was right to be so stubborn.

Viola went back to the drawing room to do some work on CROSS. A manifesto was what was needed . . .

Uther drove more slowly than usual back towards his house in a Polkerton side street. Up until now, Viola's schemes had been either too small to be of any significance (the municipal roses were an example of that) or too cumbersomely large and diffuse to pose any threat to anybody. But this latest idea showed that Viola's confidence in the strength of her position had been growing steadily under their noses. Now she'd come up with something that was a lot larger than municipal rose gardens and yet sufficiently smaller and more tangible than AWARENESS; with Viola in charge and with no strong opposition, eventual success seemed feasible. That would never do, Uther thought. Viola was wonderfully awful as she was; an added flush of triumph would make her all-powerful, and Uther didn't want that to happen. All-powerful people weren't funny at all.

No, she would have to be stopped – though not by Uther, of course. That wasn't the way he did things. Other people got their hands dirty; all Uther did was show them where

The Polkerton Giant

the mud-pies were . . . but who was to fling the pies this time?

The Beaufort-Lyonses headed Uther's list. Not only were they mustard keen on all the latest and dottiest of fads but, recently, Rapunzel had been showing signs of increasing confidence in her abilities to lead – and mustard keenness and confidence were what was needed if they were to have the ghost of a chance against the juggernaut that Viola showed signs of becoming. Certainly, the Beaufort-Lyonses were the only members of the opposition who might dare to stand up against her.

When Uther got home he went straight to his study and telephoned Grassmere. Eric answered with his customary 'Hullo, hullo, hullo-ho,' managing in one breath to sound like a cross between a music-hall policeman and a Swiss yodeller.

Uther said, 'Hello Eric, it's me, Uther. I wonder if I might come round? It's a matter involving Viola Pomfret, art, nature conservancy, and the Obscene Publications Act. And Rapunzel ought to be there too . . . in fact, she *must* be there otherwise I won't come. And don't tell me you're busy, Eric, because I shan't believe you.'

Twenty minutes later he was sitting on the ugly, brown naugahyde sofa in the Beaufort-Lyonses' living room, pretending to drink a cup of nettle tea. Rapunzel sat on a low stool at his feet, her long thin legs folded awkwardly under her, her eyes owlishly large behind steel-rimmed glasses. Eric leaned against the fireplace, directly underneath one of Rapunzel's nude portraits of him. It was a particularly revealing version, and Uther found himself directing his conversation Rapunzel's way so that he wouldn't have to look at the thing.

He told them about Viola's plan and was gratified when he saw Rapunzel's eyes narrow behind her spectacles. Whether the Beaufort-Lyonses would be up to the job remained to be seen, but at least Rapunzel had cottoned on quickly and was showing her colours – nailing them, it seemed to Uther, to the mast of her long nose.

'That's nothing short of outright vandalism,' she said. 'There are laws to protect ancient monuments. She won't get away with it.'

'We-e-ell,' said Uther, 'with Viola one can never be sure. She's got some powerful friends.'

'So have we,' said Rapunzel.

Uther glanced at Eric and saw doubt in his eyes, so he turned back and looked enquiringly at Rapunzel.

'The People,' said Rapunzel importantly. 'The People will never allow such a thing.'

Uther wondered whether 'the people' cared very much about an ill-executed drawing of an aroused man on an out-of-the-way hill, no matter how ancient the thing was, but he nodded slowly as if their mere mention were enough to clinch the matter in their favour.

'So, what ought we to do?' he asked innocently.

'We must form a committee,' said Rapunzel.

Uther sighed happily. The day was proving to be one of the very best. He clapped his hands together and leaned forwards. 'Of course,' he said, his voice trembling with enthusiasm. 'And what shall we call it?'

There was a silence. Uther watched as Eric and Rapunzel tried out a number of letter combinations in their heads. When twenty seconds had gone by with no result, he said, 'Um, I have a thought.'

'What?' Rapunzel said with eagerness. Uther Tregeffen's thoughts were always of value.

'Well, I think with committees it's frightfully important to have a name that everybody remembers, don't you? And with that in mind, what do you think of this? The Society for the Protection of Ancient Monuments. SPAM.'

There was another silence, lasting this time a full half-minute. Then Eric said, 'Mm. SPAM. I like it. Very catchy. Mm.'

Rapunzel blinked a couple of times behind her glasses. Then she said, 'SPAM. Yes. A familiar word, given new significance. And with its long association as a staple food of the working classes, we can attract the *real* people to the cause. You'll be our first member, won't you, Uther?'

Uther felt a small jolt of irritation. 'Real' was not a description he would have applied to himself, since surely the whole point of being alive was to create oneself as a piece of art, with all the artifice one could manage? Realness was

The Polkerton Giant

for those who lacked the talent to be artificial, and Uther didn't mix with people like that – not if he could help it. He held up his hands in a defensive gesture. 'No, no, dear Rapunzel. Not me. You know my rule.'

'But surely, just this once . . .?'

'No. I never break my own rules. Everybody else's rules, of course – but never my own. I'm a great believer in discipline. No, SPAM will have to do without me – and SPAM will do very well, I'm sure.'

'But you'll help?'

'Yes, in my own small way. I shall be SPAM's spy. You know how close I am to Viola . . . Well, I shall be a double-agent and report everything back to you.' He paused, allowing a little frown to crease his forehead. Then he said, 'Of course, I've promised Viola exactly the same thing.'

'You haven't!' said Rapunzel.

'Yes, I have. Of *course* I have – she's my friend. But not to worry, I'll only spy a bit for her. I'll spy a lot more for SPAM, I promise.'

'I don't know why she's a friend of yours,' Rapunzel said sourly. 'She's a horrible snob.'

'So am I, dear Rapunzel. That's why I love her. That's why I love you and Eric, too.'

'We're not snobs,' said Rapunzel.

Uther smiled. 'Of course you are, dear. And I love you all the more for it.'

Eric laughed and said that he didn't know about that, and what was Uther doing for dinner? Uther, who avoided eating at Grassmere because everything on the plate looked like it might have been cut from the Grassmere undergrowth, said that he had a very important date with his television set and couldn't possibly stay, and a short time later he left them and drove home. He whistled snatches of *The Gondoliers* as he manoeuvred the Morris round Polkerton's narrow streets. What a perfect day it had been – CROSS and SPAM formed, battle-lines drawn, cause and effect in place . . . and all before teatime. Bliss.

Chapter 4

Mick Jenson stood at the foot of Giant's Hill and stared bitterly up at Polkerton Pete. If anybody had come up to him at that moment and asked him to express his feelings for the thing, Mick would have spat savagely out of the side of his mouth and said, 'Oy can't aboide the bloody thing, and that's the bloody truth.'

The Jensons had farmed this small corner of Somerset for almost two hundred years, and not one single generation had managed to scrape more than a bare living from the land. The Jenson family was partly to blame; they were genetically predisposed to laziness and had thumbs that were so far from green that the crops they bothered to put into the ground mostly withered and failed. The land itself was pretty but poor, so it would have taken more talented farmers to make it work.

Over the years successive Jensons had tried to leave the farm, but something always held them back. One year it might be an unexpectedly decent harvest, the next a sudden rise in the price of milk that temporarily turned their bank balance from red to black – whatever it was that lifted their spirits, it seemed enough to hold them in place, at least for another few years.

And Polkerton Pete was always there. Perhaps he had something to do with their reluctance to leave. Generations of Jensons had tended Pete, regularly cleaning away the grass that threatened to cover the wide lines of exposed chalk and generally maintaining him in a decent condition. They had done it not because of any desire to preserve the thing for posterity, but in the vague hope that some day, and in some unspecified way, Polkerton Pete would repay them. It was this hope, as much as any sudden and temporary lifting of their fortunes, that kept them attached like limpets to the farm.

Mick had recently finished his annual maintenance of the giant, and the work had been back-breaking as usual. He was getting too old for this sort of labour – bent double on a thirty-degree slope, scratching away at the grass roots and patting back clods of escaping chalk. It had taken the better part of a week and he'd had nobody to help him this time. His son Buster had refused, for the first time ever, to have anything to do with it, and had roared off on his motor bike to Polkerton where he'd got so drunk that he'd lain in bed, moaning, for a whole week. Why he bothered with the bloody thing, Mick couldn't imagine. Pete had never done anything for the Jensons and never would. The trouble was that Giant's Hill couldn't be seen from anywhere, unless you were actually standing at its foot, so nobody outside the neighbourhood even knew Pete existed. The sale from the postcards (taken several years before by an enterprising hot air balloonist) never amounted to more than a couple of pounds a week. And since so few people came to visit the giant in person, it seemed pointless to try and charge admission. Charging admission to their land would have meant either Mick or his wife Maggs, or Buster – who couldn't be counted on for anything these days – having to man the sagging gate that led to the field all day long, leaving the farm itself understaffed.

Mick cleared his throat, hoiked, and spat neatly on to the giant's foot. He'd spat a lot at the giant during this past week, leaving his small expressions of disgust all over the chalk outlines from top to bottom – but now he was done with the bloody thing for a year and perhaps old Maggs had cooked something decent for his dinner. He took one more bitter look up at Pete – and then a sound behind him made him turn.

A small group of people were emerging from the woods. They were led by a short, stout woman with a tight perm under a tweed hat. She had on a matching tweed suit and her feet were encased in a pair of yellow Wellington boots. Behind her were three men, and Mick saw that two of them were wearing their collars back to front.

The Polkerton Giant

Mick curled one corner of his lip into a sneer. He didn't like clergymen – particularly around Harvest Festival time, when (according to the Reverend Pargiter) they were all supposed to give thanks to Almighty God for the bountiful crops He'd supplied, which seemed ridiculous to Mick, considering the regular poor showing of his own wheat yield.

And one of the dog collars *was* Reverend Pargiter, in a pair of Wellington boots that were black and shiny new. Mick didn't recognise the other priest (and the cut of his clothes was subtly different from Reverend Pargiter's), but he too was wearing new black rubber boots. The third man was older and smaller than the priests, red-faced, wearing the same sort of waxed jacket that Mick sported (although much cleaner) and a brown trilby on his head. His boots were green and well-used, with little straps near the tops, and he carried a walking stick, with which he prodded the ground as though looking for land mines.

The woman and her three companions saw Mick and stopped and, for a moment, caution held all of them still. Then the woman waved and began to walk towards him, her short legs pumping her busily up the slope. The three men followed. Mick waited for them to come to him, secure in the knowledge that this was his land and he was the only one with the unchallengeable right to be there.

'Good afternoon,' said the woman, arriving within five feet of him and panting slightly. 'Mr Jenson?'

'Aarrr,' said Mick.

'We've come to view your . . . object,' the woman said, waving her right hand vaguely at the hill above them.

'Aarrr?'

'One does hope you don't mind . . .'

'Aarrr.'

It was remarkable, Viola thought, how the rural working classes could make one simple, guttural sound – produced, it seemed, from the very back of the throat – convey so many varieties of meanings. Of course the limited vocabulary was distressing, but what could one expect? She smiled with just her mouth at the disgusting old man. His hands were caked with what looked like mud but might have been some sort of fecal matter, and Viola certainly wasn't going to shake either one of them. So she said, 'Just a quick look, if you don't mind, and then one will be out of your hair. Thank you so much.'

She wrinkled her nose and abruptly turned her back on Mick before he could say anything in reply. All he would have come up with, no doubt, would have been his usual, all-purpose 'Aarrr', which could mean whatever the utterer wanted it to mean, but Viola gave him no opportunity to use it.

Mick, who picked the easy life whenever it was offered, shrugged his shoulders under the dirty waxed jacket and moved away.

When the disgusting old man had taken himself off to a reasonable distance, Viola forced herself to look square at the terrible thing that loomed over them. There was a moment of silence and then she said in a small, broken voice, 'Too horrid. Too horrid for words.'

Geoffrey Pargiter had successfully managed to ignore the Polkerton Giant for all the years of his ministry, because nobody had ever thought to mention it to him. He'd been vaguely aware of its existence through the picture postcards on sale at the antiqué shop in Polkerton High Street but, since no official body – like the National Trust or English Heritage – had ever expressed any interest in it, he hadn't felt the need to either. But now, with Viola Pomfret involved (not to mention the Catholic Church), it was going to be difficult to ignore it, which was why he was standing in a muddy field looking at a prehistoric chalk figure instead of enjoying a cup of Earl Grey in his study.

'Egregiously – ah – prominent,' he said, wondering a moment later if the remark was sufficiently opprobrious to please Viola Pomfret. Geoffrey Pargiter was a little afraid of Viola Pomfret. His appointment had not been entirely uninfluenced by a certain industrialist, close to the seat of power and not unconnected with lawn care, and quite often Viola had made small but pointed criticisms about the way that the Church of England was handling its affairs, implying in the subtlest of ways that perhaps Reverend Pargiter had had something to do with the decision making and wasn't it time that he took another look at the matters in question?

The Polkerton Giant

Geoffrey Pargiter translated this outspokenness as a clear manifestation of Pomfret Power which, obviously, was to be respected.

Father Roget was there because, whatever the event, if the Church of England was to be represented then the Church of Rome must make a showing too. Between him and Geoffrey Pargiter there existed a strained bonhomie; Father Roget thought Geoffrey Pargiter a pompous fool and Geoffrey found Father Roget – who looked a little like the Buddha – altogether too blandly secretive. Besides, Father Roget had a habit of peppering his conversation with snippets of French, which was irritating. They met only on broadly based, mostly secular occasions, where they were insincerely jovial with each other.

Father Roget thought the Polkerton Giant a fine joke – but if Pargiter was going to come down heavily against it, then he would perhaps have to start thinking about taking it seriously. On certain matters, it was necessary for the opposing faiths to be seen to agree.

Precisely the same thought was going through Geoffrey Pargiter's head.

Commodore Billingsworth was there because he was in love with Viola Pomfret and had been in love with her ever since he'd first set eyes on her. He had attended a meeting Viola had organised (the title on the posted flyers had intrigued him: 'Teenage Curfew – Past Time?'), and at the end of the meeting he'd approached her and said, 'Jolly good title that. "Teenage Curfew – Past Time?" Damn clever.' Then he'd signed her petition with a flourish and asked her to dinner. Viola had dimpled prettily and explained that she was, unfortunately, married; otherwise, she would have been delighted to dine with so distinguished an officer as he. Commodore Billingsworth, glowing from the compliment and misunderstanding Viola's rhetorical use of the word 'unfortunately', clung to the hope from then on that Victor Pomfret might fall under the blades of one of his more powerful machines, thus releasing Viola into his loving care. Her compact body, her short, powerful legs and her bright, brown eyes all reminded him of a favourite Jack Russell terrier he'd once owned, and he enjoyed watching Viola bustling after her causes as much as he'd enjoyed watching Lucy chase after rabbits she could never catch.

The Commodore was a small man, not much taller than Viola. His title (although few knew it) dated from a period in the sixties when he'd been the senior member of a small yacht club in Lowestoft. If people chose to believe that he'd been in the Navy – well, that was their look-out; he didn't see any reason to broadcast the fact that his connection with the sea was limited to commanding a twenty-five-foot fibreglass yacht around Lowestoft harbour. To strengthen the impression of a service history, he adopted a distinctly military bearing. A shortage of small, famous admirals had forced him, in terms of emulation, to abandon his own adopted branch of the services for the Army, where there were plenty of small, famous generals to copy. Thus he modelled himself after Montgomery, walking with the same swagger and talking through his nose (under which the short, bristly patch of hair was as exact a replica of Monty's moustache as he could manage). Sometimes, when he was on level ground and didn't need its support, he would swing his walking stick up under his arm and carry it like a Field Marshal's baton.

Commodore Billingsworth was thinking that this chalk chap with the stupendous stiffy was obviously going to be the latest of Viola's causes, and since he joined all of them with cheerful alacrity as soon as Viola thought them up, he stepped forward now, sidling close to Viola and staring up at the giant with an angry frown.

'Bloody disgusting,' he said. 'Pardon my French, but bloody disgusting.'

'I knew you'd feel that way,' Viola cooed. She was perfectly aware that Commodore Billingsworth was in love with her, and it didn't surprise her in the least. Lots of men were in love with her – darling Uthie for one, and dear Victor for another, and all those others to whom at this particular moment she couldn't put a name – and it made her happy that she could still engender such passion.

'Aarrr,' said Mick from several feet away, and Viola and Geoffrey and Father Roget and Commodore Billingsworth turned to him. Mick wasn't looking at them, however; he

The Polkerton Giant

was staring down towards the spot where the path emerged from the woods.

Viola followed his gaze and saw three figures emerge from the trees and start up the hill towards them. She peered at the group, trying to recognise the members . . . Oh, good heavens, it was those awful Beaufort-Lyonses, she in one of her ghastly brown sacks and him in his almost equally ghastly rust-coloured corduroy. And Mr Beaufort-Lyons was chatting to a familiar-looking figure with yellow hair who was strolling by his side . . . Good heavens again! The familiar figure was Uther Tregeffen, who was smiling and nodding as if in complete agreement with what Mr Beaufort-Lyons was saying. This surely couldn't be right, Viola thought. Whatever he was saying would be a lot of pseudo-intellectual, left wing, New Age gobbledegook.

Uther was so deep in conversation with Eric that they almost bumped into Rapunzel, who had stopped dead in her tracks.

Rapunzel said, 'Oh look, it's Viola Pomfret,' and Eric made a muted submarine klaxon noise and said, 'Enemy off the port bow.'

Uther concentrated on his next move. Being caught fraternising with the Beaufort-Lyonses was unfortunate, and he could guess what sort of thoughts must be flying through Viola's head. Those thoughts would have to be diverted quickly, or a flood of recrimination would be upon him. He spoke under his breath and managed not to move his lips. 'I think we're probably looking at the president, the chairman, the vice chairman and the general secretary of CROSS. Which one is which, I can't say. Now might be a good moment to be the SPAM double-agent, don't you think? I shall pop up there and fawn for a bit. I shall say frightful things about you and with any luck Viola will open up like a daisy in the sunshine.'

'Do a bit of a James Bond, eh?' said Eric, and Uther wondered how he had known that Eric would say something like that.

Commodore Billingsworth leaned towards Viola's ear and

muttered, 'Here comes that Tregeffen chap with his damn silly wig.'

The Commodore didn't care for Uther Tregeffen. He found him effeminate and a little too clever. The odd appearance bothered him, and sometimes Uther said things that he didn't understand and that made him irritable.

'Ah! Our friend *avec son perruque*,' said Father Roget in Viola's other ear and, for a second, she felt a flash of vexation. What did these two acolytes know of Uthie, that they could so openly sneer at him? And yet here he was, caught in the open with the awful Beaufort-Lyonses. No doubt there was an explanation . . .

'Viola, dear heart,' Uther cried, walking up to the group. 'And Commodore Billingsworth, if my eyes don't deceive me – in a pair of the most fetching boots imaginable. And Geoffrey too, and dear Father Roget. All of you in these wonderful boots and here's shabby me in a dismal pair of galoshes that belonged to my uncle Theodore, who died, would you believe, of the mumps! I never thought anybody could die of the mumps until Uncle Theodore managed it, but then he was always the clever one.'

'Uthie,' Viola said in a voice dripping with reproach, 'what are you doing with those people?'

'Ah,' said Uther, winking and laying one forefinger along the side of his nose. 'SPAM.'

'Spam?'

'That's what they are, Viola. They're SPAM. The Society for the Protection of Ancient Monuments – SPAM for short. Isn't that wonderful?'

'SPAM? Damn silly if you ask me.' Commodore Billingsworth moved a few feet away from Uther and looked grimly up at the giant. Let Viola deal with the chap; it looked like woman's work anyway.

'But what are you *doing* with them, Uthie?' Viola asked, more querulously this time. It was all very well for him to look so jolly, but fraternising with the other side simply couldn't be tolerated.

Uther managed to look surprised that she should ask such a question. 'I'm spying on them, dear. Like we agreed – you remember? I can't spy on them effectively if I don't

The Polkerton Giant

spend some time with them, can I?'

Viola felt silly. Of course Uthie was right, and it was indeed what had been agreed upon . . . it just felt so odd, seeing him with the awful Beaufort-Lyonses and looking so happy. 'Sorry, Uthie. Silly little me. Of course, you must do whatever you think best. What are they doing here?'

'The same as you, I imagine. What *are* you doing here?'

Viola looked around furtively, as though the bare hillside might somehow be concealing a host of invisible enemies. Then she said, her voice lowered to a whisper so that only Uther could hear, 'We had to see what we were dealing with, Uthie.'

Uther bent his head to hers and muttered, 'I see you've brought your big guns. The Reverend and the Father and the Commodore. Canterbury, Rome and the Senior Service – an unbeatable combination. Much better than poor old SPAM, who can't seem to muster any sort of troops at all. What's CROSS's next move?'

'Well, a petition to start with. And then I'm hoping Geoffrey will write something about it for inclusion in the *Polkerton Press* – perhaps the letters page, they always publish senior churchmen, don't they? And perhaps Father Roget can get something into the *Catholic Herald*, and I'm pretty sure the Commodore will want to do something with the *London Gazette* . . . And then we shall probably start petitioning in the high street on Monday morning. You must help us write it, Uthie.'

Uther held up both hands, palms outwards, and oscillated them from side to side. 'No, no,' he said. 'No writing for me. I'm a source of information, not a pamphleteer. You'll do it much better without me.'

'Well, if you won't, you won't.' Viola paused for a moment and her brow furrowed. Then she said, 'Uthie, dear – it's just occurred to me. If you're spying on them for us, what will they think, seeing you talking to me? Won't they think you're betraying them?'

Uthie sighed. 'No, they won't, because they think I'm spying on you.'

'Oh, I see. How frightfully clever.'

'And, of course, I am.'

'You are *what*?'

'Spying on you, Viola. I shall rush back to SPAM in a minute and tell them everything.'

'You wouldn't!'

Uther sighed again, more heavily. 'Do try to keep up, there's a dear,' he said. 'I'm a double-double-agent. That means I spy for everybody. That's the *point* of being a double-double-agent.'

'You didn't say you were going to be a double-double-agent. You just said you'd report everything back. That's just being an agent, isn't it? No double-double about it, I mean.'

'But I can't report everything back unless SPAM *tells* me everything I'm supposed to report back. They have to believe I'm *their* spy. That's what being a double-agent means.'

'But you said you were a double-*double*-agent.'

'That's because you have to believe it too, dear heart.'

'But surely . . .' Uncertainty made Viola's voice quaver. 'Surely if you tell everybody else's secrets, doesn't that cancel everything out, so there's no point in doing it in the first place?'

'Exactly!' cried Uther, and he grabbed Viola's plump little hands and, using her as a pivot, danced a jig around her. 'Oh, you're so clever. You've seen clear to the heart of the matter.' He stopped dancing and stepped closer to her so that their noses were almost touching, and very softly, so that there was no chance of Viola's companions overhearing him, he said, 'However, to tilt matters slightly in your favour, I shall be selective about what I tell SPAM. Very selective indeed, if you catch my drift . . .'

'You won't tell them everything?'

'By no means. By no means whatsoever. Now, I must go. The mission awaits.' Uther winked and put his finger back along the side of his nose. Then he waved at the two priests (and at the Commodore's back) and hurried off to rejoin the Beaufort-Lyonses.

Commodore Billingsworth turned from his contemplation of the giant. 'Gone, has he?' he asked truculently. 'Off to his friends again?'

'They're not his friends,' said Viola. 'Far from it.'

'Then what's he doing with them?'

It was not necessary for her subordinates to know everything, Viola decided. In fact, knowing everything could be dangerous – particularly for the Commodore, who may or may not have seen active service but whose military experience almost certainly didn't extend to running such exotic creatures as double-double-agents. Besides, the Commodore had been known to let slip certain secrets that Viola had expressly forbidden him to let slip; so the less he knew about what Uthie was up to the better. As for Geoffrey Pargiter and Father Roget – well, churchmen were supposed to be above the seamy side of warfare, protected from the dark and nasty underbelly by their spiritual natures – so they would probably be grateful if Viola kept them both in ignorance.

So she simply said, 'He's on our side – that's all I can tell you. And if it ever appears that he isn't, well, let me assure you that in reality he *is*. I do hope that is clearly understood . . .'

Geoffrey Pargiter and Commodore Billingsworth exchanged a quick glance. When Viola's voice changed from girlishness to military resolution, it was time to shut up and nod in a thoughtful but humble way; they nodded thoughtfully and humbly, and Viola nodded back, knowingly and with no humility whatever. Father Roget, secretive to the last, beamed Buddha-like at them all.

In order to avoid the chance of a meeting with the members of CROSS, the Beaufort-Lyonses had moved sideways across the base of the hill and had started to climb up the left-hand leg of the giant. The slope was steep, and by the time Rapunzel (whose long legs took her into an early lead) reached the base of the penis she was out of breath. She paused in the centre of the oval scrotum for a moment, letting Eric catch up, and the two of them stood for half a minute, panting and looking out over the tops of the trees far below them.

'Exquisite,' said Rapunzel.

'"Oh to be in England, now that April's here",' said Eric, and Rapunzel twitched the end of her nose in irritation. Sometimes Eric said the stupidest things; they were already in England, and it wasn't April, it was September.

Rapunzel's arm described an arc that encompassed all of the woods beneath them and a large section of Somerset beyond. 'Wonderful old woodlands,' she said, reverently. 'You don't see too many of them these days. The natural habitat for so many of our native species. Fast disappearing, I'm afraid.'

'Too fast,' said Eric.

'Blessed Gaia,' Rapunzel whispered, bending her long frame double and patting the grass with the palm of her right hand.

'Blessed, *blessed* Gaia,' said Eric.

Rapunzel climbed upwards until she was standing on the tip of the penis. She threw her arms out wide and cried, 'Marvellous! There's magic here! One feels so . . . *alive* – almost as if the spirit of those ancient peoples who laboured to create this masterpiece were infusing one with . . . with . . .'

Quite what those ancient people were infusing her with, Rapunzel was for the moment unsure, but it was certainly something wonderful and terribly meaningful. She felt a most extraordinary sense of occasion, as though Fate had brought her here, on this day and to this spot, with some sort of purpose for her to fulfil – and Rapunzel was in no doubt as to what that purpose was.

Two hundred yards away, Viola said, 'Oh, good heavens, look at that woman. Trust her to stand there, of all places. She's making an absolute exhibition of herself.'

'An – ah – unfortunate choice of location,' said Geoffrey Pargiter.

Father Roget said, '*Un peu risqué, n'est ce pas?*'

Commodore Billingsworth growled, 'They're hippies, you know. She's doing it on purpose.'

Uther strolled up and joined Eric on the perimeter of the chalk oval. He was hardly out of breath at all. 'Well, I see you've found it,' he called up to Rapunzel, and she waved and started down towards them.

'Did you discover anything?' she said when she joined them.

The Polkerton Giant

Uther told them about the plan for the petition and the letters to the newspapers. 'I don't know how far up they intend to take this,' he added. Then, to season the mix, he said, 'I think Geoffrey Pargiter mentioned the Archbishop of Canterbury, although I can't be sure I heard it right. He might have said something else entirely. But if I *did* hear the Archbishop of Canterbury . . . well, that's a bit of a poser, isn't it?'

'The Church is irrelevant nowadays,' said Rapunzel. 'Both of them. I don't think we need to worry about them – Canterbury or the Vatican or whatever they want to threaten us with. I don't know anybody who cares a jot what Canterbury or the Vatican says.'

'The Queen has been known to listen to the first,' said Uther, politely. 'And several million listen quite intently to the second.'

'But this is a piece of history,' said Rapunzel. 'English Palaeolithic history. Nobody, least of all the Queen – and I don't know why you want to bring her into it – is going to argue against conserving that. I mean, look at it.' She flung out both her arms again, embracing as much of the giant that would fit between her splayed fingers. 'It's too magnificent for words. All that energy in those flourishing arms, all that power in those thrusting legs, and, between the two, all that fecundity in this perpendicular phallus . . . And now some mealy-mouthed prudes who see dirt where there is only beauty want to obliterate him, willy-nilly . . .'

Uther snorted with involuntary laughter, and when Rapunzel looked sharply at him he said, 'Sorry. Touch of hay fever,' and pulled out a cream silk handkerchief to scrub at his nose.

Then Eric, who had been staring fixedly at the ground for the last few moments, suddenly dropped to his knees and put his eyes very close to a patch of nondescript, purple flowers.

'Oh, just look at this,' he said. 'We've really got something here.'

'What?' said Rapunzel.

'It's only purple butterwort, that's all,' said Eric, breathing heavily.

'Is that good or bad?' said Uther.

'It's marvellous,' said Eric. 'It's frightfully rare. Confined to just a few patches here and there in the West of England. A real find.'

They crowded around the patch of colour and stared down at it respectfully. Uther could have sworn that he had some of this stuff right in the middle of his lawn – in fact he'd been trying to get rid of it but the bloody thing kept coming back – but perhaps he was wrong (he certainly wasn't going to blurt out that one of those few patches was in his garden and he'd been trying to eradicate it for years with Pomfret gardening equipment).

'Purple butterwort,' Rapunzel breathed, as though she was looking at the Hope diamond. 'How lovely. How delicate. Could we get a restraining order?'

'Possibly,' said Eric, getting to his feet. 'A temporary one, I should think. Enough to stop any kind of disruption of the area until after an investigation has concluded.'

'Splendid. That'll put a spanner in their works.'

Eric tried to think of a line of poetry that might fit the occasion. He liked finding appropriate bits of poetry when Uther Tregeffen was around. For some reason, it was important to impress Uther, and Eric knew of no better way to impress than to quote an apt line of poetry. Ah . . . here was one now.

Eric cocked his head to one side and looked wistfully down at the purple butterwort. '"To me the meanest flower that grows can give thoughts that do often lie too deep for tears".'

'Thank you, Eric,' said Rapunzel, 'that was lovely, but we've gone past that now. Now we're on court orders.'

'What do you think they're looking at?' said Viola.

'Smut,' said Commodore Billingsworth, slashing at the grass with his stick.

From where they were standing, it did indeed look as though Uther and the Beaufort-Lyonses were engrossed in a study of the giant's genital regions and that was too distasteful for Viola to dwell upon. 'Ought we perhaps go, do you think?' she said.

'I've seen enough,' said the Commodore, and he looked

The Polkerton Giant

fiercely at Geoffrey Pargiter. Geoffrey nodded in what he hoped was a thoughtful way and Father Roget nodded in what he knew was a serene way, and they all turned downslope and started back towards the woods. As they passed Mick Viola said, 'Thank you so much. Most kind.'

'Aarr.'

Eric was looking at his watch. They'd been there for hours, it seemed, and now that the enemy had left the field there couldn't be much point in staying any longer. He clapped his hands together in a breezy, decisive way and said, 'Marvellous. A lot accomplished. Well – I think a spot of tea, don't you?'

Rapunzel said that she thought some tea would stimulate their thought processes and give them a really good impetus for planning, but Uther said he thought he'd stay for a while. 'It's so lovely,' he explained in a dreamy voice. 'A few moments alone, perhaps?' and in deference to his spirituality, Rapunzel and Eric nodded sympathetically and started down the hill.

As they passed Mick, Rapunzel said, 'Lucky you, to live in Arcadia.'

Mick didn't reply because his mind was elsewhere. He was thinking that Pete had just had eight visitors in one afternoon, which was more than he'd seen in a month. If this happened again, for any reason, manning the gate into the field below the woods might turn him a profit after all.

When Rapunzel and Eric had disappeared among the trees, Uther walked slowly down to where Mick was standing.

'Seems to be a bit of interest in your giant,' he said.

'Aaarr.'

'Get many visitors, do you?'

'No.'

'But if you did, would you consider charging admission at all?'

Mick looked sharply at the tall man in the yellow wig, but he was staring blandly up the hill, his face smooth with innocence. 'Thought about it,' Mick said. 'No point, though. Not enough people interested to come up 'ere.'

'Supposing lots more were to come?'

'Loike today, you mean?'

'More than today. Much more.'

'Moight be worth whoile, then.'

'It might, mightn't it? And supposing – just supposing, you understand – that a particular person was in some way responsible for generating the interest in your giant that resulted in large and regular crowds coming to see him? Crowds more than willing to pay for the privilege? Would that person, do you suppose, deserve some sort of recompense?'

Mick shot another glance at the man but he was still gazing up at the hill with a lazy, enraptured look on his face. Mick followed his gaze and, together, they stared up at the giant. Then Mick cleared his throat and spat politely away from the man.

''E moight.'

'Perhaps fifty per cent?'

'Fifty?'

'Or forty-five, say?'

Mick considered forty-five. That meant fifty-five for him. Fifty-five per cent of something was better than a hundred per cent of nothing.

'P'raps.'

'Splendid,' said Uther, reaching down and taking hold of Mick's mud-encrusted right hand. 'How do you do. My name is Uther Tregeffen. And you are . . .?'

Chapter 5

Uther sat in his drawing room sipping a dry sherry. The lunch that his housekeeper had prepared for him (his favourite – smoked salmon on thinly sliced brown bread, a quartered tomato and a plastic pot of lime green jelly) was on a tray at his side. Outside the sun was shining and inside Tai-loo was purring noisily at his feet, so the world and its affairs – from Uther's point of view – were progressing very pleasantly.

Most pleasant of all was the progress made by the antagonists on the Polkerton Giant affair. The events so far had been unexciting but significant; they had started, predictably, given Viola's announcement on the giant's hillside, on Monday morning.

Viola was to be seen passing out flyers from behind a fold-up card table that was set on the pavement at one end of Polkerton High Street. Commodore Billingsworth was doing the same at the other end of the road, at a similar table.

Uther had received his flyer from Viola and had spent a few minutes with her, allowing her to point out the details of the paper's contents. Its headline read: 'THE POLKERTON GIANT – A MONUMENT TO *GRAFFITI*?' Underneath there was a rough drawing of Pete, with a banner set diagonally (and discreetly) across his pelvic region, bearing the words 'IS THIS NECESSARY?' Beneath the picture, it said: 'C.R.O.S.S. SAYS GRAFFITI!!!'

The rest of the flyer expressed, in small print, what CROSS was, and what Viola and her supporters in the organisation felt about the Polkerton Giant and what they would like done about it. Readers were invited to sign a petition (copies of which rested on the tables in front of Viola and Commodore Billingsworth) that recommended Polkerton Town Council to consider removing the offending object.

So far, Viola didn't seem to be doing very well. Her name was prominent at the top of the list; next came Geoffrey Pargiter's (Viola had added, in her own hand, his full title) and below him was Father Roget's neat signature (Viola had added 'of Saint Mary's Catholic Church'). Next was Commodore Billingsworth's name, written in cramped letters. Uther counted eight more names, none of which he recognised. He added his own below the last one, signing in such an indecipherable scrawl that nobody would ever have known it was Uther Tregeffen's autograph, then strolled to the other end of the high street and got a flyer from Commodore Billingsworth, who handed it over with a certain reluctance, as though he didn't really want Uther to have any part of the business.

Uther pretended to read what he'd already read at the other end of the road before saying, 'And may I sign?'

Commodore Billingsworth grunted and handed him a biro.

Uther scrawled a series of jagged lines, like a cross section of the Himalayas, across the paper. He saw that the Commodore's petition had even fewer names on it than Viola's had (which might perhaps have had something to do with the belligerent jut of the Commodore's jaw, which gave him the air of a man who would rather you didn't go anywhere near him and his folding table, let alone have the audacity to muck about with his paperwork).

'Thank you so much,' Uther breathed. 'A wonderful effort.' He bowed his head to the Commodore, and went to the pub and had a gin and tonic. A good start. A very good start indeed.

Later that evening he telephoned the Beaufort-Lyonses and told Rapunzel about the petition.

'I know,' said Rapunzel. 'I was there. Saw them at it. Didn't read their idiotic paper, of course.'

'And how will SPAM react?'

'We'll do a petition of our own, of course. You could help with it, if you like.'

'No I couldn't. I'm not good at that sort of thing. Just leave me to do my bit, there's a dear.'

'Oh, all right.'

It was interesting, thought Uther, how the note of

disappointment in Rapunzel's voice today so exactly matched the note of disappointment in Viola's last Saturday afternoon. 'What will you do?' he asked. 'Sit behind a table like CROSS?'

'No. That was too static for words and quite the wrong way to go about things. I'm sure they didn't manage to get much support doing that. They certainly didn't deserve to. It was obvious that Viola doesn't know much about activism. No, you have to be outgoing if you want to succeed. We shall move among the people, approaching them rather than trusting that they will approach us. We shall go to their pubs.'

'My dear, how enterprising.'

On Tuesday morning Rapunzel and Eric could be seen darting in and out of Polkerton's five public houses, sheaves of luminous green paper under their arms. Uther followed them at a discreet distance. At the end of their expedition, the Beaufort-Lyonses seemed to have almost the same amount of luminous green paper under their arms as when they started. Uther managed to find one, on the floor of the saloon bar at the Horse and Hounds. It had a muddy footprint on it and was soggy with spilt beer, but Uther bravely picked it up and took it to a table under a window.

It was headed: 'THE POLKERTON GIANT – THREATENED!!! DO YOU WANT TO SEE YOUR HERITAGE DESTROYED?' The footprint obscured much of the rest of the pamphlet, but Uther could make out the occasional phrase here and there. 'NATIONAL TREASURE', said one bit, and 'CULTURAL VANDALISM' another, and down at the bottom was a paragraph, mostly now unreadable, which contained the words 'PURPLE BUTTERWORT' and 'THE POINT OF EXTINCTION!'

All in all, thought Uther, swallowing the last of the lime jelly, it was a good start. Small and undramatic as yet, but there was plenty of time for things to develop. Nothing in the newspapers yet – perhaps a small nudge from him might be timely. He telephoned Viola.

'My dear, I've perused the papers from front to back, but nothing. Absolutely nothing.'

'Well, the Commodore wrote a marvellous letter to the *London Gazette* but they haven't published it yet.'

Uther told Viola about the SPAM pamphlet and Viola said, 'Green? How horrid.' After about twenty minutes, which was as long as Uther cared to talk on the telephone, he said goodbye and put the receiver down. Then he went to his address book, looked up the numbers of the *London Gazette* and dialled.

'The letters page. Simon Spillman, please. Uther Tregeffen calling.'

A minute later, Simon came on the line. 'Uther, you old bugger! How the hell are you?'

'Better before you shouted in my ear. We're not at Twickenham, dear boy. You are obviously hale, if a little too hearty. Now listen. Have you had a cross letter from a Commodore Billingsworth? About the Polkerton Giant?'

'What's the Polkerton Giant?'

'If you'd read the letter you'd know. Perhaps a minion?'

'You want me to find out?'

'Yes, please.'

Simon went off the line for a few minutes. While he was gone, the telephone played selections from Andrew Lloyd Webber musicals in Uther's ear. When Simon came back, Uther said, 'Mozart next time, please, or at a pinch Debussy. Well?'

'Apparently we did get one yesterday. Cross is right, Camilla says. Written in big letters along the top. A bit loony, Camilla says. We thought not.'

'Well, think again. It could be a rich vein to mine. You haven't thrown it away, have you?'

'No.'

'Good. Stick it in tomorrow's issue. You won't regret it.'

While Simon Spillman had done several stupid things in his life and had regretted all of them, he had never regretted any of his past actions that had been taken on advice from Uther Tregeffen, because every one of those actions had turned out well. So, when he put the telephone down, he said to Camilla, 'We'll do the loony tomorrow. Down the bottom in the funnies section. It's not filthy, is it?'

The next morning, the telephone trilled in Uther's bedroom.
'Hello?'

The Polkerton Giant

'Uthie, dear, it's Viola. Have you seen the *London Gazette*?'
'I have yet to open my eyes. Why?'
'The letter. The Commodore's letter – they've printed it.'
'Whoopee.'
'Shall I read it to you?'
'If you do, Viola, I shall never speak to you again. I haven't had my coffee yet. But I promise I'll look out for it.'

Later, over breakfast, he opened his paper and found the letter down at the bottom of the page.

Sir,
   I wish to draw your attention to an open obscenity currently despoiling one of the more scenic spots in the West of England. I refer to the so-called Palaeolithic chalk outline figure known, locally, as the Polkerton Giant. That this crude representation of a male figure, in a state that I can only describe, in a family newspaper, as one of arousement, has been tolerated and even admired for so many centuries is yet another example of the apathetic attitude towards the upholding of decent standards into which this country has been so long falling. It is time that a stand be taken against this kind of insidious filth and I and my colleagues at C.R.O.S.S. (Campaign for the Removal of Obscene Signs and Symbols) hereby give notice to the Public that a stand is currently being mounted to counter the blind acceptance of licentiousness in our fair land. The so-called Polkerton Giant must go!
Commodore Edwin Billingsworth, Retired.
CROSS

Uther telephoned Viola. 'Tremendous letter, I thought. Full of sound and fury. I should think there'll be lots of reaction to it. Is the Commodore pleased?'

'Tickled pink. He's never had anything in the *London Gazette* before.'

'What about the others?'

'Well, a bit of a disappointment with Father Roget – but then what can one expect from the Romans? He says the *Catholic Herald* doesn't really concern itself with this sort of thing, so it would be unlikely that they'd publish a letter about it. One would have thought, wouldn't one, that a voice for decency would find a welcome there?'

'One would.'

'Geoffrey Pargiter had promised to write to the *Polkerton Press* but there's no sign of it yet and, anyway, it won't have the same effect as a letter in the *London Gazette*.'

'Hardly.'

'I think they're both a bit mealy-mouthed, our clergy, I'm afraid.'

'They're just being meek. They want so desperately to inherit the earth.'

'Yes, well. Not good enough, in my book. I shall write to the bishop.'

Uther spent the rest of the morning working on his own letter. By lunchtime he'd come up with something that he thought would do.

Sir,

The Polkerton Giant: In reply to the letter from Commodore Billingsworth, may I suggest that where he sees licentious depravity, those more enlightened among us see nothing but a primitive beauty. The Polkerton Giant, far from being 'an open obscenity, currently despoiling one of the more scenic spots in the West of England', in fact represents Man's early struggle to understand his nature, in particular that part of him that responds in so oedematous a manner to the procreative urges that Nature instils in him, and those Palaeolithic peoples who created him did so with their simple innocence intact, which is more than can be said of Commodore Billingsworth's innocence, which seems far from simple and, indeed, appears to have been begrimed from birth. To destroy or deface the Polkerton Giant in any way would be an act of criminal vandalism. What next, I wonder, from the bigots? Bathing drawers on Michelangelo's David?

G. Flagstaffe, London.

'Simon? It's me again.'

The Polkerton Giant

'We put it in, Uther.'

'Yes, I know, and it looks very nice. Have you had any rebuttals?'

'Not the sort we're looking for. Just one really barking mad letter, claiming the giant is a fake.'

'Really? Who from?'

'Hang on a sec . . . here we are. It's from somebody with the unlikely name of Lysander Blount.'

'Well, well,' said Uther, slowly. 'Um, look – don't publish that one, Simon. We don't want the subject to go off at a tangent, do we? Obscene or not obscene, that is the question, not whether the thing's a fake. That's irrelevant.'

'All right. But we haven't had anything else.'

'I promised you a rich vein and you shall have one. From somebody called Flagstaffe. Wonderfully loony. You'll have to look up one of the words, which is always fun, isn't it? I shall fax it to you forthwith.'

'I say, Uther – it's not you writing them, is it?'

'Simon, how could you? What an idea! Certainly not. I merely have an interest, that's all. Mr Flagstaffe is a friend.'

'You said he was loony.'

'Am I not to be allowed any loony friends?'

'Is it any good?'

'Superb. Down the bottom again, I think.'

'If you say so. Camilla!'

After lunch, Uther decided to go for a drive. He went to the bathroom and adjusted Quentin, who had slipped a bit from all the literary effort of the morning. Then he tucked his folded copy of the *London Gazette* in his pocket and stepped outside. The day was sunny, so he wound down the window of the black Morris and went bowling along the lanes around Polkerton. One of the lanes happened to pass by Grassmere, and Uther casually turned the steering wheel and swung into the weedy gravel driveway.

Eric opened the door. He was puffing on his pipe and there was ash on the front of his corduroy jacket.

'Ahah! Hail to thee, blithe spirit.'

'Hello, Eric. Have you seen this?' Uther pulled the *London Gazette* from his pocket and waved it in front of Eric's face, managing in one stroke to catch Eric's attention and to force the tobacco smoke away from his own nostrils and back into the house, where rather a lot seemed to have collected, miasma-like, in the hallway.

'We're *New Independent* people, actually,' said Eric, his eyes watering.

'Well, never mind, perhaps you can't help it.'

They went to the drawing room. Rapunzel was there, at the table, half hidden behind a wall of books. When she saw Uther, she said, 'We're doing research on the chalk figures. Nobody seems to know much about them at all, and there's no mention of our giant anywhere. A bit about the Cerne Abbas one, probably because he's more complex and more visible than ours. Certainly, given the priapic nature of both of them, they are fertility symbols. They definitely date from the Stone Age, though.'

'I think I read somewhere that it's believed that couples from the local tribes used to fornicate on the member,' Uther said in a dreamy voice. 'They thought it would guarantee conception. So quaint.'

Rapunzel looked at him with interest. 'Where did you read that?'

He shrugged. 'I honestly can't remember. Funny how things stick in your memory though, isn't it? Oh, have you seen this?' He handed her the newspaper and she and Eric read it together.

'By jingo,' said Eric. 'I didn't know people like that still existed. Extraordinary.'

'Why on earth would they publish such nonsense?' Rapunzel said.

Uther shrugged noncommittally. 'Will you reply?' he asked.

'I don't think so. Why lower oneself to their level?'

Uther felt relieved. If there was to be an ongoing correspondence on the subject, it would be so much better if it was left to him to supply the letters. Somehow, he didn't think the Beaufort-Lyonses had the literary skills to keep the matter buoyant – they would be sure to sink the boat with their own earnestness.

'Besides,' said Rapunzel, 'we're rather more excited by our court order.'

'Oh yes. The purple butterwort. Have you got one?'

'Not yet.'

Uther turned down the offer of some nettle tea and left soon after. Small doses of the Beaufort-Lyonses (and even smaller doses of their nettle tea) went a long way. He resumed his afternoon drive. This time, the black Morris took him, circuitously, to the gates of the Grange. He drove up the drive between high banks of rhododendrons and, when they petered out, past the sweeping lawn with its three great oak trees, and up at last to the front door with its brass knocker in the shape of a dolphin.

Viola was in her reading room, a small space tucked to one side of the morning room. There were books in the reading room – leather-bound editions of Dickens and Thackeray and Surtees – but Viola was looking at a copy of the *Tatler*. When Uther came into the room she put the magazine down quickly. Then she saw the newspaper poking out of his jacket pocket. 'You've read it? Isn't it marvellous? Clever Edwin.'

'Even cleverer SPAM, I'm afraid. They're talking about a court order.'

'To do what?'

'To stop you, dear. And everybody else, it would seem.'

Uther told Viola about the purple butterwort and Viola snorted.

'I cannot see how some obscure little plant could possibly matter more than the necessary obliteration of an obscene eyesore. Really, sometimes these conservationists go too far.'

It had occurred to Uther that the purple butterwort might be just a weed. He'd looked closely at the stuff growing so vigorously in the middle of his lawn and, as far as he could tell, it was the same plant as the one growing between Pete's legs. He said ruminatively, 'Of course, if it was shown to be just a common little weed – well, so much for the Beaufort-Lyonses court order, eh? And they'd be absolute laughing stocks too, wouldn't they?'

Viola hugged herself. Then she frowned and said, 'But what if it's really rare? What then?'

'Well ... couldn't you find a botanist friend to go up there quietly one evening, when nobody was about, and take a look at it? It's right there, just under the . . . the – ah – the giant's thingy.'

'Where you were looking the other day?'

'Right there. You can't miss it.'

'Splendid. I shall send Norfolk.'

Norfolk was the Pomfrets' gardener, and the Pomfrets had hired the best. The gardens at the Grange were the finest for miles around and Norfolk had made them so. Norfolk's salary was high, but the Pomfrets didn't mind – it was, Victor Pomfret reasoned, a sensible investment, if only to persuade visitors to the Grange that Pomfret equipment, in the right hands, could produce vistas equally as lovely in their own back yards.

'Oh yes – send Norfolk. Now do tell, how did the petition go?'

'A bit measly, if you must know. People are so apathetic.'

'Aren't they just? Take heart, dear. I don't think SPAM did well either.'

'Well, of course not, Uthie. We at CROSS at least have right on our side. Even the most apathetic people can see that the Beaufort-Lyons lot, with their liberalism, are actively promoting lewdness.'

Any couple less likely to make lewdness attractive, Uther couldn't imagine. But he said, 'Yes, terrible. Quite terrible. So, what's next?'

'Well, I'm not sure. We don't really have enough to go to the council, and poor little me is a bit stumped. Do you have any ideas?'

'Well,' said Uther, 'I did have a thought.'

'Do tell.'

'Well . . . perhaps we might question not only the purple butterwort but also the authenticity of the giant. Perhaps it isn't really Palaeolithic at all. Perhaps it's much, much later? And if it is, then all that guff about "national heritage" and "priceless treasure" and "ancient monument" goes for nothing. What do you think?'

'But it *is* Palaeolithic, isn't it?'

Uther sighed. 'Probably, probably. But it doesn't matter, does it? It's the controversy we're after. Controversy sets the match and publicity flares – and that's what we need. The

The Polkerton Giant

more people made aware that there is a difference of opinion, the more will flock to your banner. Of course, they'll flock to SPAM's banner in equal numbers, I expect, but that's the nature of war and you can't have a war with only one side, can you?'

Viola put her head on one side and screwed her eyes tight shut, giving her head a little shake that made the permed curls quiver. It was all so confusing. Surely it didn't have to be. Right was right, no matter what sort of clever spin one put on things – and yet here was Uther talking about the dreadful Beaufort-Lyonses getting just as much support as she; and saying that that was to be expected! Viola had imagined a simple movement, unopposed, that would be carried to a successful conclusion, the quiet efficiency of it all raising her still further in the esteem of her friends. She certainly hadn't envisaged any sort of organised resistance . . . 'But I don't want a war, Uthie.'

'Yes you *do*, Viola. You think you don't, but you do. And anyway, you've got one whether you like it or not. So you'll simply have to make the best of it, and the best of it is the newsworthy qualities of the story. Now, what you really need is some national attention. Get the topic out of Polkerton and even out of Somerset. You'll never get anywhere if it remains a local issue.'

Viola had never imagined that her campaign would be anything other than a local issue, and she was impressed that Uther thought otherwise. Images of herself speaking on the radio and even, perhaps, appearing on television (like that wonderful if common woman who tried to get the dirty programmes stopped all the time – although with singular lack of success it seemed) leaped into her mind. She would wear her new blue suit with the white piping round the edges, and she'd wear the treble row of pearls round her neck and the matching drop pearl earrings, and everybody would come up to her after the broadcast and tell her how wonderfully she had come across and how very attractive she had looked . . .

'Now, Viola, dear heart, you've gone off somewhere. Come back this instant.' Uther was waving his hand across her eyes.

'Sorry, Uthie. I was thinking . . . Victor knows somebody at the BBC. He's on the board of governors, I believe.'

'That's good,' said Uther. He knew quite a lot of people at the BBC and several more at the independent television companies and, while some were on their boards of governors, others (and one in particular) were the sort of people who made the actual programmes and were therefore much more useful to know. (The boards of governors were unlikely to know anything about making programmes and probably knew only about being on boards of governors, which was useless as far as Uther was concerned).

Uther drove home that day feeling a strong sense of satisfaction. The hornet's nest that he'd stirred, so very gently at first, was humming. Humming was, at this stage of the proceedings, acceptable; later, when there'd been some more stirring, the humming would build to a proper buzzing; and with even more determined and vigorous stirring, the buzzing would rise in pitch and belligerence until it would be sensible to move away some distance and watch the fury from a safe vantage point.

Paris, perhaps. And then on from there. Lots of people to see, lots of places to go . . .

But not for a while yet.

Chapter 6

Evie Billingsworth sat at one end of the kitchen table, listening to her husband chewing on a piece of toast at the other. It was a noisy business. Edwin's teeth didn't fit well, and keeping them in place while coping with toast required effort. At least she couldn't *see* him doing it. As usual, Edwin had his newspaper propped up between the coffee pot and the milk jug. All Evie could see of him were his little hairy fingers curling round the edge of the paper.

Chomp, chomp, chomp.

Why couldn't he get a new set? Evie wondered. It wasn't as though they were so poor that they couldn't afford them (although Edwin was always harping on about the cost of everything). They both had their pensions, and Evie had a little money of her own, which paid for all the housekeeping and the rent on the flat, so they weren't all that badly off, really. The biggest expense came when they had to go to the Pomfrets' cocktail parties. Edwin didn't like Evie to wear the same dress, so she was forced to buy something new (with her own money, of course) almost every time they were invited. The dinner parties were worse, although there weren't as many of them. With the evening engagements, she really had to push the boat out and get something in satin or even silk – and that meant going without all sorts of nice things, for months it seemed, until the pot grew back to its original size.

It was all so pointless, really. She didn't even like going to the Pomfrets'. Once they were there, Edwin seemed to want to pretend that she didn't exist – and if she *must* exist, then he pretended she wasn't his wife at all, just some acquaintance he'd met up with at the party. If she pressed herself on him, then he'd talk to her as if she were a stranger.

As far as she was concerned, she'd be happy if she never had to go to another Pomfret party. Besides, it was obvious that Viola Pomfret couldn't care less if Evie came or stayed at home. It was Edwin she wanted, and her consequent disregard of Evie was almost rude.

But then, nearly everybody ignored Evie Billingsworth. She was a quiet, grey woman – grey hair, grey eyes, grey face – who rarely said anything unless she was asked a direct question, to which she would reply with such paucity of volume and such economy of speech that her audience either couldn't hear what she'd said, or came away knowing so little more about the subject that asking the question became waste of breath.

One set of hairy little fingers disappeared from the edge of the newspaper and a moment later Evie heard Edwin take a slurp of coffee, his teeth clicking against the rim of the mug. It would be quite pleasant, she thought, if Edwin would choke on his toast and coffee and die right here on the kitchen floor. She had decided, twenty-six years before, that she didn't like Edwin very much. After a year of not liking him very much, she decided she actively disliked him, and after a year of that she entered her Seriously Hating Edwin phase, which had lasted up to the present day. Once, when the boys were little, she'd thought of leaving him, but she'd lacked the confidence to believe that she could manage on her own, so she had stayed. Then the boys had grown up and one had gone off to New Zealand and the other to California, and by then she and Edwin had settled into an existence together that, while endlessly depressing, was at least familiar; so the thought of being anywhere other than with him hardly arose any more.

All the same, Edwin was easy to hate, being a hateful creature. And when Evie described him to herself as 'hateful', she meant literally that he was *full of hate*: for her, for anybody socially beneath them, for all religions other than Anglicanism, for homosexuals and the unemployed and the Labour Party and the unions and foreigners and foreign food . . . everything, in fact, that wasn't Commodore Edwin Billingsworth (or Viola Pomfret, whom he regarded with awed respect).

The Polkerton Giant

However, he reserved most of his spite for Evie, simply because she was handy and because she didn't answer him back. Commodore Billingsworth had a horror of being answered back. His small stature had long aggravated a pre-existent paranoia, and he was endlessly fearful of being punched on his nose, so he kept his hatreds concealed from everybody but Evie, who had to bear not only the diatribes against her own shortcomings but also his rantings about everybody else's.

Yes, Edwin would certainly be improved by death.

A page of the newspaper was turned. Then a faint tremor began at the top right hand corner of the newspaper, a tremor that became quickly a shudder, then a furious shaking – and Evie wondered if her wish had somehow been answered and Edwin was undergoing some sort of attack?

The paper was slowly lowered, revealing Edwin's face. It was purple, with veins bulging on both temples. 'Bloody hell!' he shouted, staring pop-eyed at Evie.

She shrank back in her seat. 'What?' she quavered.

'What? *What? This* fucking what! That's what!' Edwin's finger was stabbing at the newspaper. 'Some filthy fucking bugger has replied to my letter! Bastard says I was begrimed from birth! *Bastard!*'

'Oh dear,' said Evie, very quietly.

'Is that all you can say? Some filthy fucking buggering bastard says I'm begrimed from birth and that's all you can say?'

Evie shook her head. It was so awful when Edwin got like this. She'd discovered that it was best to stay silent, staring down at her plate. Edwin didn't want answers to his roared questions anyway. Just let him rant.

'What's his fucking name, eh? Flagstaffe. Filthy fucker. Lives in London. Well, of course. Might have known. Fucking little *shit*! Writes like a nancy boy. Probably looks like a nancy boy, too. Says the fucking thing on the hill is beautiful, so he must be a nancy boy. Filthy little pervert. Buggering little bastard. Little prick.'

The rage was subsiding into muttering imprecations. Evie watched as Edwin tore out a rough rectangle of paper from the bottom of the page and crumpled it in his hands. Then he threw it on the floor and stamped down on it with his heel.

'Hah! Squash you like a bug, little nancy boy. I'll begrime *you*.'

Evie began one of her daydreams. It unrolled in front of her eyes like a film, and it was so pleasant that a small smile hovered about her lips. A man is ringing on the doorbell of the flat. He is handsome – and when she goes to the door and opens it, he smiles down at her. 'Where is he?' he asks, and Evie replies, 'He's in the bedroom.' She leads the man down the passage and opens the bedroom door. Edwin is asleep on the bed. The man pushes past her and bends over Edwin and shakes him by the shoulder. 'Wake up, little fellow. Wake up.' Edwin wakes and stares at the figure looming over him. 'Who are you?' he says in a shaky voice, and the man says, 'I'm G. Flagstaffe, and I hear you think I'm a nancy boy.' And then the man starts hitting Edwin, forehand then backhand, across his face . . .

'What are you grinning at?'

Evie's dream blew apart like smoke in a sudden gust of wind. Edwin was staring crossly at her.

'Nothing, dear.'

'Nothing? Why do it then?'

'I don't know, dear.'

'Stupid.'

A tiny bubble of rage – all that Evie Billingsworth could manage – rose in her throat. How dare he say she was stupid? For a start, she was much better educated than he was. Edwin hardly knew anything and she knew lots about all sorts of things. And then he was always doing really stupid things – like calling himself 'Commodore' just because he'd run a second-rate yacht club in Lowestoft. That was ridiculous.

Then the bubble burst and the small fury went away – but it left behind a seed of rebellion. She would show him, she thought. She'd do something quite apart from their usual dull lives, something that didn't involve him and, indeed, excluded him completely. Something just for her. Something . . . something . . .

Something what? What *could* she do? Sadly, she opened

The Polkerton Giant

her paper, the one Edwin didn't like to read. To be honest, she didn't like reading it either. It was boring. The *Polkerton Press*. Advertisements for second-hand washing machines. Announcements of agricultural machinery sales. Winners of livestock prizes. A picture of a smirking schoolboy clutching a rosette. Notices of church services

Then, catching Evie's eye at the bottom of the third page, there was an outlined rectangle, headed by the masks of Tragedy and Comedy. Under the masks, the words 'The Polkerton Players'. Beneath that it read: 'Forthcoming Summer Production: *Peer Gynt* by Henryk Ibsen. Brady Street Community Hall. Reserve your tickets NOW!!!' There was a telephone number, and down at the bottom of the rectangle, in smaller letters: 'Wanted: *Enthusiastic!!* Backstage Volunteers needed for help with Wardrobe, Box Office, Scenic Construction and Stage Management. Contact Rapunzel Beaufort-Lyons at the above telephone number.'

The beating of Evie Billingsworth's heart accelerated. Rapunzel Beaufort-Lyons. The name of the enemy. Edwin had spent half an hour telling Evie what horrors the Beaufort-Lyonses were, and how they were to have nothing to do with them. Well, having something to do with the Beaufort-Lyonses could be her own little rebellion against Edwin's tyranny. And here was something she could do. Certainly not act – that was out of the question: the thought of standing up on stage and having all those eyes staring at her . . . no, no, she couldn't – but helping out with some of the technical problems . . . Wardrobe, for instance. Well, that wasn't beyond her capabilities. She assumed that 'wardrobe' didn't mean a cupboard, it meant the costumes that went in the cupboard – and that was something she could be useful at. She had a sewing machine and she was quite good with it. She'd done a bit of painting at school too, and her art teacher had said she had talent – so perhaps they might let her try her hand at the scenic construction. 'Box office' was surely just counting money, and she could do that too. Quite what 'stage management' entailed, Evie wasn't certain. It sounded a little executive, a little high-powered, and she lacked the confidence for anything with the sort of responsibility that it suggested. But everything else . . . well, what did she have to lose? The worst that could happen would be that they would turn her down, and she could bear that. It had happened before. Perhaps she might give Rapunzel Beaufort-Lyons a ring – after Edwin had left for one of his now-daily meetings with Viola Pomfret. Evie wondered if they were having an affair. Then she dismissed the idea as being too preposterous. Nobody could possibly find Edwin attractive enough to want to go to bed with him.

After he'd gone, she went to the phone. She dialled the number from the paper, feeling nervous.

A man answered with a noisy 'Hellohellohello?' and Evie said, 'Oh! Er – Mrs Beaufort-Lyons, please,' in a tiny voice.

A minute later Rapunzel said, 'Yes?'

'Oh, Mrs Beaufort-Lyons. It's me, Evie Billingsworth.'

Rapunzel couldn't think who this might be. 'Oh, hello,' she said, in the warm tones people use when they don't recognise either the name or the voice of the person on the other end of the line.

'Oh dear, I don't suppose you remember me. We met at the Pomfrets'. I was with my husband, Commodore Billingsworth.'

Ah, the little grey woman with the awful man who looked like Monty. The same man who'd written the letter. One of Viola's allies. So what on earth could the wife want? Rapunzel made a face at Eric, who was standing close by.

'Yes, of course. How are you, Mrs Billingsworth?'

'Oh, I'm well, thank you. How kind of you to ask. Oh dear . . . The reason I'm calling you is the advertisement in the *Polkerton Press* – about the Players.'

'Yes?'

'Oh, well, I was wondering if you might be able to find something for me to do. I would love to help . . . Oh dear, perhaps you'd rather not. That's quite all right and I do understand and I hope you'll forgive me for calling—'

'No, please, Mrs Billingsworth . . .'

'Oh, do call me Evie – unless you'd rather not, of course. So forward of me to suggest it, I'm so sorry—'

'We'd love to have you, really.'

'Oh, good heavens. Really? I'd be very quiet.'

Any quieter than she was being right now, Rapunzel

thought, and Evie Billingsworth might as well not bother opening her mouth at all. 'Really – we need volunteers desperately. Everybody wants to act, you see, and nobody wants to work backstage.'

'Backstage?' It sounded so glamorous, Evie thought.

'Yes,' said Rapunzel. 'You don't want to act as well, do you?'

'Oh, no. Oh dear, no. Oh, I couldn't. Would I have to?'

'No, not at all. We've got more than enough actors. No, we need technical people. What sort of thing would you like to do?'

'Oh, well – I thought perhaps help with the costumes.'

'The wardrobe?'

'Oh, yes, the wardrobe. And perhaps . . . oh dear . . . perhaps I could do a little painting too. I wasn't bad at school. Not *good*, of course, but not too bad. But I expect you've got experts doing that, haven't you? So you probably wouldn't want me—'

'Really, Evie, we need you desperately. Why don't you come to our next little gathering? Then you could meet everybody and we could talk about fitting you in.'

Fitting in. What a wonderful phrase. Evie had never fitted in anywhere. Nobody had known what to do with her, and so they'd ignored her for the most part. It was as though she was nothing but an afterthought. That was how it had felt all these years – and now Rapunzel Beaufort-Lyons was proposing to *fit* her *in* to a group of glamorous people who used words like 'wardrobe' and 'backstage' and 'scenic construction'.

'Oh, thank you, Mrs Beaufort-Lyons. Thank you so much.'

'No – thank *you*, Evie. Well, look, our next rehearsal is actually tomorrow. At the Community Hall in Brady Street at seven in the evening. Can you come?'

Seven in the evening was exactly the time that she and Edwin sat down to supper. Well, tomorrow, Edwin could sit down by himself. She was surprised by her sudden determination and wondered why she'd never done this before – gone out somewhere when the mood came on her, without thinking to ask Edwin if she may. She realised with a start that she wasn't actually frightened of him at all. It hadn't been fear that had kept her at home in front of the television screen; it was just that she'd never had anywhere to go before, and therefore had no reason to ask Edwin if she might. But now she had somewhere to go, and the feeling that she ought to ask Edwin simply wasn't there – and the decision to let Edwin eat a solitary supper was surprisingly easy to make. She'd leave him something on a tray . . .

'Evie? Hello?'

'Yes, Mrs Beaufort-Lyons. Oh, yes. I shall come tomorrow.'

Rapunzel put down the receiver and looked at Eric. 'Very odd,' she said. 'That was the Billingsworth woman. She wants to join the Players. Technical only.'

'Do we know her?'

'Sort of. We met her briefly years ago at that ghastly party Viola gave. I don't think she spoke once.'

'Technical, eh? Well, that's marvellous, isn't it?'

'Yes, unless she's just spying on us. We'll have to keep our eyes on her.'

The rest of the Beaufort-Lyonses' morning was spent discussing G. Flagstaffe's letter and how they could get in touch with him. They telephoned the *London Gazette*; but the man said the paper never gave out the addresses of its correspondents. He suggested the Beaufort-Lyonses might like to write a letter of their own (which the paper would not guarantee printing), inviting G. Flagstaffe and anybody of a like mind-set to join their organisation.

So Eric and Rapunzel sat together at the table and composed a letter, deploring the bigoted attitude of Billingsworth and lauding the response of G. Flagstaffe.

When they'd finished, they telephoned Uther and read it to him; for some reason his approval seemed necessary. When he expressed it, they faxed it to the *London Gazette*.

Viola was having a hard time with the Commodore. The fact that she too had come across G. Flagstaffe's response to his original letter seemed to outrage him even more, and she was having difficulty bringing him out of the stratosphere of his fury and back to earth without burning up entirely.

'And Evie – damn her! (pardon my French) – just sat there, saying "what?".'

The Polkerton Giant

'Poor you.'

'If I could get my hands on that bas— that damn fellow, I'd tear him to pieces. I don't mind telling you, Mrs Pomfret, when my dander is up, there's no stopping me.'

'I'm sure there isn't, dear Commodore – but you must call me Viola and I shall call you Edwin.'

'Ah. Ahah. Right. Good. Viola and Edwin it shall be. Ha ha.'

He seemed mollified by this. Viola took him companionably by the arm and walked him to the drawing room and poured him a whisky and soda.

'Thing is, Mrs Pom— Viola, the thing *is*, we ought to reply. Put the fellow in his place. Any ideas along those lines?'

Viola fetched several sheets of blue writing paper and a couple of matching envelopes. There was a small, embossed drawing of the Grange on the head of the writing paper and another on the flaps of the envelopes. They sat together at Viola's desk in her reading room, their hipbones joined by the daintiest of pressures, and worked over a second letter to the *London Gazette*, in which G. Flagstaffe and any who thought like him were dismissed as the most misguided and foolish of New Agers. Those readers who agreed with the opinions expressed by the authors of *this* letter (Commodore E. Billingsworth, Mrs Viola Pomfret, and the fast-growing membership of CROSS – too numerous to name individually) were invited to join the battle to remove the Polkerton Giant in their first step towards the cleansing of the British countryside.

After Edwin had gone, Viola called Uther and read their letter to him over the telephone. Uthie's taste was impeccable and his opinion invaluable.

With his unreserved praise ringing in her ears, Viola faxed the letter to the *London Gazette*.

This time Uther wrote two letters.

One was signed 'Gloria Wattle, R.N.' and was vehemently in favour of leaving the Polkerton Giant alone on his hill. Nurse Wattle also said that she thought the members of CROSS must be a bunch of sorry souls, obsessed by sex, whose prurience so discoloured their attitudes that their opinions on this (or any) subject should be regarded with suspicion by the rest of us.

The other letter came from an Indian shopkeeper in Bradford, Mr Durbhan Singh, who wholeheartedly concurred with the aims of CROSS, accused G. Flagstaffe of latent pederasty, and condemned all depictions of genitalia, both male and female, as being deeply offensive to his religion (which he carelessly omitted to name).

Not owning a fax machine, Uther took his letters to the Polkerton post office and faxed them to the paper from there. While he was in the post office, he slipped into a telephone booth and called Simon Spillman.

'Some more coming, Simon. Four, I believe. Landing on your desk as we speak.'

'*Four?*'

'I think four, yes.'

'And you're really not writing them?'

'Cross my heart and hope to die, spit, spit.'

'All right. I believe you. Thousands wouldn't. Any good?'

'Getting better. All worthwhile, I think. Pros and antis, so you've got a definite correspondence going. I believe – and keep this under your hat – but I *believe* there's some interest in this from Satellite West, and even a nibble from the BBC, so the *London Gazette* can take credit for starting something, can't it?'

'Not something we really go in for, Uther. We leave all that "starting" stuff to the tabloids. Still, it's quite fun, so we'll go along with it for the time being. But if it looks like it's getting boring we'll have to drop it. Even if it's fascinating, we can't carry anything for more than a week. The readers don't like anything longer than that.'

'A week is fine,' said Uther. He was getting tired of the letters, anyway. It was time to move on to greater efforts.

Chapter 7

Brady Street Community Hall was an ugly, single-story, redbrick building off Polkerton High Street. It had a tar-paper roof, a small parking lot, and a peeling notice board screwed to the side of the structure, so that any passer-by could read the list of forthcoming events and attractions that could be found within its walls. It was used by a number of organisations, and the Polkerton Players had to fight for their rehearsal and performance times with claims on the space by the Mother's Union, the Women's Institute, the Boy Scouts, the Girl Guides and the British Legion. Other, lesser groups like the Knitting Club and the Polkerton Chess Society fitted in when they could.

Tuesday and Thursday evenings, between seven and tenthirty, were reserved for the Polkerton Players' rehearsals. At ten-thirty, the sour old Polish janitor, Mr Skidelski, would arrive to lock the place up for the night. He didn't care if Rapunzel was right in the middle of one of her long speeches – he would crash open the doors of the rehearsal room and stand foursquare in the opening, the bunch of keys rattling in his hand, and he would keep rattling them until the cast stopped whatever they were doing and gathered their belongings together and ducked past him into the night.

Tonight, with three and a half clear hours before Mr Skidelski would make his uncompromising entrance, Rapunzel, Eric and the core members of the Polkerton Players were gathered in the rehearsal room. They sat in tubular steel and canvas chairs and sipped at the fawn, opaque liquid that Grace Stanley called coffee and which she had taken upon herself to provide at every meeting. They nibbled at her biscuits too, which were a little nicer than the coffee. At the back and several feet away from the nearest player, sat Evie Billingsworth. Her eyes were wide with excitement until somebody looked at her – then she would lower her eyelids and stare at the linoleum. Even further back, in the shadows of a far corner of the room, sat Uther Tregeffen.

Rapunzel looked at her watch. Seven forty-five. Time to start. She got up and moved to the front of the room, where the low stage had been built across the space. She perched her angular rear on the lip of the stage and looked out over her actors.

'Hello? Everybody? Could we start? Jack? Hello-o? Full attention, please, everybody. Thank you. I've rather a lot to say. First of all, as you've no doubt noticed, we have our good friend Uther Tregeffen with us. Hello, Uther – you're right at the back, I see. Wouldn't you like to come forward a little? No? All right, stay where you are, then. Uther asked if he might visit and I said he was very welcome, so here he is.

'Now, I would also like to introduce everybody to Evie Billingsworth. Evie, please stand up. Ladies and gentlemen, this is Evie Billingsworth.'

Evie half rose to her feet and stood bent over in embarrassment, her crimson face turned down towards the floor.

'Evie has expressed an interest in joining the Players – on the technical side, you'll be pleased to hear.'

There was an ironic cheer and Jack Lunn said, 'Thank God for that.'

Rapunzel continued. 'Evie has very kindly volunteered to take over our wardrobe department.'

'Oh,' squeaked Evie, inaudibly even to Grace Stanley, who was sitting closer to her than anybody else. 'Oh dear. I'm not sure I could manage actually taking over – just a bit of sewing . . .'

'Thank you, Evie. We're all most grateful. And perhaps when you know your way around, we might press-gang you into a bit of assistant stage management.'

'Oh . . .'

'Thank you again, Evie. Everybody please introduce yourselves to Evie – no, not now, Jack. Right now I need everybody's full attention, please. I'm going to propose something rather radical, rather daring and just a little bit scary for us all.'

'You're not going to bring the opening forward, are you?' said Maureen Lodson, who was still working on her Arabian dance and was counting on at least another three weeks before the public would see it.

'No, no, Maureen. No, we still open on the twenty-fifth. No – I'm afraid my proposal is even bolder than that. Now, first of all, may I say how wonderfully well rehearsals of *Peer Gynt* are going. You're all being splendid. It's a tremendous effort from everybody, in a difficult piece, and Eric and I have been deeply, deeply impressed by everybody's commitment to Ibsen's wonderful masterpiece.'

There was a brief ovation, which would have been thunderous had the Players numbered more than they did.

Rapunzel held up her hands. 'Eric, your Peer is, if I may say so, peerless.'

'Hear, hear!' cried Jack Lunn, beating his beefy hands together with great force, in the belief that if he showed sufficient admiration for Eric Beaufort-Lyons's performance, then perhaps Rapunzel Beaufort-Lyons might look more kindly on him when casting the next production and let him play a part that had more than five lines to it.

Eric got up and bowed. He said, 'We can't do it without our superb director, whose Solveig is, in all our estimations, unsurpassed.'

'Bravo!' shouted Jack Lunn.

Rapunzel smiled graciously. 'You're very kind. As for my direction, when one moulds clay one hopes for the finest quality – and I think I can say, without reservation, that you are all of clay that Pygmalion would have been proud to knead.'

'Marvellously said!' yelled Jack Lunn, wondering what Rapunzel was talking about.

'Now,' said Rapunzel, putting on her serious, let's-get-down-to-business face. 'Now, that being said, on to the matter in hand. Eric and I have been discussing this at length and we believe we ought to make a major change. A change that is drastic and that some might say is unfortunately in midstream, considering the work we have already put in and with regard to the work that is yet to come.'

Rapunzel paused, muddled for a moment by her own syntax. Perhaps she was sugar-coating the proposal too much and should simply come straight out with it? She glanced at Eric and he nodded back encouragingly.

She took a deep breath. 'In fact, what Eric and I have discussed is the idea that we ought to stop doing *Peer Gynt* and do something else instead.'

There was a long silence and several of the Players looked questioningly at one another.

Rapunzel explained: 'A different play, you see.'

There was another silence and then Jack Lunn put his hand up.

'Yes, Jack?'

'How about *Journey's End*? Marvellous play, that.'

Rapunzel breathed a sigh of relief. She and Eric had assumed that there would be violent objections, mostly concerning the fact that there were only three weeks left before their proposed opening night and it was a bit late to embark on something new – but here was Jack Lunn looking perfectly ready to drop his part in *Peer Gynt* in favour of a First World War uniform.

'Superb play, Jack. One of the very best. But, unfortunately, no parts for women, Jack.'

There was a low rumbling of discontent, and all the women except Evie looked at Jack Lunn with disfavour.

'Ah. Right. Sorry. Didn't think of that.' Damn. He'd set his heart on playing Stanhope.

Now another hand was waving hopefully.

'Yes, Maureen?'

'Well, if we're not going to do *Peer Gynt*, I was wondering if we might do something a bit lighter?'

'Lighter?'

'Yes. We always seem to do these really serious plays, and I was wondering if we couldn't do a comedy. A Noël Coward or something.'

Rapunzel smiled sweetly at Maureen, as though the plump, middle-aged woman in the front row were a pretty, wayward child. 'We could, Maureen, we could. But do we really *want* to? That's what we have to ask ourselves – do

The Polkerton Giant

we really want to? There are so many wonderful, profound, significant plays – plays that instruct and illustrate and illuminate, plays that lift the spirit to realms of wonder, plays that light up the dark corners of the human condition and show us the path to self-improvement – so many deep and truthful plays just begging to be performed, that there honestly seems little point in bothering with the shallow froth of Noël Coward.'

'It's just that they're a bit gloomy,' said Maureen stubbornly. 'I think that's why we don't get many people coming to see us. They want cheering up and all we do is depress them.'

Perhaps, Rapunzel thought, she ought to have stepped aside and let Maureen Lodson play Solveig rather than fobbing her off with the Arabian dancing girl. Of course, Maureen wouldn't have been any good as Solveig (and was an ungainly and overweight Arabian dancing girl), but this minor mutiny from a normally cheerful and useful member of the Polkerton Players demonstrated to Rapunzel that Maureen Lodson was becoming disaffected – and disaffection was the last thing she needed at the moment.

'Well, Maureen may have raised a very interesting point,' she said. 'Perhaps we might consider putting on something a little lighter in the Autumn – and, if we do, I hope Maureen will take a leading role. We know how adept she is at raising chuckles.'

During rehearsals Maureen had been raising several chuckles as the Arabian dancing girl – mostly from Jack Lunn – but, fortunately, she hadn't heard any of them. She'd been putting a lot of effort into her dance – and it had been strenuous, full of clashing finger cymbals and tinkling ankle bells and lots of swirling pink chiffon – and the effort had been so noisy that the muffled laughter from some members of the cast had been drowned.

'I'd love to,' she said now with eagerness. 'Why not *Private Lives*? I've always wanted a stab at Amanda.'

A stab it would undoubtedly be, thought Rapunzel. Anybody less equipped to play Amanda than Maureen Lodson she couldn't imagine. Maureen weighed almost fifteen stone, bleached her hair a startling shade of yellow and looked like a farcical barmaid (of course there was nothing wrong with barmaids – on the contrary, they were the absolute essence of salt-of-the-earth – it was just that Amanda in *Private Lives* really oughtn't to look like one). Rapunzel thought she might, at a pinch, cast Maureen as the maid – always supposing they were going to do *Private Lives* in the first place, which was, she determined, unlikely.

'*Private Lives*? Now there's a thought. We shall certainly keep it in mind. Thank you, Maureen. However, back to the present production. Eric and I have had some discussions on this, and we came to believe that perhaps we ought to attempt something more relevant to the times we live in. Something original, with a local connection, we thought. And with that in mind . . . are you all aware of the controversy currently surrounding our famous landmark, the Polkerton Giant?'

'What? Old poke-it-in-Pete?' Jack said, and he banged his fat hands down hard on his knees.

'Yes, ha ha. The very same, Jack.'

'Bit hard, Rappie, for anybody *not* to know about it.'

Rapunzel winced. *Nobody* called her 'Rappie' – except Jack Lunn, whose position as Polkerton's only ironmonger hardly gave him the licence for such familiarity (of course, there was nothing wrong with being an ironmonger – on the contrary, ironmongers represented the very best of the working man – it was just that Rapunzel preferred – when buying a hammer, perhaps – to keep the relationship between them a purely professional one, while dear Jack seemed determined to make it personal).

'So, you all know what's at stake here?'

There was a nodding of heads but no vocal agreement, which led Rapunzel to believe that perhaps the Players weren't as familiar with the situation as she and Eric were – so she spent the next five minutes on a brief but imaginative history of the Polkerton Giant, stressing the importance of preserving such an ancient and priceless monument.

She noticed that Evie Billingsworth was staring at the floor. 'Now, you all know where Eric and I stand, and I'm sure I don't need to wonder where all of you stand either.

The Polkerton Giant

You would hardly be a Polkerton Player if you were among the ranks of those who would wish to destroy such a significant artefact, so I am confident that we are on the same side. If anybody feels differently, perhaps they would like to raise their hand . . .'

Ever since Rapunzel had introduced Evie Billingsworth, it had been dawning on the Players one by one that Evie must be the wife of the appalling Commodore Billingsworth, who was so openly allied to the equally appalling Viola Pomfret. Now Evie felt twelve pairs of eyes boring into the top of her bent head. Oh heavens, they knew – about Edwin, and his passion for Viola, and how he hated everything else including his wife, and all about his silly attitude to the giant – and now they probably thought she was a spy or something . . .

Evie raised her head and met Rapunzel's steady gaze. Oh dear. It was no good. She would have to say something.

'Oh . . . please . . . I don't agree with my husband. Not at all. About anything. Well, some things, of course. But not this. No. He's quite wrong. They're all wrong. You're right. There's nothing dirty about it. About the giant. Oh dear. I just want to help. I don't agree at all. Not with them. I agree with you . . .'

Her voice, whisper-quiet, petered away to nothing. There was a moment of silence. Then Rapunzel raised both her hands to one side of her head, pressed the pulse points of her wrists together, and clapped, with just the tips of her fingers meeting in a series of dry little taps.

'Thank you, Evie, and well said! Well *said*!'

Eric started to clap as well, then Jack Lunn joined in, banging his hands together like a sealion – and then all the rest of the Players began applauding her and Evie felt a sudden elation. They were going to *like* her and, perhaps, even take notice of her and talk to her and listen to her . . .

'So, we are *united*,' said Rapunzel. 'How marvellous. Without unity, there can be no teamwork and, without teamwork, there could be no Polkerton Players. Which brings me to our production. It occurred to Eric and me that, with this controversy raging, perhaps we might try to mount an *original* work rather than a Norwegian classic and, to that end, Eric himself has been working on the outline of a play all about the Polkerton Giant.'

To most of the Players the controversy didn't seem to be raging at all, but if Rapunzel Beaufort-Lyons said it was raging then, in her mind at least, it was; and since Rapunzel Beaufort-Lyons was the artistic director of the Polkerton Players, with the power of casting in her hands alone – then raging it would be.

'The play that Eric and I have in mind,' Rapunzel said, 'will take the audience back to Palaeolithic times. It is set in a Stone Age settlement, here where Polkerton presently stands. The set is a composite, representing various caverns in the side of a hill, and it is in the main one of these caves that the tribe – which Eric has called the People of the Polk – meet and discuss the day's events. A sort of council chamber, you see. There are some marvellous parts for everybody. Maureen, I see you as one of the leads, playing Pomunka, the fierce chief of the women, who is unable to conceive by her warrior husband Harga, who has, unfortunately, lost the ability to procreate during a battle with another tribe – that's you, Jack, I thought, in another leading role – and it is Pomunka and Harga who bring the idea of creating a giant statue to the god of fertility to the council chamber. Poppy and Roger, you will be playing the young lovers—'

'What are *you* going to play?' Jack said, torn between his excitement over finally landing a leading part and his disinclination to act somebody who would appear, to the audience at least (and if he understood Rapunzel correctly), to be missing his manhood.

'I shan't be in it, Jack. Not this time. I shall just be directing this time.'

The Polkerton Players, as one, sat up a little straighter. This was a first. Rapunzel Beaufort-Lyons had never 'just directed'. She was always in the play as well, always in a leading role. Why not this time?

'What about Eric?' said Jack.

'Eric will be too busy putting the piece together to play any parts in it. And here's the really exciting part, everybody. Eric would like *your* input on this project, so what we're going to do is *improvise* scenes during the rehearsal period, and

The Polkerton Giant

whatever works will be put into the script – so let your imaginations run wild on this!'

Looking out over the dozen faces that were looking dumbly back at her, Rapunzel wondered if there were any Polkerton Players who had imaginations that ran to wildness. But she supposed between them they might manage to generate enough collective Palaeolithic spirit to convince the audience that they were transported back in time to the Stone Age . . . particularly if the Players would accept, without question, the next two ideas she was about to suggest.

'Now, because this is a new venture for us – a truly original piece, created by ourselves – and because our time is limited, I am going to ask that you all drop everything and try to rehearse every night of the week. Tuesdays and Thursdays from seven-thirty, as usual. The rest of the week – well, I have spoken to Mr Skidelski and he has agreed to let us have the hall from ten-thirty until two o'clock in the morning. If we use all those lovely extra hours and really put our backs into it, this will give us, I think, just enough time before the twenty-fifth to whip ourselves into shape. I take it that all of you will be able to manage this new schedule?'

There were no sounds of dissent. It was rather wonderful, thought Rapunzel, how the promise of good parts to amateur actors overcame any objections they might have to the disruption of their social lives. (It was also rather wonderful what the gift of £500 did to the personality of irritable Polish caretakers, although there was no necessity for the Players to know anything about that side of things).

She and Eric had been right to step aside and take no acting parts – besides, they had agreed the night before that neither of them cared to subject themselves to what Rapunzel visualised for the rest of the cast, or at least those who might be willing.

'Oh, splendid. Thank you all. Now, I do think it's important that we get it absolutely right. Authenticity must be one of our main goals here. Our attitudes to life, our ways of speaking to one another—'

'Ayahh. Hi did they tork, thin?' said Aileen Beresford.

(Rapunzel did a swift translation in her head: *'Oh. How did they talk, then?'*) 'Well, of course we don't really know,

Aileen,' she said, wondering for the hundredth time where, exactly, Aileen Beresford had found her accent. It was undoubtedly upper-class, but the vowels were so mangled by her gentility and the consonants so often missing entirely that sometimes it was hard to understand what she was trying to say. Aileen, she thought, would have to take a non-speaking role this time. There would be, she decided, no Knightsbridge modulations in the cave of the Polk People.

'However,' Rapunzel continued, 'I think we can be fairly sure that the language was in its infancy, so simplicity must be our watchword.'

'Ooga ooga,' said Jack Lunn.

'Perhaps a little more advanced than that, Jack. Ideas were certainly exchanged during this period – the giant is proof positive of that – and I think such complex communication would have been difficult, if not impossible, with just "ooga ooga", don't you? So, we will work on our attitudes and on our speech – and, of course, on our appearance.'

Rapunzel paused, letting the last word gather weight. This was the crunch, the moment she had been building towards. She took a breath and said, firmly, 'Animal skins, of course. Bare feet. And legs. And arms. And – ah – tops.'

'Bare tops?' said Maureen, in a puzzled voice.

'Well of course, Maureen. It was a primitive society.'

'Hurr, hurr,' said Jack Lunn. He turned in his seat and grinned lasciviously at Maureen and she blushed and looked away.

'What – all of us without tops?' said Poppy Boscombe. She was the youngest Player and the prettiest, and Rapunzel had let her play Irina in *Three Sisters*.

'Some of them covered themselves up, surely?' said Maureen. 'I mean, surely they didn't all go around showing everything all the time, did they?'

'Probably not all the time, no,' said Rapunzel. So far, she thought, she was pleasantly surprised at the Players' reactions. It seemed that prudery didn't have that strong a grip on them. She had expected a lot of resistance and, so far, it had been mild. No volunteers, it was true, but no outright refusals either. Now was the moment to let those that wanted no part of this off the hook, before any serious dissension could be voiced.

'Look, I realise that some of you would have a problem with this – although I can't think why, the human body is a beautiful thing . . .'

'Not everybody's,' Maureen said darkly. She stared hard at Jack Lunn's back.

'Everybody's,' said Rapunzel firmly.

'"Age cannot not wither her, nor custom stale her infinite variety,"' said Eric.

'I don't know about wither,' said Maureen. 'I just know I'm not taking my top off for anybody.'

'And as Pomunka you won't have to, Maureen. Pomunka is a senior member of the People of the Polk and, as such, would be richer than the others. So she would have more skins than the rest, you see. Enough to cover the top.'

Her modesty no longer in jeopardy, Maureen subsided in her seat and began to think of how she would do her hair.

Jack Lunn put his hand up.

'Yes, Jack?'

'What about old Harga, then? What's he wear?'

'He too is a senior member, Jack, and could be covered if you'd rather.'

'Righto. Don't want the girls to get too excited, eh?'

Maureen Lodson snorted loudly and said, 'Silly bugger. You couldn't excite a blind nymphomaniac, you couldn't.'

Aileen Beresford was waving her hand in small circles, like the Queen Mother at a parade.

'Yes, Aileen?'

'Ay wouldn't maind, ectually. Be a hoot.'

'Thank you, Aileen.'

And Rapunzel gave silent thanks to the muse of exhibitionism – assuming there was one, of course. Aileen Beresford had a plain face, but she had a spectacular figure. She wore tight shirts or sweaters, cut to accentuate the swell of her bosom and the thinness of her waist, and she manipulated her torso in such a way that the eye was drawn not to her long, horse-like face but to the twin points of her breasts. When talking to her, most men's eyes drifted downwards (Jack Lunn openly addressed all his remarks to her chest). Aileen had never taken offence at any of this and, indeed, seemed pleased with the effect, so it came as no surprise to Rapunzel that Aileen would be the first to volunteer.

'Whoo, whoo,' said Jack Lunn, and Aileen stuck her tongue out at him.

'Anybody else?'

Young Roger Gower (who, when he wasn't being a chartered accountant spent most of his leisure time in the gym) coughed and cleared his throat and said he wouldn't mind particularly, so long as he and Aileen weren't the only two. Then Poppy Boscombe, who had no bosom at all, said she thought it might be rather an interesting experiment and would certainly think about it, but only if she had a really long wig and a roll of Sellotape. And everybody began to join in a general discussion of the matter – mostly jocular, Rapunzel was relieved to notice.

She drifted over to Evie Billingsworth and sat down next to her. 'What do you think, Evie?'

Evie didn't know what to think. It was shocking and absurd and exciting and unbelievably brave. While she couldn't conceive of doing anything like it herself (and could hardly bring herself to glance at the those who had volunteered), she wanted desperately to be a part of it, to show everybody that she wasn't the dull grey mouse everybody thought she was. Most of all, she wanted to outrage Edwin. She wanted to turn him purple, make him splutter and choke, make him gape and gasp and, with a bit of luck, cause him to have a decisively nasty cardiac arrest so he would never turn purple or splutter or choke at anybody ever again.

'Oh, well . . . I think it will be – oh – innovative.'

'Exactly, Evie. *Innovative*. Now, what about you helping out with the costumes?'

'Oh, well, yes. Perhaps I could draw something for you? I'm not very good but perhaps you could – oh – get some sort of idea?'

Rapunzel patted Evie on the shoulder and said some drawings would be wonderful. Then she went back to her perch on the edge of the stage and began to talk about

The Polkerton Giant

Palaeolithic motivation, which Evie didn't understand. She stopped listening and began to think about animal skin clothes, without tops to some of them. Did Mrs Beaufort-Lyons mean *real* animal skins, or did she mean that fake nylon fur stuff? Whichever, they could be cut like nappies, perhaps. One size to fit all. That wouldn't be too difficult, surely? And the men could have a sort of strap of fur going over one shoulder, like the old strong man in the circus . . .?

Perhaps they had fur hats as well . . .?

She felt movement at her side and turned to see the nice-looking man with the yellow wig settling himself into the chair next to her. He held out his hand and Evie took it.

'Uther Tregeffen,' he said, in a whisper. 'I'm new too. Isn't it terrifying?'

Chapter 8

Eric Beaufort-Lyons was having second thoughts about the purple butterwort. What if it wasn't purple butterwort at all? If it wasn't, then there was some danger that he was going to look silly. It might be best to drop the whole thing – but, of course, Rapunzel would never let him. She was already impatient that he hadn't yet contacted their lawyer and was threatening to do it herself. He really ought to get hold of a botanist but he didn't know any. Perhaps if he bought a book...?

Norfolk's position in the Pomfret household was a powerful one. The Pomfrets were justly nervous of him, and Viola's airy remark that he would be dispatched to Giant's Hill had been nothing more than bravado on her part. She would no more dream of ordering a man like Norfolk on an errand like that than invite him to one of her dinner parties. While Norfolk was, indeed, the gardener of the Grange, he was – to Viola and Victor at least – a lot more besides. He was riddled with agricultural qualifications, with letters after his name to prove it; he was a member of the Royal Horticultural Society, and had several times received telephone calls for gardening advice from a woman whose voice (although distorted by her beseeching tones) Viola thought she recognised, and who (if Viola was right) was connected by marriage, if not by birth, to the royal family.

Norfolk was tall and imposing and looked like the Duke of Edinburgh. When Viola had approached him that afternoon and had (carelessly it seemed) brought the subject round to the possibility of a patch of purple butterwort existing on Giant's Hill, Norfolk had listened with only half an ear (Viola Pomfret all too often prattled horticultural nonsense).

'Is it, in fact, Mr Norfolk, as rare as my friend says it is?'

'Rare enough, I suppose.'

'How interesting to see such a thing! Would one, perhaps, enjoy it?'

'It's a dull-looking plant, Mrs Pomfret. Most of the rare ones are, you know.'

'But for us to have an example here in Polkerton! A feather in one's caps, don't you think? One would want to make every effort to preserve it, wouldn't one? One's position gives one responsibilities in many areas, doesn't it? Not just town matters but country matters too. Nature conservancy is so important, don't you think?'

Norfolk had raised one eyebrow and lifted the corner of one nostril. Only the week before, Viola had suggested that Norfolk might care to see to the cutting down of two of the ancient oaks that dotted the front lawn of the Grange – trees that had been there for five hundred years at least. Naturally, Norfolk had politely refused.

'Of course,' Viola had stared at Norfolk's toecaps, 'one would have to be sure. It would take a real expert to tell, wouldn't it?'

Norfolk acknowledged that purple butterwort looked quite like lots of other more common plants, and would therefore need proper and expert identification.

'Oh, Mr Norfolk, one wonders if one dares to ask. Such a favour, one knows, but what a thrill for all of us! And one would have to protect it, of course, from hikers – and no doubt there would be some publicity for whoever identified it! Too exciting!'

Norfolk's vanity was so tickled by the thought of the publicity that he found himself agreeing to take a look at the plant sometime that week and, on Friday afternoon, he abandoned the planning of the orchid house and drove his Land Rover to Giant's Hill.

It wasn't purple butterwort at all. It was barrow sedge, a common wildflower found practically everywhere in the British Isles. Norfolk felt a small disappointment. It would have been nice to have his name in the papers again, (the last time had been in the *Gardener's Gazette*, when he'd produced a rather nice hybrid cross between a damson and

The Polkerton Giant

a yellow plum for the Wisley orchards); but barrow sedge wasn't purple butterwort, no matter how much you wanted it to be, so that was that.

He strode back down the hill and climbed into the Land Rover and drove to the Grange. Viola was waiting by the front door.

'Barrow sedge,' Norfolk said laconically through the open window of the car.

'Not purple butterwort?'

'No. Barrow sedge. Very common.'

'*Very* common? Really?'

Norfolk thought he detected a note of happiness in Viola's voice, which was odd. He'd assumed she'd be disappointed, and had looked forward to seeing her face fall. Hadn't she been excited at the prospect of finding purple butterwort?

'Common as grass, practically.'

'Oh dear. What a pity. Well, it can't be helped. So sorry to have wasted your time, Mr Norfolk. One is *most* grateful. How is the orchid house coming along?'

When Norfolk had gone, Viola hurried to the telephone. 'Uthie? You'll never guess. It's not purple thingy at all, it's just some frightfully common little plant called barrow sedge. Norfolk went up there just now and came back five minutes ago and told me. Barrow sedge – it even *sounds* common, doesn't it? Found *everywhere*, my dear. Isn't that marvellous? So much for SPAM's silly court order – which, I may say, seems slow in coming. Do you think they might have changed their minds?'

Uther said that he would try to find out, and he said it in such a mysterious voice that Viola felt a thrill run through her body as her mind filled with visions of Uther, dressed all in black, creeping around Grassmere with a torch in one hand and a pistol in the other.

In fact, Uther simply hung up on Viola and called the Beaufort-Lyonses.

'How's the court order coming?'

'It's not,' said Rapunzel. 'Eric is dragging his feet.'

Uther was silent for a moment, wondering whether to let Viola have this small victory. But he decided he wouldn't. It would mean that SPAM would lose a lot of credibility too early in the game, while CROSS would gain a premature ascendancy. Besides, he hadn't liked the crowing tone in Viola's voice. He told Rapunzel about the purple butterwort not being purple butterwort at all but merely the common little barrow sedge.

'I don't believe it,' said Rapunzel. 'It's a clumsy plot to put us off.'

'I don't think so. Norfolk identified it. He's got too much to lose if he's seen to be wrong.'

'But Eric said—'

'My dear, when it comes to flora identification, whom would you believe? Norfolk or Eric?'

'I suppose the Norfolk man, Uther. Botheration. Well, thank goodness we found out before anything serious happened. I shall have words with Eric immediately.'

Rapunzel put the telephone back in its cradle, and was beginning to work out exactly how cross she would be with Eric when, almost immediately, it rang again.

She picked it up. 'Hello? . . . Yes, this is Rapunzel Beaufort-Lyons . . . Who? . . . Satellite West? . . . Oh, yes, of course. What can I do for you?'

Then she listened, with growing excitement, while Satellite West told her what she could do for them.

Five minutes later, Viola received an almost identical call from Satellite West. She too listened with her hopes rising – and with a deal more attention than she usually gave to people who wanted something from her. This, she thought, was what Uther meant by a wider audience.

Mick Jenson was sitting at his kitchen table counting five-pound notes. There had been a trickle of local visitors to the giant over the past few days – enough to warrant the presence of one of the Jenson family at the entrance to the lower field. While the hordes which Uther Tregeffen had insinuated might arrive at any minute had not yet appeared, Mick was well satisfied. So was old Maggs, for there was the prospect of a new dress.

She put his tea in front of him with more than customary

care. "Ow much did you get?' she asked.

'Twenty-foive today. Twenty yesterday. Not bad.'

Buster stopped looking at the page-three girl and lowered the paper. 'Bloody great, Da,' he said.

'Aaarr.'

There was a knock at the front door and Maggs said, "Ooever could that be?' which was what she always said when they had visitors, because visitors to the Jenson farm were rare. She waddled out to the hall and Mick heard a mumbling of voices and then he heard Maggs say, 'Weli, you'd better come in.'

A tall young woman stepped into the kitchen and Buster forgot all about the page-three girl. He stared at the visitor, his mouth agape. Her hair was long and blonde; her eyes were large and pale blue; her nose was straight, her lips were full, her chin small and pointed. Fully dressed, in a Shetland sweater, jeans, a pair of old cowboy boots and, on her head, a cloche cap made of cream wool, the girl exuded more sexuality than a whole host of topless page-three girls – and Buster fell into hopeless love.

'Hello,' said the girl. She looked around the kitchen and smiled. 'Sorry to intrude. I would have telephoned but there was a problem.'

'We 'aven't got one,' said Maggs, peering over the girl's shoulder.

'Right,' said the girl. 'That was the problem. Are you Mr Jenson?'

'Aaarr.'

'I'm Pamela Gibbons. From Satellite West.'

Mick stared at her blankly, so the girl said, 'You know? Satellite West? The television company?'

'Oh, aaarr.'

'Uther Tregeffen gave me your name. And your address. We tried to call. When we found we couldn't, they sent me along in person. So here I am.'

She was so pretty, thought Mick. Obviously Buster thought so too. His eyes were bulging and his mouth was hanging open. Silly little bugger. That was no way to impress a girl.

'Oh yurr?'

'We want do to a story on your giant, Mr Jenson. A sort of

documentary. Just a short piece, to put in one of our news magazines. We'd like to interview you and several other people, and obviously take some shots of the giant. Would that be possible, do you think?'

"Ow much?' said Mick, staring hard at the heap of five-pound notes on the kitchen table.

'We'd pay fifty pounds for the interview and something for filming on your land.'

"Ow much?'

'Another fifty,' said Pamela. Mick thought for a moment and then he nodded. A hundred pounds had never come so easily.

'Oh, good,' said Pamela. 'Shall we say tomorrow? Round about eight in the morning? It shouldn't take more than an hour.'

Buster walked her silently to her car and, when she said, 'Goodbye. So lovely to meet you,' he could only gulp and nod and grin.

Pamela Gibbons ignored the boy gaping at her through the windscreen. She was used to boys doing that. She flipped through the pages of her leather-bound organiser, glanced at the road map of Somerset that lay open on the passenger seat beside, and then drove out of the rutted Jenson yard and pointed the car in the direction of the Grange.

Ten minutes later, she was sitting with Viola Pomfret in the drawing room.

'We thought we'd do it at the actual site, you see,' said Pamela. 'It would be so effective to hear the CROSS point of view with the frightful giant in the background, don't you think? It would make the argument that much more convincing, wouldn't it?'

Viola thought that her first impression, when she'd spoken on the telephone with the girl, had been absolutely correct. What a pleasant creature this was, with such charming manners and such an incisive mind – and quite well-bred too, which was a surprise. Viola had thought that the days when well-bred people worked in television were long since over.

The Polkerton Giant

'Would you like the rest of our committee to be there, or just little me?' she said.

'Oh, just you, I think. Perhaps one other, if you feel it's necessary. After all, you are the founder of CROSS, aren't you? Again, in television terms, a single spokesperson is more effective than a group. Besides, you are so articulate, and you have, if you don't mind my saying so, a really lovely voice. A wonderful quality to it. Quite musical. Have you ever done any broadcasting? No? What a pity . . .'

Viola glowed. Soon, she was showing Pamela her walk-in closet and, together, they picked out her wardrobe for the interview – which was difficult because Pamela exclaimed with pleasure over every outfit that Viola produced. At last, they settled on the dark blue with the white piping, and the treble row of pearls and the matching drop earrings, which was how Viola had always seen herself if ever the opportunity to appear on television had ever arisen. Now it had, Viola, pink with anticipation, promised to be at the lower field, dressed and ready to go, at nine the following morning.

Pamela played out the same scene at Grassmere, although it was quickly apparent to her that the Beaufort-Lyonses came as a matched pair. However, it was also quickly apparent that Rapunzel saw herself as the undisputed mouthpiece of her organisation and Eric seemed content to let her – so his presence, possibly slightly out of focus behind Rapunzel's shoulder, would hardly be noticed.

When it came to discussing wardrobe, Rapunzel smiled gently. 'I think you will find, Miss Gibbons, that we know how to present ourselves. Both visibly and audibly. Eric and I are quite used to public appearances. The camera holds no surprises for us, I can promise you.'

'Oh, you've done this before?' Pamela asked.

'We are not without experience, shall we say?' said Rapunzel, and Eric nodded and solemnly said, '"We are such stuff as dreams are made on."'

'Oh, good,' said Pamela. 'Shall we say nine-thirty, then, at the base of the giant?'

* * *

Twenty minutes later, Pamela was sitting in Uther's living room, sipping a dry sherry.

'I do hope,' she said, 'that this works. I've put myself on the line on it, I want you to know.'

'What do you mean, dear?'

'I mean, Uther, that I've absolutely *promised* Alan that it'll be worth doing, and if it turns out that it *isn't* my arse will no longer be mine.'

'Well, whoever gets it will count themselves blessed. It's a very pretty one, if I may say so.'

'You may not. Look, I like my job, that's all. I don't want to lose it.'

'Now, dear Pamela, do relax. You've met the protagonists. It can't fail, can it?'

'No. Well, *you* don't think it can fail and *I* don't think it can fail. Let's just hope Alan won't think it can fail either.'

Uther smiled mysteriously and said, 'I rather think I've taken care of that.'

'How?'

'Well, with a little Machiavellianism here and there, I rather think I've managed to interest the BBC as well.'

'Do you know everybody, Uther, or does it just seem that way?'

'I know *everybody*. Don't interrupt. The BBC, with their customary sluggishness, will probably be following you in within the next few days and, if they follow you, then your independent rivals can't be far behind. So, whatever the outcome, Satellite West can at least claim to have scooped both dear Auntie and the others, can't it? I think Alan would like that, don't you?'

'I think,' said Pamela, 'that Alan will probably have an orgasm.'

'Given the subject matter, a not inappropriate reaction,' said Uther, gazing at his ceiling.

Quite soon – and within half an hour of each other – both Viola and Rapunzel had telephoned to tell Uther their exciting news. To both, Uther said the same: 'My dear, you shall be a star . . . Well, of course I shall be there. Wild horses wouldn't keep me away . . . No, no, I shall observe from a discreet distance. I wouldn't want to steal your thunder. Too exciting for words.'

Later, to Pamela, he said, 'And you, dear, don't know me. Understood?'

'Duh,' said Pamela. 'I'm not a complete idiot.'

'I know,' said Uther, 'but your grandfather was, poor old sausage, so there's always the possibility of an atavistic slip. Just be careful, there's a good girl.'

'Duh,' said Pamela again.

Chapter 9

Viola accepted Commodore Billingsworth's suggestion that he should escort her to and from the interview. One ought, she thought, to have some sort of support from one's organisation at times like this, and since Edwin was, *de facto*, most of the rest of her organisation, it was only right that he should accompany her. Besides, for some reason she felt a little sick, so his support would be doubly welcome. (Probably the Dover sole from last night's dinner. She would have to have words with Cook.)

However, she was nervous that Edwin might want to join in the interview. That would be disastrous. Edwin had a tendency, when speaking, to appear angrier than he was. He blustered and roared and spluttered about the most inoffensive things, and Viola feared that, if asked questions about the Polkerton Giant and its effect on the morality of the inhabitants of Somerset, Edwin might become incoherent.

She sat him on the sofa and gave him some coffee and then said, 'I'm so glad it's you coming with me and not Father Roget or Geoffrey Pargiter. They are wonderful men, of course, and most sincere in their support of us, but I'm quite sure they would want to be part of the interview and I always feel that there should only be one spokesman, don't you? So muddling for the viewers if the questions are answered by a committee.'

Edwin had been hoping to get on television. Not to say anything – he didn't want to do that – but just to have his mug up there. Now that would be something. Viola saw his face fall and said smoothly, 'That is not to say you shouldn't *be* there, Edwin. You *must* be there, at my side, perhaps, and a little behind me, so that the viewers can see you quite clearly. And that will show them that CROSS has the support of all right-thinking *men* as well as women – and that's so important, don't you think? To have both sexes represented in matters such as this?'

Edwin cheered up and slurped his coffee and said he thought it was a damn fine thing Viola was doing (pardon his French), and he was proud to stand at her side and a little behind her, so that he could support her in any way she saw fit.

Soon after, they stepped through the front door and got into Edwin's old Rover, which smelled of stale cigar smoke and damp tweed, and fifteen minutes later they were bumping over the cattle grid that led into Mick Jenson's field. Viola was feeling a little sicker – almost certainly, she decided, from the Dover Sole – but the smell inside Edwin's car was no help.

A young man, his face patched with acne, was there, leaning on a stout stick, barring their way. Edwin stamped on the brakes and the Rover crunched to a stop. The young man walked slowly round to the driver's window and tapped on the glass. When Edwin wound down the glass the young man thrust a hand through the opening.

'Foive pound,' he said.

'What are you talking about?' said Edwin. 'Five pounds for what?'

'It's foive pound to come in 'ere.'

Edwin felt his rage bubbling to the surface like magma, but the young man's stick was big and black with ugly knobs all along its length, and now he wasn't leaning on it he was hefting it in his other hand, as though feeling its weight for the first time. Edwin breathed heavily for a few moments, his anxiety about the stick dampening the embers of his fury. Then he leaned sideways, away from the young man and, making delicious contact with Viola's right shoulder, he stuffed his hand into his trouser pocket. He fumbled in there, feeling the coins with his fingers. He knew what was there: seven pounds and thirty pence, which was all he had left until the end of the week. He fumbled some more, grunting with effort, making a performance out of it in the hope that Viola would offer to pay, but Viola was staring fixedly out

The Polkerton Giant

through the window at the cluster of cars and vans that were parked on the far side of the field.

'How much was it again?' he said.

'Foive pounds,' the youth repeated in a dogged voice.

'Five pounds, eh? Right you are. Bit steep, I must say. Five pounds, just to drive into the field.'

'It's for the parking,' said the man. 'You can park all day for that.'

'Yes, well, even so. Five pounds?'

'You don't have to come in if you don't want to. Oy don't give a rat's arse.'

The man made a movement away from the car and Edwin said, 'All right. Hold your horses. Here.' He poured five of the precious coins into Buster Jenson's hand and Buster dropped them into his trouser pocket and then produced, like a conjurer, a small rectangle of orange cardboard with the word 'PARK' printed on it. He pushed the ticket at Edwin and said, "Ere you go, squoire. We close at six. Still 'ere and you're buggered.'

Edwin ground his teeth. Fucking little oik bastard. He'd show him. Fucking arrogant yokel shit oik bastard. He wound up the window in a series of fast, furious jerks. Then he crunched the Rover's gears and spun the back wheels in the grass, and they lurched towards the group of cars and vans that were parked near the entrance to the woods on the far side of the field. As they got nearer, they could see that the largest of the vans had the words 'Satellite West' printed on its side. There was a man by the van, sitting in a deckchair, reading a newspaper. He got out of the deckchair as Edwin drew up, and watched Viola and Edwin get out. Then he said, 'Mrs Pomfret?'

'Yes? That's little me,' Viola said gaily.

'Right. Well, they're up there.' He waved vaguely towards the woods and then, his job done, settled back into the chair.

When Viola and Edwin approached the gap in the fence that led into the woods, they saw a big, red-faced woman was there, apparently waiting for them. She was sitting on a kitchen chair. She wore a flowered print dress and Wellington boots and there was a glass jar at her side.

'Good morning,' she said pleasantly as Edwin and Viola

reached the gap in the fence. "Ere to see the giant, are you? That'll be three pound for each adult. Six pound in all.'

'Bloody hell,' said Edwin, feeling the rage rising again into his throat. 'What's going on, eh? What's all this malarkey?'

'Excuse me,' said Viola, curling up the ends of her mouth and wrinkling her nose. 'One hardly thinks one has to pay, since one is here on official business.'

'All the rest of them 'ave paid,' said Maggs defensively. 'All them television people. They didn't moind.'

Viola shook her head. 'One would like to speak to Mr Jenson. Is he anywhere around?'

Maggs nodded. "E's 'aving 'is make-up taken off.'

'One begs your pardon?'

"E's been interviewed and now 'e's 'aving 'is make-up taken off,' repeated Maggs, as much for her own benefit as for the lady's, since she was still finding the concept of Mick allowing some slip of a girl to smear make-up on his face as hard to comprehend as the lady in front of her evidently was.

Viola's startled reaction had nothing to do with whether Mick Jenson had been wearing make-up. She was mortified to find that the farmer had not only been interviewed before her, but had been interviewed at all. What could an uneducated, working class person like that possibly have to say that would be of interest to anybody? Good heavens, half the country wouldn't even be able to understand a word he said, so thick was the local dialect. It was, she thought, absurd – and yet another indication of the increasing stupidity shown by those who might, reasonably, be expected to demonstrate a greater degree of responsibility, given their enormous influence over the television viewing public.

'And you are?' Viola said, after a long pause, during which she had stared wide-eyed at the big woman in the print dress, as though doubting the evidence of her eyes that the woman existed at all.

'Oi'm Mrs Jenson. 'Is woife. And 'e said it was three pound each to see the giant, so three pound it is. Take it or leave it.'

'Look here,' said Edwin, turning red. 'Dammit all, this isn't on, you know. Public land and all that. Right of way. Footpath. Ancient law of the bloody land, pardon my bloody French.'

The Polkerton Giant

'It's proivate,' said Maggs. 'All of it.'

'Oh, bugger that for a game of soldiers . . .'

'It's all right,' said Viola, sensing the advent of one of Edwin's tantrums. 'One will pay this once. After all, it's unlikely that one will ever be here again and one shall make sure that one's friends don't come either.'

'Well, but look here, Viola . . .' said Edwin, in a voice quivering with barely suppressed anger. When Viola did just that, with a look in her eyes that seemed to be pleading for peace, he fell back a pace and stared at the ground. Feeling sick, he stuffed his hand into his pocket. He rattled the remaining coins together and then plastered a look of mild chagrin over his face. 'Ah. Ha ha. Dammit, how embarrassing. Not sure I can quite come up with the goods—'

Viola patted his arm. 'No, Edwin. It's my turn. You did the parking.'

Relieved, Edwin watched as Viola rummaged in her handbag. She dropped the coins into the glass jar at Maggs's feet as though dropping money into a beggar's hat. Then she turned away from Maggs and said, 'Come, Edwin.'

They tramped silently through the wood, each thinking how pleasant it would be to exact some sort of revenge on the Jenson family. Their motives were different – Edwin's desire to get even was based on financial considerations, while Viola's had everything to do with the affront to her social position – but the depth of their desire for vengeance was the same.

When they came to the base of Giant's Hill they saw a small knot of people standing near the giant's feet. Viola, whose eyes were sharper than Edwin's, could see that the group had a camera and that its lens was roving over the giant's body. A figure in the group turned and saw them and broke away and started down toward them. Viola saw that it was that charming girl, Pamela Something-or-other, and she waved.

Pamela waved back and doubled her pace to a downhill trot. 'Hello,' she cried, still twenty yards away. 'Good morning. You made it all right? Well done.'

Viola simpered at her triumph. She introduced Edwin.

'Commodore Billingsworth, one of CROSS's most loyal supporters.'

Edwin stared at Pamela, daunted by her beauty. She shook his outstretched hand firmly and then, ignoring his gaze, turned to Viola and said, 'Oh, you were so right, Mrs Pomfret. The blue is perfect and so are the pearls. Attractive and, at the same time, authoritarian. Such a good choice.'

Viola simpered again. Strangely, she was finding it difficult to make her voice work. Ever since she had seen the camera up on the hill, something had happened to her throat. It felt as though some of her breakfast was lodged there, and she swallowed convulsively several times to see if she could shift the obstruction. Swallowing didn't seem to do any good, though, and merely made the Dover Sole churn about in her stomach, just as if the horrid thing was still alive and swimming about in the sea.

Pamela chatted on. 'We're just doing a little coverage of the naughty chap and then we'll get on to you, Mrs Pomfret.'

Viola nodded, her throat tightening harder round whatever it was that was stuck in there. She felt sick.

'I say,' said Edwin, 'these pictures your chaps are taking . . . I mean to say, can you show that sort of thing on television?'

'Well, of course, it's not up to me, Commodore Billingsworth. I'm just a humble production assistant. If it *was* up to me, I certainly wouldn't allow it, but you never can tell nowadays, can you?'

She had a lovely mouth, thought Edwin – and a lovely chin and a lovely neck and lovely shoulders and really lovely breasts . . . He forced his eyes back up to her face and saw that she had seen him looking at her chest and that she didn't seem to mind in the least. She was smiling at him, her head cocked to one side and one eyebrow raised half an inch higher than the other. She looked at him like that for several seconds and then switched her eyes back to Viola.

'Now,' she said, 'if you wouldn't mind waiting here for a moment. I'll send a couple of chairs over for you and then Marion – that's our make-up person – will be along to check you over. Not that you'll need any, Mrs Pomfret, I'm sure. You've done a wonderful job with that already. But perhaps Commodore Billingsworth could do with a little touch up.'

The Polkerton Giant

Edwin blushed and said, 'Well, look here, I'm not actually here to say anything, you know.'

'No, right – but you will be in the picture, surely? As a CROSS member?'

'Oh well, that's up to Viola . . . Mrs Pomfret, of course.'

Pamela turned Bambi eyes on Viola again. 'Oh, Mrs Pomfret, you will let him be in shot, won't you? A loyal supporter, and with such a photogenic face – it would be such a shame to exclude him . . .'

Viola shook her curls vigorously and squeaked, 'No, no – I want him there.'

'Oh, terrific. Thank you. Definitely the right decision. Well, I'll just go and organise everything.'

Pamela turned and walked briskly up the hill and Edwin watched her, admiring the smooth, liquid stride of her long legs and the way her buttocks twitched from side to side. Beside him, Viola cleared her throat delicately and then coughed in a series of sharp little terrier yaps.

'I say,' said Edwin, 'we're going to be film stars.'

The camera crew had moved up the hill and were standing high between the giant's legs, their feet churning the barrow sedge into pulp. Pamela came up just as Alan was saying, 'All right, I think we've got everything pretty well covered. Let's get on to the humans, shall we?'

Pamela said, 'The antis have arrived, Alan. Both priceless. The man looks like Montgomery and talks like him too, and the woman's trying to look like Thatcher but she's far too small. It's going to be great, I promise.'

Edwin sat in a canvas chair while the make-up woman dabbed foundation on his face. It was, he thought, rather a pleasant sensation. He wished it was that Pamela girl doing the stroking – the Marion person was overweight and her hair was grey – but, on the whole, he was rather enjoying the process. No woman had been this close to him for ages. Bloody Evie had kept herself at a safe distance for years now – which was fine by Edwin, since the feeling was mutual – but all the same, he missed the feminine touch. He closed his eyes, feeling the sponge on his eyelids.

'Cooee!' cried Viola, and Edwin's eyes flew open. Viola was waving vigorously from her matching chair at somebody downslope from them. Edwin, with instructions to keep quite still, please, couldn't turn his head to see who it was.

'Cooee!' Viola cried again. 'It's Uther, Edwin. He's come to watch.'

The idea of Uther Tregeffen watching him having make-up applied was, Edwin thought, too awful to contemplate. 'Not coming up here, is he?'

'I don't think so. He's got his shooting stick and he's sitting down on it. Cooee! Uthie! Oh good, he's seen us. He's waving back at us, Edwin. Now he's got up. Now he's sitting down again. I think he's going to stay where he is. He said on the telephone that he'd watch from a little way off.'

'Good. Thank God for that.'

Pamela returned. She looked critically at Edwin's face. Marion was dabbing on some powder. 'Much better,' Pamela said. 'You look years younger, Commodore. Doesn't he, Mrs Pomfret?'

Viola stopped waving at Uther, who wasn't waving back anyway, because he had taken a newspaper out of his jacket and seemed to be reading it. 'What? Oh, yes. Marvellous. You look quite handsome, Edwin.' She said this with some surprise, and Edwin felt a pang of hurt that she hadn't considered him handsome before the make-up had been applied.

'Are we ready then?' Pamela said.

'What – now?' said Viola, shrinking in her chair.

Pamela led Viola and Edwin up the hill towards the feet of the giant. The crew were there, five men in nylon anoraks, doing intricate things to a television camera and a tape recorder. When Viola and Edwin and Pamela appeared, they carried on doing the intricate things just as if the new arrivals weren't there at all. There was a younger man in a leather coat, standing at the edge of the group and looking through narrowed eyes out over the woods below them. To him, Pamela said, 'Alan? They're here. Mrs Pomfret and Commodore Billingsworth – from CROSS, you know?'

Alan tore his gaze away from the scenery and walked forward and shook Viola's hand, then Edwin's.

The Polkerton Giant

'Hi. Lovely to meet you. I'm Alan Littler. The director. Thanks so much for doing this. We'll try and make it fun, I promise. Now, Mrs Pomfret, if you'd just stand over here, so we can get a line-up on you? And perhaps Commodore Billingsworth would be very kind and stand here – yes, just behind Mrs Pomfret's shoulder, that's perfect. Great. That's great. Won't be a sec.'

Alan turned away and rejoined the crew, leaving Viola and Edwin to stand where he'd placed them. A small, detached part of Viola's brain was relieved to see that Alan Littler had organised matters so that the camera would be facing away from the giant, with the Jenson woods as her backdrop. Of course, that meant that while she was talking she would have to suffer the full-frontal effect of the giant as background to the camera crew – but it was certainly preferable this way, if perhaps a little distracting for her. She felt the comforting presence of Edwin, just behind her and to one side. She could hear his breathing and wondered if he could hear hers. For some reason, she seemed to be having difficulty with that now. Perhaps the air up here was thinner than down below, or perhaps she was coming down with something. Too tiresome. First the Dover Sole and then the throat business and now some sort of congestion of the chest. What next? she wondered, and was instantly notified what next by the sudden, unexplained trembling that took over her knees, a quivering that took her so much by surprise that she staggered and almost fell.

Edwin's hand was on her elbow. 'I say. You all right, Viola?'

'Fine, thank you, Edwin. It's rather steep here, isn't it?' And now (oh really, it was too much) her silly mouth had gone all dry. She wished now that it was Edwin – or perhaps Geoffrey Pargiter or even Father Roget (as long as he kept off the French) – who was going to be doing the talking, but she had doggedly kept everybody but herself out of it and now she was going to have to pay the price of her conceit. Although of course it wasn't *conceit* at all that had driven her, but a desire to get it absolutely right – and there was only one person she could trust to do that . . .

And, oh heavens, here they came, with their camera and their tape recorder, all those men in nylon anoraks, looking at her as if she was just another person, not who she *really* was: Mrs Viola Pomfret, of the Grange; Town Councillor and wife to Victor Pomfret, Admiral of Industry . . .

'Right, Mrs Pomfret – if you'd just look this way . . . thanks. I'll ask you a question and you do your bit to me, not to camera, OK? All right, everybody, nice and quiet . . . roll camera.'

Uther sat on his shooting stick looking up at the activity on the hillside. How he wished he could be up there . . . but of course he couldn't because Pamela might let something slip, or Alan might be momentarily too familiar – and, besides, SPAM was due any minute now and it wouldn't be advisable to be too close to the action.

He sighed and looked back at his paper. Then slowly he became aware of a familiar musty smell, of old clothes and rotting rubber.

He looked up from his paper and smiled. 'Mr Jenson! And how was your interview?'

'Oy 'ad make-up on,' said Mick proudly. 'They took it off, though.'

'I'm sure you looked very handsome.'

'Oy did,' admitted Mick.

'And how much have we made so far?'

Mick bent down and whispered – unnecessarily, Uther thought, since the nearest person was a hundred and fifty yards away – into his ear. The sum was respectable, given the early days of the campaign, and Uther nodded in a pleased way. But when Mick plunged his hand into the pocket of his old coat, Uther waved one hand gently in the air and said, quietly, but firmly, 'Not here, Mr Jenson. And not now, thank you all the same.'

'All right,' Alan said. 'If you'd just face this way, Mrs Pomfret . . . That's it, lovely. Got her all right, Bob? Great. Tuck in behind her, would you, Commodore? That's the ticket. OK. Now, Mrs Pomfret, in your own words, what is your objection to the Polkerton Giant?'

Viola's tongue suddenly stopped being a tongue at all, and became a wet, flabby, useless thing, hopeless at forming words and occupying far too much of her mouth for comfort. Alan was looking at her with his eyebrows raised and the camera lens was a black hole of enquiry; an answer for both of them was obviously expected within the next few moments.

She opened her lips and took a breath.

'Blathuthluh,' she said.

'Whenever you're ready,' said Alan.

Viola opened her mouth again and tried to spit out her tongue.

'Flaugh.'

'Take your time,' said Alan.

Viola decided to try talking without using her tongue at all.

'Wha, whe a' whoff . . .'

'Not quite getting that, I'm afraid,' said Alan. 'We have to have the odd consonant, you see.'

A single tear appeared at the corner of Viola's right eye which Edwin, standing tight against her shoulder and craning round to see what was ailing her, spotted. He took Viola by the shoulders and moved her gently to one side, shielding her from the camera lens. Then he stepped on to her mark and looked fiercely at Alan. There was an elation in his narrow chest and the words were lining up in his mind in the most wonderfully orderly way. He was Monty at El Alamein and the world was watching. He put his hands behind his back, planted his feet well apart and leaned forward slightly at the hips.

'What my friend, Mrs Viola Pomfret, means is this,' he said, and Alan heard the unmistakable lilting whine of the Field Marshal's voice, complete with the uncertain R, which was almost a full-blown W, but not quite. This, coupled with the familiar military stance, was a piece of wonderful televisual luck.

Edwin had paused, impressively, shooting piercing little glances this way and that. Then he nodded, as if acknowledging the fact that the troops were paying him the fullest attention, and said, 'She means that we at CROSS – which stands for the Campaign for the Removal of Obscene Signs and Symbols – we at CROSS fully intend to clean up the *filth* that threatens to mire this country, starting in our own back yard with the long-overdue removal of the thoroughly disgusting thing up there behind you. The so-called Polkerton Giant has outstayed its welcome, and we at CROSS invite all right-thinking people to join us in this campaign. Any questions?'

Alan said, 'What, exactly, do you find offensive?'

'Dammit all! If you can't see that, then all I can say is – well, you must be blind as a bat. Ha ha. Thing's pretty bloody obvious, isn't it? Pardon my French. Can I say that on television?'

'Say whatever you want.'

'Right. Well . . . ha ha. There you are. Yes.' And suddenly, given so much freedom of speech, Edwin lost the ability to produce any at all. He'd said everything there was to say, surely? What else *was* there? He'd covered CROSS and the disgustingness of the giant – what else had Viola been about to say before she became unwell?

He looked at her. Her little mouth was working from side to side and he bent towards her to catch the words she was struggling to produce.

'Church . . . support . . . Indian shopkeeper.'

'Ah, yes. Right. My friend, Mrs Viola Pomfret – and I'm damned proud to call her my friend, because she's a *wonderful* woman, a wonderful, wonderful woman – has – and this is important so you'd better listen carefully – has reminded me that we have the support of the Church, both of them actually, and also the support of a section of our ethnic minority friends from . . . I believe . . . the Indian community – which is, I think you'll admit, pretty damn impressive.' Edwin stopped abruptly and looked around him with an air of triumph. Viola was staring at him with grateful eyes, which made his chest swell.

Alan said, 'What about the opposition?'

'Opposition? Paltry. *Paltry*. See them off in a jiffy, I don't mind telling you. Lot of liberal idiots.'

'But your wife is one of them, isn't she, Commodore?'

Edwin became very still. The only movement that revealed he wasn't turned to stone was the breeze-ruffled hair at the nape of his neck. Then one eyelid twitched. 'What did you say?'

The Polkerton Giant

'Your wife, Commodore. I understand she's not one of your supporters.'

The other eyelid twitched. 'What are you talking about? You don't know my wife. Her name's Evie.'

'That's right—'

'Of course it's right. I should know, dammit.'

'Well, we understand that Mrs Billingsworth actively supports the movement to preserve the Polkerton Giant. Does this cause any friction at home?'

Edwin stared uncomprehendingly at Alan. What the hell was the man talking about? How could he *possibly* know anything about their home life, or Evie, or whose side she was on? And even if they did know something, then they must surely have got her supposed allegiance to the opposition quite wrong – because dear, dull, grey little Evie had never, in his experience, had any opinion about anything that differed even an iota from his own. In fact, she hardly seemed to have any opinions at all. Any suggestion that she might have allied herself to the frightful Beaufort-Lyonses must be wrong. And yet this Alan man and the rest of the film crew were all looking at him with innocence smooth on their faces, as though the suggestion was as true as the fact of them standing on a Somerset hillside.

There was only one way to handle this. 'Rubbish,' said Edwin firmly. 'Absolute nonsense. No friction whatsoever. Happy as Larry. Soulmates. Always have been, always will. Right, that's it. Stop now. Turn it off. No more filming, thank you very much. Come along, Viola.'

He cocked his arm in a gallant gesture and felt Viola's little hand, trembling noticeably, take his elbow. They turned and began to walk down the hill.

'Thank you, Edwin,' whispered Viola. 'You were wonderful. I'm a little unwell. Influenza, I suspect. Please take me home.'

She leaned heavily on Edwin's arm, feeling the sickness of her shame flood through her. How could she, Mrs Viola Pomfret, Town Councillor, Chairwoman of AWARENESS and CROSS and wife of industrial giant Victor Pomfret – how could she, of all people, have suffered such stage fright as to render her speechless? So speechless that one of her acolytes had been forced to push himself forward and speak in her stead? The humiliation was more than she could bear, and she began (silently, so that Edwin wouldn't notice unless he looked her in the face) to cry.

When they reached the far side of the woods and Edwin's Rover came into view, her tears ceased to flow and she managed, without drawing Edwin's attention to her actions, to extract a fragile lace handkerchief from her handbag and dab at her face. Then she saw Rapunzel and Eric Beaufort-Lyons walking towards her, and she gave a little squeal and tugged at Edwin's arm.

'Walk away! Walk away!' she whispered, with such urgency that Edwin changed his course across the field in such a dramatic way (turning at a sharp right angle from his previous track and heading fast towards a blackberry hedge on the far side of the field) that it was obvious to Rapunzel and Eric that they were being deliberately avoided.

Rapunzel didn't care, other than feeling a mild irritation that Satellite West had obviously seen fit to interview the opposition as well – why else would Viola and her Commodore be emerging from the woods? – but then, it was right and proper that both sides should be represented in the matter, so long as SPAM had not only the last word but the best one as well. And Rapunzel felt sure that hers would be the best.

They passed through the woods, stepping over the muddy patches that had been made that morning by the passage of many feet and not a little equipment, and came out into the open area at the base of Giant's Hill. Uther, perched on his shooting stick and with Mick Jenson at his side, waved to them and shouted, 'Good luck!' and Rapunzel smiled sweetly in his direction with the air of a woman for whom television appearances were so commonplace that she required no such benison.

Indeed, she was feeling all the confidence that Viola had so recently lacked. She was bursting with it; had she known of Viola's débâcle, she might well have exploded. The facts were at her fingertips and she was ready for anything. This, she decided, was what she was born to; activism on a grand scale, reaching through the media to affect the thoughts and

The Polkerton Giant

opinions of millions of people all over the country and then the world . . .

'Mrs Beaufort-Lyons? Mr Beaufort-Lyons?'

Pamela was standing in front of them, smiling warmly. 'Hello. You made it. Marvellous. Well done.'

While the footage that the camera had managed to record on Viola Pomfret and the Commodore had been distressingly short, Alan Littler soon found that the footage he was getting on the Beaufort-Lyonses was so distressingly long and turgid that his only option was to try for a comedy slant. Rapunzel was intensely earnest and unbearably long-winded, answering all his questions with a numbing solemnity and using words like 'beatitude' and 'pantheism' and 'symbiosis' in a voice that began to scratch against his nerves like nails on a blackboard . . .

'So, *finally*, Mrs Beaufort-Lyons, and in *short*, you believe that it is SPAM's duty to fight for the giant's preservation at all costs?'

'Indeed we do, indeed yes – for is it not the duty of all descendants to preserve the monuments so lovingly erected by their ancestors? The essence of departed souls hovers over those still in the living world, and woe betide those who would deracinate their simulacra . . .'

'"Their monument shall be my gentle verse",' quoted Eric, who had been trying to think of an apposite line for ten minutes.

'Cut!' said Alan.

He stepped away from his post by the side of the camera and came forward to speak to the Beaufort-Lyonses. 'Well, that was . . . what can I say? Terrific. I'm sure we'll be able to get something really good out of that. Thank you so much.'

'There's quite a lot more we could say,' said Rapunzel without moving, as if stepping off the mark that Alan had given her would, in some way, be an admission that she was done with the matter.

'Thanks so much, but I think we've got all we need. It's just an item, you understand, in our programme "South West Living", and as such can't run for longer than five minutes. So, honestly, we've got more than enough. You were marvellous. Thank you.'

* * *

Later, over dinner, Rapunzel and Eric congratulated each other on the success of the interview, and Rapunzel, glowing from excitement, was kind enough to tell Eric that his choice of verse for his small contribution had been exactly right.

Viola's dinner was a more subdued affair. Victor asked her if she was all right. Viola nodded dully.

Uther took Alan and Pamela out to dinner at a small restaurant on the Bristol road. It was just far enough out of Polkerton so that any likelihood that the Beaufort-Lyonses or the Pomfrets would dine there on the same night as Uther's little party was slight. It was a pleasant dinner. They all laughed a lot and Pamela kissed Uther several times on both cheeks.

Chapter 10

Uther's prediction that the BBC and the independent television companies wouldn't be far behind Alan Littler and Satellite West proved accurate. Within two days the BBC had invited representatives of CROSS and SPAM to take part in a show called *Daytime Talk*. Radio Bath & Bristol asked Rapunzel to plead for the giant against the objections of a frosty Muslim cleric from Walsall, and three independent television companies held forums on the subject with noisy studio audiences freely expressing their opinions. More followed, until it seemed that every news and documentary programme had given time and money to the subject. The national newspapers, tabloid and broadsheets alike, all joined the feeding frenzy, each following events with the gleeful attention to detail that the media invariably devote to any story of the eccentricity of the English.

Soon Rapunzel and Eric Beaufort-Lyons (but particularly Rapunzel) were famous.

Viola Pomfret wasn't. She allowed herself to be photographed for some of the better class newspapers, but refused to pose for any that she considered beneath her dignity to appear in. While this did draw some small attention to her and CROSS, it had little impact on the wider audience of the television screen. Viola didn't attend any of the television debates. The thought of that dark, cold lens beaming her voice and face across England and possibly far beyond was enough to bring on severe gastric symptoms which sent her straight to bed for days. She accompanied Edwin to a minor local radio interview and managed to say, in a quivery little voice, that she thought the Polkerton Giant was disgusting, too too disgusting – but that was all before her mouth went so dry that it made the formation of any more intelligible words impossible.

It was, she thought, so unfair. Why was she perfectly capable of standing up in the council chamber, in front of the dignitaries of Polkerton, without a trace of nerves – but when faced with a lens or a microphone (or both) she was reduced to a state bordering on catatonia? Edwin, on the other hand, seemed able to stand the strain – although Viola could have wished that he was a little more imaginative with his side of the argument. Whenever asked for it he simply repeated, by rote, the few words that had been supplied to him by CROSS's manifesto and then fell silent. If pressed for more, he would begin his spluttering noises – which weren't, Viola felt, an effective form of debate.

Of course, he'd been badly affected by the revelation of Evie's treachery. He'd gone storming home on the day of the first interview and confronted her with it.

'I've joined their theatre group, Edwin, that's all. Surely I must be allowed to do that?'

'But that's not all, is it? Dammit, Evie, everybody thinks you're on the bloody Beaufort-Lyons side!'

'Well . . . oh dear – well, perhaps I am, I suppose. I don't agree with you at all, you see, Edwin. Not about this. I think it's – oh dear – I think it's silly.'

'Silly?'

'Yes.'

She was sitting in her armchair, looking quite calmly at him, and Edwin realised that he didn't really know this woman at all. He'd been married to her for ever, it seemed, and yet she was a mystery to him. He'd never thought she might go against him; he'd never thought she had either the wits or the courage to do anything without him – and to discover now her active participation in something that she knew would displease him came as a shock.

'But . . . but . . . but . . .' he said, sounding, Evie thought, like a Pomfret lawn mower.

'But what, Edwin?'

'Well . . . are you going to go on television with them?' he asked truculently.

'Good heavens, no. How could I? I shan't say a word, Edwin. I'll just be part of the theatre group, that's all.'

The Polkerton Giant

'What do you do with them?'

'I'm in charge of the wardrobe at the moment. Later, I might do some stage management.'

'When does all this happen, I'd like to know?'

'Perhaps twice a week, in the evening. I shall leave you supper on a tray.'

'I see. Right,' said Edwin, warily. 'Well – if that's what you want . . .'

'It is, Edwin.'

'Right. Well. All I can say is, on your own head be it. That's all. On your own head *be* it.'

It was, Evie thought, one of the lamest remarks she had ever heard Edwin utter, and she felt a fresh surge of triumph. If he wasn't going to amuse her with an apoplexy, then she would settle for some damage, however slight, to his self-esteem.

Uther, watching it all from the sidelines, witnessed the rapid ascendancy of SPAM and the equally rapid decline of CROSS. Poor Viola, he thought – to have been struck down so early in the campaign and by so unexpected a disaster. Meanwhile, Rapunzel and Eric Beaufort-Lyons were getting stronger every day. Rapunzel was particularly good on television, Uther decided. On radio, her reedy voice grated a little, but on screen the sight of her stubbly skull and her steel spectacles and her long beaky nose, all weaving about on top of her stork-thin neck, seemed to lend a sort of learned credibility to her voice.

The debates, such as they were, became lopsided. If Edwin turned up at all, he simply muttered the CROSS manifesto and then fell silent, leaving the arena clear for Rapunzel to prance about in it for as long as the programme-makers cared to let her – and there was no doubt in anybody's mind that SPAM was winning the argument. To clinch the matter (and to make the giant into a tourist attraction with a difference), it was during one of these interviews that Rapunzel let slip the fact of the giant's supposed influence on the fertility of couples who elected to sleep on its member. That single remark saw the beginning of the rush to camp overnight on Giant's Hill by couples that were divided, almost equally, between the sexually frivolous and the reproductively challenged. Within a few days, the Jensons were making more money than they'd ever seen in their lives and Maggs bought five new dresses.

It was a week later than Megan and Derek Baines arrived at Giant's Hill and found, to their disappointment, that the site on which they had anticipated pitching their tent (and making the baby that had so long eluded them) was filled with tents of every shape, size and colour, so that the shaft of the giant's penis looked like a patchwork quilt. That first night, they camped on the giant's left foot and slept poorly – so much so that Megan was too exhausted to take any notice of the shrilling of her alarm clock at seven the next morning. She rolled over and hit it with her fist, the clock stopped its noise, and Megan went back to sleep.

They both woke an hour later, stiff and sore from the hard ground. Megan's first thought was to see if anybody had left a vacant spot on the prized location. She thrust her head out of the tent flap and looked upwards. The patchwork had changed slightly – a red tent had been replaced by a green one, and there was more white canvas than there had been the evening before – but there still wasn't a square inch free.

She brought her head back into the tent. 'No good,' she said. 'You'll have to go up there and have a word, Derek.'

'Me? Why me?'

'Because you're the man, Derek Baines – or haven't you noticed?'

'But what am I supposed to say?'

'Ask if anybody's moving off and if so, can we have their space? Go on.'

Derek struggled into his clothes and crawled out of the tent. The day was warm and sunny, which cheered him, and he climbed up to the hub of the campsite and began to walk slowly round its perimeter. He asked several people if they intended moving off soon; most shook their heads and some made ribald comments about his sex life. One Scandinavian couple said that they were leaving that very morning but had promised their patch of ground to a German tourist and his wife.

The Polkerton Giant

Derek went round the perimeter a second time, asking anybody who would listen if he and Megan could possibly be guaranteed their spot when it became vacant, but everybody had somebody else waiting – some even had a short list of applicants vying for a place. Thus it became obvious that he and Megan would have to find a sponsor and join a queue.

He went back to the tent and told Megan.

'I'm sure you just didn't ask properly,' she said crossly.

'I did,' said Derek, smarting at her unfairness.

'Well, I'll just have to do it myself, won't I?'

They had a silent breakfast of raspberry pop tarts and lukewarm tea from the thermos, and then Megan got up and climbed purposefully up to the penis. Derek watched her, a speck against green. He saw her slowly move up one side of the shaft, round the top and then slowly down the other side. Several times she stopped and talked and, towards the end, she stopped for some time, talking to two people outside a yellow tent. Then she turned and started back towards him, almost running down the hill.

'Whew, what a slog,' she said, echoing Derek from the night before, and Derek knew he was forgiven.

'Any luck?'

'Well, sort of. I was talking to ever such a nice couple, from Wallasea actually, and they said they were leaving the day after tomorrow and there was one other couple that they'd promised their place to, but after they go – and assuming this second lot haven't promised it to anybody else – then we can have it. Which is great, isn't it?'

'When are the second lot going, then?'

'Well, the first lot don't know. That's the only problem.'

'But we've only got a week, Megan.'

'I know that, Derek Baines, thank you very much.'

'I mean, perhaps they won't go at all and we'll have wasted our time. Do you think we might as well pack the whole thing in?'

'I most certainly do not. We've come all this way and just because it's a bit crowded, you want to give up and go home?'

'No, no I don't. I thought we might go somewhere else, that's all.'

'Oh, you did, did you? Well, you've got another think

coming, that's all I can say. Don't you *want* a little tiny baby?'

'*Course* I do, Megan.' Derek wanted a little tiny baby quite a lot. He looked warily at his wife and saw the set of her jaw and the determination in her eyes, and he knew in that instant that all hope of getting to the motor show had flown away in the morning breeze.

'So,' he said, 'so – we'll just sit and wait, right?'

'Yes,' said Megan. 'That's exactly what we'll do.'

Uther found himself torn. On one hand, the media attention was making the Polkerton Giant notorious and the number of visitors to Giant's Hill was increasing every day, which made Mick Jenson happy and that meant that Uther was happy too. Cash was always welcome, and there was quite a lot of it – although the small bundles of fivers and tens that Mick was passing over weren't very clean and sometimes smelled bad, so that Uther was forced to wear a pair of gloves when handling the stuff. The local tradespeople were happy too; Polkerton was getting a surge of tourism where there had been none before, and even the sales of the old black and white postcards of the giant were selling fast.

All this was very pleasant, Uther decided, but money wasn't everything. More important by far (to Uther at least) was the up-and-down, in-and-out surge of the human tide. Uther – who regarded himself as the moon, insofar as influencing that tide was concerned – was prepared to disregard money entirely if the ebb and flow that he was dictating proved sufficiently entertaining. Naturally, having a lot of money of his own allowed Uther this nonchalant attitude to the stuff, so the fact that he was getting more than he needed and certainly more than he deserved was pleasant, but not crucial.

What *was* crucial at this moment was the awful collapse of CROSS. Uther blamed himself, although it was hard to see how he could have known of Viola's camera-shyness, given the forcefulness of her personality when dealing with human beings. All the same, he thought, when one is directing the affairs of men and women one should (like God, although of course He doesn't) show impartiality to all sides – and SPAM's present domination of the scene was unacceptable.

The Polkerton Giant

There was a way, he knew, of cutting the ground from beneath the triumphant Beaufort-Lyonses without destroying them completely, of course.

Plotting this reversal of fortune took most of one morning. Uther well remembered (although Viola, lifted high in the heat of excitement over being in television then plunged deep in the damp shame of not being able to cope with being on television at all, had obviously forgotten) his off-the-cuff suggestion that they ought to find some way to question the giant's authenticity. When he put forward the idea he already knew how to do it, but when Viola had seemed more interested in discussing the potential of a wider audience he'd put the thought on the back burner. Now, with Viola's collapse and the imminent failure of CROSS, it was time to bring it forward.

There was a problem. The professional debunker that Uther had in mind, the expert who had hinted that he possessed the kind of knowledge that Uther needed, was one of the most horrible men Uther had ever known. If he could overcome his reluctance to get in touch with the man, there was still the strong likelihood that he would refuse to have anything to do with Uther's scheme. (That was the trouble with experts, horrible or otherwise – they tended to be far too obsessive to allow their subjects to be trivialised). However, Uther knew he couldn't produce anybody who was *not* an expert who would be credible enough to sway the balance. He couldn't do it himself, of course, because that would be openly taking one side against the other.

There was no alternative. He was, finally, going to have to get in touch with Lysander Blount. Lysander Blount was mad and unpleasant and obviously despised Uther, although they had been to school together and even shared (then and for the rest of their lives) several interests, like history and making people do what they wanted. Lysander had been Uther's fag, and Uther had discovered quickly that the small, thin boy wasn't in the least bit frightened of him – in fact, he seemed to regard him with contempt. This had hurt Uther, until he discovered that little Lysander Blount regarded everybody with contempt. After that, he and Uther settled into an easy sort of relationship in which Uther told Lysander what to do and Lysander ignored him and went off to torture ants.

Lysander's interest in history had translated itself (for a short time) into a chair in that subject at Bristol University, but Lysander had made himself so detested that the student body threatened to go on strike if he wasn't removed, so the authorities (who hated Lysander even more than the students) got rid of him quickly. Ever since, Lysander had lived, unknown, unloved and in poverty, in a nasty flat near the old Bristol docks. The only reason that Uther knew of Lysander's whereabouts was because Lysander, for reasons known only to himself, sent Uther a recycled Christmas card every year. (Not that the paper from which it was made had been used before, but it had been sent earlier in the season to Lysander from some other well-wisher and Lysander had simply crossed out the personal, hand-written message and substituted one of his own, usually along the lines of: 'Why don't you convert to Islam, you ghastly thing? Then I wouldn't have to send you any more of these. All the best, Lysander Blount.'

Uther knew that Lysander had some knowledge about Polkerton Pete (or was pretending to, which was just as good), and not just because of the letter to the *London Gazette*. Lysander had also written, in last year's Christmas card, a line that at the time had puzzled Uther: 'Happy Christmas, you fake, you. Not unlike Big Pete, actually. And I'm the only one who knows about both of you, hee hee.' At the time, the words had meant nothing and Uther had put the message down as being some sort of obscure reference that he wasn't supposed to understand. Then, when the Polkerton Giant began to take a position of importance in his life, and when Simon Spillman jogged his memory with the letter sent to the paper, Uther had made the connection.

Uther decided to suppress his distaste for the man and talk to him. He knew from past experience that if he telephoned him, Lysander would simply tell him to piss off, so he filled the Morris's tank and drove to Bristol. He bought a street map of the town and found Lysander's block of flats down near the old docks.

The building was sooty and uncared for, and several panes

The Polkerton Giant

in the ground-floor windows were boarded over with plywood. Uther parked the Morris and entered the flats through a grimy archway. The area by the lift smelled of old urine and there was a roughly pencilled sign hanging on the lift door that said 'Out of Order'.

Uther walked up three flights of concrete stairs. There was graffiti everywhere and the smell of urine was stronger the higher he climbed. Lysander's flat was on the third floor. Uther pressed the doorbell button and, when he heard no ring from the inside, rapped sharply on the door. There was a shuffling sound and then the noise of several bolts being retracted.

Then Lysander's voice.

'Who?'

'Uther Tregeffen, Lysander.'

'Piss off.'

'In a minute. What do you know about the Polkerton Giant?'

There was a short silence, then Lysander said, 'A tremendous amount, actually. I was wondering when you would get to me about it. You're right in the thick of it, aren't you? You got my Christmas card, then?'

'Yes. And all the other ones, too. Thank you so much, Lysander. Do you think I might come in?'

'You never send me a Christmas card.'

'I'm sorry.'

'Why don't you?'

'I can never find one I think you'd like.'

'I like robins. Robins in the snow are nice.'

'Next year you shall have a whole flock of them.'

'What do you want, Uther?'

'I'd like to come in, if you don't mind. It smells rather nasty out here.'

'Hee hee. It smells a lot nastier in here, I promise you.'

Uther decided to stop playing this game. He stood patiently and in silence for several moments, and then Lysander said, 'You still there?'

Uther didn't reply. There was another pause and then the sound of more bolts being withdrawn. The door opened a crack and Uther could see one of Lysander's small, black eyes peering at him through the opening.

'Still got that stupid wig, I see.'

Uther smiled politely.

'What do you want?' said Lysander, opening the door a little wider.

'I want some information about the Polkerton Giant.'

'Why?'

'I'll tell you why if you let me in.'

Lysander sniffed and then slowly opened the door just wide enough to let Uther slide his body crabwise through the gap. Inside it was very dark and did, indeed, smell rather worse than outside. Lysander closed the door and carefully shot all the bolts back into their slots. The inside face of the door, Uther saw dimly in the gloom, was like a bank vault.

Lysander pushed past him and led the way down a short corridor. The corridor led into a cluttered nightmare that Uther assumed was Lysander's living room. There were cardboard boxes filled with newspapers scattered about the floor, dirty glasses and smeared plates balanced on the arms of the chairs, and everywhere a pervasive smell of decay. Lysander stood in front of where the fireplace might have been if it wasn't obscured by a tottering pile of magazines.

Uther found a chair and lowered himself into it. He looked up at Lysander with interest. It had been many years since he'd seen him, and Lysander seemed to have shrunk. He was very thin, and he carried his shoulders high about his ears, his head thrust forward like a turtle's. He was dressed in a suit so rumpled that Uther guessed he had slept in it. When he met Lysander's eyes, he saw a look of bitter derision in them.

Lysander said, 'Comfy?'

'Thank you.'

'Because that's my best chair. You know what you look like?'

'No, Lysander. What do I look like?'

'You look like one of those disgusting baby birds, sitting in its nest with its beak agape for food. All naked and scratchy, except for a silly patch of yellow feathers on its head.'

Uther nodded, smiling distantly. He remembered that you

The Polkerton Giant

always had to go through this when dealing with Lysander Blount; there was always this prologue to endure, filled with insult and invective and, if you could stand it without cracking, then sooner or later Lysander would calm down and allow a conversation to take place.

'You've aged dreadfully,' said Lysander. 'You look a hundred and forty-two.'

Uther smiled again, secure in the knowledge that he'd hardly aged at all since turning forty-five. Lysander sniffed again impatiently and shifted his weight. Then he said, 'All right. What do you want to know?'

'Have you heard of CROSS?'

'Unfortunately, yes.'

'And SPAM?'

'Again, unhappily, I have. There is a television somewhere in here.'

'I'm responsible for both.'

'And a lot more, I have no doubt. I hope you're ashamed of yourself.'

'Not at all. I'm inordinately proud. Now, you mentioned Pete in your card, and I know you also wrote a letter to the *London Gazette*.'

'They didn't publish it.'

'I know. The letters editor is a friend. I begged him to put it in but he wouldn't. He said it was altogether too scholarly a piece for them. What about Polkerton Pete?'

'Scholarly, eh?'

'Far too much for them these days.'

'A sad day. Of course, I don't read the *London Gazette* any more. I prefer *Exchange & Mart*. Altogether meatier. Hee hee. Well, I want to be paid, Uther. I will not divulge expensive facts for nothing.'

'How much?'

'Sixpence a word.'

Lysander had not made it into the seventies at all. Uther translated sixpence into two and a half new pence.

'Done – but be brief.'

There was a pause, while Lysander seemed to be collecting his thoughts. Then he said, 'Well, of course, the Polkerton Giant is not Palaeolithic at all. Not in the leastways. Not anyhow, not in the slightest, not no ways—'

'This is not brief. You're like a crooked taxi driver. I shall pay only for essentials, Lysander. Stick to the bones, please.'

'You're a cheapskate. All right. The Polkerton Giant is early seventeenth century – and that's three and six already, old chum. Are you sure you want the rest of it?'

'Absolutely. Go on.'

'It was carved round about 1624 by one Nathaniel Pyne, who owned the land. Nathaniel was in love with Miss Anne Bathwell, a beautiful and rich maiden who lived at Bathwell House. Do you know Bathwell House?'

'No, Lysander.'

'No, well, you wouldn't. It's not there any more. Hee hee – got you there, didn't I? It *was* on top of the hill next door, Hay Hill, the one that rises adjacent to what is now known as Giant's Hill. If you go up there and dig about a bit, you will find some foundations. From the front elevation of Bathwell House, Miss Anne Bathwell would have been able to see, quite clearly unless the day was foggy, whatever appeared on our hill, which at the time was known as Pyne Hill because Nathaniel Pyne happened to own it – and I'll let you off that last ten bob because the information is perhaps a touch superfluous.'

'Thank you, Lysander.'

'God, but you've still got that stupid little voice, haven't you?'

'The Polkerton Giant, Lysander.'

'Well, the thing was that little Anne Bathwell thought Nathaniel Pyne a complete arsehole and refused to have anything to do with him. Wouldn't see him, wouldn't answer his letters, would walk in the opposite direction if they chanced to meet. So Nathaniel, who was indeed a complete arsehole, took his revenge by carving the priapic monster on his hill so that Anne would be forever reminded of her cruelty towards him whenever she happened to look out of her bedroom window. Or her dining-room window, or her drawing-room window, or her sewing-room window, or any window, in fact, that faced towards Pyne Hill. Of course, it didn't work out happily. Anne's father, Mr Bathwell, went round and had some serious words with Nathaniel, and when

The Polkerton Giant

Nathaniel refused to say he was sorry Mr Bathwell lost his temper and stabbed him through the heart with one of Nathaniel's own pitchforks, which killed poor Nathaniel instantly. Mr Bathwell claimed that Nathaniel had fallen over on to the implement and, since there were no witnesses, he got off. Then the Bathwells sold their hill and razed Bathwell House to the ground so that nobody would have to look at the insult again. They went to Stoke Poges and lived, as far as I know, happily ever after. It was found that Nathaniel, who was quite alone in the world, had died with considerable debts, so his land was sold off by his creditors. Nobody mentioned the giant ever again.'

'How do you know all this?'

'It's in a satirical gazette. A pamphlet from some scribbler, dated 1627 and privately published. I've had a copy for ages.'

'But why didn't the truth follow the giant down the years? Where did the Palaeolithic stuff come from?'

'Well, I suspect that the giant was left to its own devices and probably became obscured over the years. It's not exactly visible to the passing crowd, is it? And grass grows back quickly. Then, perhaps late in the eighteen hundreds, some farmer discerned the outline through the turf and cleared it off and then some idiot probably came along and said it was Stone Age, simply because all the others are, or at least are supposed to be. Good God, this is costing you a fortune.'

'How do I know it's true?'

'You don't, you dullard. It's a bloody good story though, isn't it?'

'Do you think it's true?'

'Well, I do, yes. Nathaniel Pyne certainly owned the land – I've been into that – and the Bathwells certainly lived in Bathwell House on top of Hay Hill – I've researched that, too. And Nathaniel certainly died suddenly of what was coyly and discreetly described as an agricultural accident, and the Bathwells certainly knocked down Bathwell House and moved away immediately, and there is absolutely no mention that I can find of the Polkerton Giant before 1885; if the thing had been a Stone Age artefact then I think one would reasonably expect to find some reference to it somewhere before that, and there isn't one that I could uncover . . . so, on the whole, yes, I think it's true.'

Uther stared up at Lysander and Lysander, a self-satisfied grin turning up the corners of his lipless mouth, stared back. They stayed quite still, gazing unblinking at each other for twenty seconds. Then Uther said, very quietly, 'Lysander, would you like to be a little bit famous? And a little bit better off? The two often go hand in hand, you know.'

Chapter 11

Rehearsals were going as well as could be expected, given the conflicting temperaments and blazing egos of the Polkerton Players and given the fact that nobody was getting paid for all the extra work that Rapunzel was demanding of them. The tentative title of their play was *Giant!* Jack Lunn had pointed out that *Giant!* was already the name of a film with Elizabeth Taylor and James Dean, and perhaps the film's producers might not like the Polkerton Players appropriating their title.

'It's a *working* title, Jack,' Eric explained. 'By the time we open it'll probably be called something else entirely. Besides, I don't think the film used an exclamation mark, which makes us sufficiently different, I think.'

'Righto,' said Jack agreeably. He decided that now was not, perhaps, the right moment to suggest the play be called *Harga's Saga*, which, apart from rolling pleasantly off the tongue, was a more appropriate title than *Giant!* – since it was he, Jack Lunn, who had contributed the most to the improvisations and it followed that Harga was, at the moment at least, the central character in the current version of the script.

Maureen Lodson wasn't bad at creating a part for herself either. Between them they'd come up with all sorts of good bits, which Eric had scribbled down on a big pad of yellow paper. Jack had developed a style of speech that closely resembled the delivery of fake Red Indians in old cowboy films, and this had been generally accepted as a worthy compromise between the foolishness of 'Ooga ooga' and completely contemporary dialogue. The trick, Jack explained to the rest of the cast, was to leave out all the words that weren't strictly necessary like all the definite and indefinite articles, refer to oneself by name, and speak in a deep, ponderous voice that rumbled up from somewhere in the stomach.

'Harga no can make child. Harga lose goolies in battle against bad tribe down road thataway. Harga kill many warriors. Harga heap powerful, with arms like oak trees and legs also like oak trees but a bit thicker – but still cannot put wife Pomunka in club.'

'That's good, Jack,' said Eric, scribbling fast on the yellow pad. 'Not sure about "goolies", and perhaps "heap" is a bit Hopalong Cassidy, and I think "in the club" might be a little too colloquially modern . . . but otherwise very good. Well done, Jack.'

Maureen, not to be outdone, caught on quickly and contributed many powerful lines to the script.

'Pomunka strong and healthful. Pomunka can make baby, no problem. Problem is with husband, Harga. Harga no longer a man. Harga eunuch. Harga soft and flabby. Harga getting really fat. Harga no use to anybody, least of all Pomunka. Pomunka pretty damn fed up, don't mind telling you.'

'Very good, Maureen,' said Eric. 'I like "healthful" very much. Perhaps she might still like Harga a bit, though, don't you think? It's sounding rather as though Pomunka doesn't like him at all – and that's wrong, surely? I mean, he's still a powerful warrior, isn't he? She'd admire that, don't you think?'

'Yes, go easy, Maur,' said Jack. 'I may be stocky but I'm not fat. Or flabby.'

Poppy Boscombe and Roger Gower were playing the young lovers, Fern and Fin, and they seemed to be entering into the spirit of the thing in a wonderfully committed way. Their love scenes were tender and they did a lot of kissing. Rapunzel had suggested that perhaps Palaeolithic people hadn't discovered kissing, maybe they rubbed noses when they wanted to express affection for one another . . . but Poppy and Roger said that they'd much rather kiss because they had tried rubbing noses and it had been quite painful and had made their noses run, which wasn't hygienic. Neither Rapunzel nor Eric had felt strongly enough about

The Polkerton Giant

the matter to make a fight of it, particularly since Poppy and Roger charged their love scenes with a lot of Stone Age eroticism. In performance, Rapunzel thought, when they were both bare to the waist and rolling about on the floor like a pair of puppies, their scenes might well be the highlight of the play.

Of all the players, Aileen Beresford seemed to be having the most trouble getting into the skin of a Stone Age woman. In fact, she was the only Player who seemed unable to become anything other than what she was – a plain girl with sallow skin and a long, mare-like nose, a pair of splendid breasts that jutted out over an impossibly small waist, and an accent that was so mutilated by her Knightsbridge upbringing as to be barely distinguishable as English. By giving Aileen a non-speaking part (which she had accepted with good grace), Rapunzel had managed to overcome the last hurdle, but the rest of Aileen was hard to suppress. It wasn't that there were no plain, sallow girls with wonderful bodies in Palaeolithic times – Rapunzel was sure there had been plenty – but none who carried herself quite like Aileen Beresford.

The problem started early in rehearsals. Having established that she would be one of the cast who would be going topless, Aileen seemed determined to conquer any embarrassment she might feel on the first night by rehearsing without her blouse. The first evening she kept her bra on, but the following night, at one-thirty in the morning when the spirits of the cast were beginning to flag, Aileen decided to take it off.

'Efter orl, Ay maight as will. So thit evvybuddy can get used to it.'

Aileen was playing Zena, Pomunka's mute slave-girl. Her main duty was to dress Pomunka's hair with a wooden comb and listen dutifully to Pomunka's thoughts of the day. The part was designed by Eric to be an unobtrusive female presence, there simply to give Pomunka somebody to talk to when Harga wasn't around, and that would have worked well if Aileen had kept her blouse on. Once it was off, then Zena, silent but voluptuous, became the centre of attention – or rather, the twin cones of her breasts did. Whenever Harga came into Pomunka's chamber (which he did rather more than seemed strictly necessary, Eric thought) he would address all his portentous remarks to Zena's chest. Even Maureen, when she turned round from having her hair combed, seemed hypnotized by Zena's bosom.

This eye-catching distraction from the play was the price, Rapunzel realised, that they were going to have to pay for the controversy that the partial nudity was sure to raise. On the other hand, if the audience devoted all its energies to looking at Zena's torso, then the play would surely fail. Perhaps it was Zena's muteness that made her breasts so magnetic? Perhaps . . . perhaps if there was some sort of animation going on in Zena's face, the eyes would be less inclined to settle on her chest . . . some sounds, possibly . . . No dialogue, of course – unless . . .

The only person who attended all the rehearsals and who didn't look at Aileen's breasts was Evie Billingsworth. Though it was hard not to look – Aileen's breasts seemed to be everywhere – Evie managed it by looking at the floor every time they made an appearance. Looking at the floor was easy; Evie had done it for most of her life.

She felt most at ease with Billy Sherman. When he wasn't playing the tribe's elder he would come and sit with her and chat about his past without ever expecting an answer, so Evie just sat and nodded and stared at the floor while he talked. Billy claimed to have been a professional actor when he was young, although Evie didn't think he was very good in the part of Galf. He was small and skinny, with a face that was permanently tanned. He looked like a hairdresser from the fifties. He had an impossibly thin white moustache, and his white hair was swept up in two curvaceous waves above his ears. He had a fine pair of sideburns too, and they were teased into going straight backwards, the ends curling cunningly over his ears and almost concealing the small hearing aid he wore. Galf, thought Evie, was altogether too coiffed to be a Stone Age man – but Billy Sherman had charm and was being nice to her, so she decided to forget that he wasn't any good.

Evie had made several costumes and had brought them in today, well ahead of schedule, for Rapunzel's approval. In a coffee break, Rapunzel came over to the trestle table

The Polkerton Giant

where Evie had lain them out.

'Well, let's have a look, shall we, Evie? I must say, you're wonderfully efficient, bringing stuff in so early.'

'Oh, well, I don't suppose they're any good. Not at all what you wanted . . . I can start again, if you like . . .'

Rapunzel held up a fur loincloth. The fur was nylon, a dusky brown and quite long. Evie had found the material in Needles & Pins in Godber Street. Rapunzel turned the garment this way and that.

'I think it looks marvellous, Evie. Who's it for?'

'Oh, well, that's Fin, I think . . . Mr Gower's. Yes.'

Rapunzel turned away. 'Roger? Do come and try this on.'

Roger Gower came over to the table and, one by one, the rest of the cast arrived to take a look. The loincloth was passed from hand to hand and everybody murmured noises of approval and Evie became pink with pleasure.

'Should I take my trousers off?' said Roger.

It was generally agreed that he should. Roger went as pink as Evie, but he undid his belt and slipped off his trousers and stood there in a pair of brief underpants. Rapunzel handed him the loincloth. There was a short debate as to which was the front and which was the back; then Roger stepped into it and pulled it up about his waist. There was a moment of silence. Then Maureen Lodson said, 'I don't think the shoes and socks help much.'

Roger took off his shoes and socks and there was another moment of silence. Evie held her breath. They hated it, it was no good, it was awful, they were going to be cross with her, she knew she shouldn't have joined . . .

'Perhaps the shirt too, Roger,' said Rapunzel. The pinkness in Roger's face deepened and he glanced at Poppy for encouragement. She smiled prettily at him and he tore at the buttons of his shirt and threw it on the floor, and all those hours in the gym finally gave him his reward.

Roger Gower had a magnificent body. The pectoral muscles of his chest were sharply defined, his stomach rippled as though he was harbouring a six-pack of beer cans under the skin, and the tops of his arms bulged with muscle.

There were several sharp intakes of breath and Jack Lunn muttered, 'Bloody hell.'

'Oh, dear . . . I'm so sorry . . .' started Evie, staring miserably at the floorboards.

'But it's *wonderful*,' said Rapunzel. 'Don't you think so, Eric? It's magnificent, Evie. Now he really looks like Fin.'

'Just the ticket,' said Eric. Then inspiration grabbed him. '"The *accountant*, a mighty man is he, with large and sinewy hands, and the muscles of his brawny arms are strong as iron bands." Ha ha.'

Roger looked at him with a puzzled frown and Eric smiled modestly and said, 'With apologies to Longfellow, of course.'

'You look like Tarzan,' said Poppy, her eyes glittering. Roger stopped staring at Eric and looked at Poppy instead, and that made him stand up a little straighter and flex the slabs on his chest.

Instantly, everyone wanted to try on *their* costume, and the loudest was Jack Lunn.

Evie looked horrified. 'Oh dear. I'm so sorry, Mr Lunn, but I haven't finished yours yet. I ran out of fur, you see.'

'Surprise, surprise,' said Maureen.

Poppy took her skirt off but refused to remove the top until she got the long wig that had been promised her. She had pretty legs, and the nylon fur wrap draped over them alluringly. Fern, thought Poppy with satisfaction, was going to be the prettiest character in the play.

Rapunzel touched Aileen on her shoulder. 'Might I have a little word?'

They moved away from Evie's costume table and went and sat in the far corner of the room.

'First of all, I think your Zena is coming along marvellously. So marvellously, in fact, that Eric and I have had a thought about her – and we believe, to make it more interesting for you, that Zena would almost certainly have been captured from another tribe – possibly during the battle in which Harga was wounded – and brought back to serve Pomunka as her personal slave. Perhaps she was a *present* from Harga to his wife . . .'

'Oh yah?'

'Yes. And Eric and I both feel that Zena is an important role; we do so much want to build it up.'

'Ay wouldn't maind a lane or two,' said Aileen hopefully.

The Polkerton Giant

Rapunzel clapped her hands together and bounced excitedly in the canvas chair. 'Oh! Oh! I've got it! This is marvellous. What a good idea of yours! Of course! She isn't mute at all! The thing about Zena is – she doesn't speak their language! She doesn't speak Polk! She probably *wouldn't*, you see, coming from a different and more advanced tribe. She has her *own* language and, whenever she speaks, that's what she uses.'

'What lengwidge does she speak?' said Aileen dubiously.

'Well, her *own*. I mean, not any recognisable language of today – that wouldn't be right at all . . . No, you'd have to make it up, Aileen. Oh, this is going to be terribly exciting!'

Aileen thought that making up an entire language was going to be a lot more difficult than learning some ordinary English words like everybody else, but she was flattered that Rapunzel thought she might be able to do it. Since Rapunzel had started going on television, Aileen had developed a powerful respect for her. Television was, after all, the domain of professional actors, and somehow Aileen had managed to confuse the interviews Rapunzel took part in with real performances by real actors in television dramas.

'What sort of lengwidge should Ay make up?'

Rapunzel thought for a moment. Whatever Aileen was to say had to be as far removed from English as possible. 'I know, what about something like the click language?'

'Cleck?'

'Yes. You know – the one they use in Africa. All the words start with a clicking of the tongue, and sometimes you click in the middle of the word as well . . . but never at the end, I think.'

Aileen clicked her tongue, experimentally, several times.

'Marvellous. Now try saying something.'

'*Click*-what should Ay *click*-say?'

'Just do made up words, Aileen.'

'*Click*-um, shlombo wally boo boo. *Click*.'

'Well, that's definitely along the right lines, Aileen. Work on that and we'll really have something, I think.'

Uther Tregeffen glided out of the shadows and made a small bow to Rapunzel. She smiled back at him with real pleasure. Uther had, unobtrusively, attended all their rehearsals. He would sit at the back of the hall, his legs and arms elegantly crossed, and he would watch, with the stillness of a statue, all the actors' improvisations and all Eric's scribblings on the yellow pad and all Rapunzel's lectures about the essential *happiness* of the simple People of the Polk and how Grace Stanley really hadn't quite got there yet.

Uther had come up with several good ideas, which made him doubly welcome at rehearsals.

'It's going tremendously well,' he would say, drawing Eric or Rapunzel aside. 'I'm so impressed. You're all so talented. It makes me quite sick. One little thing I thought of – it's probably not at all what you want but I shall say it all the same. Billy, I think his name is . . .'

'Billy Sherman, Uther.'

'That's the chap. He's terrific, isn't he? Very much the tribal elder. Well, I wondered if his character – Galf, is it? – might not be something else besides being the elder of the tribe. I wondered if it might perhaps humanise him more if we saw him doing something quite ordinary, as though being the tribal elder was more of a part-time job, you see? Perhaps he's the weapon-maker, or . . . no, better still, perhaps he's the tribal *barber*. Yes, that would work – because barbers were surgeons as well, weren't they? And that would have earned him the respect of the tribe – which was why they elected him the elder, you see. Just a thought, of course.'

And, being a thought from Uther Tregeffen, Rapunzel or Eric would invariably adopt it with enthusiasm.

Now Uther straightened up from his bow and looked, more gravely than usual, into Rapunzel's eyes.

'My dear, just *entre nous*, I've heard rather an unsettling rumour. Curiously, it's about a man I used to know. We were at school together – he was horrid then and he's horrid now, I'm told. One Lysander Blount. Historian. Expert about this part of the country. Anyway, I've heard, from a small bird which shall be nameless, that Mr Blount is going to be on television this evening, Satellite West to be precise, and he is going to be talking about the Polkerton Giant.'

'Well, what's so bad about that? Or is he on CROSS's side?' said Rapunzel.

The Polkerton Giant

'I don't think he's on anybody's side, other than his own. However, I think it's safe to say that what he will be divulging, to an audience of several million people, will hurt poor SPAM a lot more than it will hurt CROSS.'

'What's he going to say?'

Uther took Rapunzel's arm and led her to the stage. They perched their bottoms on the edge of the platform, looking down the hall to where the cast was still gathered round the costume table, and Uther told Rapunzel all about Nathaniel Pyne and Anne Bathwell and the pitchfork, and Rapunzel's face became even more pinched than usual, and her cheeks went pale and the end of her nose (pink under normal circumstances) turned a pillar-box red.

'It can't be true,' she whispered.

'Probably not. But Lysander Blount *does* command some respect in historian circles, and whatever nonsense he utters will certainly be taken, by some people, as the gospel truth, I'm afraid. He's on tonight, at eight o'clock. We shall simply have to watch, won't we?'

Chapter 12

It wasn't only the Beaufort-Lyonses and Uther Tregeffen who watched Lysander Blount's interview that evening. Viola Pomfret watched as well, because Uther had telephoned several hours earlier and advised her, in a thrilling and mysterious voice, that the programme promised to be an absolute *must* and she was not, on any account, to miss it.

A lot of viewers tuned in throughout the country. *Contention* was a popular, long-running show, hosted by a young woman of beauty, brains and charm (some unkind people said she had not enough of the first, far too much of the last, and almost none that could be detected of the middle) called Samantha Sagamore – and it was she who faced the unknown but visibly reptilian Lysander Blount.

'Mr Blount, I understand you have an alternative theory to explain the origins of the Polkerton Giant. Would you like to tell us what it is?'

The camera switched to Lysander, who sat still and unblinking under its scrutiny.

'Mr Blount?'

The reptile stirred. The lipless mouth opened a crack and a pale yellow tongue slithered out. It oscillated from side to side and then disappeared. The corners of the mouth twitched. 'You *understand* I have a theory? You know *perfectly well* that I have! You came to my house and I told you then, didn't I?'

'True, Mr Blount, but our viewers don't know about your theory, you see—'

'Well of course they don't. I haven't told *them*, have I? The trouble is, they shouldn't give pretty girls like you such a responsible job. You won't mind me saying this but I have the feeling that it's just a bit beyond you. You'd probably be much happier being a receptionist or something. Viewers? What viewers? There are *viewers*?' He looked into the camera lens and frowned angrily. 'Is that thing looking at me?'

'Yes it is, Mr Blount. Now, about the Polkerton Giant . . .'

'The viewers can see me through that thing?'

'Yes. Now . . .'

Lysander waved dismissively at Samantha Sagamore and fixed the camera lens with his small black eyes. He said, 'Well, look here, everybody. I'm Lysander Blount and I don't stand for any nonsense, see? So if any of you don't agree with what I'm saying, well you can bloody well stuff it as far as I'm concerned, all right?'

The camera switched back to Samantha Sagamore, catching her with her mouth wide open and a stricken look in her eyes (and those detractors of her talent who were watching the programme turned to their partners and said they'd always known she was a silly cow).

Lysander was hitting his stride. 'There's a whole lot of stinking rubbish talked about the so-called Polkerton Giant, and I'm here to give the hard facts of the case. If you don't like what you're about to hear then you can do one of two things: you can turn your receiver off, or you can piss off – I don't give a monkey's. Right, here we go then . . .'

'Mr Blount, I wonder if I might stop you there—'

'My dear girl, you're very pretty, but the fact is the viewers don't want to *hear* from you . . . although perhaps they might like to *look* at you. Of course, they feel quite the reverse about me. I shall do all the talking; you just sit there and be decorative. You do that very nicely.'

Samantha Sagamore's gasp was heard throughout the land – but the director, who knew good television when he saw it, resisted the temptation to cut back to her. 'We've got a real live monster, people. Doesn't happen often. I want to stay on Camera One all the time. I don't want to miss a syllable of this.'

Lysander pushed one little finger deep into his left nostril and poked about in there reflectively for a few seconds. Then he withdrew the finger, wiped it down the front of his ill-fitting suit, glared fiercely at the camera and embarked on the story of Nathaniel and Anne.

Uther, sitting at home with a glass of red wine in one hand and a small cigar in the other, watched Lysander's performance with fascination. It *was* a performance, Uther decided. It was certainly not an interview, because after the first few salvos from Lysander, Miss Samantha Sagamore was neither seen nor heard from again.

What sort of reptile was he? Uther wondered. At the nasty flat by the old docks, Lysander had been a turtle . . . but there was too much vibrant life in this manifestation for a turtle. There was something about the sloping shoulders raised high about Lysander's neck, the slow, rhythmic swaying from side to side and the coiled energy in that rapier-thin torso . . . and the way that yellow tongue flickered in and out . . . Of course! Lysander Blount was a cobra, its hood spread wide, swaying to the tune from the snake charmer's pipe.

Lysander was, Uther decided, one of the most unpleasant objects ever to be captured by a television camera – and yet there was a deadly vitality in the man which made his nastiness most fascinating to watch (and which, Uther realised, could make Lysander a star).

Lysander wound up his story and sneered into the camera lens for the last time. 'Well, there you have it,' he said. 'The object holds no historical interest for anybody of the smallest intelligence – which I suspect applies to most of you out there watching this idiotic show. All right, turn it off now, I'm not going to say any more. Who's got my money?'

The picture cut back to Samantha Sagamore. There was a sheen of sweat on her upper lip. She turned to her camera and smiled painfully. 'There you have it,' she said, her voice trembling. 'A fascinating alternative theory of the origins of one of Somerset's most notorious landmarks. A Stone Age fertility symbol – or a seventeenth-century act of revenge?'

From off camera (but still close by) Lysander's voice muttered, 'Christ, girl, I've just spent the last ten minutes telling the cretinous viewers that it's seventeenth century, haven't I? Weren't you listening?'

Samantha Sagamore took a breath and arranged the features of her face around a smile of such rigid brightness that it threatened to crack her head into two. She said, 'Well, that's all from *Contention* this evening. We'll be back, next week at the same time, to talk about the unprecedented rise in pre-teen crime in the lovely old city of Bristol.'

'It's a *sewer*. I live there and I ought to know.'

'Goodnight,' said Samantha Sagamore, abruptly, and the picture faded to break.

Almost immediately, Uther's telephone trilled. He picked it up.

'Uther! What a find! He's stupendous! Thank you *so* much.'

'Why are you excited? It's not your show, is it, Pamela?'

'No. I just happened to catch it on a monitor here in the office.'

'Then why are you thanking me?'

'Because Satellite West has another coup on its hands, that's why, and that makes us *all* look good. Where on earth did you get him?'

'Get him? What can you mean? Are you implying I had something to do with this, Pamela?'

'Oh come on, darling. The whole thing had Uther Tregeffen written all over it.'

'Well, I very much hope it didn't. I can't be seen to be taking such a prominent position in this. I shall lose my friends, and I can't have that.'

'Don't worry. They won't guess it. It takes a professional relative like me to ferret out the truth. I hope you've bribed that wonderful man not to tell on you?'

'I have donated a small *pourboire* to Lysander, which will, I think, keep him quiet. He seems to be very fond of money. I can't think why . . .'

'That's because you've got so much of it. The rest of us poor mortals are rather fond of it too. Now you'll have to give me some as well or I'll talk.'

'I shan't and you won't.'

'Scrooge. By the way, he did a wonderful job on that Sagamore bitch. I've had several run-ins with her and it was glorious to watch her sweat.'

'What a cruel thing you are, to be sure.'

'And you're not? By the way, while the Blount man was still talking, we got a couple of calls asking about him. One

The Polkerton Giant

from the Beeb and one from Carlton. I think he'll be going big time any minute now.'

'And Satellite West discovered him. A feather in your cap!'

'All due to you.'

'Oh, hush.'

The moment Uther put his phone down it rang again.

'Uthie? It's little me.'

'Hello, Viola. Did you watch?'

'Of course I did. I've been ringing and ringing but you've been engaged for hours. Who were you talking to? Well, never mind. What a very peculiar man that was. Quite ugly. Rather horrid, I thought. So rude to that poor girl. But, one has to admit, he seems well bred. He went to school with you, I think you told me . . . ?'

'Indeed he did.'

'And which school was it, Uthie? You've never told me.'

'Haven't I? It was Winchester.'

'Ooh. You brainy-poos.'

'What did you think of the content?'

'Oh, well, that was marvellous for us, of course. Fancy it being a fake. That'll scotch all those silly claims that it's historically valuable, won't it?'

'Among those who believe Mr Blount – yes, I think it will.'

'Don't you think everybody will believe it, Uthie?'

'Not everybody, Viola. Not those who passionately *want* the giant to be Palaeolithic. That's a funny thing with people – if it's important to them, they will continue to believe, obstinately, in something that has been proved to be false. You can argue with them until you're blue in the face, it won't make any difference.'

'Oh dear. What do you think we should do?'

'I think, Viola, that CROSS should stay discreetly quiet for the moment and let Mr Blount do its work for it. CROSS has been lagging behind lately, and perhaps Mr Blount will turn the tide. Somehow, I don't think we've seen the last of him.'

After he'd finished with Viola (he could detect in her voice a hint that her old confident complacency was returning), Uther sat by his telephone and waited for Rapunzel and Eric to call. But his telephone trilled no more that evening and, at midnight, he went to bed.

The next day Uther received several calls but none of them from the Beaufort-Lyonses, and he began to wonder if perhaps they had missed the programme. He thought about calling them and decided that he wouldn't: it would be inadvisable, he thought, to appear too eager in any of this.

Instead, that evening at seven o'clock, he checked in his bathroom mirror to see if Quentin was properly seated on his head before trotting downstairs, the polished toecaps on his black shoes twinkling. Out of the door, into the Morris, a zip down one street, a sharp right turn into another, a negotiation of a roundabout, into Polkerton High Street then a left turn into Brady Street . . . and a swing into the small car park by the community hall. Uther could see, in the dimming light, the poster on the notice board by the door: 'Coming Soon! A brand new, entirely original play from the Polkerton Players!' Then, in bolder letters: 'GIANT! (THE STORY OF POLKERTON PETE) SEE THE PAST UNFOLD! LEARN THE MARVELLOUS TRUTH ABOUT OUR HERITAGE! TICKETS AVAILABLE NOW!'

Uther looked at his watch. Ten past seven. They'd all be there now, gathered round the urn, sipping Grace Stanley's coffee. Rapunzel insisted on punctuality.

He got out of the car and went to the door at the side of the building and quietly pushed it open. Everybody was there, but they weren't gathered round the urn and they weren't sipping Grace Stanley's coffee. They were sitting on the tubular steel chairs, clustered up front near the stage. Rapunzel was perched in her usual place on the edge of the platform, looking out over her cast; Eric stood beside her, clipboard under one arm. His head, Uther noticed, was hanging low.

Rapunzel saw Uther and gave him a wan smile, and Uther wiggled his fingers back at her then moved to sit in his usual chair at the back of the hall.

'Uther, dear – do come up to the front, won't you?' Rapunzel called. 'We need all the input we can get.'

Uther went to the front row of chairs and sat down next to Evie Billingsworth. He saw that she was frowning so he

The Polkerton Giant

leaned over and whispered into her ear, 'Whatever's wrong? You all look so gloomy.'

Evie shook her head and stared at the floor.

Rapunzel said, 'Well, as I was saying, there's no doubt about it – we have received something of a setback. It's not the end of the world, but it might be the end of *Giant!*. Personally, I don't believe a word of what that dreadful man said and, even if I did, I see no reason to have the giant removed just because there's a faint possibility that he might not be quite so old as we thought. However, *I'm* still convinced he *is* Palaeolithic, and therefore of even greater value. I suspect lots of people will pick up the seventeenth-century theory, though, and if we simply go ahead and present *Giant!* we might get some unwelcome jocularity from some members of the audience . . . not to mention an even more scathingly rude review than we got for *Three Sisters* from that ridiculous young man who calls himself a critic.'

'Hear, hear,' said Jack Lunn.

'I think, knowing him as we all do,' Rapunzel continued, 'I think we can be sure that he will embrace this latest theory rather than ours, simply in order to be unpleasant to us. And I do *not* want to expose this wonderfully talented and sensitive group to ridicule.'

Uther marvelled at the blindness of some people, who couldn't see that they were ridiculous already, without making any effort at all.

'So, rather than do that, I feel we ought to postpone *Giant!*. We can always resurrect it when the time is right, so all your marvellous work and Evie's wonderful costumes won't go to waste. Meanwhile, we are committed to mounting a play before the end of this month, which gives us very little time, I'm afraid – particularly since I will most probably be called on by the television companies to refute this nonsense. I can see a busy time ahead for Eric and myself. So – any suggestions?'

There was a glum silence.

Rapunzel said, 'Uther? What about you? Although you're not technically part of the group – and how we wish you were! – your suggestions are always so helpful.'

'Hear, hear,' said Jack again.

Uther inclined his head modestly and frowned as though deep in thought. Everybody was looking at him now, and he wanted them to believe that the notion he was about to come up with was quite spontaneous.

'We-e-ell,' he said slowly, as if the light bulb over his head that contained the notion was on a slow dimmer-switch, and all that could be seen at that moment was a dull red glow from the filament.

'Yes?' said Rapunzel, leaning forward with eagerness.

'We-e-ell, I wonder if you *really* have to postpone *Giant!*'

'What else can we do?'

'Here's my thought. What about doing *Giant!* first and then doing a version of the unrequited love theory afterwards?'

'Do *two* plays?' said Maureen Lodson.

'Yes,' said Uther, apparently warming to his idea (and moving the dimmer-switch up a notch – now the filament was glowing yellow). 'Why not? The Polkerton Players, in the interest of impartiality, can present both tales – and the audience can choose whichever one they like better. You'll get lots of brownie points just for being fair.'

'But won't that very impartiality weaken SPAM's cause?' Rapunzel said. 'Don't forget, the concept of *Giant!* was always to promote his historical significance and thus his future conservation.'

'And *wonderful* propaganda it will be too! Let me explain. By presenting the other admittedly idiotic theory too, you not only appease its adherents but you confound your horrid critic – and at the same time glorify Pete in not one but *two* historical perspectives, thereby doubling his significance and making him more worthy of conservation than ever before!' Uther finished in a rush of enthusiasm then sat back, panting slightly. The idea that the Polkerton Players had the kind of influence over local affairs to alter the way people thought and thereby change the course of events was, of course, ridiculous. On the other hand, the Players had between them an ego as big as the Ritz, and probably believed already that their cultural inspiration was easily up to the job.

A glance at their faces settled his doubts. Gone was the air of dejection. Now they were all looking at him with varying degrees of excitement in their eyes, as though his

The Polkerton Giant

light bulb was burning as brightly as the sun.

'Might the evening be, perhaps, a little on the lengthy side?' said Eric. '"Deserts of eternity" and all that?'

'Yes,' said Uther, injecting a grace note of disappointment into his voice. It wouldn't do to let this new idea appear to be germinating too quickly. 'Um . . . on the other hand . . .' He trailed off, apparently deep in thought.

'On the other hand . . . ?' Rapunzel prompted.

'On the other hand – and, of course, I'm no expert in these matters and you'll probably tell me it can't be done – but what if the pieces were presented as a double bill of two *one-act* plays? It would mean a cutting back on *Giant!* a bit, and the other one would have to be of a similar length, but what if you could present *both* plays in two hours? How would that be?'

Rapunzel turned to Eric, and Eric, feeling her eyes on him, turned to Rapunzel. Her eyebrows were raised, so he knew an answer was expected from him.

'Well, it could be done, I suppose. We'd have to lose some marvellous material to get it into an hour—'

'But we could put a lot of marvellous material in the other piece, couldn't we?' Rapunzel said sharply.

'Ah, well, yes we could.'

'And what an exciting contrast it would be, wouldn't it?' said Uther. 'An evening of wonderful opposites. In the first half, we experience the animal skins of the ancient past, the simplistic language, the unsophisticated straight-dealing between people . . . and then, in the second half of the show, we get the elaborate Restoration dresses, the courtly, almost ceremonial language, and the almost contemporary complications of human relationships that several thousand years have developed—'

Rapunzel broke in. 'Oh, but this is marvellous!' she cried. 'This is so exciting! And, apart from all the wonderful contrasts that Uther has mentioned, the audience will see how versatile we all are – how we can change, in just a few minutes, from half-naked noble savages to elaborately dressed and coiffured Restoration ladies and gentlemen . . .'

'How *we* can change?' said Maureen. 'I thought you weren't going to be in this?'

'Well, naturally, Eric and I will play Mr and Mrs Bathwell, Maureen. Roger will play Nathaniel Pyne, Poppy will play Anne Bathwell—'

'And who will *I* play?' Maureen said in a tired voice, knowing perfectly well whom she would play.

'Well, Pomunka, of course . . . in the first play, and . . . and the Bathwell housekeeper in the second. A very important part, naturally.'

'What about me?' said Jack.

'You, Jack, will be the Bathwell butler. Another pivotal role and a marvellous contrast to Harga. And Grace and Billy will be Nathaniel Pyne's elderly retainers – gardeners perhaps . . . yes, and it's Grace and Billy who actually carve the giant at Nathaniel's orders.'

'End me?' said Aileen Beresford (who, since the rehearsal hadn't yet started, was still modestly dressed).

'Ah. I'm not sure yet, Aileen, but we will fit you in somehow. Perhaps a visiting duchess, come to call on the Bathwells for tea? Something along those lines. But it won't be terribly big, I'm afraid. You won't mind, though – not after such a fabulous part as Zena.'

'The frocks were quaite low cut, weren't they, in thaose days?' said Aileen hopefully.

'Very low cut, Aileen.'

'Lovely,' murmured Aileen.

'And Evie shall make all the costumes,' said Rapunzel. 'We've seen how good you are, Evie, so you simply can't say no.'

'Oh dear,' whispered Evie. 'I really don't think . . . I mean, fur loincloths is one thing, but . . .'

Rapunzel began to talk about wigs and fans and brocade and lace, and how to bow and curtsey, and Uther got up and glided silently and invisibly to the door at the rear of the hall. When he got there, he turned and wiggled his fingers and pointed at his watch and made some apologetic faces, all in the direction of the stage, but nobody seemed to notice that he'd slipped away, so he opened the door quietly and stepped outside.

The night sky was dark and clear and the moon was full. He stared at it, thinking how pleasant it was to be him. And

The Polkerton Giant

tomorrow was Friday, which meant lunch with Viola. Another treat.

'Goodness, how spoilt I am,' he said to the moon.

Chapter 13

'Uthie, dear, do come in. I have such a treat for you.'

'Not that ambrosial salmon dish again?'

Viola slapped him playfully on his wrist. 'Naughty Uthie. Always thinking of his tummy – although you never seem to get any fatter, whatever you eat. Look at poor little me! An endless battle! Too unfair for words. Now, come along and see your treat.'

Viola led him, almost at a trot, to the big drawing room. Usually, while they waited for luncheon to be announced, Uther would find himself sequestered with Viola in her reading room – unless there were other guests, which was rare, but when it did happen they would all gather in the big drawing room. The room was very big indeed, with a great limestone fireplace and fat, red leather armchairs and matching sofas scattered about the place. There was a portrait of a younger Viola, winsomely dressed in pink lace, hanging over the vast fireplace, and a matching one of Victor (who didn't look any younger than he did in real life, even though the portrait had been painted at the same time as Viola's, which was puzzling) at the opposite end of the room. Overhead, the ceiling was painted sky blue and some impossibly fluffy clouds floated motionless over its surface. In the corners of the ceiling were groups of gold-leafed cherubs, blowing lustily into cone-shaped trumpets. There were Persian rugs and marble and ormolu tables, gilded clocks and two life-sized statues of Nubian boys . . . and, on every horizontal surface, back-copies of *Country Life*.

For several moments after entering the room Uther thought he and Viola were alone, but then she called out, 'Cooee! He's here, the naughty thing!' and out of one of the fat armchairs – and so dwarfed by it that Uther thought he must have shrunk overnight – rose Lysander Blount.

Not many things surprised Uther Tregeffen, but the sight of Lysander Blount standing in Viola Pomfret's drawing room, clutching a glass of dry sherry in one claw-like hand and grinning nastily at him by twisting up just one corner of his slit of a mouth, made him stop in his tracks.

'Hee hee,' said Lysander. 'Gobsmacked you there, didn't I, Uther? Flabbered your gast, I do believe.'

'Hello, Lysander,' said Uther carefully. He wondered if Lysander had said anything to Viola about his involvement in the affair.

Lysander saw the query in his eyes and put his forefinger to what passed for his lips, shaking his head and grinning even more fiercely. 'Not a word, Tregeffen – not yet. But I shall be requiring additional moolah sharpish or the limas will have to be spilled.'

Viola was looking from Uther to Lysander – and then back again to Uther – with a bright smile of incomprehension on her carmine lips. 'What are you talking about, you naughty things?' she said.

'It's schoolboy slang, Viola,' said Uther. 'Lysander is referring to a minor episode in our past. Something that happened at Winchester. I'm surprised you still remember that, Lysander.'

'He beat me,' said Lysander, investing the word 'beat' with venomous resentment.

'Uthie! You didn't!'

'Well, yes I did, Viola. Lysander had been very wicked. I didn't beat him very hard.'

'Yes, you did,' said Lysander.

'Oh, pish. I had arms like toothpicks. It couldn't have hurt at all.'

'I bled, Mrs Pomfret,' Lysander said darkly. 'There were weals.'

'How awful for you,' said Viola. 'Cruel, cruel Uthie. Well, I think you must both have been quite horrid back then . . . but now you're not, are you? Which just goes to show what a dose of maturity and a spoonful of clean living will do. Which reminds me – and I don't mean to pry, Mr Blount – but I understand that you, like Uthie, are not married.'

The Polkerton Giant

'No, Mrs Pomfret. I am a virgin.'
'Oh.'
'I am waiting for Miss Right.'
Viola simpered. Mr Blount seemed to be looking at her in a yearning sort of way, so she blushed prettily. What a gift she had, to be sure. So many gallants at her feet ... but no, she mustn't allow them to retain even a smidgeon of hope. 'I'm sure Miss Right will be along any day now,' she said and, to emphasise the point, she patted Lysander encouragingly on the back of his hand.

Uther was positive that Miss Right had always kept, was still keeping, and would (if she had any brains at all) continue to keep the greatest possible distance between herself and Lysander Blount. Miss Right was, Uther thought, probably lying low somewhere in New Zealand.

Luncheon was announced and they trooped into the dining room. Lysander offered Viola her arm [←his], and to Uther's dismay she took it. He wondered what was going on. Why was Lysander being so courteous, so attentive, rather than his usual spiteful self?

When they had sat down at the great refectory table — Viola at the head and Uther and Lysander sitting either side of her — Uther looked closely at Lysander and found his answer. Lysander was staring about him, obviously deeply impressed. He hadn't looked particularly interested in the drawing room, but Uther reasoned that the odious creature had been alone in that room long enough for the awe to have died away by the time he and Viola had entered. But the dining room was making Lysander gape.

There was much to gape at. The room was the same acreage as the drawing room, but longer and narrower. The table at which they sat was twenty feet long, a massive slab of polished oak. The chairs were tall, with Gothic backs. They looked like thrones and were upholstered in the most royal of red velvets. All protuberances on the walls and on the ceiling — and there were many — were covered in gold leaf. The ceiling was painted in a series of panels that exalted the art of gardening. There were wheelbarrows and watering cans and spades and forks; pots of geraniums and banks of flowering rhododendrons and borders of roses; a charmingly rustic potting shed, with ivy growing over it; and in the centre panel, and most prominent of all, there was an old gardener, leaning on a rake. He had a pleased, almost smug, expression on his face and looked a little like Victor Pomfret. A Persian carpet covered most of the floor. The napkin rings were gold (Uther saw Lysander rub his thumb slowly over the surface of his).

Lysander's little black eyes, usually dull with rancour, were glistening with envy.

Of course, Uther thought: *wealth*. That was the only thing that impressed Lysander, the only commodity that had any meaning for him – and, apparently, the only stuff which curbed his malice towards the human race – or at least towards the few people who possessed enough wealth to awe him.

They progressed from lobster soup to a fine *Boeuf en Croute*. Lysander continued his obsequious behaviour towards Viola, referring to her during almost every sentence as Mrs Pomfret, and congratulating her on her cook and enquiring where the carpet had come from . . . and asking who, precisely, was the model for the splendid painting of the gardener on the ceiling?

Viola, with not one but two inamorati sitting next to her, was at her most flirtatious. Uther was strangely quiet – jealous, she surmised – so she concentrated her efforts on the peculiar looking but undeniably charming Mr Blount.

'You must call me Viola,' she cooed. 'Mrs Pomfret makes me feel just a teeny bit ancient.'

'Dear lady,' said Lysander, leaning viper-like towards her, ' or Viola, should I say . . .?'

'Oh, yes,' squeaked Viola.

'Viola – dear lady. You don't look a minute over thirty-nine.'

Viola wriggled with pleasure. 'Oh, Mr Blount, you mustn't say such things! Whatever will Uthie think?'

'I don't give a monkey's what Uthie thinks,' said Lysander with sudden savagery. Then the skeletal grin reappeared. 'It's what *you* think that matters, dear lady. And no more Mr Blount. You must call me Lysander.'

'Such a big name. I shan't be able to get my little mouth

The Polkerton Giant

around it. I shall have to shorten it.'

'You could call him Lice,' suggested Uther.

'Naughty! Take no notice of him. I shall call you Sandy.'

Later, over coffee in the reading room, Viola told Uther how Lysander came to be there.

'I was so impressed by Mr Blount . . . Sandy – on the television the other night, that I thought we ought to get to know him. He had such a presence that I just *knew* he'd done it lots of times before and was quite probably a star – although I couldn't have known that because I don't usually watch television, you understand. Anyway, I thought it might be rather wonderful if he could be persuaded to join us in CROSS. I felt that his wonderful, fresh opinions on the matter would be so useful in our cause – so what do you think I did?'

'I can't imagine,' said Uther, who could imagine only too well.

'Well, I took my courage in both hands and looked up Blount in the Bristol telephone book. Then I telephoned him. Didn't I, Sandy?'

'You did, dear Viola. A red letter day if ever there was one.'

'He was rather rude at first, Uther – but then I expected that. Brilliant people are often rather rude, I've found, and always quite without meaning to be.'

'I thought you were somebody else,' said Lysander. 'Somebody horrible. She will remain nameless.'

'But then I explained about CROSS and who I was and who Victor was, and all about you too, Uthie, and then Mr Blount . . . Sandy became sweetly charming, so I wasn't frightened of him any more. So I invited him to luncheon and here he is.'

She turned to Lysander and put her head on one side. 'Now, I wonder if I can tempt you at all? CROSS *so* needs your wonderfully accurate, truly historical approach – so refreshing after the silly, Stone Age mumbo-jumbo we've been hearing from the idiotic SPAM people lately – and, indeed, it needs your advice as well. We are, I'm afraid, a teensy bit deficient in the spokesman department. Impoverished, even.'

Then she added quickly: 'But not impoverished in any other

areas, I assure you. We are – CROSS is, I mean – quite . . . comfortable.'

'Um, yes. I see,' said Lysander pensively. 'Well, I would be most pleased to help in any small way that I can. However, there is a difficulty. I hardly like to mention it. Rather embarrassing . . .'

'You mustn't be embarrassed, Sandy. Speak out.'

'Well, Viola – dear lady – my schedule is quite full at the moment and any time spent away from work – poorly paid though it is – would, inevitably, render me even more impoverished than I am at the moment. The profession of historian is not generously remunerated, I'm afraid.'

Uther was fairly sure that, apart from the fee Lysander had just earned from Satellite West, the man didn't actually do any historical work at all (or work of any kind, come to that) – and so he was unlikely to be getting paid for doing nothing. Uther was also fairly sure that Lysander lived entirely on welfare and was in fact much poorer than he appeared. But he kept his mouth closed and watched to see if Viola would take the bait that Lysander was dangling in front of her.

She did.

'Oh, Sandy – but of course you would be paid! One of the official spokesmen of CROSS, and a television star too, taking time away from his valuable work to help us in our campaign . . . for you not to receive some recompense would be too absurd!'

'But, dear lady,' Lysander muttered, waving his hands in front of him in protestation, 'I couldn't . . . it's not *possible* to take money from so gracious a lady . . .' And he sunk his chin down on to his narrow chest and let the rest of his speech trail away, apparently overcome.

'I think it's a very good idea,' said Uther. 'You ought to be paid, Lysander. Besides, it won't be coming from Viola's pocket, it'll be coming from the coffers of CROSS. Won't it, Viola?'

'Oh, well – yes, of course,' Viola stammered, wondering how it was that Uthie didn't know that CROSS had never had such things as coffers and that the entire cost of the campaign came from the depths of her Thatcherite handbag.

The Polkerton Giant

'There you are, you see,' said Uther. 'No need to worry yourself about it. Now, how much do you think you ought to get?'

Lysander shot him a glance of naked malignity. Then, in a flash, he turned the look away from Uther and towards Viola, and in that instant his furious little eyes became embarrassed and even tragic.

'Ah. My friend Uther is so much of this world and I am so detached from it. Far be it from me to decide on a sum. Whatever you say, dear lady, will be most humbly and gratefully accepted.'

Viola was in a quandary. What sort of money did historians get? What if they were television stars as well? Television stars got quite a lot of money, she thought – or at least quite a lot for *them*, though to Viola it didn't seem so terribly much. And what did campaign spokesmen earn? If they were campaigning on behalf of the President of the United States they probably got quite a lot, being in the news and everything. It was, she decided, an impossible figure to guess.

She looked desperately at Uther, who was sitting a little behind Lysander. Seeing her desperation, he discreetly raised his right hand so that it stood vertically in the air in front of him, four fingers pointing at the ceiling, his thumb curled out of sight.

Four. Yes. Viola got that.

Then, lifting his left hand so that it was next to the right, he joined the tip of his left forefinger to the tip of his left thumb, making an O.

Yes. A nought. All right.

Then Uther moved the O three inches to the left . . .

Another nought.

. . . before putting both hands back in his lap and lifting his eyebrows, waiting for Viola's nod of comprehension.

Viola's brain worked overtime. A four and two noughts was four hundred. Did Uthie mean four hundred pounds? It didn't seem very much – not for an historian who was also a television star and possibly a national spokesman too. Unless, of course, Uthie meant . . .

'Would four hundred pounds a day cover it?' Viola said in a small voice.

Lysander's face turned white and he opened his mouth wide.

'Viola means four hundred pounds a *week*,' Uther said quickly.

'Do I?' asked Viola, and then, when Uther nodded (a little curtly, she thought), she said, 'Yes, of course – four hundred pounds a week. But I'm not sure that's quite enough, Uthie.'

'It's *quite* enough, Viola. Isn't it, Lysander?'

'Most generous,' Lysander muttered.

Viola went off to write a cheque. The moment she was gone, Lysander whirled on Uther. 'Bugger you, Tregeffen. I could have got four hundred a day out of her.'

'Let's not be greedy, Lysander. You've got a pot of money out of me—'

'More, or I'll tell. I ought to get some sort of additional compensation for "Sandy", for Christ's sake.'

'I shall have to think about that. There has to be an end somewhere. You've got your fee from Satellite West and four hundred a week from Viola. There'll probably be more from other television companies too. You've probably never seen so much money in your life.'

'You forget, I was at Winchester. Mummy and Daddy had plenty of loot.'

'And since?' Uther said, acidly.

Lysander relapsed into a short sulk. Then he brightened. 'I got a telephone call from the BBC,' he said. 'They want me to appear on a programme called *Discourse*. It sounds just like that *Contention* thing. They made a special point of asking me to be as rude as I was on the Satellite West thing. I can't imagine what they mean. I wasn't rude at all.'

'Of course you weren't,' said Uther. 'How odd of them to suggest you were. If I were you, I should behave exactly as you've always behaved. I believe being oneself is encouraged nowadays.'

Viola came back with an envelope in her hand. She gave it to Lysander. 'The first of many, I hope,' she said. 'And I've made it out to cover the month, "in advance" I think it's called. I do hope that's all right?'

Lysander said Viola was too generous for words and that in consequence he was quite dumbstruck – which was untrue because he continued mouthing words of gratitude for the next five minutes, until Uther got sick of listening to them and said it was time he was leaving.

'Can I take you anywhere?' he asked Lysander, hoping he was happy where he was.

'No, you can't,' Lysander replied. 'I won't be seen in that revolting little car of yours. It looks like a baked potato. No, I'm being chauffeured in Viola's beautiful silver Rolls-Royce. It brought me all the way here in hedonistic comfort, and will take me all the way back in identical circumstances. The chauffeur's name is Frobisher. Viola is exceptionally benevolent.'

'Exceptionally,' said Uther, heading for the door.

Chapter 14

During the following week, Lysander appeared four times on nationally broadcast television programmes. He was vilely rude on every occasion, both to the programme presenters and his fellow guests, and the fan mail forwarded to him by the television companies began to cascade through his letterbox.

He talked mostly about the Polkerton Giant and its historical worthlessness and, following the line that he and Viola had agreed on, he repeatedly called for its destruction.

'The bloody thing is no more than a late-seventeenth-century prank. It has no relevance for us today and is nothing more than a blot on the landscape. Rip the bloody thing up, that's what I say, and give the stinking hill back to the sodding sheep.'

At first – and in the interests of fairness – Rapunzel was invited to appear as well to present the other side of the story. She and Lysander Blount appeared together once (and only once) on the first programme recorded, which was the BBC's *Discourse*. They were driven to London in separate cars, and were kept apart from each other until the studio came alive. Then, each was introduced. From opposite sides of the backdrop and to applause from the studio audience, they took their places next to each other on a white leather sofa.

During the presenter's short preamble, one camera moved to a shot of Rapunzel and Lysander. The moment Lysander saw the bright red light on top of this camera flash on he turned to Rapunzel and, using both hands and all of his limited strength, shoved her violently away from him.

'Don't *do* that!' he screamed.

'What?' said Rapunzel, bewildered.

'Don't press up against me like that! What's the matter with you?'

'But I—'

'If I *wanted* sexual congress on television – and I do assure you that I don't – I'd pick somebody a touch more engaging than you, madam.'

Rapunzel stared at him, mouth agape. Lysander brushed at some imaginary specks in the region of his lap, took a deep breath, as if oxygen were the cure for his injured feelings, and said in a voice of calm and reason, 'Now, that's enough of that. Why don't we try to suppress whatever morbid feelings we might be having and generally pull ourselves together, eh? Let's try to regain our composure and attend to the matter in hand.' He forced a small smile of what looked like forgiveness on to his lips and then turned to the presenter. 'You were saying, pretty child?'

When it was Rapunzel's turn to speak, she found that her usual eloquence in front of the camera had deserted her. For one thing, her position on the white leather sofa was now dreadfully uncomfortable. In an effort to distance herself as far as possible from Lysander (who remained firmly planted in the centre), she had shuffled herself to one end of it. When her hip had met the base of the arm and could shuffle no further, Rapunzel had simply continued to move those parts of her body that had not yet met an obstruction. Her upper torso had draped itself over the arm, which was as far as it could go, leaving only her head still capable of travel, which had continued moving away from Lysander until the tendons in her neck were strained to breaking point. Now, at last, the voyage was over. Now her head was several inches off centre from her torso, which was almost a foot off centre from her hips.

It was in this racked position that Rapunzel was forced to listen to the Blount Theory, and it was in the same painful pose that she tried to deliver her ringing repudiations. It was no good trying to appear relaxed – there was nothing natural about her pose – and, anyway, the constriction against her ribs and the difficult angle of her head in relation to her neck was forcing her to breathe in a series of shallow gasps that took all the practiced eloquence out of her piece

The Polkerton Giant

and made her sound nervous and hesitant and even a little demented. Lysander's muttered interruptions didn't help her, either.

'Dating the artefact has yet to be initiated but, when it is, I believe the Polkerton Giant's Palaeolithic origins will no longer be challenged—'

'Oh yes they will.'

'Er . . . legends abound on the subject, legends that obviously come down to us from our ancient forebears, thus proving the giant's – um – considerably earlier fountainhead—'

'*Fountainhead*? What *is* the woman talking about?'

'Um . . . Had the figure been carved in the – er – seventeenth century, surely there would have been some attempt at placing the figure in its – um – time-frame, rather than creating so obviously . . . primitive an outline—'

'Oh, hee hee! Sorry, but hee hee. Sorry. Do go on.'

Soon, Rapunzel was to flop and flounder and stammer and lose her place. 'Um' became the word she used most, followed by 'er'. 'Ah' came in a close third. Her glasses fell off twice and two patches of dampness, one under each arm, appeared on her dress. It was, for her, almost unbearable to speak at all – and for her audience, almost unbearable to listen.

At last, she stuttered to a finish. 'So – um – *historically* speaking, it seems – er – that . . . that . . . well, whatever theory one sort of accepts, as it were – ah – the giant must still, I feel, retain its significance, you know, so we mustn't – um – indeed we can't . . . destroy it. No, no. Er, thank you.'

'Testicles,' said Lysander. Then he turned to the live audience and said, in a conversational manner, 'You can say that on television, you know. "Testicles" is, apparently, acceptable. Or *are* acceptable, rather. Hee hee. They don't like "balls" or "willy" at all, I'm told, or any of the really naughty ones either, so I shan't say any of them. Don't want to lose my license, hee hee. So – "Testicles" – which sums up, I think, my opinion of the beliefs of this most gullible example of an already foolishly gullible sex . . . is as far as I'm allowed to go. How I wish I could go further, but there you are. Where's my car?'

* * *

All the way back to Somerset, through the darkness, Rapunzel cried silently in the back of the limousine. When she got home to Grassmere, she wouldn't answer any of Eric's questions or react in any way to his expressions of sympathy. That he'd *watched* her public humiliation was the last straw. She went straight to bed in the spare room and stayed cloistered inside Grassmere for the next two days, leaving Eric to run the Players rehearsals at the community hall – which worked out all right, since *Nathaniel's Revenge* (another working title, Eric said) was still in the improvisation stage, with the actors and Eric working on the script together. Rapunzel's direction and her lectures on the mores of the late seventeenth century would come later.

Uther spent the two evenings talking to Rapunzel on the telephone and saying soothing words of comfort to her. Perhaps, he thought to himself as he listened to her complaints, perhaps I should have been a psychiatrist . . . No, not a psychiatrist – the learning process would have been too tedious for words.

Besides, he knew all that stuff already. To Uther, it came naturally.

Meanwhile, there was another call to make.

'Pamela, dear. I was wondering if you knew anything at all about feminism?'

'Oh, you were, were you?'

'So fascinating, all this militancy one has heard about. Mrs Pankhurst all over again. One wonders about it.'

'One does, does one?'

'One does, rather. So . . . what and whom do you know?'

Megan and Derek had at last found a vacated spot on the penis, and their tent was pitched with all their equipment safely stowed inside. The young couple who had taken over from the people from Wallasea came from near Chester, so Megan and Derek had spent time chatting to them and getting in their good books until they all became quite friendly. After a few days the young couple had promised that they could have their site when they left. Derek was pretty sure the couple weren't married, because they laughed all the time. (In Derek's experience, married people only

The Polkerton Giant

laughed when something was funny.) He kept his thought from Megan, who didn't quite approve of people sleeping together unless they were married.

The spot had come free a week later, and the Chester couple came all the way down to the giant's foot to tell Megan and Derek that they could have their place – which was nice of them, Megan said. In fact, quite suddenly, there were several places empty – although none better, Megan insisted, than the one promised to them. Derek said he thought it was a bit funny, a whole lot of people going suddenly like that, and Megan said she didn't think it was funny at all, just normal because they probably had to get back to work and hadn't been able to come up with excuses as good as theirs.

Megan's determination had kept them there long past their allotted holiday, and they were now in the third week of their excuse. Derek wondered how much longer they could keep it up before they both lost their jobs. The excuse was that they'd been in a car accident just outside Walsall. Derek had been in a coma for five whole days and Megan had been in one for three, and now they were out of hospital and were recovering under the care of Derek's friend Birmingham Paul (who was a registered nurse but who didn't, unfortunately, have a telephone).

That last bit, Derek thought, was the weak link in the excuse, and was probably the bit that would do them in.

Getting the tent up had been difficult for Derek, although Megan had refused to see why he was having such a problem and had been quite critical as she watched him struggling with the ropes.

'Just hammer the peg in, Derek. No, not there! Where you're standing. Honestly!'

'I've got to get it straight, pet, or it'll fall over.'

'Well that's not straight at all, is it? It's all sort of leaning uphill. I don't call that straight at all.'

'It's straight in relation to the angle of the hill, pet. That's what matters, you see. The angle of the slope.'

The angle of the slope was extreme, and getting the tent support poles to adopt the perpendicular without distorting the canvas into a series of wrinkles and folds like the hide of a rhino was almost impossible. The final result, which left Derek hot and irritable, looked like a sinking ship.

'It's all funny looking,' said Megan. 'None of the other tents look like that. You've done it all wrong, Derek Baines.'

For the first time since he'd been a small boy (when he'd been prone to temper tantrums until they were smacked out him by his mother), Derek's irritation inflated into a small balloon of anger.

'You don't know *anything* about it, Megan,' he snapped. 'It's not a question of what it looks like. Not a question of that at all. It's a question of physics. What you don't understand is that the other tents are *different* to ours – and even if they're not, they've done it wrong and I've done it right. Right?'

There was a moment of silence. Even the flock of starlings wheeling overhead seemed to stop their shrilling. In that moment Derek's balloon of anger, thin-skinned and fragile, popped and fell in tatters, leaving Derek with no anger and no irritation – just a cold, sick horror that now he'd done it and no mistake, and Megan was going to fly right off the handle at him . . . and then probably stamp off down the hill in a rage and drive away in the Morris and he'd never see her again, not ever.

'All right, love,' said Megan, quietly. There was a mild, conciliatory tone to her voice, almost soothing, as though she was talking to a dangerous dog. It was not a tone Derek had heard her use before, and he watched her warily through lowered lids. Then Megan said, 'I'm sure you're right, and it's ever so clever of you to know about it. Physics – fancy!'

'Right, well. As long as we're clear on that,' he said.

'Quite clear, love. You know best about things like that. I expect you'd like some tea, now, wouldn't you? All that hard work . . . I couldn't have done it, I don't mind telling you.'

'Right. Well. That's all right then.'

Derek managed to drink his tea with composure, but inside he was seething with excitement. He'd let his temper out by accident and, instead of snapping his head off, Megan had become uncharacteristically meek. There was always the chance that she might exact retribution at a later date, but her reaction had been so unexpected and so gratifying that

The Polkerton Giant

Derek suspected he'd stumbled upon a key to release a placatory, submissive aspect of Megan's personality. It was a question of standing up to her, that was all. Of course, that was easier said that done. He couldn't have done it if he hadn't got angry, and Derek couldn't see himself getting angry with Megan very often. In fact, he couldn't imagine ever doing it again – he simply wasn't the type. Still, it was nice to know he could and, if ever she made him really cross sometime in the future, it was comforting to know that he could retrieve, if only temporarily, the little dominance that Megan had taken from him, so easily, the day they first met.

Later, when they were both pressed tightly together in Megan's sleeping bag, something awful happened. It was what Derek had always feared would happen, and now it had. After two whole weeks of abstinence, he thought, it oughtn't to be this difficult; it *ought* to be as easy as anything. But it wasn't, it was bloody impossible. This was partly because of the extreme slope of the ground, which made any sudden movement into an adventure where gravity played a leading part; partly because of the thought of all those people crammed about them, with only canvas walls to muffle the sound; but mostly because he just couldn't stop thinking about where they were. Right on the tip, they were. There was something about being right on the tip that shamed Derek, because he'd never been into that sort of thing. But the idea of one bloke pumping away while lying on another (never mind the disproportion in their respective sizes, or that there was a real live woman coming between them) was a bit repellent . . . and Megan wasn't helping, she was just lying there, trying to stroke his back (which was difficult because of the confined space inside the sleeping bag.

'Bloody hell,' Derek said, rolling off her.

'Language,' said Megan. 'What's the matter?'

'I dunno. I just . . . I dunno. It's not your fault. It's me. I'm really sorry, pet.'

'Don't be sorry, Derek. It happens sometimes. I read it in something. It's not serious.'

'It's serious to me.'

They lay on their backs, squeezed together in the sleeping

bag, until Derek said he was getting hot. He wriggled out of the bag and slipped into his own and, quite soon, Megan heard his breathing deepen with sleep.

There was no question about it, she was disappointed. After all this time waiting on the giant's foot, then going past their holiday break and lying to their employers, and two and a half weeks of abstinence – which, to be honest, she hadn't minded at all but it must have been hard for Derek – and now the poor old silly couldn't manage it, which had never happened before. Derek could always manage it, any time, any place, so this freeze-up was peculiar. However, that article she'd read also stated that the best way to cope with such an occurrence was to relax your partner (there were a number of methods, apparently, some of which Megan hadn't heard of and which she wasn't sure she'd be able to cope with either) and never, on any account, make him feel bad about himself. Because Derek – or so the article had said – would be feeling quite bad enough without any help from her.

It was ever so noisy up here, she thought. People rustling and giggling and moaning all around her. It had been quieter down on the foot, like living in a country lane; up here, it was like living on the Chester High Road during rush hour, only without cars or buses or lorries, just lots of people making love. And it was more uncomfortable up here too – the slope was much steeper and the ground lumpier. If it hadn't been for Derek finding that piece of timber (which exactly fitted across the floor of the tent; when you lay down you could brace your feet against it, which stopped the feeling that any second you were going to slide out of the tent and straight down the hill) she doubted she could have borne it for longer than a night. She had to admit, Derek was good at things like that.

And then, this evening, when he'd snapped at her . . . well, that had been wonderful. It had even made her feel a bit – well, a bit more loving. She had worried that it wasn't in him, that he was marshmallow all the way through, and now he'd shown that it *was* in him after all and that the marshmallow only went so deep. This new knowledge would make their lives together that much more fulfilling, if only

The Polkerton Giant

Derek could overcome his little problem. A baby would complete the picture. Or two babies – that would be even nicer.

Soon, her breathing fell in step with Derek's. She had a bad dream about being at the hair stylist's in Quincy Street. For some reason, she kept slipping out of her chair and landing flat on her back on the lino, among all her own cut hair . . . and Sharon kept shouting at her that if she wasn't more careful, she couldn't be held responsible for what might happen with the scissors. Derek was there too. Every time she fell on the floor he applauded.

Commodore Edwin Billingsworth was angry and hurt, and when he was angry and hurt he sulked. He stayed in the flat, sitting for hours in front of the dark television, brooding over the injustice that Viola had inflicted on him. Until this ghastly Blount man had come on the scene he had been Viola's confidant, her helpmeet, her trusted associate. He'd been on television several times as her spokesman, and she had always congratulated him on his performance. He had been entrusted with her plans; she'd confided her aspirations to him. She had even allowed him to think that there was a measure of affection between them. And yet, now she treated him in this cavalier manner. He was – dammit! – her second-in-command. And now, with no warning and certainly no apologies, she had apparently transferred her approval from him to the awful Blount – who was, Edwin thought, among the foulest creatures ever to walk the earth. He was rude, he was ugly, he was arrogant . . . What on earth could Viola see in him? Whatever it was, it was enough to uproot Edwin from her immediate circle and plant Blount in his place.

It was rare now for Edwin to be called to the Grange, and when he was there would always be other people there and the opportunity for private words with Viola never arose. At home, he kept his feelings to himself. Evie had become somebody he no longer recognised, and Edwin had been taught from a young age that you didn't talk to strangers. Of course, Evie still *looked* like Evie; the difference, as far as Edwin could tell, lay deep beneath the surface. There was a quiet strength about her now. Sometimes a steely look would creep into her eyes when she glanced at him. She held herself differently, too – as though there was an iron rod running up her spine. She still looked at the floor most of the time, but now Edwin imagined that the floor no longer stared impudently back. Now, the floor, after locking eyes with Evie for a few seconds, would drop its gaze shyly and turn a little pink and even admit that, yes, Evie was absolutely right, it *was* there to be walked on, and being walked on by Evie would be a real honour and a privilege.

Evie had taken over the dining room. Her sewing machine sat square on the table and there were mounds of nylon fur everywhere. The day before, inexplicably, piles of multi-coloured satins and rolls of cheap lace had appeared as well. Edwin wanted to ask her about the new material (surely she'd told him that the play was about cavemen or something – what was all this fancy stuff doing all over the place?) but it was impossible; Edwin had never asked Evie for information about anything, apart from when dinner was going to be ready and why it wasn't ready now.

The silences between them grew, leaving Edwin more time than was healthy to simmer against the injustices that Viola had heaped upon him, and to brood about ways to discredit the dreadful Blount. He had indulged for several days in a mindless, raging sulk, which effectively prohibited his brain from working at all. At last the rage was cooling and Edwin's mind could begin its limited processing again.

Blount was, he admitted to himself, the better wordsmith, there was no doubt about that. Blount used words that Edwin had never heard of, and he was fluent and literate and witty – in a disgustingly offensive way, of course. So offensive, indeed, that it was impossible to fathom why the man had become a media star overnight. But the fact was that Blount *had* become one and Edwin, who had been on television almost as many times as his rival, hadn't.

It was the words, Edwin decided, that made Blount the man of the moment. Well, the vile creature may have possessed the eloquence, but that was all he had. He certainly wasn't a man of action. His physique would preclude that, whereas Edwin's military bearing surely cried out to the world that here was a man of action, a man of deeds. A little

The Polkerton Giant

tongue-tied at times, a bit hesitant occasionally, but all the great soldiers and the great sailors and even the great bloody airmen were like that . . . except perhaps for Winston and Nelson and Bomber Harris. And Monty, of course – now there was a man who could talk and act, a bloody marvellous bloke all round, really. But apart from them, surely most men of deeds did the deeds without talking about them much at all. That was the point, wasn't it, about being a man of action? The very phrase implied you weren't much cop with words, but give you a battlefield and you knew what was what. The man of action belonged not at HQ, jawing away with the generals, but on the battlefield, leading the troops to the fore. Waving a sabre. Cutting off a few heads. Bloody but unbowed at the end of it, standing proud amidst the corpses of the enemy. Not sitting primly in front of a lot of television cameras, sprouting theories and being hateful to everybody. Leave that to the clever chaps.

Right. Well, that was the easy part. Now to come up with the action. A bit of a poser, that. It had to be something that would impress Viola enough to make her recognise his worth to her and to her organisation. It had to be something that would obliterate Blount and, at the same time, reinstate him . . .

What would Monty do? Well, Edwin knew what Monty would do. Monty would make a concentrated attack, with all his big guns blazing, right at the heart of the enemy. That was what he'd wanted to do after the invasion – go straight for Berlin and clobber the Nazis where it really hurt – but bloody Eisenhower wouldn't let him. Well, there was no bloody Ike to stop Commodore Edwin Billingsworth doing the same thing now, was there? Not this time round, chummy.

Only one question remained, then: who to attack? Well, that one was a doddle. Attack the blasted giant, that's who. Go straight for its head and work your way downwards until you've wiped it off the map. Pretty obvious really, when you came to think about it.

All that drivel on the television was just a waste of time. Talk was cheap. Action, though – well, actions speak louder than words. A bird in the hand is worth two in the bush.

The pen is mightier than the sword. No, that wasn't quite right – but one got the gist. While everybody else was just talking about it, he – Commodore Edwin Billingsworth – would mount a surgical strike and destroy the object under so much pointless discussion. That would shut up the Blount chap for ever, and impress Viola no end. He'd be the *real* hero in her eyes, if only for showing the initiative, the gumption, to make such a startling clean sweep of it all. Actually, that was rather a good name for the operation: Operation Clean Sweep. That's what he'd tell the troops at the first briefing – that the attack was to be named Operation Clean Sweep and that they were all to keep mum about it because walls have ears and loose lips sink ships . . .

Hang on. What troops? Edwin searched through his mind for some names of likely pals who'd jump at the chance of some damned fine action. He couldn't think of any names at all and, with a pang, he realised that he didn't have any pals who might thrill to the adventure. In fact, he didn't know anybody at all, not *that* sort of person anyway – and precious few of the other sort, either. But there must have been some in his past, surely? He thought back to the days in Lowestoft, when he was the Commodore of the yacht club; there must have been one or two good eggs there? He remembered a chap called George Something-or-other, with whom he'd been quite pally. George was small and pale and bald, with a scrubby moustache and white, bony knees under his shorts. He had a constant cold and he'd sniff every ten seconds and the wife (Penny, was it?) would click her tongue at him and slap the back of his head. They both drank lager and lime in half-pint glasses and ate bags of Smith's crisps. They owned a small wooden dinghy and only took it out of the harbour when there was no wind at all and the sea looked like a sheet of blue glass. They were wallies, Edwin remembered. No. George was out. Certainly not the stuff that Lovat's commandos were made of. Anyway, he couldn't remember George's other name. Forget George.

Who else? Edwin thought hard for ten minutes. There was nobody. Nobody at all. Well, dammit, that was all right. He'd always been a bit of a lone wolf. Kept himself to himself, minded his own business, a solitary hunter. No harm in that.

The Polkerton Giant

If you wanted to do something well, it was best you did it yourself, that's what he'd always said. Right, then. He'd do it alone. A big job, but he was up to it. He'd sneak up there one night under cover of darkness with a pickaxe and a spade, and he'd go for it. Well, perhaps not *all* of it. That was asking a bit much – the thing was about four hundred feet long . . . No, he'd just attack the how's-your-father bit – after all, that was the part that was giving offence. The rest was just a crude outline of a vaguely human figure, and there was nothing particularly wrong with that.

Thing was, what would it look like when he was done with it? If he just ripped up the turf between the lines he'd be exposing even more chalk – and still in the shape of a how's-your-father – and that was no good at all. No, the thing had to be obliterated, covered over. Disguised, even, so that it looked like the giant was sexless. Yes, that was it . . . and, of course, there was only one way to do that. He wouldn't need a pickaxe or a spade after all.

It was brilliant, and he'd thought of it. A real plan. A real bit of strategy.

Edwin fumbled in his jacket pocket for his diary. It was a question of the moon. It mustn't be full, or even crescent. This operation was undercover and covert, and as such must be carried out in total darkness.

Sitting at her sewing machine in the dining room, Evie could see through the archway into the living room. Unexpected movement there drew her eyes from the yellow satin that she was hemming. She watched Edwin pull his diary out of his breast pocket and flip feverishly through the pages. Then he stopped flipping, arriving at a page he obviously needed. He squinted down at it. Then he stabbed the diary with his forefinger and said, 'Hah!'

Whatever could he be doing? Evie wondered. Surely Edwin's diary was empty. It had always been empty, because Edwin never had any appointments to go to, no meetings to attend. He only carried a diary because he thought everybody else carried one. So what on earth could he find there that would give him the kind of satisfaction that would make him smile (albeit in a rather ferocious way) for the first time in four days and say 'Hah!' with such enthusiasm?

It was a puzzle, to be sure. Not a very interesting one because it was about Edwin, and nothing about Edwin was interesting. But still a puzzle . . . as was this satin, which seemed to be resisting the hemming with the most extraordinary determination.

Chapter 15

Uther's Morris Minor was, perhaps, his favourite belonging. There were other objects he liked tremendously – the little Degas horse was one, the Utrillo in the dining room another – but the Morris was the one possession that he held most dear. It had belonged to an aunt, who had decided one day that she no longer cared for driving and given him the car on the same day.

'Look after it, dear,' she had said. 'It has behaved immaculately and deserves a cosseted life.'

The Morris was now cosseted rather more than the aunt had envisaged. It was the shape of the bonnet, Uther decided, that made the little car so appealing. It had the rounded chubbiness of a small child's face and Uther liked small children, as long as they belonged to someone else and were removed when they became tiresome. The Morris never became tiresome – so, while some of his friends (Viola, in particular) urged him to get something new and expensive, Uther saw no reason to have it replaced.

Uther rarely drove very far; the trip to Bristol to see Lysander had been a major expedition. Mostly he used the car round Polkerton, to visit the shops and his friends; if ever he went to London he took the train. Today, it was a quick trip to Sainsbury's for his weekly supplies.

When he came out of the supermarket, there was another Morris Minor parked right in front of his. The other car was green and a little shabby, but the shape of the bonnet was as appealing as ever, and Uther stopped to admire it. His gaze travelled slowly over the front of the car and then on up to the windscreen. There was a girl sitting in the driver's seat and Uther saw that she was crying. Their eyes met for a moment and then the girl looked away in embarrassment, ducking down suddenly as though looking for something on the floor. Then she reappeared, a paper tissue to her nose. She looked up, obviously hoping Uther had moved on, but when she saw he hadn't – and was, in fact, still looking at her – she smiled wanly at him and made a small, rueful shake of her head.

Uther walked to the side of the car and tapped on the window. The girl sighed and wound the glass down a few inches and said, 'Am I not supposed to park here?'

'My dear, you can park wherever you like, but you mustn't cry while doing so. You must never cry in a Morris Minor, you understand. They don't like it and are inclined to mope if you do so. I never cry in mine. It's right behind you. You see how shiny it is? That's because I shriek with laughter the whole time I'm in it, no matter how sad I feel. Now looks at yours – all dull and dowdy. So you see I'm right. Anyway, what's the matter?'

Ten minutes later, Megan and Uther were having tea and scones in the coffee shop in Clark Street, and Megan was telling Uther all about what had gone wrong.

'But it's been on television for a week now,' Uther said.

'We haven't got one, not in the tent, you see. Nobody up there had one, except for some people who had a little battery one. They watched sport all day long, so they probably never saw anything about it. It was only today, when I came in to get some food, that I saw the newspaper on the stand and it said all about the giant not being Stone Age at all and being a fake and everything ... So, what with getting all our hopes up about a baby and then wasting all that time and money coming here and probably losing our jobs as well ... well, I was ever so upset, I don't mind telling you.'

Not only did she not mind telling him everything – Megan was finding it impossible to do anything else. Uther had started out by making her laugh about his wig, and nobody had ever done anything quite like that to Megan. It was so disarming and friendly that she'd found her reserve melting sufficiently to allow her to accept tea and scones from a stranger. And here she was, feeling ever so much better. It was all because there was something comforting about the man sitting opposite her, something that was making her

The Polkerton Giant

relax her guard and encouraging her to chatter like a monkey. She was pouring out the sort of stuff she usually kept to herself – and that was funny because Megan had been taught not to reveal personal matters to strangers and, quite often, not to friends or relatives either.

'You want a baby?' said Uther, stirring his tea.

'Ever so much. That's what we came for.'

'And you really believed . . .?'

'Well, yes and no. I mean, if there was the slightest chance, you see . . .'

'Of course. I would have done the same thing myself. And who knows – perhaps there *is* something in it. But . . . no luck?'

'No. Well, it's difficult.'

'So I've been told.'

'Well, we've been sort of saving ourselves, if you see what I mean . . .'

'Ah.'

'. . . until we could get a better place, you see. On the . . . the . . . you know. We've been waiting ever such a long time, and now, finally—'

'And now you've got a place, have you?'

'Yes. Well, lots of people suddenly upped and left, you see. Now I know why. Still, we thought it was a good spot. But all of a sudden Derek can't seem to . . . you know. I mean, it's probably the stress and everything, but he can't . . . Anyway, I suppose it doesn't matter now, does it? Not if the giant's a fake like everybody says.'

'And you've lost your jobs?'

'Probably. By now.'

Megan told Uther about her work at the building society and Derek's job with the double-glazing firm, and all about the excuse and its diminishing plausibility – and then, to her surprise, Megan found herself telling him, to the penny, exactly how much the expedition had cost them so far.

'A lot of money,' observed Uther, thoughtfully.

'We'll manage,' said Megan.

Uther, looking intently at the girl and noticing the strong set of the jawline and the bright intelligence in her eyes, thought to himself that indeed she would manage, although there might be hard times along the way. And that would never do – not as long as the author of her predicament, presently sitting opposite her in a coffee shop, retained even a particle of conscience.

'You know what I think you ought to do? I think you ought to go back to your tent and not tell Derek a thing. I think you ought to spend a few more days where you are, just having a little holiday.'

'But what about our jobs?'

'Oh, I shouldn't worry about them, if I were you.'

And, to her surprise, Megan did stop worrying about them, and felt immediately better.

The Islington chapter of FEFA, which stands for 'Free Eve From Adam', was holding an extraordinary emergency meeting in Caitlin McCarthy's basement flat. (In fact, all meetings of the Islington chapter of FEFA were now hold in Caitlin's basement flat, because the other members had discovered that Caitlin had more generous ideas about hospitality than any of the rest of them and free food and free drink were always there for the taking). Caitlin was the newest member of FEFA and she was flattered that the Islington chapter – according to Beatty Summerfield the most militant of all the chapters of FEFA – chose her flat for their meetings. What Caitlin didn't know was that FEFA was a brand new organisation, formed only recently by Beatty Summerfield (who had broken away from a prominent feminist group to form her own, more aggressive league), and that the Islington chapter of FEFA was still the only one around.

So Caitlin was proud to be a member, although there were times when she wished Beatty Summerfield would talk a little less loudly, and other times when she wished a more senior member would propose that some sort of remuneration be arranged to repay her for all the coffee and biscuits she provided for the meetings. But on the whole she was pleased they were here in her flat and not somebody else's, because that meant that she was well and truly *in* with the Islington chapter of FEFA, and that was so important to her.

Ever since Matthew had gone off like that, without so

The Polkerton Giant

much as a word, leaving her to pay the rent and all the utilities . . . well, men could go hang themselves, as far as she was concerned.

Meanwhile, this wasn't just an emergency meeting, this was an *extraordinary* emergency meeting, and Caitlin had never been to one of those. She checked again to see that everybody had a full cup of coffee in front of them and access to one of the plates of digestive biscuits scattered about the room, and when she saw that everything was as it should be, she pulled her attention back to what Beatty Summerfield was saying.

'It is not uncommon, as we all know, to be confronted by anti-fem attitudes wherever we look. But that this *creature*, masquerading as a member of the human species, has been allowed, even encouraged, free rein with his dangerous, antediluvian attitudes to our sex, is intolerable. We members of FEFA must make our outrage known to this so-called Lysander Blount. We must put a stop to his patronisation, his repression of our gender, his blatant misogyny—'

'Smash him!' shouted Sue, banging her fist down hard on the coffee table.

'Thank you, Sister Sue. We cannot tolerate the proliferation of such anti-fem attitudes within our so-called free press, or on our so-called free broadcasting media – attitudes which seem unopposed so far by all responsible parties—'

'Smash 'em all!' yelled Sue, thumping both hands down on the table – dangerously near, Caitlin couldn't help noticing, one of her quite nice Wedgwood plates.

'Thank you, Sister Sue – your dedication to the cause is noted and appreciated. But I think we must direct our hostility towards a single target, namely the monster that calls itself Lysander Blount. And this time, sisters, words will not be enough! This time, actions are called for! Actions that will demonstrate, as clearly as possible, that such behaviour as the monster Lysander Blount currently indulges in cannot and will not be tolerated!'

There was a cheer. Caitlin joined in a fraction late but nobody seemed to have noticed. All eyes were on Beatty Summerfield. During her brief tenure as chairfem of the

Islington chapter of FEFA, Beatty had never before suggested that words were not enough; indeed, sometimes it had seemed to the other members that words were all she had. But now, at last, Beatty seemed to be suggesting something else.

There was a glitter in her eyes as she paused for dramatic effect, and her fellow members leaned forward in anticipation. 'It's time to get personal, sisters. It's time to confront the enemy head on, face to face, eye to eye. *Mano a mano*. We must take our fight to the front lines, sisters – and we must start with the greatest criminal of them all: the beast that calls itself Lysander Blount!'

'And sisters . . .' Beatty's voice dropped to a thrilling whisper, so that those at the back of the room found themselves straining to hear her words. 'Sisters, to that end I have a proposal to put to the members. A proposal which will, I feel confident, meet with the *full* approval of said members.'

Caitlin doubted that any member would be likely to voice disapproval of anything Beatty Summerfield proposed; it was rumoured that she carried a Bowie knife in her boot and had once used it to frighten off a mugger in Camden High Street.

'I have received a letter,' Beatty said, waving a sheet of writing paper in the air, 'a letter which contains much useful information about the habits and daily movements of the subject. Armed with this knowledge, I propose immediate and drastic action be taken on the body of the problem—'

'You mean smash him?' Sue asked hopefully.

'I mean, Sister Sue, the implementation of a fully-covert and unannounced abduction scenario for the eventual purpose of the re-education of the subject in order to reinstate, among those still spiritually unchallenged members of society, one fully worthy of the same nomenclature.'

'Not smash him then?' Sue asked doubtfully.

'Well, not unless he really asks for it,' said Beatty.

Caitlin, along with several other FEFA members equipped with vocabularies, had caught the words 'abduction' and 're-education', and suddenly her little anxieties about the cost

The Polkerton Giant

of the coffee and the biscuits seemed to dissipate like steam in cold air. Could it be true? Were they *really* going to kidnap Lysander Blount and brainwash him (actions which Caitlin had dreamed of performing on Matthew in the long sad days after he'd abandoned her)? And if they were, would she – the newest member – be expected to take her part? So far all they'd done was talk, and talk was cheap (until you added up the jars and jars of Nescafé and the packets and packets of McVitie's digestives), but action was something else entirely. Caitlin looked around the room; from the rapt expressions of those whose vocabularies had been up to it, quite clearly action – any action at all – was welcome.

Pru, the brave one, was waving her hand in the air.

'Yes, Sister Pru?'

'That letter . . . who's it from?'

'As to that, Sister Pru, all I can say is that it's from a well-wisher. An anonymous supporter of our cause?'

'Anonymous?'

'Anonymous, yes – but clearly a fellow sister. One can tell these things. The style, the sympathies expressed . . . well, I don't have to explain further, do I? This is clearly a sister who feels that the despicable party to whom I have been referring has overstepped the mark, continued beyond the bounds of what even low mankind considers acceptable. Unable to take action herself – apparently she is ambulatorily disadvantaged to the extent that she can't get out of bed – she proposes that those more mobile sisters than she take up the flag of positive action, which is why she's written to us, enclosing such a wealth of detail.'

'How do we know it's not fake?' said Pru.

'We don't.' Beatty folded the letter and put it into the back pocket of her jeans. 'That's why I propose we check out the daily movements of the subject as detailed in the letter. This afternoon, for instance, at four o'clock, he is supposed to be appearing at a meeting of the Hendon Archeological Society. I propose we send an agent to verify that fact. We can do this for several days, until we are fully satisfied that our informant is on the level. Then, we can act!'

'Smash him!' shouted Sue, who had decided at an early age that education was not for her.

To Caitlin's mild disappointment, when it was time to pick the spy, Beatty didn't choose her. It was Winnie who was dispatched to Hendon – alone, Beatty insisted, over Sue's objections. Caitlin felt her confidence in her leader growing; Beatty was probably right not to pick her, the newest and least experienced member, and even righter to stop Sue from accompanying Winnie on this first assignment. Sue, Caitlin had decided, was a bit of a loose cannon. Obviously Beatty Summerfield thought so too.

'I think,' said Viola, 'it's time I took the matter of the giant to the council. What do you think, Uthie?'

They were having coffee in the drawing room, after a particularly excellent lunch. Uther was feeling a little sleepy and it was several seconds before Viola's question made any impression on the relevant section of his brain.

'Well,' he said slowly, wondering what his response ought to be.

'Dear Sandy has made such an impression all over the country. I really think we have enough evidence on our side to entirely debunk the Palaeolithics, don't you?'

Uther screwed his eyes tight shut and then opened them wide, in the hope that the sudden glare on his retinas would shock his synapses into some kind of decision – either for or against, it didn't really matter. But he found his mind centring on the extraordinary inaptness of Viola's choice of nickname for the frightful Blount. How she could have extracted the relatively harmless and friendly sounding Sandy from the utterly brutal and animosity-driven soul that was represented by the name *Lysander* was beyond him – but then, *Uthie* was equally beyond him, so he withdrew from that area of examination and tried to concentrate on what Viola was saying.

'I know there are plenty of council members who support our point of view, and I feel sure – when the rest are persuaded that the giant has no archeological value whatsoever and is merely causing us all to look ridiculous – that they will all flock to our side. I thought, perhaps, at the next council meeting . . . It's this Wednesday, you know.'

Uther couldn't think of any objection to Viola's plan, so he

The Polkerton Giant

made encouraging murmuring sounds and sipped his coffee. It was amusing, he reflected, that Viola failed so utterly to see that the reason they all looked ridiculous was *because* of the campaigns for and against. If they had left the giant alone, they would only have been seen to be normally ridiculous – just like everyone else, in fact – but now, with all Uther's secret manoeuvres paying such dividends, they were all figures of fun. And that was exactly as it should be.

'Do you have a tremendous number of names on your petition?' he asked slyly, knowing the answer.

'Oh, petitions are such silly things, I always think. Such a waste of time. Who needs a petition when there is such a wealth of evidence on our side – and on television too?'

Uther knew that there was exactly the same number of names on Viola's petition today as there had been at the end of her singular petitioning session in Polkerton High Street: Viola had no taste for jostling with the crowds, particularly if they were disinclined to rally to her cause. The situation was probably the same with the Beaufort-Lyonses: for all their talk of an affinity with the working classes, Uther had never seen a member of that social division at Grassmere. No, one day of traipsing about the Polkerton pubs and actually having to talk to a lot of them had almost certainly been enough for Rapunzel and Eric.

Besides, who cared about petitions when Lysander Blount loomed large? A little too large, Uther thought. The pendulum had swung again, too far as usual, and now poor old SPAM was, to all intents, out of the picture. That wouldn't do.

Chapter 16

As is the case with all who are heartily disliked, a degree of paranoia had always been part of Lysander Blount's psychological profile – but it had never been as exercised as it had been over the last few days. The feeling that he was being watched and followed had grown from a vague suspicion to an absolute certainty.

It had started at Hendon. He'd emerged from a bracing meeting with their ridiculous Archeological Society (ridiculous because too many of their opinions differed from his own) and, on his way to the car they had provided, he'd been overwhelmed by the suspicion that the drab young woman in the camouflage jacket, leaning negligently against a lamp post, was staring at him with an interest that had nothing to do with his new-found celebrity. He continued on towards the car park, the Hendon Archeological Society's chairman chattering nervous trivialities into his left ear and, all the way along the pavement, Lysander could feel the young woman's eyes still on him. When he got into the back of the chairman's car, he glanced back towards the lamp post; the young woman was writing something on the palm of her hand with a biro.

Later, when he got home to Bristol, he thought he saw another young woman loitering in the shadows near the entrance to his block of flats, but when he walked nearer there was nobody there. He let himself into his flat and hurried to the window, staring down at the pools of orange light cast by the sodium street lamps. Again, there was nobody there. It was, he decided, merely a seasonal bout of his old paranoia.

The next day he had an appointment with Viola at lunchtime and then, in the afternoon, an interview with the editor of the *Bath Chronicle*'s women's page (who wanted Lysander's views on how many times the average Roman citizen would actually have used the city's baths in the course of a Roman week). As usual, Frobisher came to collect him in the Rolls. As Lysander was stepping into the back of the car – inhaling, as he did so, the rich aroma of somebody else's money – he thought he caught a glimpse of movement out of the corner of one eye, the swirling of a skirt perhaps, or the flash of a leather jacket . . . Whatever it was, it wasn't there any more.

Forty-five minutes later, they swept up the drive of the Grange and Lysander began to relax. It was easier not to feel threatened behind high stone walls with broken glass embedded in cement along their tops, and he managed to loosen up enough to help Viola with her address to the council. Uther had already helped her quite a bit with it, and Lysander, recognising his style, managed to maul several of the more elegant sentences, rendering them into small monuments of inelegant vituperation, which Viola pretended to admire while vowing to herself that she couldn't possibly say such things in the privacy of her own bathroom, let alone in a crowded council chamber.

Lysander relaxed even more during the wonderful lunch, becoming quite expansive and, under the influence of an exceptional Chablis, even a little amorous – which made Viola blush and giggle and smack the back of his hand.

They had coffee in the drawing room, and Lysander admired for the tenth time the Georgian silver coffee pot. Then he looked at his pocket watch and said, 'Ah! Alas, dear Viola, I must tear myself away from you. Oh, what a bitter sorrow such a parting proves to be, not sweet at all, which makes the Bard of Avon an arrant fool as far as I'm concerned.'

'Naughty Sandy,' said Viola, wishing she'd invited Uthie as well, because it was such fun watching him get cross when Sandy said such dear, wicked things to her. 'Where are you going now, you bad creature?'

Lysander told her about the *Bath Chronicle* women's page.

'How exciting,' said Viola. 'You're such a celebrity now. And do they pay you?'

Lysander admitted that they did.

The Polkerton Giant

'Lovely,' murmured Viola, allowing a splinter of resentment to enter her soul. She'd known Lysander was not being quite as exclusive with his services as she might have hoped and was indeed occasionally moonlighting (such a pretty phrase for such a naughty deed!), but she supposed the four hundred pounds a week she was giving him wasn't quite enough to demand that every moment of his days and nights were hers and hers alone. All the same, he did seem to be spending a tremendous amount of her time making quite a lot of money from other people ... and then there was this business of using Frobisher and the Rolls as if they were his own ... Her smile as he kissed her hands on his departure wasn't quite as warm as when he'd done the same thing on his arrival.

Viola watched as her car glided away down the drive, with Lysander wiggling his fingers in the rear window. Perhaps she should say something about it next time Sandy came to visit.

Lysander's sense of well-being vanished as they swept through the great iron gates at the end of the drive. For a moment Frobisher slowed the Rolls as they approached the main road, and Lysander saw a slight figure sitting astride a motor bike on the other side of the road. There was a full-face helmet covering the person's head, but the visor of the helmet was certainly facing in the direction of the gates. Lysander felt that familiar pricking sensation along his spine, a feeling he always experienced when he thought he was being watched. Frobisher accelerated the Rolls down the main road and Lysander craned round to look out of the back window. The figure on the motor bike was diminishing fast, but he could have sworn that the person was writing something on a pad that he or she was holding in one black-gloved hand.

Rapunzel felt sufficiently recovered to take back the reins of the Polkerton Players, and announced to Eric that she would be back in charge on Wednesday evening.

'How are they doing?' she asked, hoping that he would say they were doing very badly indeed and it was due entirely to her absence.

'Jolly well, actually. Marvellously, in fact. You'll be pleased, old girl.'

Rapunzel smiled the smile of one who seriously doubted the possibility of being pleased by anything ever again. 'We shall see. In fact, we shall have a run-through on Wednesday. With costumes.'

'Ah. Right. Um . . . not sure we're quite ready for that, old girl.'

'Time is getting on, Eric. SPAM needs the victory that I feel sure our double bill of drama will provide. Besides, if the Players are as good as you say they are, then there will be no problem, will there?'

'Well, no – but *Nathaniel's Revenge* is nowhere near ready for a run-through. I mean, I don't think Evie's done any of the costumes for that yet, and nobody knows their lines either . . .'

'I see. So not quite as marvellous as all that? What about *Giant!*? How are we progressing with that?'

'Better. Pretty much there with *Giant!*'

'Then we shall have a full-costume run-through of *Giant!* on Wednesday evening. I shall telephone everybody and tell them. We shall see how ready they are.'

Rapunzel went to the telephone and Eric pinched himself quite hard on the upper thigh, in the hope that the pain might remind him in future to keep his false optimism to himself. Why couldn't he have admitted that the Players were in the fairly hopeless state they always were at this stage of rehearsals? Most of them didn't know their lines, (except for Aileen Beresford, and since she was just spouting gibberish anyway it didn't matter if it came out differently each time). Perhaps their idea of creating the script from improvisations hadn't been such a good one after all. It meant that every time Eric pointed out their apparent unfamiliarity with the words, the actors could (and invariably did) retort that they were, in fact, trying out some new stuff, and if Eric would only give them a chance, they were sure he would agree that it was better than the old stuff they'd presented on the day before . . . and Eric would patiently point out that that was all jolly fine but, since they opened in less than ten days, perhaps now would be a good time to settle

The Polkerton Giant

on whatever stuff it was they intended saying to each other on the night?

A little later, Rapunzel joined him. She was smiling grimly. 'Well, that put the cat among the pigeons,' she said. 'There were several objections. However, I pointed out that there can be only one captain of any ship and, since I am that captain, my directives are not there to be questioned. So, it's all settled – we shall have our first dress-rehearsal on Wednesday evening.'

Eric shuddered. Wednesday evening was going to be ghastly and it was all going to be his fault.

Jack Lunn's mind wasn't where it should have been – on the box of four-inch nails and the hickory-shafted hammer the customer was trying to buy from him. Instead, it was in the Brady Street Community Hall, trying to deal with the prospect of Wednesday evening and wondering if there was any hope at all of getting through Harga without any trouble. If only he could remember what came after Maureen's stupid speech about her part in the battle, a speech that seemed to be getting longer every time he listened to it – and more full of Pomunka's heroics too, if he wasn't mistaken.

'And a small bottle of turpentine, please.'

It was beginning to sound, Jack thought, as though Pomunka had won the battle pretty much single-handed. There were all too many references to how Harga had suffered his debilitating and embarrassing wound, and how Pomunka had stood over his recumbent body, defending him from his enemies through the rest of the fight.

'How much is that, please?'

If only he could remember what happened after she got to the end of it! Was he supposed to growl and sharpen his knife? Or was he supposed to grunt and fetch a goatskin of water from the well? And, what happened after that? What he ought to do, he knew, was shut up shop and pop off home and really have a good go at the script, but he'd been a bit of an idiot and not written all his stuff down, of course. Perhaps Eric had got a full copy . . . But he couldn't ring up Eric and admit he was missing a lot of his own material. That would look so unprofessional . . .

'I suppose you would like me to *pay* for this?' said the nails/ hammer/turpentine man petulantly, and Jack dragged his mind back into his shop. There were several others lined up behind the petulant man and Bob was in the back doing stock-taking, so now was not the moment to be thinking of Harga. Jack dealt with the man and then turned his attention to his next customer in line. It was Commodore Billingsworth, looking distinctly nervous.

'And what can I do for you, squire?'

Commodore Billingsworth lowered his head and looked furtively out from under his trilby.

'Paint,' he whispered hoarsely. 'And a really big brush.'

Derek wondered if he ought to say something to Megan, explain to her why they were now the only people left camping on the giant's thing (apart from a couple down near the bottom who hardly ever came out of their tent). He looked at her out of the corner of his eye. It was a lovely day, warm for the time of the year, and they'd been outside all the morning. Now Megan was sitting with her back against the front tent pole, reading her book. The book was called *Getting the Best out of Baby*, and as Megan read it a little smile hovered round the corners of her mouth.

She was so pretty, he thought. How he'd managed to win her in the face of all that competition he couldn't imagine... and how he was going to hang on to her, in the face of this seemingly insurmountable problem, he couldn't fathom.

No, he decided – he wouldn't tell her. She'd be so disappointed. Coming all this way and then waiting all this time, only to find out that the whole thing was a fake, a hoax, a complete non-starter – at least as far as the fertility whatsit went.

He'd found out while Megan was shopping. Lots of people were packing up their gear and starting down the hill to the car park and he'd wandered about, making conversation and asking people what was up. That fat Scots git had laughed at him and told him all about how the story had been out for a whole week and what a wally he must be for not knowing about it.

His first thought had been for Megan. Being a practical

The Polkerton Giant

sort of bloke – well, you had to be in double glazing, didn't you? – he'd never really thought there was anything to the story. Quite honestly, he'd been a bit surprised to find that Megan apparently did, but that was women for you – all sensible and down-to-earth one minute and all believe-anything-anybody-tells-you the next. And she had believed, enough to decide to make the trip and camp out for days and days in not very comfortable circumstances, surrounded mostly by the sort of people that she would normally go out of her way to avoid. Her belief in the giant's powers must have been pretty strong, Derek thought – and that was going to make her disappointment hard for both of them to bear. No, he wouldn't tell her. At least, not now. Not when she seemed so relaxed and calm and everything, reading her book about babies and smiling like that and looking so very pretty.

All the same, there wasn't much point staying on here now, was there? Maybe he ought to bring up the subject of going home to Chester . . .

'I think we ought to go home the day after tomorrow,' Megan said, suddenly, shutting her book and turning to look at him.

'Day after tomorrow?' said Derek, wondering for the hundredth time whether she could really read his mind.

'Mm. On Thursday morning. That'll give us just one more day. Because with everybody gone and the whole place practically to ourselves, it's ever so much nicer, don't you think? We might as well take advantage, mightn't we?'

'Great,' said Derek, looking about him. It was true that, without all the tents in the way, the view was smashing. He could see clear over the tops of the trees to the hill opposite, and there were trees on the top of that, too. He liked trees; there weren't all that many in their bit of Chester.

'We don't have to do anything,' said Megan quietly. 'Just relax. Be ourselves. You know?'

'Right,' said Derek, wondering how to do that.

'A little bird—' began Geoffrey Pargiter.

'*Un petit oiseau,*' said Father Roget helpfully.

'Indeed,' said Geoffrey, pouring them both cups of tea. 'Well, this little feathered companion has whispered in my ear that dear Viola Pomfret will be making certain – ah – representations to the council tomorrow, regarding our over-stimulated friend on the hillside.'

'*Quelle surprise,*' murmured Father Roget. 'Was the *oiseau* a canary, by any chance?'

For a second or two Geoffrey wrestled with the curious-sounding rhyming juxtaposition of 'was' and '*oiseau*', and having sorted them out, puzzled momentarily over 'canary'. Father Roget, seeing his blank look, helped him out by patting the top of his own head.

'Ah,' said Geoffrey. 'Yes, indeed. He of the Arthurian nomenclature.'

Now it was Father Roget's turn to look blankly at Geoffrey who, suddenly irritated by these coy conundrums said briskly, 'Uther Tregeffen.'

'As I suspected,' said Father Roget, sipping his Earl Grey.

'He telephoned me. Said he thought I ought to know. Rather decent of him, I think. Thing is, what ought we to do about it?'

'Do?' said Father Roget, raising both eyebrows.

'Yes. In response, as it were. If we should be questioned on the matter.'

'What would the Church of England's position be?' said Father Roget.

'I think,' said Geoffrey, choosing his words with obvious care, 'our reaction would be similar – if not identical – to that of the Church of Rome.'

Father Roget smiled beatifically. 'Sometimes I wonder why King Henry bothered, you know. I'm sure he wouldn't have if he could see how well we all get on these days.'

'Possibly,' said Geoffrey, keeping to himself his fervent admiration for the author of the Reformation. 'However, I think it – ah – expedient if we agree to appear with a united front on this matter. Have you been in much contact with Viola recently?'

'Not at all. Have you?'

'No.'

'Perhaps she has given up on us,' said Father Roget hopefully.

'Even if she has we will be asked questions. I have been

approached already, several times, by the media—'

'*Les journeax jaunes,*' said Father Roget.

'Indeed – and television and radio, too. I assume you have as well?'

Father Roget tilted his head sideways in mute acknowledgement that he too had suffered the same intrusions.

'So far, I have been able to fend off the requests for an opinion on the subject,' said Geoffrey.

'*Moi aussi.*'

'However, I think we shall be pressed even further if Viola's proposition gets a serious hearing by the council. To deal with that eventuality, I feel we should present a front that demonstrates that we are, ecumenically speaking, in the same boat – if only to avoid any consequential controversy between the two churches, if you see what I mean?'

'Well, I do, Geoffrey,' said Father Roget, 'but doesn't it rather depend on which of the two theories is the *right* one? I mean, if the thing is genuinely Palaeolithic, then one could argue that not only does it have a profound historical importance for all of us but also – since pre-Christian man knew no better and was entirely innocent of our modern prurience, and indeed placed the object on the hill in the simple and unsmutty belief that it would encourage the primitive gods of the day to look kindly on their procreative efforts – that it should be maintained and kept open to the public. On the other hand, if the thing is merely a crude seventeenth-century act of petty revenge, then both churches might be encouraged to condemn it as a piece of ugly, sexually-depraved graffiti, of little historical value and deserving of no place in these more enlightened times.'

It was the longest speech entirely devoid of French that Geoffrey had ever heard from the mouth of Father Roget, and it seemed to have drained the priest, so that he appeared to slump a little in his chair. Geoffrey poured him some more tea and Father Roget recovered sufficiently to take a sip.

'Well, I quite agree,' said Geoffrey. 'But how do we know which is the correct explanation?'

'Oh, well, we don't,' said Father Roget, rather too cheerfully for Geoffrey's taste. 'We are in the dark. We haven't the foggiest. That's why I'm off to Bury St Edmonds by the morning train. Starting tomorrow, I'm going on a much-needed sabbatical, to spend a month of meditation at the Retreat of Saint Benedict The Blessed. There are no telephones at the retreat, nor televisions, nor even a transistor radio. Newspapers and periodicals are strictly forbidden and casual visitors are discouraged. Just *le billet*, if you see what I mean? As far as my duties here are concerned, well – some eager young creature will take my place on a temporary basis. I feel for him, I really do. *Pauvre petit*.'

Geoffrey stared admiringly at Father Roget. Why hadn't *he* thought of that? It was so obvious, really. In times of trouble, run away. There were plenty of precedents for it in the Christian Church: priest holes sprang instantly to mind, and Saint Patrick popping off to France; then of course there was Friar Tuck, if one was prepared to stretch one's case. If he got a move on, there was still time. He could take his annual holiday right now if he wanted to. Tessa might be a little peeved, but that couldn't be helped – needs must when the devil drives. Besides, it would provide a wonderful excuse not to go to Torquay, as they usually did, to visit her frightful relatives. They could follow Saint Patrick's example and dash off to the continent. They could go to Antibes. He'd heard that Antibes was very nice in October. Tessa might like Antibes so much that she wouldn't mind forgoing Torquay this year . . .

Uther sat like a fastidious spider in his fastidious house, waiting for all the separate elements of his grand design to coalesce. Quite what would happen when they did he could only guess at – but half the fun, he knew, was in the waiting. The other half was in watching the cascade of fireballs from the exploding rocket and being so pleasantly surprised at all the different colours.

The detonation, he felt sure, was imminent. There was a small but noticeable itch in the area between his shoulder blades, and that always happened just before the fuse was lit. He'd watch the display for as long as it lasted and then, just before anybody started to ask questions, he'd do what

The Polkerton Giant

he always did under similar circumstances – pop across the Channel to the relative safety of the continent and stay there until the blaze died down.

Chapter 17

Wednesday, though it would later be referred to as 'Bloody Wednesday' or 'What On Earth Was Everybody Thinking Wednesday', began peacefully enough for most people.

For Evie Billingsworth, it began quietly but with urgency at five o'clock in the morning, when her alarm clock shrilled in her ear. Edwin moaned and shifted in his twin bed, and Evie thought she heard him mutter 'Green, green, green,' in a despairing sort of way, which she took to be a comment on the state of his golf game. But he didn't wake up, which was a relief.

Evie got out of bed and pulled on her candlewick housecoat, then tiptoed out of the bedroom and closed the door silently behind her. A quick cup of tea, standing up in the still-dark kitchen, and then a deep breath and into the dining room, where the table was all but hidden by the piles of nylon fur and the multi-coloured bolts of rayon trying to pass itself off as satin and the yards of polyester lace on cardboard rolls.

She swept the half-made costumes for *Nathaniel's Revenge* on to the floor and began to rummage among the pieces of fur. If only she'd known what Mrs Beaufort-Lyons intended to do. She'd been concentrating her efforts on the more difficult costumes for the second play, which meant there were still several pieces missing for the first: Jack Lunn's loincloth with matching top was yet to be finished, she hadn't even started on Aileen Beresford's costume, and she still had no idea what Billy Sherman ought to wear as a tribal elder. She had finished Grace Stanley's costume, which was basically a ten-foot strip of the nylon fur, the material doubled over, the edges roughly sewn together and a circular hole for Grace's head cut into the middle of the fold. Perhaps she could do the same for Billy's outfit, since it was fairly quick to sew, although the fur was inclined to snag the needle and she had had to clear the mechanism on the sewing machine several times.

Evie looked at her watch. If she worked steadily all morning and then most of the afternoon, she might have everything done for the run-through of *Giant!* by seven o'clock that evening. If only she'd known. If only Mrs Beaufort-Lyons had told her earlier . . .

Another early riser – although two hours later than Evie Billingsworth – was Viola Pomfret. Her presentation still needed work.

Victor had been no help at all. She'd shown it to him the previous evening and he'd hemmed and hawed over it and said 'Jolly good' several times – which meant nothing, of course.

She sat at her desk, swathed in her dusky pink peignoir, and pored over the paper. The speech seemed a little cold, she thought, a little impersonal. Between them, Uther and Lysander had submerged the essential *her*, obliterating the fundamental sweetness of her personality. That, Viola thought, might well chill her audience and thereby weaken her case. She began to make small alterations to the text, removing some of the more obvious Tregeffen/Blountisms and substituting some more Pomfretish ones, and then she added a few Violettic phrases in the margins to be used as softening fillers in her pauses. When she finished an hour later, well satisfied, she put down her pen and sighed. She was, she admitted to herself, just a little nervous, but it wasn't anything like the horrible terror that had assailed her in front of the television cameras; it was just the normal, manageable butterflies in the stomach she always had before addressing her people, and that was perfectly all right and quite to be expected.

Victor thumped down the stairs just as Viola heard Frobisher drive the Rolls up to the front door. She wondered for a moment if she ought to go and say goodbye, but decided against it. Normally she would be asleep at this time, and Victor would be curious as to why she was up. Viola didn't feel up to explaining – so she kept still until she heard the

The Polkerton Giant

front door close and the Rolls crunch away down the drive. Then she went back to her bedroom and rang the bell by her bedside. When Chambers put her head round the door, Viola asked for a cup of tea and some thinly sliced brown toast – and when she had swallowed it all down, the butterflies settled themselves and almost went away altogether. Now Viola felt ready to face the day. The crushed raspberry suit, she thought, with the black piping round the lapels and the pockets. Cheerful and eye-catching, but still reserved enough for even the oldest of fogies on the council.

For some, there had been little or no sleep for all of Tuesday night. Wednesday morning found even the most active members of the Islington chapter of FEFA in an exhausted state. All six of them had crammed themselves into the back of the old Volkswagen van which Sue had provided, and had spent an uncomfortable night parked in a lay-by on the Bath road. Sue had provided three futons to cover the floor of the van, but futons didn't seem to cushion Caitlin's hipbones against the rivets or the chill of the steel floor, and by the time dawn appeared over the hedgerows she was cold and stiff and sore. Several of the women groaned when they sat up, their hair tousled, their faces slack, and Caitlin realised that probably everybody was just as cold and as sore as she was so it would be best if she kept her complaints to herself. Sue was probably going to be the most rested of all of them – she was still sleeping, stretched out across the front seat (which, Caitlin reasoned, was her right, since she'd supplied the van).

When she woke up, Sue did indeed look more refreshed than the rest of them. She sat up and stretched, then started the engine and drove the last few miles in to Bath. They all had breakfast in a transport café and Caitlin began to feel a little better. Then they drove to the Satellite West studios and parked, unobtrusively, down a nearby side street. Winnie and Pru were posted as look-outs at the Satellite West gates. They mingled with the small group of autograph hunters that gathered there every morning, and were generally accepted by them as fellow collectors (until Winnie brought her walkie-talkie to her lips and whispered into it, which impressed the autograph hunters so much that they debated, briefly and in undertones, whether she might be some important person's assistant and, if she was, whether they ought to ask *her* to sign their books).

Geoffrey and Tessa Pargiter only just made it to Heathrow. Both of them were out of breath by the time they finally sank into their seats.

'I just don't understand why it all has to be so last minute,' Tessa said tersely.

'I thought you'd like a surprise,' said Geoffrey.

'Why on earth would you think that?'

Geoffrey shrugged and looked out of the window. She'd come round soon, he thought. A whiff of garlic, the scent of a Gauloise, a nice glass of country wine – give the old girl a cuddle or two. That would do the trick, and then they could relax and really enjoy themselves.

All in all, he was quite pleased with himself. It had taken some organising and he'd spent a long time on the telephone, but he'd managed it all in less than twelve hours, which was something to be happy about. This was better than some dreary old retreat of Father Roget's. Their hotel, he understood, was near a golf course. Once he'd done the romantic bit, he could spend the rest of the time improving his game; Tessa could read or something. Either way, he could forget about the Polkerton Giant for a bit.

Lysander hated getting up early. In fact, he disliked getting out of bed at all. He was happiest dozing in the semi-darkness of his flat, with his eyes closed so that he couldn't see anything and a pillow over his ears so that he couldn't hear anything. Only when there was money to be made (and very good money, at that) did Lysander overcome his distaste for the whole business of wakefulness and drag himself out of his foetid bed. If the money was good enough, he even attempted punctuality.

This morning, the money was more than enough to warrant getting out of bed *and* being on time. The Satellite West people were sending a car for him at eight o'clock, so Lysander was in his bathroom by seven-thirty. By seven-forty-five he was dressed and ready, and by seven-fifty he was downstairs, standing hunched against the chill morning air and peering out from the shadows of the entrance way. At five past eight the car arrived.

'You're late,' said Lysander balefully. 'I've been standing here for half an hour. I'll have you fired, you shitbag.'

The driver, who had driven Lysander twice before, smiled amiably. 'Go fuck yourself, you silly old bugger,' he said, and Lysander cackled and got into the back seat.

They exchanged good-natured insults for the next twenty minutes, until the car swept through the gates of Satellite West. The group of autograph hunters craned to see who was passing. As the car slowed to negotiate the entrance, Lysander raised two fingers and jerked them at them. As he did so, he caught sight of a young woman standing a little apart from the rest of the group. She wasn't craning her head to see him like the rest of them – if anything, she seemed to be turning away in an attitude of disinterest – but there was something familiar about her back. Lysander wondered where he'd seen her before. Well, he'd met so many people during the last few weeks – how was he expected to remember them all? Meanwhile, here was pretty Miss Pamela Gibbons standing by the double glass doors, a welcoming smile on her face. Lysander liked Pamela Gibbons. She'd called him a ragged hyena during their first meeting and he'd called her a painted trull – and after that they became, if not friendly, then at least grudgingly respectful of the other's spirit.

The idea for the short series of programmes had been Pamela's, and she'd sold Satellite West on the idea of her writing and directing them with the promise that she could get Lysander Blount to present them. Having delivered on her promise – Lysander had been fairly easy to land once she'd discovered the sort of bait to load on her hook (money and flirtation in equal doses) – Pamela sat down and hurriedly cobbled together six half-hour scripts. The series was to be called *Blount's Britain*, and the premise involved Lysander discussing the origins and significance of six famous English landmarks. The first programme was to be on Stonehenge.

A week before, Lysander had been brought in to Satellite West to discuss the details.

'I know nothing about Stonehenge,' he'd said, leering mistily at Pamela's bosom.

'That's all right, we don't expect you to. We'll do all the research. All you have to do is be filmed at the location and read what we've written for you from the autocue.'

'What if you write rubbish, which you are certain to do?'

'Then you can say it's rubbish – so long as you put forward your alternative explanation.'

'And if I don't have one?'

'You are so tedious, Lysander. If you don't have one, then just read our rubbish, take the money and scuttle off home. All right?'

Lysander, after hissing for a while like an irritated snake, had agreed that in principal it was a fair deal, and now he was ready to begin the first programme. The fact that he knew no more about Stonehenge now than he had at their last meeting didn't bother him in the least. He'd seen the script that he was to read, and if it wasn't accurate – which was a fair bet – at least it *sounded* good, and that was all anybody could ask from a thirty-minute, potted history television programme.

Pamela opened the door of the car and slipped in beside him, eyeing his narrow frame with obvious distaste. 'Is that honestly your best suit?'

'It's my only suit, you slut.'

'And you paid good money for it?'

'What is this, a fashion parade? I thought I was just going to be jawing about megaliths?'

'Well, I suppose it'll have to do. We might make a feature of it, in fact. Come to think of it, television eccentrics have always been known for their dreadful clothes. All right, you'll do. Now, Stonehenge, Ted, and step on it or we'll lose the morning light.'

Lysander protested feebly that nature was calling and couldn't he take just five minutes to answer it, but Ted already had the car in motion and they drove back out through the gates, leading a convoy of cars and vans that had tucked in behind them. Nobody noticed the two figures

The Polkerton Giant

scurrying away from the autograph hunters and, shortly afterwards, the battered old Volkswagen van joining the rear of the convoy.

Sue kept the van at least a hundred yards behind the last vehicle, so as not to excite suspicion, and everybody inside kept out of sight to the rear of the Volkswagen, crammed together over the back axle, every bump in the road sending jolts through their bruised and aching bodies.

Caitlin began to wish she hadn't come. What had sounded exciting and decisive in her flat in Camden Town now looked foolish and dangerous. They could get into the most awful trouble, surely? She hadn't joined FEFA to get into trouble; she joined it to feel better about rotten Matthew. And yet here she was, rattling headlong into trouble – and it was too late to back out now. The others would never understand. They all seemed so keen, as though trouble was the last thing they feared. They all seemed to be looking forward to it . . . whatever *it* was. Beatty Summerfield hadn't been very precise in her briefing, other than telling them all to wear black nylon anoraks and black jeans and to be sure to put on their masks – and keep them on – when the time came. That was pretty much all she had said to them. If only Caitlin knew what, exactly, they were going to do . . .

'Where are we going?' she whispered to Pru, and Pru rolled her eyes and shrugged. Then the Volkswagen went over a particularly big bump in the road and Caitlin stopped worrying about criminal charges in her future and concentrated instead on protecting the base of her spine.

'Are we nearly there?' asked Lysander querulously, like a small child on a long trip.

Pamela looked at her watch. They had been on the road for an hour and a quarter. 'Not long now,' she said.

'I am about to wee-wee in my trousers.'

They let Lysander out at a café, and he came back to the car five minutes later with a family-sized packet of crisps which he munched noisily, scattering crumbs all over himself. When he'd finished, he threw the empty packet out of the window.

'Litterbug,' said Pamela.

'Mealy-mouthed environmentalist,' snarled Lysander, spitting crisp crumbs into her lap.

Ten minutes later they parked in a field in sight of Stonehenge and the convoy clustered to a stop around them, and the business of unloading the equipment and carrying it up to the location began. Nobody noticed an old green and cream Volkswagen van bumping to a halt fifty yards away from the rest of the vehicles.

The Stonehenge authorities – knowing a good bit of publicity when they saw one – had agreed to close the site for the day, so Satellite West had the monument to itself. There was a local policeman with his bicycle in attendance, and a man from English Heritage. Other than them, the place was deserted.

Pamela began setting up her opening shot: a slow pan down from the sky, across the tops of the sarsen lintels, the sun flaring dramatically into the lens; then a slow downward tilt revealing one of the sarsen uprights . . . and then Lysander – so the theory went – stepping out from behind the menhir and saying, 'Hello. I'm Lysander Blount. Welcome to *Blount's Britain*.' And that would be the end of the first set-up. They rehearsed the camera movements several times, with Pamela standing in for Lysander, who was still at base camp having his make-up done.

Twenty minutes later, when Pamela was beginning to wonder what the make-up girl could possibly be doing to that reptilian face that could take so long, she saw their car bouncing over the rough ground towards them. It drew to a halt beside her and Lysander emerged from the back seat, blinking in the sunlight.

He stared up at the great blocks of stone with distaste. 'Pointless,' he said. 'Utterly pointless. What a monumental – to coin a phrase, hee hee – waste of time. Not to mention effort. Silly, silly people.'

Pamela took him through his paces and Lysander fought her at every step. 'You want me to come from behind *there*? Why? Wouldn't it be better to come from behind *here*? And where's the autocue thing? What do you *mean* I don't get it for the first shot? Why don't I get it for the first shot? Oh,

The Polkerton Giant

you expect me to be able to remember eight words, do you? You said I could have an autocue. Anyway, I can't say anything, the sun's in my eyes. I shall walk into one of these stupid rocks and hurt myself, and then you'll be sorry, and a lot poorer too after my lawyers have had their way with you.'

It took half an hour of flirtation and insults before Lysander grudgingly agreed to perform the scene Pamela had imagined, and by then some dark clouds had drifted across the sun, ruining the artistic lens flare she had planned. Indeed the whole sky now had a grey, lowering appearance and a sharp little wind had kicked up, a hint of rain in its bite.

'We ought to get on with this,' said Frankie, the cameraman, looking at his light meter.

'Right. Positions, everybody!' Pamela called. 'Lysander, a bit further back behind the stone, please, we can still see a bit of you – and the less the better at this point. That's it, thank you. I'll shout "Lysander" when you're supposed to come out – we've got that bit of establishing shot to do first. All right, let's go. When you're ready, Frankie.'

The camera whirred and the lens began its slow tracking across the now dark sky. It was a pity about the sun, Pamela thought, but these heavy, brooding clouds were rather dramatic. Just so long as it didn't rain.

The camera panned down the massive upright stone and Pamela called, 'Lysander!'

Lysander slithered from behind the stone and smirked into the camera lens. 'Hello. I'm Lysander Blount. Welcome to—'

'Hang on,' called the sound man, twiddling with the knobs of his recorder. 'We've got an engine running. Who's the silly bugger . . .'

Pamela turned and saw an old Volkswagen van rattling across the ground towards them. The policeman and the official from English Heritage saw it too, and they both started towards it, waving in an attempt to slow it down and stop it. But the van neither slowed nor changed its course. It came barrelling towards them, and the policeman and the official moved – uncertainly at first and then, when the van driver seemed intent on mowing them down, with sudden urgency – out of its path. The Volkswagen shot past them, racing on towards the knot of people gathered round the camera. At the last moment it swerved to one side, skirting the crew, slithering to a stop five feet short of two of the great upright stones with the massive lintel lying across the top ... under which, at the moment, cowered a hunched and goggling Lysander Blount.

As in all situations when the unexpected happens quickly, nobody made any move at all as the rear doors of the Volkswagen van burst open and six figures, dressed in black with rubber Prince Charles masks enveloping their heads, leapt out on to the grass and ran straight for Lysander. Although it must have been obvious to him within seconds that he was their target, Lysander was also rooted to the spot. The only indication that there was any life in him at all was the faint mewing sound that was coming from between his lips, and that stopped with a gasp when the two leading assailants stepped close to him, one on each side, and grabbed him by the arms. Their grips were powerful, almost painful, and Lysander whimpered. The Prince Charles on his right snarled, 'Shuddup!' and Lysander gulped and held his breath.

The rest of the Princes clustered around. One of them carried a shotgun, held at an efficient angle. Their leader was a big person, with enormous chest muscles under the black sweater. The figure moved, turning sideways to Lysander – and he realised with a start that they weren't muscles at all. The figure was quite obviously a woman. A big woman. Certainly a lot bigger than Lysander, which made his knees sag with terror.

'Stand up, you little worm!' hissed one of his captors, and Lysander straightened his knees with a jerk and stood, trembling.

The big woman stared at him through the rubber eyeholes and Lysander closed his eyes to shut out the terrible sight. When he opened them a moment later the woman had turned her back to him and was looking out at the immobile crew and the statue-still policeman and English Heritage official, who looked like a nervous dormouse.

Then the leader raised a loudspeaker to her mouth. There

The Polkerton Giant

was a squeal of feedback. The sound seemed to galvanise the policeman. He stepped forward and said 'Oi!' in a commanding voice, and the Prince Charles with the shotgun lifted the barrel so that it was pointing directly at him and shouted, 'Stop right there, you fascist bastard reactionary Tory pig!'

The policeman froze in his tracks with a hurt expression on his face. He was a staunch Labour Party supporter and an admirer of Tony Benn, and being called a fascist and a reactionary and a Tory was, he felt, unfair. 'Bastard' and 'pig' he could live with.

There was a click from the bullhorn and another squeal of feedback. The big woman blew into the mouthpiece a couple of times. In a gruff roar that was so muffled by her mask and distorted by the poor quality of her amplifier that many of her words were lost in a blare of noise, she began her announcement: 'RIGHT! NOW HEAR THIS! EVERYBODY DO AS THEY'RE TOLD AND NOBODY GETS HURT! WE ARE HERE TO REDRESS THE NUMEROUS WRONGS PERPETRATED BY THE CREATURE THAT CALLS ITSELF LYSANDER BLOUNT, ON WHOM THE ENTIRE RESPONSIBILITY FOR THIS OPERATION RESTS. THE NAZI BLOUNT HAS BROUGHT THIS ACTION UPON HIMSELF AND IS TO BE HELD FULLY ACCOUNTABLE FOR WHATEVER BEFALLS HIM OR ANYBODY ELSE AND NO BLAME IS TO BE ATTACHED TO ANY PERSON OR PERSONS, LIVING OR DEAD, OR TO ANY ORGANISATION, REAL OR FICTITIOUS, WHATEVER. WE SHALL TAKE THE NAZI BLOUNT INTO PROTECTIVE CUSTODY. RESISTANCE IS USELESS. ANY ATTEMPT TO LIBERATE HIM WILL BE MET BY FORCE. A FURTHER STATEMENT WILL BE ISSUED AT A LATER TIME.'

The bullhorn was waved towards the Volkswagen and the other five Prince Charleses, Lysander pinned in the middle of them, moved towards the van.

'Couldn't we have a bit more statement now?' said Pamela, stepping forward.

'You what?' said the big woman, stopping and looking fiercely at Pamela. The fierceness was – unfortunately, for

Beatty Summerfield – entirely concealed by Prince Charles's benign, caricatured features. Any terror Pamela might have been supposed to feel was transmuted by the gently smiling mask with the big ears into an impression that they were about to start up a friendly conversation of the sort one might expect to have with the heir to the throne during a garden party at Buckingham Palace.

Pamela gestured towards the camera. 'I think we're still running,' she said. 'Are we still running, Frankie?'

'Oh, we're still running,' muttered Frankie, his eye screwed to the viewfinder.

'We're still running,' said Pamela. 'We can get all this on the news, if you like.'

'The news?'

'Satellite West. And nationally, too, I should think. Isn't that what you want?'

All princely movement towards the van had stopped and the big woman, after narrowing her eyes in a cautionary glare at Pamela which Pamela failed to catch, turned to her followers. There was a brief, muffled discussion, then she turned back.

'Are you in charge, then?' she said, and Pamela detected a sneering, incredulous tone to the question – as though the idea that a woman who looked like Pamela Gibbons could be in charge of a bunch of tough-looking men was too ridiculous for words.

'I'm the director.'

'Oh yes?'

'Yes, I am. We could film your whole manifesto, or whatever you have to say, right here and now – if you like.'

'Not here. And not now. Not in front of that lot.' Prince Charles's chin was jerked in the direction of the policeman and the man from English Heritage.

'All right. Where?'

'You'll have to come with us. What will you need?'

Pamela thought fast. 'Me, of course, and the cameraman and somebody on sound. Three altogether – that's if you don't want make-up and hair.'

Prince Charles looked at her and sighed theatrically. 'Hair? *Make-up*? I don't think so, *bitch*.'

Pamela smiled apologetically. 'Sorry. Three, then. If they'll come, of course. Hang on a second . . . Frankie? John?'

Frankie and John nodded carelessly, as if joining an armed gang of political kidnappers was something they did, on average, once a month. In fact, both of them were a little in love with Pamela Gibbons and were happy to follow her wherever she wanted to go. Besides, there might be a nice little technical award in the offing for scooping an event as dramatic as this.

Pamela nodded her thanks and turned back to the big Prince Charles. 'Perhaps a couple of your people could carry some spare batteries and a few lights?'

'We're not cripples,' said the woman scornfully. Then she jerked her head at two smaller Prince Charleses and said, 'Help them. Get the stuff.' She turned to the rest of the gang and barked, 'The rest of you – immobilise the vehicles.'

Three minutes later, Pamela, Frankie and John crammed themselves and their equipment into the back of the Volkswagen. The rest of the Princes piled in behind them, hustling a badly frightened Lysander in their midst. They made him lie face-down on a futon and one of them sat on his legs so that he couldn't move. Beatty got into the front passenger seat and Sue, at a nod from her leader, crashed the gears and stamped on the accelerator, and the overladen van groaned and lurched away across the grass. Pamela peered through the rear windows of the van and saw the man from the National Trust running towards his car (which was pointless, since it no longer had a distributor) and the policeman running towards his bicycle and the remaining crew members from Satellite West, leaderless and with their cars and trucks disabled, standing aimlessly on the spot.

She turned forward and leaned on the back of Beatty's seat. 'Aren't you nervous about that policeman getting your number plate?'

'We are not nervous of anything, sister,' said Beatty. 'Let them do their worst. We are in control here.'

'Anyway, it's nicked, isn't it?' said Sue. There was a gasp next to Pamela from a very small and slender Prince Charles, who said in a frightened voice, 'Nicked? Stolen, do you mean?'

'Yeah, Caitlin – fucking stolen,' sneered Sue, and Beatty

nudged her hard in the ribs and said, 'No names, remember? Now shut up and drive.'

'Where to?'

There was a moment of silence between the two Princes in the front seats, and Pamela, immediately behind them, looked delightedly at the back of their rubber heads.

They had no plan.

John tapped her on the shoulder and mumbled in her ear, 'I think they're all women.'

'Of *course* they're all women,' whispered Pamela, wondering again why the minds of men seemed to move just that little bit slower than hers. 'Are you running?' she hissed, nodding at John's recorder in his lap.

'I can be.'

She nodded again, and John inched his fingers over the controls and switched on the recorder. Under the perspex cover, the reels began to turn. Pamela turned back to the big woman in the passenger seat.

'Can I know the name of your group?'

'FEFA. Free Eve From Adam.'

'I thought you said no names, Beatty,' whined the driver, and Beatty leaned over and thumped her hard on her left shoulder.

'Not personal names, you stupid bitch,' she snarled.

'Ow! Oh. Right. Sorry.'

'It's all right for them to know the *organisation*,' Beatty said in a conciliatory tone. 'In fact, there's no point them *not* knowing – not if we want to broadcast our message – is there?'

'Right. Got it. Where are we going?'

Pamela watched the back of Beatty's head and saw her stiffen with the birth of an idea.

'That giant thing he's always on about, the one with the prick. Where's that?'

'I dunno.'

Pamela tapped Beatty on the shoulder.

'The Polkerton Giant? I know where it is. It's not far, either.'

A fat drop of rain splattered against the windscreen. Then another – and another – and then there was a sudden

drumming of water on the roof and the rain was sheeting across the glass and Sue was reaching for the wiper switch.
'Right,' said Beatty. 'We'll go there, then.'

Chapter 18

Buster Jenson was fed up.

It had been all right at first, when the customers were coming through in droves and the money was rustling in their pockets, but all that had stopped and now nobody came at all. In fact, for the last few days, the traffic had been all departures, with not a single new arrival.

He looked around the sodden field. There was just one car left now, an old green Morris Minor. It had been there for a long time, and Buster wondered whether he ought to walk through the woods and check that its owners were still camped up on the hill – but then he decided he couldn't be bothered. He'd have to leave the shelter and the polythene sheet that he'd stretched between the gatepost and his kitchen chair, and with this rain pissing down as hard as it was – well, he wasn't about to get himself soaked for anything.

He looked at his watch. He'd missed his dinner, that was for sure. Mum always put something on the table at twelve sharp and here it was nearly one o'clock, so whatever had been steaming on the kitchen table was certainly back in the larder by now. The next time food appeared would be at teatime, at four, and he was buggered if he was going to miss that too.

How much longer was he expected to hang about here? It was stupid, that's what it was. There was nothing to do and he was cold and damp and the polythene sheet wasn't going to hold out much longer, not with this downpour, which had been going on for hours now. And nobody was going to come anyway. Not in this weather. It was bloody stupid. He'd give it another five minutes and then he'd pack it in, no matter what Da said.

There was the sound of a labouring engine and Buster turned and peered through the driving rain. An old Volkswagen van, very low on its springs, was lurching up the lane. When it got to the gate it turned into the field and slowly rocked its way towards him.

Buster sighed. Hippies, probably. It was the sort of transport they seemed to favour, anyway. He hated hippies. They never had any money and they left a worse mess than anybody and half the time their vehicles would break down and he'd have to tow them out with the tractor . . . and this lot looked like prime candidates for his poor opinion, or at least their battered, bald-tyred, rusty old van did. Buster was prepared to lay odds that he'd be getting the Ferguson out for this one.

The van drew level with him and stopped and Buster stepped out from the shelter of his polythene sheet and tried to ignore the rain drumming on his cap. He moved close to the van and tapped on the window and, a moment later, it was rolled down.

'Camping or for the day?' said Buster, failing to notice – through eyes squinting against the pellets of rain that beat against his face – that he was talking to the Prince of Wales.

'Never mind all that,' said Beatty, thrusting the shotgun through the window and pressing its barrel against Buster's forehead – and the pressure of the cold, dripping steel between his eyes focused Buster's mind with sudden clarity, and he saw the famous face smiling at him and, beyond that, in the driver's seat, what appeared to be Prince Charles's twin brother also smiling identically at him and an awful fear rose in him and he felt the sudden prickling of sweat break out under his arms – and then he saw that the two faces were just rubber masks and he felt a wash of relief because Da had always said that Prince Charles was nothing less than the Devil Incarnate because he talked sympathetically to plants, which meant that he sided with Nature and Nature was, in Mick's estimation, the farmers' enemy in general and Mick Jenson's in particular. Mick hated Nature. Given the money – and if he thought there would be a profit in it – Mick would gladly have spread a foot-thick layer of ready-mixed concrete all over his unproductive acres.

The Polkerton Giant

That would show Nature who the boss was. Meanwhile, Prince Charles sided openly with the enemy – and that, Mick told his family, meant that Prince Charles was bad to the bone.

Buster had, in consequence and for years, suffered from a dread of meeting the Prince, so it was with much relief that he saw now that it wasn't Prince Charles at all – neither of them was, in fact. It was just a couple of jokers with a shotgun, which wasn't anything to be afraid of . . . unless you took into account the fact that the barrel of the shotgun was currently pressed against his forehead and the eyes of the gun-wielder – clearly visible through the rubber eyeholes – were glittering with a deadly intent . . .

Buster's mind, which was less of the InterCity Express variety and rather more of the sleepy, stop-at-every-little-station milk-train sort, took a number of small, slow, logical steps and came, after several seconds, to the conclusion that the shotgun ought, perhaps, to be taken seriously.

'Get in the van,' said Beatty. 'And no funny business, buster.'

It was bad enough, he thought, that these robbers (or murderers or whatever) were holding him at gunpoint, worse because they both looked like his most feared public figure, but it was truly terrifying that they had done such a thorough casing of the joint that they even knew his name. It occurred to him that the reason they knew it was because they weren't robbers or murderers at all, at least, not primarily – no, they were *kidnappers*, and he was their victim. All those warnings about being abducted by a gang of brigands if he didn't behave himself – issued by both Mum and Da whenever he'd been a particularly naughty little boy – were coming to pass.

'Roight,' said Buster, squinting up at the gun barrel and wondering how much his ransom was going to be.

The gun was withdrawn and the passenger door was opened and a brawny hand reached out and captured the front of Buster's coat. He was dragged into the front seat and the hand released his coat, reached past him and pulled the door closed. Buster, who had seen enough films to know how to behave in such circumstances, stared straight ahead and kept his mouth shut. The bulk of the person next to him was such that there was very little room left for him on the bench seat, but even in that confined space the gun was still levelled at him, the end of the barrel unpleasantly close to his chest.

'Right,' said Beatty. 'Let's go.'

Sue released the clutch and the Volkswagen, which had been sinking slowly into the mud, spun it's rear wheels and sent two plumes of muddy water shooting out behind it. Sue tried again and the rear of the van settled deeper into the field.

'We're stuck.'

'Oh, shit.' Beatty turned round in her seat, her hips crushing Buster's narrower ones against the door.

'Everybody out,' she said. 'Everybody out and push.'

Frankie shook his head. 'Can't do it, miss,' he said. 'Can't leave the equipment. Too delicate to leave, you see.'

John, squashed next to him, nodded. 'Precision instruments, you see, miss. Need to be cradled, as it were.'

'Everybody *else* out, then,' snarled Beatty and, a moment later, the subordinate members of the Islington chapter of FEFA (apart from a heavy girl called Letty, who had been detailed to sit on Lysander's supine body and make sure he didn't move) were straining their shoulders against the back of the van while, up at the front end, Sue revved the tired old engine and spun the wheels and splattered everybody at the back end with geysers of watery mud.

The engine roared and the wheels churned and Sue cursed and stamped on the accelerator, and the mud-caked members of the Islington chapter heaved against the van as hard as they could . . . and the van went nowhere at all apart from a little closer to the centre of the earth.

Inside, Pamela leaned forward and tapped Buster on the shoulder and said, 'Hello, Mr Jenson. We meet again.'

Buster didn't have to turn round to recognise the voice. Even if he wanted to, he had the feeling that shifting his body might be misinterpreted by the kidnapper as a threatening motion. So he stayed as still as he could, suppressing his surprise that the goddess from Satellite West was apparently in the same trouble as he was, and said, "Ullo, miss. Loikewoise.'

The Polkerton Giant

'Shuddup,' said Beatty.

The van rocked and roared and the rear section settled a little deeper into the mud.

Lysander whimpered piteously under Letty's weight.

'It's no good,' said Sue, taking her foot off the accelerator and putting the gears into neutral.

Winnie presented her wet, rubber Prince Charles face at Sue's window and shouted, 'We can't budge it!' through the glass.

'We'll just have to walk, then,' said Beatty.

'Ah,' said Pamela, thoughtfully. 'What, with all that gear?'

'If I say so.'

'Mm. That might be a problem. Frankie? John?'

Frankie cleared his throat. 'Oh, yes. Definitely a problem. Can't be done, you see. Not in all this rain. Plays havoc with the celluloid, rain does.'

John nodded. 'Death to recording equipment, is rain. Instant death.'

Pamela said, 'I expect Mr Jenson's got a tractor. Haven't you, Mr Jenson?'

Buster nodded slowly.

'Could you tow us to the giant?'

'What – through the woods an' all?'

'I bet you could,' said the goddess, leaning close, and Buster could feel the little puffs of scented air from her lips ruffling the hairs on the back of his neck.

'Oh, yurr,' said Buster. 'No problem. Except for the gate by the wood. Pedestrian traffic only, there. Tractor won't fit through that.'

'You could smash it,' said Sue. 'Smash it down with the tractor. Couldn't you?'

'No problem,' said Buster, rubbing his hands together. Smashing through the gate would be a lark.

It was some time before the alarm was raised.

The policeman, hardly expecting any trouble from a cushy little morning duty at Stonehenge, had ridden his bicycle to the location and had left much of his equipment, including his communication gear, at the station. A quick survey among everybody else revealed that the only cellular phone the crew had brought with them had, apparently, been taken by Pamela on to the Volkswagen van. Since the only working vehicle remaining was the bicycle, the policeman jumped on to it and pedalled off in the direction of Salisbury.

The storm hit him a minute after it hit the Volkswagen van, which was now several miles to the North of him. Quickly soaked and half-blinded by the sheeting rain, the policeman rode four miles and unwittingly passed two working telephones boxes before noticing a third one. He slithered to a halt and ran to the box but the handset was missing. Another three panting miles brought him to the outskirts of Salisbury and another telephone box, also with its handset missing. Almost in tears, the policeman hammered on the door of the nearest house but nobody answered. He tried the next one, with the same result. The third one revealed, after much heavy knocking, a very old lady, who let him in and ushered him through to the tiny parlour and tried to interest him in a cup of tea. It took several minutes of questions and answers to reveal that the old lady didn't actually *have* a telephone, by which time a good part of an hour had gone by since Lysander Blount's abduction.

Fleeing from the old lady's arch enquiries as to whether he took two lumps or three, the policeman struck the motherlode with the next house, finding not only a co-operative householder but a working telephone as well. Twenty minutes later, a siren-shrieking, light-flashing, tyre-squealing convoy of police cars, drawn from the constabularies of all the local forces, converged on Stonehenge.

The information they gathered contained several contradictions: the Volkswagen might be green and cream or it might be fawn and brown; the gang numbered between seven and twenty-two; they were mostly men, or all women; they were armed with shotguns and cricket bats, or possibly Uzis and knobkerries. The one fact that everyone was sure about was the business of the Prince Charles masks.

Armed with these facts, most of the police convoy tore away in the direction of Salisbury, which was where (most witnesses agreed) the Volkswagen had been heading. In fact,

The Polkerton Giant

Beatty had reached the decision to go to Polkerton after driving only a mile and a half down the Salisbury road, and Pamela had directed them on to a cross-country, back-lane route that had, in fact, taken them in the opposite direction. The squad of police left behind at Stonehenge took names and addresses and statements, and relayed messages to the next of kin. Satellite West sent out a coach to retrieve their crew. They also sent a news team to cover the story – a story which would, the executives gleefully told each other, put Satellite West on the front pages of every paper in the country. That Lysander Blount had been kidnapped at gunpoint was wonderful enough – but that the lovely anchorwoman Pamela Gibbons had volunteered to go with him, together with two brave and resourceful crew members (who had thoughtfully remembered to take their equipment with them) – well, that was just too serendipitous for words.

A search by helicopters was proposed by the chief constable and quickly rejected. The rain was falling too hard, the light was going, and visibility was down to a few hundred feet. Until the storm passed on, low-level flight in the area was out of the question.

As the ground search got under way in Salisbury, the Islington Chapter of FEFA, who had headed in the opposite direction, were sitting huddled in their van, up to the axles in mud, in a hidden field outside the town of Polkerton forty miles to the north.

Beatty had dispatched Buster, escorted by Sue and Winnie and the shotgun, to get the tractor. Sue and Winnie walked three yards behind their captive down the rain-soaked lane to the old farmhouse.

Buster crossed the farmyard and headed for the front door and Winnie said, 'Where are you going?'

'Keys're insoide,' said Buster. 'Got to ask me Da, anyway.'

Winnie and Sue held a whispered discussion and then Buster felt the touch of the gun barrels at the base of his spine. 'Right,' said Sue. 'Remember, we're right behind you and we've got you covered.'

Buster grinned. This was just like in the films. He pushed open the front door and Winnie and Sue crowded in behind him. They went down the passage to the kitchen. Maggs was there, scrubbing potatoes at the sink, and Mick was sitting at the kitchen table, the innards of an electric motor spread out on a newspaper in front of him. Mick looked up as Buster lounged in the doorway. He saw a pair of shadowy figures behind his son, lurking back in the dimness of the corridor. They looked oddly similar, as though they might be brothers, but it was too dark back there to tell for certain.

'Need the tractor, Da,' said Buster.

'Stuck in the mud, are they?' said Maggs, without turning from the sink.

'Yurr,' said Buster, raising his eyebrows as high as they would go and opening his eyes very wide, in the hope that Mick would somehow interpret this facial distortion as a sign that there was something more unusual going on than the mere unsticking of a stuck tourist's car.

But after his first glance, Mick had gone back to his tinkering. 'Go on, then,' he said, in a disinterested voice.

Buster took the key from its hook by the side of the door. Then he coughed loudly, in a theatrical sort of way, and cleared his throat and said, 'Whoops! Coo, dear oh dear,' which was exactly the right thing to say, because Mick, at last, looked up from his work and stared at Buster with a frown.

'Whassamatter with you?' he said.

'Nothing, Da,' said Buster, winking furiously.

'Got summat in your eye, 'ave you?'

'No, Da.'

'Well, go on then. Don't stand there loike a lummox. An' it's foive pound, remember – an' don't take no bloody cheques, noither.'

Buster felt the gun barrel poke into his back, so he gave up winking and said, 'Roight,' in a sad voice, because that wasn't how it was supposed to happen at all. His Da was supposed to narrow his eyes and nod meaningfully, and a bit later in the scene come charging in with guns blazing and rescue him, and that didn't look like it was going to happen now, not with Mick dismissing him with a wave of his hand and bending his head back to the electric motor on the kitchen table.

The Polkerton Giant

The gun poked him again and a voice behind him whispered, 'Let's go!' which was exactly the right phrase for that moment. Buster took the scenario that was offered him and turned and followed the two women (who walked backwards down the corridor, the one with the gun holding it aimed at his chest) all the way down the dark passage until they reached the open air.

The rain seemed to be coming down even harder than before.

'Don't try that again,' Sue shouted over the roar of the storm.

'Try what?'

'That coughing shit. Stupid bastard. You nearly got it then, I don't mind telling you.'

Buster was pretty sure that nobody he knew had ever come close to 'getting it' – and certainly not from an all-female gang of desperadoes. The cinematic quality of the danger he was in made him feel increasingly glamorous. He led the way to the barn, adopting a forward-tilted, pigeon-toed gait which he hoped looked like the way John Wayne walked. When they reached the big tractor he pointed out, in his best West-Country-Western voice, where they should position themselves – one on either side of him, standing braced against the big rear mudguards. Then he swung himself up into the steel saddle and started the big diesel and pumped the accelerator several times, making the tractor shake and the exhaust stack belch black smoke. A moment later they rumbled out into the rain, across the yard and out of the gate.

In the kitchen, Mick raised his eyes from the table and looked out of the window and saw the tractor passing by. Through the curtains of rain and the fast-receding daylight – and across the hundred feet of farmyard – Mick could have sworn that the two figures perched on either side of Buster were almost identical twins . . . and twins with an uncanny resemblance to the detested Prince of Wales.

By the time Buster had crawled under the front end of the Volkswagen and attached the towing chain to the front axle he was caked in mud. He clambered back up into the saddle and Sue, wet but still unmuddied, leaned away from him, trying to avoid getting any of the muck on her clothes. Winnie leaned away as well, although she needn't have bothered. Buster gunned the engine and eased the tractor forward until the chain took up the slack. The motor took on a deeper note, the tractor strained for a moment, then with a sucking noise the Volkswagen was pulled free from the trough it had dug for itself and lurched off across the field after the tractor.

Viola's motion had been placed well down the list, almost at the end in fact, sandwiched between a proposal to repaint the municipal park benches and a quite unnecessary vote of confidence for the planning committee (they had received some adverse criticism lately from the local press and were, apparently, in need of some consolation). Consequently she had been forced to listen to several hours of irrelevant and time-wasting nonsense before they reached the only motion that held, for her at least, any significance at all.

The argument over the benches was droning to its end and Viola began to feel the first prickles of excitement at the prospect of her speech. She had been slightly nervous all morning, but much of that feeling had dissipated in the sleepy atmosphere of the Town Hall. Indeed, when the light outside had dimmed under the approaching storm clouds and the overhead chandeliers had been switched on, bathing the chamber in a genial glow, her sense of belonging in this privileged seat of power had warmed her, melting the small icicles of anxiety and filling her, instead, with confident strength.

The motion to repaint the benches was put to the vote and Viola was pleased when it was defeated. She hadn't actually seen the benches, they were scattered about in the park and she saw no point in going there when she had a much larger and nicer park at home, but it seemed to her to be an unnecessary expense. Particularly as they were going to need money to remove the awful giant.

The secretary was reading her motion out loud and Viola, at a resigned-looking nod from Gerald Barker, rose to her feet.

The Polkerton Giant

'Ladies and gentlemen,' she began – and there was a sudden loud gasp from across the chamber and a voice exclaimed, 'Good God!'

All eyes left Viola and looked, instead, at the one member of the council who could (until now, at least) be counted upon to be entirely silent. At every meeting of the Town Council this member sat quietly at the back of the hall, his only contributions to the proceedings being his predictable votes. He never uttered a sound, never proposed a motion, and voted for whatever the Mayor proposed. He sported a small pink piece of plastic in his left ear, in the pretence that he was deaf. In fact he could hear perfectly well; the earpiece was connected by a thin wire to a transistor radio he kept in his coat pocket. The member was keen on sport, and liked to listen to whatever was on offer. This afternoon there was some rather exciting golf going on somewhere in Surrey. The golf was interrupted – irritatingly, the member thought – every hour for a news update, and it was during one of these breaks that the member had heard something that made him, so thoughtlessly, draw attention away from Viola Pomfret and on to his own, unassuming self.

'Good God Almighty,' he said loudly, then, looking up and becoming aware that every eye was on him, he blushed deeply and pulled the earpiece out of his ear and tried to stuff it into his breast pocket.

'Is something the matter?' asked Gerald.

The member gulped. 'Sorry about that. Just heard something.' He stopped abruptly. Dammit, he'd let out his secret. Oh well, he'd never *said* it was a deaf aid. Not his fault if everybody assumed it was. Anyway, no point pretending any more. 'On the radio. Extraordinary thing. That Lysander Blount chap, the one on television all the time. Talks about the giant . . .'

'We know who he is,' said Gerald. 'What about him?'

'Well, the chap's been kidnapped, would you believe?'

Viola screamed and sat down hard. Dimly, she could hear a jumble of disjointed phrases, emerging out of the background buzz of conversation like fish rising for mayflies: *broad daylight . . . Stonehenge . . . terrorist gang . . . no demands as yet . . . disappeared into thin air . . . Pamela*

Gibbons . . . Wasn't that the name of the pleasant young person from the television company? . . . *Volkswagen van* . . . Whatever could that be? . . . *countrywide alert* . . . *Prince Charles*. Whatever could he have to do with it?

When it became apparent that no further Council business was likely to get itself done since everybody's attention was firmly on the exciting news, Gerald Barker looked at his watch and declared the meeting over and that any business not reached today would be held over until the next time.

Viola, her hand pressed to where she thought her heart might be, tottered from the council chambers and found Frobisher waiting for her under the portico, umbrella unfurled. The Rolls was at the foot of the Town Hall steps and she ran down, Frobisher holding the umbrella over her head. Several fat drops of rain made it through the defences and spattered on to the raspberry suit. Frobisher pulled open the rear door of the Rolls and Viola scrambled inside and sank gratefully into the soft leather seat.

'Home, Frobisher,' she gasped, dabbing at the rain spots with a Kleenex. 'As quickly as you can. Something too, too terrible has happened. One must telephone the chief constable and find out what he intends to do about it. He will need one's advice.'

Most Polkertonians received the news of the kidnapping at six o'clock, either from their televisions or their car radios – but some, like Edwin Billingsworth, didn't hear it until much later.

While the news was breaking Edwin was busy loading the boot of his car, and getting quite wet doing it. He had on his military-type mackintosh and a fairly new pair of galoshes and the old umbrella was doing its best, but the rain was coming down very hard now, no sign of stopping, and some dribbles of icy water had trickled down his neck.

Perhaps, he thought, taking into account this storm, he ought to think again about the operation . . . but he'd planned this for some time and – dammit all, a little rain never stopped Monty. And if the storm continued unabated, it would provide cover and he'd be pretty sure of remaining undiscovered. That was a definite plus. No, tonight was the night.

The Polkerton Giant

He loaded the last two cans into the boot. The car was parked in the street – the flats had been built before anybody saw the need for garages – and that was rather too public for Edwin's liking. On the other hand, a chap had every right to pack perfectly legal items into the boot of his car, day or night, rain or sunshine. Let the twitchers of lace curtains think what they liked!

Evie didn't hear the news either; she was still hard at work in the dining room. There was just an hour to go now before the seven o'clock deadline. The sewing machine was hot with use and her fingers were sore and her eyes were tired, but she was nearly done – just another twenty minutes. Edwin had said that he'd drive her to Brady Street, and she'd been surprised at the offer. Usually she would catch the bus because he didn't like her driving the car, especially at night. He'd never volunteered to take her – but tonight he'd said that he wouldn't mind taking the car for a spin and would be happy to drop her off in Brady Street first. Evie thanked him and meant it; she hadn't been looking forward to carrying all those bundles of nylon fur on the bus – not on a night like this, anyway.

The needle jammed – for the hundredth time that day, it seemed to Evie – and in the sudden silence she heard the rain drumming against the windows. She hoped Edwin wasn't getting wet out there – or, if he was, that it would be sufficiently drenching to give him a properly fatal dose of pneumonia rather than just an irritating little chill which would mean she'd have to nurse him. Edwin was as bad a patient as he was a husband, and both versions were very bad indeed. When she'd cleared the tufts of nylon fur from the needle and started the machine humming again, she thought again about Edwin's peculiar offer to drive her. He'd said that, having dropped her off, he'd be taking the car for a spin. Why on earth would he want to do that, especially on such a wet and windy night? Perhaps he was going to do a Titus Oates on her, valiantly disappear into the night, never to return . . .

'Ready for the off?' Edwin poked his head round the door. He looked nervous and damp, Evie thought, and not at all like Titus Oates.

'Five minutes,' she said, and Edwin said, 'Righto,' in a falsely cheerful voice and withdrew his head. Titus Oates, she speculated, had probably been falsely cheerful – but there had never been a trace of Oatesish heroism in Edwin (nor, indeed, any other kind). Whatever this sudden bonhomie of his was supposed to conceal, it was not likely to be an act of gallantry. It was much more likely to be something underhand and caddish and petty – a reprisal, perhaps, against some imagined wrong.

Edwin, Evie decided, was up to something.

There – it was done. She bundled the finished costume into the polythene bag that held the rest of them, then she took the bag out into the dim little hallway and put on her coat and her hat. Edwin was hovering by the door, smiling and clicking his finger joints.

'All shipshape, are we? All Bristol-fashion?' He didn't offer to carry the polythene bag. He led the way to the lift and they rode down in silence. They paused in the hallway, looking out through the double glass doors. The rain was coming down hard.

'I'll get the door open,' said Edwin, and he stepped outside and unfurled the umbrella before running to the car at the kerb. Evie looked at her watch. She was going to be a bit late – well, not late exactly, but she always liked to get to rehearsals a few minutes before anybody else, if only to demonstrate her enthusiasm (the advert had made a particular point of enthusiasm). Then she could have everything sorted out on the table, ready and waiting so there wouldn't be any muddle ... What on earth was he doing out there? She peered through the rain and saw Edwin folding the umbrella and opening the driver's-side door – and then he ducked his head, got into the car and shut the door. Was he not even going to come back those few yards and shelter her with his umbrella? Did he expect her simply to run across to the car in this deluge? She'd be soaked ... She saw him waving at her impatiently and she realised that escorting her had never crossed his mind. Of course – that was entirely to be expected with Edwin; Evie wondered why she was still surprised.

She took a breath and hurried out into the downpour.

The Polkerton Giant

Reaching the rear of the car she fumbled for the latch of the boot and opened it. She lifted the polythene bag over the lip and looked for somewhere to stow it – there didn't seem to be much room in there. It was full of what looked like tins of paint – big, gallon tins, they looked like—

Edwin was at her side. He grabbed the plastic bag and shouted, 'In the back seat! I'll put it in the back seat!' slamming the boot lid down and pushing Evie towards the passenger door. 'Go on! Get in! You're getting all wet!'

They drove to Brady Street in silence. All the way there, Evie wondered what on earth Edwin needed four big tins of green paint for.

'My dear, how dreadful,' Uther said in his best shocked voice.

'Isn't it?' said Viola, breathing heavily into the telephone in her excitement. 'Poor Sandy. What do you think will happen to him?'

'Well, I don't think they'll kill him . . .'

Viola screamed and Uther winced and pulled the receiver away from his ear.

'Kill him? Oh, surely not, Uthie!'

'Oh, I don't suppose so. What do they want, do you think?'

'Well, I've spoken to Sir Roderick and he said there have been no demands yet, although doubtless there will be soon. Sir Roderick reassured me that his men are doing everything they can. A nationwide manhunt is under way, and Sir Roderick feels confident that they will find Sandy quite soon. Poor, *poor* Sandy. Of course, this rain doesn't help. Sometimes one wonders whose side God is on.'

God, Uther thought, seemed firmly on the side of the unrighteous – at least for tonight. He had never thought that FEFA would be so reckless as to kidnap Lysander but, now that they had done so – and as long as nobody came to any serious harm – he hoped God would stay loyal to the cause of mischief. (Nevertheless, Uther thought that this might be as good a point as any to call Desmond, his travel agent, and organise an expensive, first-class ticket to somewhere or other. It didn't really matter where – as long as there were no phones. And it would be nice if the sun shone continuously, too. It was too late to telephone him now, but first thing in the morning . . .)

Only seconds after Viola had rung off, Uther's telephone trilled again. It was Rapunzel.

'We're having a run-through this evening. Well, probably more of a stagger-through. Do come.'

So, Rapunzel was feeling better.

'My dear, I'd love to. At seven?'

'Yes. And, have you heard about the Blount man? Awful, isn't it? Although he probably brought it on himself – if you behave like that, you must expect to make enemies. I wonder who they are?'

'International terrorists, I should think.'

'Yes, but what would international terrorists want with Lysander Blount?'

'Advice, perhaps? But really, what would *anybody* want with Lysander Blount? Well, we must hope for the best – whatever that might be.'

'Wickedly cynical. See you at seven.'

Megan and Derek were playing Snap. It wasn't easy because of the slope of the tent floor. They had to shout over the roaring, drumming rain and the only light they had came from the hurricane lantern – but somehow the difficulties made the game all the more fun and they were both laughing a lot. It was cosy inside the tent. Derek had done such a good job with putting it up, Megan thought. Here they were in the middle of a terrible downpour, and yet inside the tent they were warm and dry and ever so cosy together. Derek had been right to buy that extra storm cover, not to mention the heavy duty, built-in ground sheet. Both seemed to be doing their jobs. It was sort of fun, Megan thought, having a storm like this on their last night. Something nice to remember, anyway, while they were both trying to find new jobs next week . . . She pushed that discouraging thought from her mind because it was spoiling her mood, which had been lovely up to now – and she was determined to keep it that way.

Half an hour earlier they had heard the distant sound of a tractor coming through the woods. Derek had poked his head out of the tent flat but the darkness and the rain veiled

The Polkerton Giant

any sign of movement in the trees below. A moment later the sound had stopped and Derek, his hair dripping, shuffled back inside. Megan found a towel and she rubbed his head dry.

'Don't want you catching your death,' she said.

'Not my death, no,' said Derek. 'That would never do.'

'I wouldn't like you dead.'

'I wouldn't be much good dead, would I? Not much conversation.'

'Not much of anything.' There was a pause while Megan picked her words. She wondered if she ought to . . . well, why not? It couldn't hurt, could it? 'Not much sex, I shouldn't think,' she said, looking obliquely at Derek.

It was the first time the subject had come up since his attack of impotence, and he wondered for a moment if the remark was meant to show Megan's dissatisfaction with him. But she was smiling at him in a funny way, so she couldn't be doing that – which meant to Derek that he should keep the conversation at the same jocular level.

'Bit boring,' he said. 'Not a lot of action from a dead person.'

'I'd have to do all the work,' said Megan, making a quantum leap into the unknown.

There was a long silence, and then Derek said, 'You would, wouldn't you?'

They fell silent, each contemplating the idea of Megan doing all the work. Then Megan gave herself a little shake, as though coming out of a trance.

'We could play cards . . . if you like?'

They were almost clear of the woods when Sue saw, distantly through the trees, a faint glimmer of yellow light that seemed to hover a hundred feet in the air ahead of them. She grabbed Buster's arm and instantly regretted it.

She wiped the slime between her fingers against her sweater. 'Stop,' she said, and Buster put his foot on the brake and the tractor shuddered to a halt.

'What *is* that?' she asked, pointing the gun in the direction of the light.

Buster peered forward. 'Last of the campers, Oy think.

There's one car left back in the field. Must be theirs.'

Sue gave the gun to Winnie, jumped down the tractor and squelched back through the sodden leaf litter to the Volkswagen.

Beatty wound down the window. 'What's up?'

'There's some campers on the hill. One tent, we think.'

Beatty thought about this for a moment. One tent could hardly pose much of a threat to them . . .

She shifted around and looked back over her shoulder at the huddled mass in the back. 'Can you film in this?' she said, waving a hand at the black windscreen.

'Not a chance,' said Frankie, cradling the camera to his chest. 'Irreparable damage, that would cause. One drop and that's it, you see. No, we can't do anything. Not without our precipitation shielding.'

'Can't do a thing without the precipitation shielding,' John agreed, nodding.

'Which we were not asked to bring,' said Frankie sadly.

'Of course, once it stops . . .' said John.

'Oh, yes – once it stops . . .'

'That could be a different matter.'

Pamela smiled to herself in the darkness. She had witnessed both Frankie and John, working with identical equipment, covering a rugby match in a torrential downpour just as heavy as this, without any precipitation shielding (whatever that might be). An umbrella, probably – and to shelter them, not their equipment.

She took out her notebook and a small torch. 'Well, while we're waiting, perhaps we could get a bit of background information . . . about FEFA's aims and ambitions? What, exactly, do you want?'

Behind her and from a spot at floor-level came a faint, piteous moan.

It was amazing how much heavier the four big cans of paint seemed to become once Edwin left the level roadway and started to strike out across the fields. He'd rigged a couple of loops of rope, one for each shoulder, and he'd suspended two cans from each loop, which he figured was the best way of carrying them all. But now, stumbling over clods of earth

The Polkerton Giant

and stepping into sodden holes in the spongy ground, the weight dragged terribly on his shoulders and he wondered if, perhaps, he really needed four tins. Perhaps he could do it with two... But no, an efficient army was a well-equipped army. Monty would probably have ordered six, just to be on the safe side – so aching shoulders or no aching shoulders, Edwin would stick to the original plan.

Of course, he had chosen to come the long way round – but that had been a wise precaution. He didn't want to run the risk of meeting any of those Neanderthal farmers and having to explain why he was creeping about on their land, at night and in the middle of a hurricane, with big tins of paint dangling from his shoulders. So he'd driven round to one side of Giant's Hill, well away from the Jenson farmhouse, and had parked the car in a layby. He'd waited for half an hour, on the chance that the rain might slacken off, and when it showed no sign of doing that, he did up all the buttons on his military mackintosh, pulled his trilby down over his ears and stepped out into the deluge. He'd opened the boot and taken out the screwdriver and the six-inch brush and put both into the pockets of his mac. Then he'd lifted the cans of paint out and tied them to the loops of rope and, staggering, he'd set off up the road, covering the fifty yards to the break in the hedge (he'd scouted it out days before) at a ponderous trot. Once through the gap in the hedge, he had paused, panting. Those fifty yards had been the first dangerous part of the operation, but no car had come by and certainly no pedestrian; behind the cover of the hedge, he was reasonably safe from discovery.

He reached the far end of the field of stubble. Around its perimeter was a shallow ditch, and Edwin stepped across it. Another hedgerow (Edwin had cut a hole in this one with a pair of secateurs two days before) and another field of stubble, and then he faced the looming darkness of the woods. Somewhere round here was the place where he'd snipped the barbed wire fence – yes, here it was. He stepped through, on to the soft leaf litter of the woodland floor. There was a rough path here, overgrown in places, and Edwin followed it, pleased that he'd reconnoitred the route several times in daylight, because the darkness here was much deeper than out in the open fields and Edwin, more than once, almost blundered into a tree.

Ten minutes after entering the woods he heard the distant sound of a diesel engine, somewhere off to his left. He paused, picking out its rumble against the background pattering of the rain, and judged that it was at least a quarter of a mile away.

The sound died away, which meant that whatever the tractor was doing, at least it wasn't coming towards him. He paused for a moment, lowering the tins of paint to the ground to give his aching shoulders a rest. The rain seemed to be slackening off a little – either that or the trees grew more densely here and offered greater shelter from the downpour; either way, he thought, things were looking up a bit. If only these damned tins weren't so heavy . . .

He took a breath and set off again through the dripping woods.

Chapter 19

Neither Rapunzel nor Eric believed in naturalistic scenery in the theatre, the unspoken reason being that they had no idea at all of how to set about building scenery, naturalistic or not. Thus, all productions by the Polkerton Players were presented in the barest of sets, usually made up of a series of black drapes in the background and a number of black wooden blocks, of varying size, in the foreground. These blocks were very useful for sitting upon, or standing upon, or lying upon – which, the Beaufort-Lyonses had discovered, pretty much covered the range of human movement. Rapunzel explained when invited to talk about their presentations, they were sufficiently nondescript and unobtrusive as to allow her actors' performances to be seen in their pure, unencumbered forms.

'I do feel,' Rapunzel would continue earnestly, 'that minimalism is the right way to go. All too often in the *commercial* theatre, scenery is allowed to overwhelm the actors – and that is so wrong, don't you agree?'

The set for *Giant!* had presented just as many scenic problems as the living room of the three Prozorov sisters. No matter how the scenery blocks were arranged, the cave chamber of the People of the Polk looked more like a cubiform coal mine than a natural limestone cavern. However, once again (and to Rapunzel's satisfaction) the actors certainly stood out from their background.

The first scene was going well: Aileen Beresford had combed Maureen's hair and had listened mutely (apart from some sympathetic clicking noises) and with commendable intensity to Pomunka's lamentations on the maiming of her husband Harga in the recent battle with the People of the Dunes. Right on cue, Harga had looked in and had eyed

Zena's breasts only once before launching into a panegyric that laid particular emphasis on his own prowess on the field. And now Poppy Boscombe (as Fern) had come running in – very prettily, Uther thought, so long as you ignored the strips of Sellotape that stuck strands of concealing hair across her negligible bosom – and was asking Pomunka her opinion of the young warrior Fin . . .

'Bold and brave,' said Pomunka. 'A warrior worthy of the name of Polk.'

'Nearly as bold and brave as Harga,' said Harga, puffing out his fur-clad chest.

(Evie Billingsworth, sitting at the back of the hall, sighed with relief. The costume fitted – sort of, anyway. She had been nervous of asking Jack Lunn his measurements and hadn't quite believed the ones he'd supplied her).

'Much yet to learn,' Harga went on. 'Fin still young and foolish. What does Zena of the Hill People say?'

'*Click* lanosrep sportal *click*.'

'But Fin more fruitful than Harga,' said Pomunka, shooting Harga a look. 'Also younger and fitter and lovely as the moon.'

'Alas, poor Pomunka,' said Fern, laying a sympathetic hand on Pomunka's arm (and Rapunzel frowned from her position in the front row and made a note on her big yellow pad: *Poppy – No pink nail polish!*) Poppy Boscombe put on the soulful look that Rapunzel had taught her and looked out into the auditorium. This was her longest speech and she had worked hard at it.

'Fin seem like young god to Fern. Fern see Fin and funny feeling flood her breast.' (What breast? thought Jack, staring at the Sellotape strips and wondering how long it would be before the stickiness wore off.) 'And now, when Fern see Finn, all Fern can do is yearn for Fin. But Fin not notice Fern. Fin not aware that Fern exist. Fern foolish to feel this way . . .'

(Rapunzel wrote: Eric – *too many Fs?* on her pad, and Uther made a mental note that, whatever Rapunzel was writing, he would bring all his influence to bear so that not a line or letter of that speech would be altered.)

'Fin will notice Fern,' said Pomunka, this time putting her sympathetic hand on Fern's shoulder (and Rapunzel

The Polkerton Giant

shook her head and scribbled: *No polish anybody!*).

Jack stepped forward. 'Harga have word with Fin. Harga sort him out.'

Fern's reply was to have been an impassioned, 'Nay, nay, Harga!' and Poppy had opened her mouth to speak the line, but all that emerged was a thin scream – a thin scream which, everybody realised a moment later, was actually coming from somewhere at the back of the hall and not from Poppy Boscombe's mouth at all.

Uther, Rapunzel and Eric all turned in their seats and looked back into the shadows at the rear of the room. The actors on the stage put their hands up to shield their eyes from the lights and craned forward to peer into the gloom.

'I'm so sorry,' said Evie Billingsworth, stepping forward out of the shadows. Her eyes were wide and her face pale and both her hands were curled into fists held stiffly at her side. 'Do forgive me. Oh dear. I didn't mean to interrupt ... oh dear, please go on.'

'What's the matter, Evie?' said Rapunzel.

'Oh dear – well, I don't now if I should . . . but, on the other hand . . . Well, it does have something to do with us – with all of you. Oh dear, it's too awful. What on earth could he be thinking? Silly, silly man—'

Uther was at her side. He led her gently forward and put her into a chair next to Eric. 'Tell us about it,' he said, looking down into her face – and there was something so comforting to Evie about this tall, smiling man, in his soft grey suit and his lopsided yellow wig, that she felt her nervousness slip away.

'It's my husband. Edwin. I just realised what's he going to do. He's got all this paint, you see, gallons and gallons of it, and I couldn't think what he wanted it for. But now I know. It's green paint, you see.'

'What's he going to do?' said Uther.

'Don't you see? He's going to use it on the giant. Tonight. He's going to paint it out. Maybe not the whole thing but certainly a part of it. He's going to paint out all the chalk, so you can't see it any more. I suddenly realised that was what he was going to do. That's why I screamed. I'm so sorry.'

In the long silence that followed (a silence broken only by

Grace Stanley and Harry Sherman poking their heads round the proscenium arch on the right of the stage and Roger Gower stepping out from the wings on the left and saying 'What's up?') there was a slow, dawning recognition that something momentous was on the brink of happening – if only from the unnatural stillness of their leader. Everybody was looking at her for some kind of response, but Rapunzel sat quite still, staring blindly at a spot on the lip of the stage in front of her.

'What do you think we . . .' said Eric, but he stopped when Rapunzel held up an imperious hand.

She sat frozen for several more seconds, then stood up, her long, thin body seeming to vibrate like a guitar string. She pivoted, raking her eyes over each of the Players – and, as their eyes met hers, each of them quailed at the ferocious resolve they saw in her face. 'I think,' she said, slowly, each word quivering with emotion, 'that our duty is clear. Barbarism is in the air. The vandals have abandoned words for deeds and we must do the same. Action must be met with action. Force with force. Attack with defence. And who more fitting to mount a defence of their ancient heritage than those who created the heritage in the first place – the People of the Polk!'

'Not sure I follow, Rappie,' said Jack.

'Follow?' said Rapunzel. She stared blankly at a spot several inches over Jack's head. Then she smiled, fixing him with eyes that shone behind her steel-rimmed spectacles. 'Follow – yes. That's what you must do. That's what all of you must do. I shall lead and you shall follow and we shall smite the Philistines who threaten the sacred symbol of our tribe.'

'When were you thinking of doing this?' said Jack. His calendar was pretty full these days, what with the shop and all these extra rehearsals . . .

'Now, Harga!' shouted Rapunzel, raising both arms above her head and shaking her fists in the air. 'Now, now, *now!*'

Eric stared at his wife. He had no idea what she had in mind – and, indeed, couldn't remember ever seeing her quite like this before. Perhaps a word from him might nudge her into an explanation . . .

'"Art is long and Time is fleeting,"' he said, hoping the quotation was at least somewhere near the mark.

'*Exactly!*' Rapunzel shrieked, grabbing Eric's head and pulling it painfully against her bony pelvis. 'Oh, well *said*, Eric!'

She turned to her cast. 'Well, come along! What are we waiting for?'

The rain had stopped and so had the game of Snap. It had only been fun while the storm had raged and they'd had to shout over the noise. But now, in the silence that followed, Megan and Derek felt the strange awkwardness between them returning. Their conversation began to limp into banalities and they noticed, for the first time, how dank and chill it was in the tent.

They made the short trip down to the Portaloos together, their feet skidding on the slick grass. When they came back, Megan looked at her watch and said, 'Time for bed, I think. If we want to make an early start, that is.'

Derek said he thought that would be a good idea. They kissed awkwardly and slithered into their sleeping bags. Derek blew out the lantern and they lay, silently, staring up at the dark canvas.

After twenty minutes – and when Derek was sure she had fallen asleep – Megan suddenly reached over and laid her hand on his chest. She whispered, 'There's something out there, Derek.'

'What?'

'There's something out there. I can hear it.'

'What is it?'

'Well, I don't know, do I? Something moving about. Can't you hear it?'

Derek listened hard. There . . . there *was* something out there. It was making a funny sound, a sort of *swish-swish-swish*, like somebody sweeping . . .

'Whatever is it?' Megan whispered, reaching down and clutching at his hand.

'I dunno. I'd better look.'

'You be careful, Derek Baines.'

Derek slid out of his sleeping bag and shuffled to the tent

flap. Carefully he inched it open and peered out through the crack. It was very dark outside but still fractionally lighter than in the tent, and Derek could see the vague shape of the hill sloping away below him and then the darker mass of the woods at the bottom. There was no movement that he could see, so he kept very still and listened again . . . There it was again – *swish-swish-swish* – the sound seeming to come from above the tent, some yards upslope of them. This meant that, if he wanted to see what was making it, he would have to crawl clear out of the tent and turn round to look up the hill behind him.

'I'm going out,' he whispered.

'Don't you dare, Derek Baines. I'm not having you—'

'I'm going out, Megan.' He frowned in the direction of her voice. Her face was a pale oval against the darkness and he couldn't see her expression, but he heard the rustle of nylon as she settled back against her pillow. He reached out his hand and felt it being seized by both of hers. He let her hold him for five seconds and then pulled away, gently, until she let him go.

'I'll be all right,' he whispered.

He turned back to the tent flap and slowly eased the zipper all the way up. Then he carefully pushed himself through the opening, feeling the wet grass under his hands and, a moment later, the same moisture seeping through the knees of his pyjama bottoms. Once clear of the tent he rose slowly, staying crouched double so that the tent remained between him and the sound-maker. Then he leaned sideways, his eyes taking in more and more of the hill above him . . .

There it was. A darker shape against the slope. A man-sized shape – a smallish, man-sized shape, bent over, making regular sweeping notions with one hand – *swish-swish-swish*, then a pause and the faint *clank* of metal on metal, and then, again, *swish-swish-swish* . . .

'Hello,' said Derek.

The shape squeaked and jerked convulsively. Then it straightened slowly and Derek could see the pale shape of a face turned in his direction.

'Bloody hell,' said the shape in a hoarse whisper. 'You shouldn't do that. Creeping about like that. You shouldn't

The Polkerton Giant

creep up on a chap like that. Nearly gave me a bloody heart attack, you did.'

'I'm not creeping about, mate,' said Derek, pleasantly. 'It's you that's creeping about.'

'Well, I thought you were asleep. Didn't want to wake you up, you see.'

'Oh yeah? What are you doing, then?'

'What am I doing?'

'We heard a noise.'

'We? Who's we?'

'Me and my wife. We heard you make this noise. What are you doing?'

'Me?'

'Yes, you, mate. What are you doing?'

'Ah, well. If you must know . . . a spot of painting.'

'Painting?'

'Yes, bloody painting. Nothing to do with you, chummy. Go back to bed, I'll be done in a minute.'

'Painting what?'

'Mind you own bloody business. Pardon my French, but it's got nothing to do with you. No skin off your nose, is it? Don't bother me and I won't bother you. Curiosity killed the cat, didn't it, eh? And something you might like to know . . . I was in the army. Career man, of course. Enough said, I think.'

There was a heavy silence while Derek wondered whether he ought to pursue his line of questioning – with a man who was clearly eccentric at best and dangerously insane at worst – and before long his curiosity overcame his discretion.

'Are you painting the hill?'

'Yes, I am, dammit.'

'What for?'

'Never you mind what for. It's not your hill, is it?'

'No.'

'Well then.'

'Is it yours?'

'Is what mine?'

'The hill. Is it yours?'

'No, no – it's not mine. Not as such. What's that got to do with it?'

'What colour are you painting it?'

'What colour? What *colour*? Green, of course. What colour would you like me to paint it?'

'It's green already, isn't it?'

'Not all of it, not all of it. Now, do you mind? I've got a lot to do.'

The figure bent to its work again – *clank, swish-swish-swish* – and Derek watched for a moment before ducking back inside the tent.

'Did you hear all that?' he whispered into the darkness.

'Yes,' whispered Megan. 'Is he dangerous?'

Derek shook his head. Then, realising that Megan wouldn't be able to see the movement, he hissed, 'Shouldn't think so, if we leave him alone.'

He crept back to his sleeping bag and wriggled down into it. Megan's hand found his own and they lay, hand in hand, listening to the sounds outside. *Clank. Swish-swish-swish. Clank. Swish-swish-swish.*

'Right,' said Beatty. 'Let's get on with it. Bring him out.'

She stood with her lieutenants, Sue and Winnie, at the rear of the Volkswagen. The doors of the van were open and the remaining members of FEFA slid stiffly out, dragging the limp body of Lysander with them. Somebody had stuffed a rag into his mouth. His hair was standing up all over his head in small tufts and his eyes were wide and rolling in terror. When they stood him on his feet, his knees sagged and Letty had to hold him up.

Pamela stepped gracefully down from the rear of the van and Frankie and John followed her, cradling their equipment in their arms. Buster came out last, proudly carrying the spare batteries and the lights; if he couldn't be *in* the film (Beatty had explained, forcibly, *why* he couldn't be in the film) then the next best thing was to be involved in the technical side of things. Having begged for the privilege of being their porter, he was handed much of their cinematic burden by a willing Frankie.

Beatty hissed that everybody should shut the fuck up, and then she led the way through the last remaining fifty yards of the woods. Sue brought up the rear, her shotgun held at

The Polkerton Giant

the ready. They emerged, cautiously, from the cover of the trees and stood for a moment, staring up at the looming bulk of Giant's Hill. The clouds were thinning a little and, with the slight lifting of the deep darkness, they could just make out the contours of the giant itself. If they stared for long enough, they could see the faintly paler, rectangular shape of a tent pitched roughly in the middle of the figure.

Beatty went and stood close to Frankie and John. 'I want to see Blount in the foreground and the giant in the background,' she muttered through her rubber lips. 'All lit up nice and clear. Can you do that?'

'Phoo . . . oh dear,' sighed Frankie, squinting up into the darkness. 'It won't be very nice. Very murky. Can't promise you'll like it.'

'Show me,' said Beatty.

'What about the people in the tent?' said Pamela, who had moved, wraith-like, to join them.

Beatty curled an invisible lip under the pleasantly smiling features of Prince Charles. 'They'd just better stay out of it, if they know what's good for them.'

Frankie and John, with help from Buster, fumbled with batteries and cables and tripods, then Frankie came back to where Beatty was standing and said, 'Ready when you are, Your Highness.'

Beatty nodded in the darkness. 'Right then. Let's see it. Hang on – get Blount up there. And take the gag out.'

Lysander was led up to stand next to Buster. On seeing what appeared to be a friendly face that didn't seem to be made of painted rubber, Lysander timidly took Buster's proffered arm for support. His escort pulled the rag out of his mouth and growled, 'Don't move or make a sound, you bastard, or you'll get it,' and Lysander nodded eagerly, as if to say that movement or sound of any kind were as far from his thoughts as could be. The escort (under their masks, it was Letty and Pru) marched back to stand behind the lights. Beatty said, 'Right,' again in Frankie's ear, and Frankie waved to John, who bent down and depressed a switch somewhere near his feet. Four small but powerful spotlights flooded the grass with a hot, white light. Buster, caught squarely in the glare, threw up his arm to shield his eyes and Lysander clamped his eyelids tightly shut and gave a muffled scream.

And up on the hill, half-way round the scrotum, Edwin froze in his bent-over position and peered sideways, his eyes wide with horror, directly into the blinding beams of the searchlights below. It seemed that the lights were aimed squarely at him and that it was for him alone that they were intended. In fact, any light that spilled out beyond Buster and Lysander was diminished in comparison, so nobody noticed the hunched figure two hundred feet above them. Edwin reasoned that, as long as he remained in his paralysed state, he could easily be mistaken for a small boulder. Several moments passed, while he waited for the angry, shouted enquiries as to what the hell he thought he was doing . . . but when they didn't come he realised that he was more invisible than he'd first thought, and there was a chance that he might yet escape.

There seemed to be some sort of activity down there – shadows crossed the beams and he could hear the murmur of voices . . .

Megan and Derek were sitting up in their sleeping bags, staring at the light that was seeping through the nylon walls of the tent.

'Do you suppose it's people looking for him?' said Megan. 'Looking for the loony?'

'Could be,' said Derek. He listened for voices, shouts, running footsteps, but there was a stillness out there, as if the brilliance that had dispelled the night had also brought everything on Giant's Hill – maybe everything in the whole world – to a halt.

Cautiously, he eased himself out of his sleeping bag and shuffled on his knees to the tent flap. Behind him, Megan said, 'Derek,' and he turned and saw her face, clearly lit in the diffused light. She was looking like a frightened kitten, he thought – lips parted, eyes wide, hair tousled over her forehead . . . No, she didn't look like a frightened kitten, she looked like a model in a magazine, one of those photographs over which you linger for a long time because the face is so beautiful and you know that nothing on the next page is going to come close to it . . .

He dragged his eyes away from her and mumbled, 'Just going to have a look, love,' and then he put his face close to the zipper and dragged it up three inches. He put both forefingers into the slit he had made, pulled the nylon apart and peered through the opening.

Beatty was standing behind the lights looking up at Buster and Lysander. There was something wrong with the shot, some element that was missing . . . Beatty was prepared to admit, if only to herself, that because she didn't have a clear idea about what she wanted to do she couldn't put her finger on it. Television cameras and a professional crew had never been part of the plan which had been vague from the start; now, excellently equipped and with opportunity hammering at her door, Beatty hadn't a notion how to use it all.

She was clear on one point: humiliation of the beast was the basic element of the scheme. Lysander was to be shown the error of his ways by being demeaned by the very sex he so gleefully disparaged – but Beatty had never worked out what form this debasement would take, other than shouting at Lysander a lot and perhaps slapping his face about a bit. But given the ability to reach a nationwide audience through the medium of television, shouting and slapping seemed to Beatty to be a bit weak, a bit puerile – a bit *obvious*. The sort of tactics that a group of untrained revolutionaries might adopt before they learned the more progressive, subtler ways.

Solitude was a useful device, of course; even the strongest men were supposed to wilt if left alone for long enough. But there wasn't time to put Lysander into solitary confinement – even if they had a place in which to solitarily confine him. For a start, Beatty decided, they could deprive him of the company of the farm boy (who, at the moment, had his arm round the beast's waist and seemed to be muttering words of comfort into his ear).

Beatty muttered her own words – of command, not comfort – and Pru and Winnie disengaged Buster's arms from Lysander's waist and pulled him away. Deprived of his prop, Lysander's knees folded beneath him and he sat down hard on the wet grass. Tears welled in his eyes as he watched them lead Buster back behind the blinding lights, and a moment later he felt a cold wetness seeping through the seat of his trousers.

It was better, Beatty thought, but still not right. Lysander looked altogether too comfortable, although he probably wasn't. He certainly looked thoroughly frightened, which was gratifying, but there was still something missing in his demeanour, something which ought to be there but wasn't . . .

Her eyes wandered in search of inspiration, slowly travelling up the dark hill above them, sliding over the bulge of the scrotum (oddly, some of it seemed to be missing), over Edwin's still, hunched form – which her eyes saw as a medium-sized, dun-coloured rock – on up to the pale rectangle of the tourists' tent, pitched right where the penis was supposed to be (only it wasn't there now and surely it ought to be – she'd seen pictures on the telly), and then back to the hunched form of Lysander.

Of course. The ultimate humiliation. A fitting retaliation for all the leering, groping, tongue-lolling, eye-rolling, wolf-whistling idiocies of libidinous man, and an appropriate response to those pouting, air-brushed, simpering excuses for womanhood that find themselves spread (entirely by accident, if half of them were to be believed) across the centrefolds of the dirty magazines.

'Get his clothes off,' said Beatty.

Five heirs to the throne whipped their heads towards her. Pamela raised her eyebrows as high as they could go and said, 'What – all of them?'

'All of 'em.'

This, thought Sue, was more like it. A leader who gave orders such as this was a leader who deserved to be obeyed. During the last few hours, Sue had begun to have some doubts about Beatty's right to command them. There had been some disappointing examples of indecision, some unsatisfactory moments of deference to the woman from the television company, and several quite lamely delivered orders which the troops had obeyed in an understandably lame manner. But this was more like it. This was the Beatty

The Polkerton Giant

Summerfield she knew and respected.

Sue growled, 'Right, then,' through her mask, marched up to Lysander and yanked him to his feet. Winnie and Pru hurried to join her, and all three began pulling at Lysander's clothes in a haphazard way, tangling his tie in his waistcoat and trying to pull his trousers off over his shoes. It was a minute and a half before they stepped away from Lysander and revealed him in his nakedness.

Lysander clothed was an unpleasant sight; nude, he was pitiful. A collection of mismatched bones thrown carelessly into a mottled, blueish and hairless bag of skin that, somehow, was contriving to stand upright on a pair of legs so thin that a stork might have doubted their ability to support its weight. His hands were crossed over his groin; it was, Pamela supposed, a gesture of modesty – but he needn't have bothered. Whatever it was he was trying to hide couldn't possibly be any nastier than what was currently revealed to their eyes in the bright, white glare of the video lights. Pamela felt a surge of compassion for the man. He was shaking, his knees quivering from side to side, his mouth gaping like a fish and his eyes staring blindly into the lights. She looked at Frankie, to see if he too might be feeling that things had gone a little far and perhaps now was the moment for some sort of intervention . . . but Frankie had his eye to the camera and the lens was pointing at Lysander and the red light was on. Behind Frankie hovered John, boom extended over Frankie's head, the microphone dangling just above Lysander. Cold professionalism had taken over their souls and she could expect no support from them.

'It's awfully chilly,' Pamela said in a reasonable voice. 'He might catch pneumonia.'

'Serve him right if he does,' said Beatty.

'Right on,' growled Sue. 'Serve him *fucking* right.'

'Oi!' said an outraged voice from behind them 'Woss all this? What the bloody 'ell is all this?'

Mick Jenson had waited all afternoon for Buster and the tractor to return. When darkness fell over the farm and still neither of them had appeared back in the yard, he had snarled an oath (making Maggs click her tongue disapprovingly), snatched up a big rubber torch and set off down the lane in search of them. When he got to the field, he'd played the beam of light across the ground. The marks of the big rear tyres of the tractor showed up clearly in the mud and Mick followed them across the field. He could see the signs of another set of wheels, which seemed to criss-cross over the deeper marks of the tractor. So Buster had obviously been towing another vehicle. But the odd thing was that, instead of pulling the stuck car out of the field and into the lane, the fool boy seemed to have dragged whatever it was he was towing further and further from the road.

Now Mick was at the edge of the wood, and he was playing the beam of the torch over the broken posts and planks of the gate.

'Woss this?' he muttered, sweeping the beam past the remains of the gate. The tyre tracks continued on through the trees.

'Bloody silly little sod.' Mick stomped forward.

Five minutes later he emerged from the spinney at the foot of Giant's Hill.

'Oi! Woss all this? What the bloody 'ell is all this?'

There was only one explanation for the scene that met his eyes. A camera. A microphone. Bright lights. A naked man. People in rubber masks . . . and Buster, with that leery grin which he always plastered on his face when checking out the page-three girl . . .

'Get off!' Mick yelled, striding forward and sweeping the heavy rubber torch from side to side, making those standing in his way step hurriedly out of range. 'Get off moy land! Oy'm not 'aving no pornographic films made 'ere! Bloody filth! Get off!'

So swift and sudden was his passage through the crowd that nobody thought to stop him, and he reached Lysander without anybody making any move to restrain him. For a moment he stared at Lysander with disgust, and Lysander, quailing under his glare, hunched his shoulders and turned his awful body away.

Mick hawked and spat at Lysander's feet. 'You ought to be ashamed of yourself,' he said, his voice dripping with contempt. 'An old man loike you cavorting about in a porno film. Bloody disgusting that's what it is. Get off moy fucking land.'

Mick sniffed and swung one heavy boot as hard as he could at Lysander's rump. The blow was powerful enough to lift him clear off the ground and deposit him, still on his feet, several yards up the hillside – and the impetus that short flight imparted was enough to give him, on landing, a forward motion that propelled his legs into a shambling run. Once he'd started to run Lysander saw no very good reason to stop, and he continued stumbling, blindly and with no real hope of escape, up the steep slope of the hill.

For a moment, there was silence. Then Buster stepped forward into the lights.

'Da, it's not a porno film—'

'You shuddup. Dirty little bastard. And turn them loights off.'

Beatty said, 'Stop him,' and for a moment her troops wavered, uncertain whether she meant the irate farmer or the naked figure scrambling, like a pale ghost, up the hill. Then Beatty pointed over Mick's head and said, 'Get him back here!' and started to run herself. At the sight of their leader trundling up the slope, Sue and Winnie and Pru and the rest of the members of the Islington chapter of FEFA jerked into motion and set off at a run after Lysander.

Mick shouted, 'Oi!' again and tried to grab at a passing body.

Buster seized his father's arm. 'Da – shuddup for a bit and lissen!'

He dragged Mick away and began to whisper into his ear.

Edwin hunched his body closer to the wet ground. Somebody was running up the hill towards him. He could hear the laboured breathing and the slap of feet on the grass, and the sounds were getting nearer and nearer – he raised his head and saw a bobbing, silhouetted figure, black against the white glare from below and the figure was getting steadily bigger and bigger – and it was going to be pointless trying to pretend he was a rock, because whoever was approaching him was almost certain to pass very close by and would probably be able to tell the difference between a rock and a chap in a mac, even if whoever was doing the running kept running at the desperate pace he seemed to have set for himself – so, perhaps if one stopped pretending to be a rock and just sort of sat up and looked out over the woods in a dreamy sort of way, like a chap contemplating Nature, then the running chap might not think it so very odd to stumble on another chap sitting half-way up a hill in the middle of a wet night, although the nearly empty can of green emulsion and the extra wide paintbrush by his side might be a bit difficult to explain away – but there wasn't any more time to think about all this because the running chap was almost upon him.

'Good evening,' said Edwin, nodding politely at the bobbing silhouette a few yards below him.

'Help,' gasped Lysander, not slackening his pace.

Edwin was so intent on being a chap contemplating nature that Lysander's cry went by him unheard. 'Come up here all the time, particularly at *night* – marvellous bloody air,' he said, half expecting the silhouette to stop and take a moment's conversation with him.

But Lysander had already discarded him as a possible saviour, on the grounds that most helpful people don't sit about on wet hills in the middle of the night – and those who do wouldn't say something so inappropriate as 'marvellous bloody air' when asked for help by a distressed man. Since this fellow was doing both (and with an affected air of insouciance which, under the circumstances, was hard to understand), then Lysander had no choice other than to judge the chap not only useless in the help department but quite possibly dangerous as well, and therefore to be avoided at all costs – even if that meant he had to keep on running while his heart threatened to burst from his chest.

He veered away from Edwin, skirting him in a wide arc. It was half-way through this arc that he stopped being a silhouette to Edwin and became, in the glare of the floodlights, a skinny, naked man who looked a lot like the awful Lysander Blount but who couldn't possibly be because the awful Lysander Blount would hardly be running about naked on Giant's Hill in the middle of a wet October night.

Sounds from below made Edwin turn away from the sight

The Polkerton Giant

of Lysander's bottom twinkling its way up the hill. He looked down and saw a host of silhouettes jerking their way up towards him. He debated for a moment about becoming a rock again but decided, correctly, that since he'd sat up for the naked man, he'd probably been seen by those who were following. So sticking with the chap-contemplating-nature scenario was probably the best bet for now. If only he could have got rid of the paint and the brush . . .

Lysander's body was on the point of giving up the race and accepting death as a reasonable alternative when he saw the tent. It loomed out of the darkness in front of him, and to Lysander's wavering mind it looked as safe a refuge as a fall-out bunker. With faltering steps he pushed his body the last few yards and fell, gasping, against the tent flap. He scrabbled at the opening, caught one finger in the bottom of the zipper, and yanked it up in one swift movement. Whimpering like a puppy, he dived through the flap and into the blackness, landing with a thud between the two sleeping bags.

There was sudden movement on either side of him – a convulsive, startled shifting of bodies.

'Derek! There's somebody in here!'

'I know. Who's there?'

'Derek—'

'Who *is* this? Are you the bugger with the paint?'

'Derek—'

'Don't move or I'll clobber you one. Where's the bloody torch?'

'Derek—'

'It's all right, Megan. Stop yelling.'

'But Derek—'

'Hang on, I've got it. Right – let's have a look at you.'

The beam of torch splashed across Lysander's face. Then it travelled – hesitantly, as if it could hardly believe what it was revealing – over his naked, crouching form. When it reached his groin Megan gasped. There was silence, broken only by Lysander's heavy wheezing.

He put one hand defensively across his eyes. 'Sanctuary?' he whispered, in a voice filled with desperate hope.

* * *

Of the members of the Islington chapter of **FEFA** Sue was the fastest runner, and she quickly overtook Beatty. Winnie and Pru were almost as fit, and they stayed close behind her as she raced up the hill in pursuit of Lysander's pale form. They saw him make a sudden veering movement, widely skirting what at first appeared to be a rock but which, as they drew nearer, resolved itself into a small man in a wet trilby who was looking dreamily out over the dark woods below and making an ineffectual attempt to hide a tin of paint under the skirts of his raincoat. He said 'Good evening' pleasantly as they ran by (and Pru, who had been brought up to be polite to strangers, panted 'Good evening' back at him).

Only thirty yards separated them from Lysander when he reached the tent and dived inside. Seconds later, Sue arrived. She held her shotgun at the ready, pointing its muzzle at the tent flap.

'Right. Come on out!' she barked.

There were two squeals of fear from inside, both falsetto. Sue poked the gun barrel against the flap and said, 'Out!'

The flap parted and Derek Baines crawled out. He stood up and stared at Sue. He didn't seem in the least surprised to be confronted with a gun-toting, Prince Charles-masked terrorist – who was quickly joined by two more identically masked and panting associates – and Sue felt the first flicker of misgiving.

'What do you want?' Derek said, tying the cord of his woollen dressing gown.

'Just give us Blount,' said Sue. 'We don't want you.'

'Blount?'

'Yes. Lysander Blount. He's in there. We saw him go in.'

'The old man? You want him?'

'Right now.'

'Why hasn't he got any clothes on?'

'Never mind about that. Just get him out here.'

There was a pause while Derek seemed to consider the order. Then he said, 'No.'

'No? What do you mean, *no*? You're a fucking idiot. This fucking thing is loaded.' Sue raised the barrel of the gun and pressed the tip against Derek's chest.

The Polkerton Giant

Derek glanced down at it as though it were nothing more than an impertinent forefinger. Quietly, he said, 'Don't you point that thing at me.'

Sue gave the gun a little shove, pressing the end of the barrel harder against Derek's chest. 'Get out of the way, arsehole.'

Derek frowned. 'I said, don't point that at me,' he r_eated.

Sue gave the gun another shove, harder this time. She expected Derek to fall back a step but it was like pushing against a wall and he didn't move an inch. Instead, he raised his right hand and grasped the end of the gun barrel and casually moved it to one side, so that it was now pointing over his right shoulder. Sue was so startled that, for a moment, she did nothing – people weren't supposed to do things like that, not when you pointed guns at them. She pulled at the gun, but Derek pulled harder and added a twisting movement to his effort, which ripped the weapon out of Sue's hands with such astonishing ease that she gasped and fell back a step, bumping into Winnie and treading hard on her foot.

Calmly, Derek reversed the gun and moved the end of the barrel in a lazy circle that encompassed all three Princes of Wales. 'Go away,' he said. 'There are people trying to sleep here.'

'Give that back!' hissed Sue.

'No. Go away.' Derek raised the barrel and pointed it directly between Sue's eyes. 'Go away or I'll shoot you.'

There was something steely about his voice, something coldly impassive in his level gaze, which made Sue believe that there was a distinct possibility this young man was capable of carrying out his threat. She took another step backwards, trampling on Winnie's other foot.

Beatty cantered up, breathing hard. Behind her came Caitlin and Letty, wide-eyed behind their masks. For fifteen seconds the Islington chapter of FEFA panted at the lone gunman like a pack of wolves surrounding a caribou; then Beatty snorted and stepped forward. Sue shot out a hand and grabbed her by the elbow. 'Careful.'

Beatty jerked her arm, trying to disengage herself, but Sue held tight to the black nylon of Beatty's anorak. Beatty said, 'What's the matter? It's not loaded.'

'Yes, it is.'

'It's *loaded*?'

'Yes.'

'But I told you not to load it.'

'Yeah . . . well . . .'

'You stupid cow, somebody could've got hurt!'

It was at this instant that Sue decided to form a breakaway organisation composed solely of the fiercest and truest militants. Beatty was proving to be a horrible disappointment. She'd call it something really good, too. Not something wet like Free-Eve-From-Adam but something more belligerent and in-your-face . . . something like Kill-All-Fucking-Men! They would start with this big bully who'd taken the gun away from her.

'Go on,' said Derek quietly. 'Get out of it.'

'Perhaps we ought to do as he says?' Caitlin said. 'I mean, he's got the gun now, hasn't he?'

'Right,' said Beatty briskly. 'Good thinking, sister. Unlike some I could mention. Everybody back off. There's nothing we can do here. We shall move rearwards and regroup. A meeting is called for, I think.'

The Islington chapter of FEFA retreated down the hill in an orderly fashion until they came upon Edwin. Keen to make some sort of impression after the humiliating fiasco by the tent, Beatty halted her troops and barked, 'Who are you?'

'Ah – ahah – Commodore Edwin Billingsworth, Your Highness, sir . . . madam. Ah – At your service. Anything I can do, you just let me know . . . ahah . . .'

'What are you doing up here?'

'Ah, well . . . lovely evening, marvellous air, communing with nature—'

'Don't lie to us! It's been fucking pissing down.'

'Has it? Has it really? Good Lord.'

Beatty stirred the skirts of Edwin's mac with her toe. 'What you got under there?'

'Nothing. Nothing at all . . .' But she thrust her toe under the hem of the mac and lifted the stiff material. 'Apart, that is,' Edwin said hurriedly, 'from some paint. And a paintbrush.'

The Polkerton Giant

'Oh, yeah? What've you been painting?'

To Edwin, it seemed incredible that what he'd been painting wasn't glaringly obvious to anybody with a pair of functioning eyes. 'Painting? Ah, well – funny you should ask. Painting. Yes – well, the giant's – um – thingy, actually.' He gestured vaguely about him. For the first time, Beatty and her companions looked down at the ground and saw, at Edwin's feet, that the two-foot-wide line of chalk was roughly painted out with a thick layer of green emulsion so that, even in the glare of the floodlights, it was almost invisible. To Edwin's left, the white chalk outline of the bottom of the scrotum curved away up the hill, stopping suddenly where, presumably, it met the base of the now invisible penis.

'You've painted out his prick,' said Beatty, wonderingly. 'And now you're doing his balls?'

If only one knew which side these terrorists were taking on the issue, thought Edwin. The Prince Charles masks told him nothing of their opinions on hillside pornography. 'It washes off,' he said hopefully.

'You haven't finished,' said Beatty, jerking her chin at the curving line of the scrotum.

'No. Well – I thought perhaps that's enough for one night. Don't want to overdo it.'

Behind her mask, Beatty's face was undergoing a transformation. Coming down the hill in retreat, her features had been arranged into a scowl; now, faced with genius in the form of this little man in a mac, she began to smile with delight. It was *brilliant*, what he'd been doing, and she could've kicked herself for not thinking of it. The gesture said it all. Adam destroyed – only to become, with a bit of judicious turf-cutting (they would have to find a spade), Eve in all her glory. Of course, the little man might have picked a more celebrated landmark, one that was actually visible from a main road . . . but perhaps this was just a dry run for a series of attacks against man's monuments to himself. Beatty began to dream of sawing off Hyde Park Apollo's penis and dressing Nelson in a ballgown. Of course, inspiration or not, the little man would have to go, there was no place for him in FEFA.

'Right,' she said, reaching down and pulling Edwin to his

feet. 'You can go home now. We'll finish it off for you.'

'Oh – ah – right. Jolly good. Yes. Thank you very much. Very decent of you. Well, I'll just say goodnight, then.'

Edwin tipped is trilby and began to walk slowly down the hill. That's what you did, he remembered, when backing away from a dangerous animal. (Not the hat part, of course – hats didn't mean anything to dangerous animals.) Walking slowly was everything. Not letting them see your fear . . .

Beatty picked up the can of paint and the brush. She glanced round at her troops. Letty was the biggest and strongest. Beatty pushed the tin and the brush into her hands and said, 'Right, let's get cracking then. Caitlin, go down and tell the film crew we need 'em up here. Tell 'em we're making history.'

'Perhaps,' said Pamela, reaching into her bag and taking out her cellular phone, 'now might be the moment to exercise our civic duties and call the cops.'

'Have you had that all the time?' said Frankie, pulling back from the camera's eyepiece.

'Well, yes,' said Pamela, punching 999. 'But of course I couldn't use it before now, could I? Not with that shotgun in my face.'

'No. Right. And, of course, it *was* in your face the whole time, wasn't it?'

'You saw it. Pressed to my head, wasn't it?'

'Right between the eyes the whole time, I seem to remember.'

'And, under the circumstances, I couldn't do much, could I?'

'Not if you wanted to hang on to your head, you couldn't.'

'And I did, rather,' said Pamela – then, into the phone, 'Hello? Police, please.'

Caitlin was twenty yards away from the crew when she saw the telephone at Pamela's ear. Under the circumstances, a telephone could only mean one thing and, for a second, Caitlin was panicked into immobility. Then she saw that Pamela's head was turned away from her. The two men with her seemed intent on the phone conversation and almost

The Polkerton Giant

certainly hadn't seen her either. She risked a quick glance up the hill; her fellow members were clustered around Letty, who was bent double, her right hand moving rhythmically back and forth. Nobody was looking in her direction.

Caitlin took a breath and made a darting movement to the left, running for the hard-edged place where the darkness met the light. Ten more steps . . . five . . . and she was into the enfolding blackness. She ran on another hundred feet and then stopped to look back. Everybody was as she had left them, but she reckoned it was only a matter of a minute or two before her absence would be noticed. Now, which way to go? The police would arrive from the lane; she would go in the opposite direction. Caitlin took one look back at the Islington chapter of FEFA, decided that it would definitely be her last, and stepped into the darkness.

Chapter 20

Without warning, the rain returned. It was accompanied this time by a strong wind which blew the drops in horizontal sheets against the hillside.

Beatty and her troops ducked their heads against the sudden downpour and went on with their painting. Pamela, Frankie and John had moved up to where the action was and were filming the obliteration of the giant's private parts. It was nearly done. (Beatty, glancing up at the crew, was interested to see that the camera and the sound recording machine seemed to be functioning perfectly well, in spite of the rain drumming on the equipment.) Buster and Mick were in charge of the floodlights and were pointing them, for the most part, in the direction that Frankie had requested.

Pamela let Frankie run the camera over the scene, establishing the shot; then she stepped into the light and faced the lens. The rain plastered her hair to her head and ran in rivulets down her face, but she didn't care. This was what television was all about.

'This is Pamela Gibbons on Giant's Hill, just outside Polkerton in Somerset. Behind me is what remains of the outline of the famous Polkerton Giant, a Palaeolithic chalk outline figure – which seems to have aroused strong feelings within a shadowy feminist group, hitherto unheard of, that call themselves Free Eve From Adam. Earlier today, this group kidnapped noted television historian Lysander Blount and this television crew from Stonehenge, where we were filming an episode of *Blount's Britain*. We were brought here at gunpoint—'

'*Vandals!*' came a shriek from twenty yards down the hill and, instinctively, Frankie and John swung their equipment away from Pamela and towards the voice; Frankie waved his free hand urgently and Buster (who was beginning to understand this job) swung his lights in the same direction, illuminating the downslope of the hill.

'What the fuck . . . ?' Frankie muttered, wrestling with his focus ring, and John blinked hard and wiped the rain from his eyes.

Charging up the hill towards them, with the light of battle in their eyes, came the People of the Polk.

Rapunzel Beaufort-Lyons was in the lead, her long sack dress sodden and clinging to her bony frame. Behind her ran a pack of fur-clad savages, some bare to the waist, some brandishing massive clubs. A magnificently muscled youth was whirling his club over his head and howling like a wolf, and a statuesque, horse-faced woman, her bare breasts streaming with rainwater, was shrieking and clicking in some alien tongue.

Rapunzel had fired them to a frenzy. They had run from the community hall and piled into the Beaufort-Lyonses' Range Rover; Poppy had nestled on Roger's lap and Maureen had sat on Jack's. Aileen and Grace and Harry had crushed themselves into the luggage compartment. From the front passenger seat, Rapunzel had delivered a fiery speech about the immeasurable value of improvisation and the incredible stroke of luck that had offered them all the chance to exercise their talent at it, and provided the opportunity for a truly dramatic gesture to protect their heritage. By the time they had reached the parking field and had bumped their way across it and through the dripping wood, the cast, as one, had thrown off completely the trappings of the Polkerton Players and had transmogrified themselves into the People of the Polk (so much so that Jack, on emerging from the Range Roger, reverted to his initial concept of Harga and charged up the hill howling 'Ooga! Ooga!').

There had been no room in the Range Rover for Uther and Evie, so Uther had led Evie to his Morris and they had followed as close behind as Uther deemed safe. They had almost got stuck in the mud of the parking field, but Uther was determined to see his creation through to its uncertain finale and managed to keep the car rolling steadily through the mud. He parked next to the Range Rover, fetched his

The Polkerton Giant

umbrella from the back seat, and escorted Evie sedately up the hill towards what appeared, at a distance, to be developing into a small battle.

On the way, they met Edwin stumbling down. When he saw them he stopped and stared abashed at the ground. His trilby was shapeless with water that dripped on to his nose, and his hands and mackintosh were spattered with green paint.

'Hello, Edwin,' said Evie quietly.

'Ah – hello, Evie. Hello, Tregeffen,' Edwin muttered. 'Ah – look, I can explain—'

'I don't think you can at all,' said Evie. 'You're a silly, silly man.'

'Look here, Evie . . .'

'We're going home, Edwin, before you get into any more trouble.'

'Yes, but look here—'

'Home, Edwin. Now.'

Uther tried to press his umbrella on them but Evie politely refused. She said goodnight and took Edwin firmly by his arm. Uther watched them for a moment as they walked away into the night. When they had disappeared into the darkness, he turned and trotted up the hill, heading for the lights.

Pamela, once the attack had begun, sensibly relinquished the star spot and was letting Frankie and John roam freely through the mêlée with their equipment. She watched them with pride. Like the seasoned documentary makers they were, they treaded a sinuous path through the combatants, ducking and weaving from the blows each side aimed at the other. As long as the gear kept running, Pamela thought, this footage was going to be priceless.

She felt a cessation of the rain on her head and then a light tap on her shoulder. Uther was standing next to her, holding his umbrella over them both.

'Hello, dear,' he said. 'Isn't this jolly? I do hope you're pleased . . .'

The battle (it was more of a skirmish but the Beaufort-Lyonses were always to refer to it later as a battle) was short-lived, and had almost finished by the time Uther caught up with it. Five militant feminists in rubber Prince Charles masks were no match for seven amateur actors in the ecstasies of improvisation, armed with papier mâché clubs and led by a charismatic Amazon who, influenced by her own fiery oration to a far greater degree than any of her cohorts, and inflamed even further by the terrorists' masks (which seemed to her to be a deliberate affront to her Republican ideals), charged forward into the ranks of FEFA with no thought for her own safety.

'Vandals! Huns! Philistines!' she shrieked, swinging a bony fist and catching Beatty Summerfield under Prince Charles's protuberant right ear. 'Imperialists! Nazis! Exploiters of the Working Man!' she screamed, lashing out with her foot and connecting with Sue's shin-bone.

Close behind, her platoon was distinguishing itself in its own way. Jack broke his now soggy club over Pru's head, and Pru said, 'Ow, that hurt, you bastard.' When she saw the remains of the club rising for a second blow, she turned and ran away into the night.

Maureen, with no club, was doing a lot of pushing and pulling and scratching with her wickedly long, painted nails. Roger was methodically thumping heads with a savage glee, his damp papier mâché bludgeon doing little damage to flesh and bone but irreparable harm to FEFA's collective psyche. Poppy's Sellotape had given up the unequal struggle against strain and rain, and the long strands of her wig had come unstuck from her little breasts and were now flying out behind her. Unconcerned, she slapped furiously at the rubber masks of the enemy. Aileen lashed out with her wooden comb, jabbing its teeth into anything in black nylon.

Eric Beaufort-Lyons – always more lamb than hawk – followed his wife at a distance, muttering 'Could we not perhaps talk about this?' and trying to think of an apposite line of verse that might convert Rapunzel back from the berserker she had become and into the rational human being that he knew and loved.

Grace Stanley and Billy Sherman, being older and slower, arrived a few moments later. They hovered at the fringe of the battle, hurling clods of grass and shouting encouragement.

The Polkerton Giant

Their efforts were hardly needed. Within half a minute, the Islington chapter of FEFA had had enough. The rubber masks, while effective at concealing identity, acted like blinkers on the peripheral vision, making the members vulnerable to attack from the side. The whooping, fur-clad savages that assailed them had been so unexpected that the members found themselves paralysed by the shock of it all. Despite this, as Beauty was to point out at a later meeting (held at Letty's flat in Muswell Hill; Caitlin sent them a letter of resignation, changed the locks on her front door and refused to pick up the telephone), and though they were vastly outnumbered, they had nevertheless accomplished the task in hand – for, just as the attack began, Letty was daubing over the last patch of chalk, obliterating, at least to the casual glance, all evidence of the sex of the Polkerton Giant.

Pru had been the first to run, followed by Beatty nursing a sore jaw, and then Sue, hopping on one foot and holding tight to her bruised shin with both hands. Letty, under attack by a clicking woman with extraordinary breasts and a vicious wooden jabbing weapon, dropped the paint tin and the brush and ran away into the darkness. Winnie, seeing herself alone and about to be surrounded, screamed and dashed through the last remaining and fast-closing gap, and was quickly swallowed up in the night – and the Battle of Giant's Hill was over as quickly as it had begun.

The victors, panting heavily, grouped themselves round their leader. Their eyes were alight with the joy of victory and they stared at Rapunzel, waiting to hear her congratulations. Rapunzel was staring down at the wide line of thick green emulsion that stretched out on either side of her.

'This will all have to be cleaned up,' she said, her face thick with fury. 'Tonight, in fact. We cannot allow this vandalism to see the light of day. We will all go and fetch scrubbing brushes and detergent and we will clean this – this *mess* – up tonight.'

This was so far removed from what the People of the Polk had hoped Rapunzel would say, that they quite suddenly stopped being the People of the Polk and became a group of cold, wet, amateur actors in sodden nylon fur loincloths, with no great ambitions for their immediate futures other than a hot bath, a strong cup of tea (possibly laced with whisky) and a warm bed. Poppy suddenly realised that she was exposed – not only to the elements but to everybody's eyes as well, including what appeared to be a small but fully operational television crew – and pulled the dripping strands of her wig across her breasts. Roger shivered and dropped the remains of his club on to the ground. Jack mumbled that perhaps he ought to be off, seeing as how he had to open up the shop in a few hours' time, and Maureen began to say that she didn't really think she'd be able to help with the clean-up, not with her mother being poorly the way she was . . . and then, in the distance, came the wailing of sirens.

The police sorted everything out in their own way. They seemed uninterested in pursuing the terrorists, preferring to take detailed statements from those present. (The evidence that Aileen Beresford offered seemed of particular interest to them. Possibly, Maureen sourly observed, because the police jacket that had been thrown round her naked shoulders had a funny little trick of falling open whenever they asked her a question.)

Lysander was removed from Megan's and Derek's tent. He had to be lifted from the depths of Derek's sleeping bag, into which he'd crawled head first, burrowing down to the foot and curling himself into a foetal position. He'd stayed there while the battle had raged outside, his eyes screwed shut, his hands over his ears, and had almost suffocated in the process. Even when he heard the reassuring burr of a West Country constable, urging him to be a good fellow and come on out now, Lysander was in such a state of shock that his limbs refused to move and they had to peel back the sleeping bag like a banana skin to get him out. Frankie and John filmed as two policemen wrapped him in blankets and carried him gently to a car.

Then Frankie turned the camera on Derek and Megan, and Pamela conducted a short interview with them, during which it was suggested that Derek had behaved with great heroism. Megan stood nervously by his side – then she caught

The Polkerton Giant

sight of the man with the funny wig standing next to the interviewer and the man gave her a lovely, encouraging smile. After that, she stopped being nervous about being on television and raised her head to look proudly up at her husband. Derek kept saying that he hadn't done anything, really, and that if he *had* done something, then he'd only done what anybody else would have done under the circumstances.

Mick Jenson became aggressive, driven to a higher than usual pitch of irritation by the host of Princes of Wales that had come, uninvited, on to his land. It didn't matter that they were no longer there – nor did it matter that they weren't the real thing, but were mere terrorists in disguise – it was enough that a bunch of crazy people had the impertinence to take on the hated royal appearance and then parade those hated features all over his fields. He stamped about, shouting and getting in everybody's way. When he discovered that the police had come on to his land without a search warrant, he demanded that they not only pay the usual entrance fee but also help him extract payment from everybody else who was on his property without the proper tickets. Three of the constables took Mick to one side and reminded him that there were some various little matters outstanding, such as two unlicensed vehicles, five unlicensed lurcher dogs and an illegal cider still – and if he didn't shut up, then they might feel a need to pop round to the farm and deal with all these trifles right away, rather than in a month's time. Mick subsided, grumbling under his breath about police states and Gestapo tactics and how he'd fought the war for people like them, and when nobody took any notice of him he got the tractor keys from Buster and drove home.

Buster stayed and helped the television crew load their gear into a police car. The police (who had no intention of running about the country in pouring rain and total darkness, pursuing dangerous international terrorists and getting their boots all muddy) insisted on impounding Satellite West's film of the events for study at a later date. In compensation, they offered to drive Pamela and Frankie and John to the studios.

While they were packing the lights into the trunk of the police car, Buster, who now knew what he wanted to do for the rest of his life, sidled next to Frankie and said shyly, 'Do you think Oy could get a job doing this? Loading and carrying and holding the loights and stuff loike that?'

'Don't see why not,' said Frankie. 'You did all right. I'll put in a word, if you like. Call Personnel and mention my name. Frankie Potts.'

'Great,' said Buster. 'Bloody great.'

Uther was still sheltering Pamela with his umbrella, and together they watched as the party wound down. The Polkerton Players, elated but shivering, trudged down to he Beaufort-Lyonses' Range Rover and squeezed inside, huddling together for warmth. Rapunzel sat in the front passenger seat and was uncharacteristically silent as they drove away.

'What fun,' said Uther, taking Pamela's elbow and strolling towards his Morris.

'You've very wicked,' said Pamela. 'It was lucky nobody got hurt.'

'Pish and tush.'

'There was a gun, Uther.'

'All the more dramatic.'

'Well, I hope you're satisfied.'

'Me, dear? It wasn't for me. It was for you. For your career. If the police ever give it back, your film will be a triumph of on-the-spot reporting and you'll be a star. I did it all for you.'

'Pish and tush, Uther. Pish and tush in spades.'

By the time everybody left Giant's Hill it was four o'clock in the morning. The rain had petered out to a light drizzle and Megan and Derek sat, bundled in all their clothes, just inside the tent flap, watching the lights of the cars flicker away through the woods below them. When they disappeared and the growling of the engines faded to silence, Megan slipped her hand into Derek's and whispered, 'I'm so proud of you, Derek Baines.'

'Oh, well,' said Derek.

'You were so brave. Standing up to them like that.'

'Not really.'

The Polkerton Giant

'Yes, you were. Like Clint Eastwood.'

'No. Give over.'

'Taking the gun away. Just like that. I couldn't believe it.'

'Well . . .' said Derek, who couldn't believe it either. What on earth could he have been thinking about, doing a stupid thing like that? He could have had his brains blown out.

Megan was breathing harder than usual, which was funny since she hadn't been exerting herself in any way; she'd just been sitting next to him, quite quietly, doing nothing very much other than telling him how brave he'd been. He felt her tighten her grip on his hand.

'Are you all right, love?' he said.

'No, I'm not all right, Derek Baines,' she said, her voice shaking. 'I'm not all right at all.'

'What's the matter?'

'Nothing's the matter. I just want us to do it. I want us to do it right now, and if we don't do it right now, then I think I shall scream.'

'Oh. Right then,' said Derek, suddenly finding himself wanting to do it as well – and with a conviction that, this time, everything would go just fine. He turned towards Megan, reaching for her, but for the first time in their life together she was ahead of him, and her hands touched him first.

Over the next half-hour, Megan became somebody else entirely and Derek was glad that she had. She twined herself over him and under him and around him, her hair flying, her tongue darting, her hands sliding – and Derek found himself propelled into her erotic world and he joined her, slithering with her, both naked now, over the slick nylon of the sleeping bags, wordlessly daring her to go further and further and aping her every move when she did – until at last, gasping with suppressed passion, they joined mouths and pelvises and thrust violently together, climaxing at the very moment when the earth moved beneath them, which it did without any warning, and so smoothly and silently – at least for the first few moments – that neither Derek nor Megan was aware that anything (other than their individual raptures) was happening.

Chapter 21

Uther was still asleep when Viola telephoned him. He looked at his bedside clock – seven-thirty in the morning, far too early for the telephone, so he put a drowsy slur into his voice, to let her know he had been disturbed but she took no notice and babbled on about how disappointed she was in the chief constable's performance and how thoroughly incompetent his men had been to let the kidnappers escape into the night.

'All I can say is, it's a blessing that Sandy wasn't killed, although I understand he is in dreadful shock and will have to spend several days in the hospital. We shall have to go and see him, Uthie.'

'You shall, Viola dear. I don't think Lysander would be interested in seeing me, though.'

'Poor man. I understand they did terrible things to him, although I couldn't quite fathom what Sir Roderick was saying. Something about taking all his clothes off, although I can't believe anybody could be so savage, and also some sort of vandalism of the giant by the terrorists . . . and something about a couple with a tent, who might or might not have rescued Sandy. It was all rather muddled, I'm afraid – so much so that I wouldn't be at all surprised if it turns out that Sir Roderick has been drinking rather more than is good for him, if you take my meaning, Uthie.'

'A tippler, eh? How shocking.'

'What can it all mean? Poor little me is quite bewildered.'

'Well . . . I was there, you know.'

'You were where?'

'There. I was there. I saw what happened.'

'You were there? How were you there?'

Viola sounded injured and a little outraged, and Uther decided to step carefully. 'I shall explain over breakfast, which you will give me in your charming drawing room. Then we shall go and view the scene together and rejoice, for there is much to rejoice about, Viola dear. Give me an hour. Goodbye.'

An hour, thought Uther, should give him enough time to concoct a believable story about his presence at the night's events – and also sort out and omit any detail which might incriminate him in Viola's eyes. By the time he arrived at the Grange, dapper in one of his pale grey suits and with Quentin secured with extra tape against the fresh, cool wind that was blowing, Uther had put together a tale involving an undercover mission for CROSS against SPAM, which had necessitated a visit to the rehearsals of the Polkerton Players. From there it was plain sailing (and truthful too), and he told Viola of Evie's revelation ('Such a pleasant, quiet little woman,' Viola murmured) and of their subsequent race to Giant's Hill, and of the battle against the terrorists and the rescue of Lysander. It was all as accurate as Uther chose it to be, which wasn't accurate at all but quite exciting. All he left out was his personal acquaintance with the leader of the kidnapped television crew, because it wouldn't be wise to let Viola know about that.

When he had finished both his story and his breakfast, Viola seemed quite satisfied with the explanation and was eager to go and visit the scene for herself. They collected their coats from the hall and walked outside to Uther's Morris.

'Your car is very muddy,' said Viola. 'Shall we have Frobisher take us?'

'Yours will get muddy, too,' said Uther. 'Frobisher won't like that.'

Twenty minutes later – and with another ten pounds of mud sticking to its bodywork – the Morris emerged from the woods below Giant's Hill and rolled to a stop. It could go no further. Its way was blocked by a twenty-foot-high mountain of folded turf.

Uther and Viola sat quite still and gazed up in wonder at what was left of the Polkerton Giant.

In the weeks that were to follow, teams of geologists and hydrologists and seismologists, experts in erosion and experts in adhesion and experts in the root systems of chalk-based grasses, and a score of others who were expert in nothing but having opinions and expressing them to anybody who would listen, wandered about, poking and prodding and taking measurements, finally reaching the conclusion that the landslide was caused by a combination of factors including the shallowness of the turf roots, the heavy rain, the recent and unusual foot traffic in the area, and the numberless hammerings in of tent pegs all over the surface of the steep slope – all of which contributed at some time in the early hours of the morning to a sudden separation of the thin carpet of grass from its underlying bed of chalk.

The vast mat of turf – in the middle of which had been cut the outline of the Polkerton Giant – had slid off down the hill, arriving at the bottom in a series of neat folds, like a blanket that had been pushed to the foot of the bed on a hot night. Its departure had denuded most of Giant's Hill, exposing a great expanse of brilliant white chalk. The rays of the morning sun fell directly on to the white surface and reflected back into Uther's and Viola's eyes, momentarily blinding them, so it was several moments before Viola, her eyes squinting against the glare, became aware that there was some sort of drawing in the centre of the chalk canvas.

'What on earth is that?' she said, pointing upwards.

The paint that Edwin had bought from Jack Lunn was of the finest quality. Its sticking properties were particularly vaunted by the manufacturers and had they known about its effectiveness in this case – and had it been put to less controversial use – they might have made a potent advertisement around the story. While the grass all around had fallen away, and several tons from further up the hill had actually slid directly over the painted chalk, most of the bright green paint had survived both the night and the landslide.

'Ah,' said Uther. 'Yes. How interesting. I rather think . . .'

'Oh, good heavens,' said Viola abruptly. 'How disgusting.'

'Revolting. Unspeakable.'

'Who could possibly have done such a thing?' Viola hadn't yet worked out what had happened. Uther saw that, as long as her bemusement lasted, a window of malicious opportunity was available. He opened it wide.

'Now I come to think of it, Viola dear, it wasn't the terrorists, you know. Not at the beginning, anyway. It was Edwin who started it. The painting, I mean.'

'Really?' said Viola, ice in her voice.

'Oh yes. He did most of it. The terrorists merely finished it off.'

'Really?'

'As sure as eggs is eggs.'

'Are you telling me, Uthie, that Commodore Billingsworth deliberately painted a crude and disgusting representation of an organ of reproduction sometime during the night? And that some international terrorists finished it off for him?'

'That's about the gist of it, Viola, dear.'

'I see.'

It would be only a matter of time, Uther reasoned, before Viola worked out the sequence of events, a sequence which ought to exonerate Edwin from any wrongdoing. But he also knew Viola well enough to know that once she had flung a little mud, no amount of absolving water would entirely eradicate the stain. The resulting chilliness between the Pomfrets and the Billingsworths would serve Edwin right for all his past rudeness to Uther. It would also, Uther realised, get poor Evie Billingsworth out of attending any more of Viola's horrible parties, for which, Uther felt sure, she would be grateful.

Viola was saying that, other than that smutty schoolboy drawing, she was thoroughly delighted with the course of events, because at last the horrid giant was no more and perhaps God had been listening after all – when she was interrupted by a tapping on Uther's side window, followed by a discreet and apologetic cough. Uther looked sideways and saw the young hero from the night before, and behind him, his pretty wife. They looked tired and muddy and Derek had what appeared to be grass stains on his forehead. Uther lowered his window.

'My dears – what happened? Are you all right?'

Derek said they were fine, except from some bruises and scrapes – not to mention the matter of the loss of most of their equipment and the fact that they were wet through

The Polkerton Giant

and rather cold and tired. But all in all they were lucky to be alive, what with riding all the way down Giant's Hill on the top of a landslide and then, on reaching the bottom, having the good fortune not to be buried under the tons of turf . . .

Uther clucked and packed Megan and Derek into the back seat and turned the heater on full.

'Viola, dear, this is the young man I told you about. The one who rescued Lysander. The one who single-handedly disarmed the terrorists and drove them off.'

'It wasn't anything, really,' said Derek

'Yes is was, Derek Baines,' said Megan. 'It was something wonderful and you know it was.' She smiled at Viola. 'He's too modest, you see,' she said proudly.

They were, Viola thought, rather an attractive couple. Of course, they were filthy dirty and their clothes were awful and cheap-looking and their accents were quite ghastly – a bit like the Beatles, only not as talented, of course – but the young man was quite handsome and the girl, even with her hair tangled like that and with those smears of chalky mud on her face, was really very pretty. There was a charming shine in her eyes and she looked adoringly at her husband and he looked adoringly at her. Altogether, Viola found herself quite taken with them both. And the young man (Derek was it? Such a common name, but that was to be expected with those accents) had been almost impossibly brave, too. She ought to do something to help them. It was always pleasant to extend a hand to the lower classes, and this young couple could be taken under her wing, as it were, so that they could realise their full potential, whatever that might be. One could never tell with people of this sort, but perhaps it would be worth a try . . . Yes, they would be her next project. She would begin with some worthwhile employment. Whatever they were doing at the moment to earn a living couldn't possibly match what she could offer them . . .

'Do you know anything at all, young man, about lawn mowers?'

Derek admitted that his parents owned one and sometimes he would go round to their house on the outskirts of Chester and cut the grass for them.

'How sweet of you. And what make is it, do you know?'

Derek said he knew, for a positive fact, since he'd had occasion to service the machine once or twice – sharpening the blades and such like – that it was a Pomfret Mark P27F, with the extra-wide grass catcher attachment and a two-and-a-half-horsepower Holcombe engine with the shielded Grissom carburettor.

Viola clapped her hands in delight. She turned to Uther. 'Come along, Uthie. We must take these young people home and get them clean and dry, and then we must take them shopping for some proper clothes, and the girl shall have her hair done and then I shall speak to Victor and we shall see what we shall see.'

On their way back along the path that ran through the woods, they came face to face with Rapunzel Beaufort-Lyons in her Range Rover. Rapunzel drove to one side of the track as they went by and Uther waved, sorrowfully but not too sorrowfully, because Viola was chatting happily beside him. He called out, 'A clean sweep, Rapunzel. A clean sweep,' which was, he hoped, suitably encouraging, commiserative, descriptive and ambiguous, all at the same time.

Once they were past, Rapunzel drove back on to the path and continued through the woods towards the base of the hill. She was angry. None of the Players had been able to come with her this morning and Rapunzel wasn't satisfied with any of their excuses. Even Eric had refused to come. Well, they would learn about discipline in future rehearsals, she decided. No more sweetness and light from her – they would feel the lash of her tongue.

In the back of the Range Rover, the buckets and mops clanked together as the vehicle swayed across the uneven path. It was going to be very hard work all on her own, and she hoped the detergent she had brought would be powerful enough to wash away the stain. Perhaps it would have been simpler to buy a lot of white paint and cover over the green – but that would have been too easy and would, in the eyes of some (Rapunzel's in particular), have merely added another layer of vandalism on to the already vandalised giant. No, proper cleansing was the only way to purify the

The Polkerton Giant

defilement. Her efforts would mean that Gaia would be pleased and would, she felt sure, reward her for her diligence ... and then she gasped and stamped on the brakes and the Range Rover pulled to a stop.

The giant had gone – disappeared – had been *obliterated*, leaving a vast white scar in his place. For several moments Rapunzel couldn't comprehend what had happened. Then her eyes took in the concertinaed mountain of grass in front of her and the clear green outline of male genitalia on the chalk above her – and she began to understand the enormity of the event and its significance in relation to her plans. Without the Polkerton Giant her campaign was at an end – SPAM was all but pointless – and both *Giant!* and *Nathaniel's Revenge* could be indefinitely postponed, if not cancelled altogether.

Nature (or Gaia – fed up, perhaps, with the priapic scratches on her belly) had decided that the horrible Viola should win after all.

For five minutes, Rapunzel cried noisily in the Range Rover, her tears misting her view through the windscreen. After a while, the blurred expanse of white in front of her began to remind her of something and, as the flow of tears abated, she realised what she was looking at.

It was a canvas. A blank canvas, waiting – at exactly the right angle, just as if it were propped up on an artist's easel – for the first stroke of the brush. Of course, the edges were ragged and the whole thing was as far from being rectilinear (as canvases usually were) as it was possible to be – but, even so, there was no doubt about it. Here was an entire hillside of unblemished whiteness, just crying out for an artist, his brushes, his paint and his inspiration. Or hers, of course.

Rapunzel began to hyperventilate from excitement. When the dizziness passed, she turned the Range Rover round and accelerated away through the woods. Within ten minutes she was sitting down at the Jensons' kitchen table.

Mick, bleary-eyed, sat opposite her and picked his teeth with a matchstick.

'I want to lease Giant's Hill from you,' Rapunzel said, without any preamble.

'All roight,' said Mick. He was fed up with the whole thing, and if this woman wanted to take it off his hands (and if she was prepared to pay him what the thing was worth) then she was welcome to it.

'In perpetuity,' said Rapunzel.

'All roight,' said Mick, wondering what 'in perpetuity' meant and adding several hundred pounds to the sum already in his head, on the off chance that it warranted it.

'Free access to the hill and I can do what I want with it.'

'All roight.' (Another five hundred pounds.)

'How much?'

The sum they agreed on was a little more than Rapunzel wanted to pay and a little less than what Mick was hoping to receive but, on the whole, it was satisfactory to both and they parted, if not friends, then mutually respectful business associates.

Later that day, Rapunzel called a meeting of the Polkerton Players at the Brady Street Community Hall and everybody turned up. There was a general feeling of guilt for not volunteering for the clean-up job, and the company was keen to show Rapunzel that, at least as far as the Players went, they were still as keen as mustard.

Rapunzel told them what had happened to Giant's Hill. Then she announced her resignation and there was a chorus of disappointed noises.

'I simply won't have the time, you see. There is much to do, and I shall have to concentrate all my efforts on the Project.'

This was said with such an air of gravitas that nobody dared ask what the Project actually was. Instead they all nodded soberly, as if in acknowledgement that a Project such as the one Rapunzel had just mentioned should, indeed, take up all their director's time.

'However,' said Rapunzel, 'Eric will continue as a leading member of the Players, and I hope you will recognise his worth and appoint him artistic director in my place.'

Nobody else wanted the job, so there was a chorus of approving noises at this suggestion and Eric smiled his acceptance.

The Polkerton Giant

'The giant is no more, so our two plays have lost their significance. Sad, but beyond our control.'

Rapunzel didn't sound very sad, thought Jack Lunn.

'In their place, Eric, I suggest *Peer Gynt*,' said Rapunzel. 'And Maureen should play Solveig.'

That bit of casting, thought Rapunzel, should ensure that all future productions under Eric's artistic direction would be unfavourably compared to all the previous productions under hers. Much as she loved him, it wouldn't do to have Eric elevated above her.

'And Evie's wonderful costumes won't go to waste,' she added. 'I'm sure that, with a little artistic adaptation, dear, clever Evie will be able to transform them into a wonderful wardrobe for our Ibsen presentation.'

Evie, sitting in her usual place at the back, nodded confidently. After last night, she could, she thought, probably do anything if she put her mind to it.

Eric noted the phrase *'our* Ibsen presentation' with a heavy heart. He would be artistic director in name only.

Megan and Derek had indeed lost their jobs, but it didn't matter. Within a week, Derek found himself in a smart office in a fashionable suburb of Chester. The building had a big sign over the front door: POMFRET & CO. THE LAWN CARE PEOPLE. In the foyer, on the wall behind the receptionist's desk, was a jazzy banner: SO MUCH MOWER FOR YOUR MONEY! Derek's office had the words *'Derek Baines, Regional Sales Director'* painted on the door in gold letters. He had a secretary, who was plain and elderly, which pleased Megan. He also had a company car all to himself. It was a new Rover and, with all the extras, a lot more expensive than the one Megan's father had bought.

Derek was an instant success, particularly when his customers realised he was the hero of that acclaimed, award-winning Satellite West television programme. Everybody wanted Pomfret machines if Derek would supply them and, after years of pushing double-glazing at reluctant home-owners, Derek found that supplying high-quality lawn mowers to garden centres was almost embarrassingly easy – so easy, in fact, that within six months there was talk of promotion to the position of sales director for the entire North Western region.

Megan was offered a very good supervisory position in the personnel department, but she declined because Derek's salary was more than enough for them both to live on. Besides, she was pregnant with Peter – or, if it was to be a girl, Peta. Either way, the giant's contribution was to be properly recognised.

Megan put her successful pregnancy down partly to the supernatural goodwill of the Polkerton Giant and partly to the passion she and Derek had shared that night in the tent. The truth, however, was more scientific than that: in all of their erotic play, they had become turned around, so that when they finally coupled their heads had been downslope of their feet. In this awkward, head-down-feet-up position, Derek's spermatozoa were given a very real advantage over all their predecessors: the initial (and trickiest) part of their journey towards their goal was downhill all the way.

Eight months after the obliteration of Polkerton Pete and shortly after Uther had returned from his long European holiday – he'd visited all his continental friends, one by one, and the process had taken a very long time, which meant he missed all the dull stuff that happens in the aftermath when the exciting bits have stopped – Uther received an invitation to a preview of an art exhibition. It was from Rapunzel, and she telephoned the next day to make sure Uther would be there.

'It's a preview, you understand,' she said. 'Just a few close friends. To view the Project.'

The next day, Uther drove the Morris down the lane that led to the Jenson farm. He turned into the familiar field. There was a young man in a white coat directing the cars to designated parking spots, and Uther followed his signals and parked next to Rapunzel's Range Rover. There were several other cars, and Uther recognised some of them as belonging to friends of the Beaufort-Lyonses.

Another young man in another white coat directed Uther to the passage through the wood. The mud and the leaf litter were covered now by a wide strip of artificial turf that

The Polkerton Giant

followed the meanderings of the path as it wound its way towards the hill. Uther, in a twinkling clean pair of brown shoes, was grateful that they would stay that way.

He walked through the trees and emerged a few minutes later at the foot of the hill. The mountain of muddy, folded turf was gone. In its place on the level ground a marquee had been set up and knots of people were gathered outside it. Two more young men in white coats glided among the guests with trays of champagne. Rapunzel and Eric stood in the centre of the small crowd, graciously acknowledging the compliments that were coming their way.

When she saw Uther, Rapunzel broke away from her admirers and came to him.

'Uther! Sweet of you to come.'

Uther was staring up at the hill and he spoke without taking his gaze away. 'Wild horses, Rapunzel dear, would not have kept me away. And I must say . . . well, I don't know *what* to say. I am overwhelmed. What a very remarkable thing.'

'I knew you'd like it,' purred Rapunzel. 'You of all people appreciate Art.'

The ragged edges of the scar on the hill had been trimmed straight, so that the acreage of bare chalk was now in the shape of a rectangle, long on the top and bottom and shorter on the sides. The exposed chalk had been smoothed somehow, the ridges removed and the holes filled in, so that paint could be applied more easily to its surface. Whether the gigantic nude portrait of Eric Beaufort-Lyons that stretched over the entire expanse of the vast white rectangle was Art, or merely a dramatic example of the craft of translating small proportions into enormous ones, Uther wasn't sure. The face wasn't particularly like Eric's, and Uther could only guess it was supposed to be him by the way the hair was arranged. The rest of the portrait was perhaps more accurate but, again, Uther couldn't be certain. He'd never seen Eric naked, and therefore couldn't express a qualified opinion. However, he felt as confident as he had always felt when confronted by one of Rapunzel's studies of the nude Eric, that at least one part of the likeness had to be an exaggeration; and for the first time, he felt confident enough to voice his doubts.

'My dear,' he whispered wonderingly into Rapunzel's ear, 'I've often wondered. Is Eric really so very well endowed?'

'Well, it's an Impressionistic piece, of course.'

'Of course. So – he isn't?'

'Oh *yes*! Yes, he is.'

'Ah well, that explains so much. But, will the sun and the rain not harm it?'

'Oh, yes,' said Rapunzel, loftily. 'That's the whole point, you see. It is a work that is designed to be at the mercy of – and to react with – the elements. It is an *elemental* work. *The* elemental work, I believe, since there is none other quite like it.'

'No. I don't suppose there is.'

'It is supposed to fade – during the course of a year, perhaps, depending on the weather. When it has achromatized sufficiently – when Gaia has tired of it – then it will be time to create another.'

'What – the same picture?'

'Oh, no. That would not be creative. That would be mere restoration. No – a quite different study. But of the same subject, naturally.'

'Eric?'

'Man, Uther. Just Man. Eric is but the example.'

'Of course. And – ah – in the same state of nature?'

'Naturally. The nude form is the apogee of all art. Even the Palaeolithics knew that, Uther, when they carved the giant.'

'So they did. You are clever.'

Uther went home. The first thing he did was telephone Viola. He told her what he'd seen.

'Oh, no,' said Viola. 'Not again. There have been rumours but I refused to believe them. And now you tell me they're true. No, no. This cannot be permitted, Uthie. It simply cannot. Something will have to be done.'

'I knew you'd say that,' said Uther, happily. 'I just knew it.'